DON'T Read THE Last Page

CATHERINE DOWNEN

ISBN-13: 978-1-0879-1219-6

First edition, January 2022

Content Warning: this novel does contain scenes discussing an eating disorder and body image.

To my mom, who's the first to read every book I write…this one is for you.

&

To those who need help opening the next door…

Chapter 1

I never read the last page in a book. I can't watch the last five minutes of a film and always hit the skip button on a song before it finishes. I hate endings, goodbyes, and finales, but I don't think that's why I'm going home.

My fingers fumble for the brown leather gloves in my mustard checkered coat. As I shift my weight to look out of the window, the worn bus seat groans beneath me. The glass bites my cheek with a cold kiss that I'm used to here in Colorado, though it's still a drastic difference from the breezy California air I left behind.

The small shuttle that takes me—and only me—from the airport slowly rounds a curve on the winding road and Rayou comes into view.

My breath tumbles from my lungs when I see my hometown for the first time since I left for Frostard University in August. *Has it always been this beautiful?*

Tonight, the mountains that enclose the little village are ominous dark shadows, their snowy edges sparkling under the moonlight. The bus works its way down the road and closer to home. From up here, I can see every block of Rayou, glittery Christmas lights twinkling along every street and lamp post, making the town glow in a grid of jolly cheer.

If there's one thing Rayou loves, it's Christmas.

Even though it's the end of January, the village seems to be stuck in a time machine, the holidays still gripping the town. I used to hate that about Rayou—that it could be the middle of February and I could still run into an inflatable Santa at the grocery store—but now the sight nearly brings me to tears.

God, I will never forgive Lindsay for making me stay in California for the holidays. *That* is probably the reason I'm sitting on this bus right now. That's why I got up at 6:30 a.m., packed a bag, and jumped on the first plane home.

As if she knows I'm thinking about her, my phone vibrates on the seat next to me. The lock screen is a picture of Lindsay and me on move-in day and it glows so bright my eyes hurt from the sudden light. A notification pops up. Another text from Lindsay asking where I am.

I blow out a sigh that fogs up the window and reach for my phone. I already texted her when I was at the airport and told her that I was going home, but she clearly doesn't believe me.

I'm not mad at Lindsay. My sudden overwhelming need to come home isn't her fault. She only suggested we stay in California over the holiday break. I'm the one who couldn't tell her no, and because of that, I can hardly believe Rayou is in front of me now. *I* chose to come home.

But it's temporary. I had a hard fall semester, and I needed to take a step back. I'm returning next fall and will continue school at Frostard. Until then, I just need... To be home. To breathe. I couldn't take it anymore. I never thought I would be homesick, but I guess that's what it is. After graduating high school, it all happened so fast that I don't even know how I ended up in that dorm room with Lindsay.

The watch on my wrist lights up with a soft buzz. An alert telling me to breathe makes my racing heart pause. Stupid technology. It has no idea what I'm even thinking.

The wheels on the bus screech and I feel the vehicle slow. I'm so distracted I didn't even realize we arrived. I yank on my gloves and slide the phone into my back pocket as I stand. My duffle bag rests on the seat next to me, and I sling it over my shoulder as I work my way to the front of the shuttle. The driver wishes me a good night as I step from the bus, and my dark brown leather boots sink into the snow under my weight. I'm hit by a sharp winter breeze, and for the first time in six months, I can finally breathe.

Careful to avoid the enormous snowdrift along the road, I find the white covered sidewalk and leave the bus stop, memories of California, and anxiety behind me. The snow crunches beneath my steps and white flakes drift through the sky, looking to add to the winter wonderland that surrounds me. The little mountain town has a population of nearly five-thousand. I've lived all eighteen years of my life in Rayou, Colorado, and yet, the sight of it takes me completely by surprise tonight.

I trek alongside Main Street, taking in every small storefront and decorated lamp post I would have overlooked this time last year. Twinkling lights wind around the street signs and posts, stretching over the road to form a tunnel of pearly white glow. Wreathes with pine cones and red bows hang on every store window, golden garland reflecting the shining lights above.

It's late—almost 10:30 p.m. on a Sunday night—so most of the businesses are closed. The strip of shops continues on both sides of me, but I stop at the main intersection. In most towns, there may be a fountain or statue. In Rayou, Colorado, there's an enormous Christmas tree.

Elaborate gold and red ornaments hang on every branch. The snow falls so perfectly against the evergreen needles that it looks deliberately placed there. It's the brightest thing in the entire town. I want to scream that Christmas has been over for a month, but instead, a grin splits my lips so wide my cheeks hurt.

God, I'm glad to be home.

Remembering where I was going, I cross the roundabout diagonally to my left and find the one door on the street that's unlocked, the windows kissed with a warm glow.

Rayou Library.

I know the door isn't unlocked because they're open to late night readers, but because she's waiting on me. With a mountain of questions, I'm sure.

The aged wooden door meets my touch with a warm welcome, the frosted windows flickering with the light inside. I push open the door and the little bell above the frame rings, announcing my arrival. A narrow, dark hall extends in front of me, the wood walls smelling of pine. My boots leave damp footprints behind me on the decorative carpet and I turn to my left.

The space completely opens up, a stark difference from the narrow entryway. The carpet beneath my boots changes to a red hardwood floor with matching bookshelves rising around me. Hundreds of books line the shelves, their colored spines like the elaborate ornaments on the Christmas tree outside. The lighting is low overhead, casting a warm and comforting aurora around the space. Through the frosted windows across the room, I can just make out the Christmas lights outside, snow clutching the corners of the panes of glass.

"Penny."

Her voice catches me off guard, even though I knew she would be in here. I look to my left, where my mom rises from her chair behind the redwood desk. Tears jump to the edges of my eyes, that suffocating feeling of homesickness erupting at the sight of her.

"Hi, mom," I say, trying to keep my voice causal, but it quivers with the tears I refuse to let fall.

In a second, she's around the desk, arms pulling me into her chest. I hug her tighter than I ever think I have before. She laces her fingers through my thick blonde curls and she mumbles into my hair, "I'm so glad you're home. Your dad and I missed you so much."

My throat closes around my words and I barely choke out, "I missed you too." I attest my tight words to her strong squeeze around my shoulders, instead of the overwhelming emotions that suddenly flared up at the sight of her. When my mom releases me and I step back, I've pulled in my tears and a tired smile spreads on my face.

"How was the flight?" she asks, directing our conversation to something easy before I know she's going to once again ask me why I came home only one week into my spring semester, after attending a few classes I'll no longer be taking now that I'm staying home until August.

I tell her about my day filled with travels, leaning my hip against the desk. My mom returns to her chair, logging off of the computer and packing up her bag so we can head home. For the most part, she doesn't interject, and just nods along, adding small responses. When she slips her cracked leather purse over her shoulder, the black material a strong contrast to her blonde bob that brushes the strap, she finally asks the question I know is coming.

"Why'd you come home, Penny?" She's not mad I'm here, or that I left school behind. I can see it in her crystal blue eyes, she's concerned.

My throat closes up around the explanation, but I knew this was coming, so I'm able to work the words out. We had talked on the phone when I was at the airport, so she knows the excuse I fed her then, but right now, this is all I can get out. "I should have come home at Christmas."

It's not the answer she's expecting, but I can tell she knows what I mean. I was already having a hard time adjusting during my fall semester. Classes Lindsay picked for me overwhelmed my days. The university felt like a jail she pulled me into, like someone convicted me for being associated with her. When she decided we'd stay on campus through the holidays, it was like prying open the crack in my heart that already longed for home. She always seemed fine with being gone from Rayou, like she talked about doing from the day I met her in the sixth grade, a dream she associated with me because I never told her otherwise.

When classes started last week, I felt it in my chest, my foundation crumbling and falling apart. I couldn't do it any longer. I couldn't live a life that didn't feel like mine. Somehow I think my mom understands all of that with my single response, even though I only tell her it's homesickness that drove me here.

"Your dad is gone for his temporary work assignment in London," she says, coming around the desk and heading for the door. I follow her, flipping off the lights like I used to do when I helped her close up.

"That's probably a good thing," I say under my breath.

While my mom may not be fuming that I'm taking this semester off from school, I know my dad will be. I didn't text him until I boarded the plane, and luckily it was already after 10:00 p.m. in London.

"Be ready to explain this to him," my mom says, echoing my thoughts.

The presence of my phone in my back pocket feels too heavy and I beg the universe to make sure my dad doesn't look at his phone until I'm already asleep. I don't think I could face him tonight.

"He's going to be mad, isn't he?" I ask her like I need reassurance of that.

When we step outside, the sharp bite of the winter air is ready to attack. My mom pulls the door closed and locks the library, pausing only a minute before meeting my watchful eyes.

"There's not much he can do from London," she says with a shrug and my shoulders drop with relief. "That doesn't mean we aren't concerned," my mother reminds me, her eyes narrowing.

I nod, letting her know I understand the weight of my decision to come home. She said as much to me on the phone when I paced around the airport in California. We spent over an hour going back and forth, but when she heard my adrenaline falter as my voice began to shake, tears seeping into my eyes and gripping my throat, she knew what I needed. Maybe my dad won't understand that, but *I* understand it. For once, I'm doing something for myself and I'm not going to change my mind now. I'll take this semester off and return in the fall, ready to continue my classes.

We follow the snow-covered sidewalk around the side of the library and I see my mom's royal blue SUV in the snowdrift. No, she's not supposed to park on the street when there's this much snow, but who in Rayou actually cares?

I toss my duffle in the trunk and head for the passenger seat. The pop of the handle is a familiar welcome and I hop in, relaxing against the grey cloth seats that hold me like a hug. My mom sits behind the steering wheel and, after the tires spin and spin, they finally grip the road through the slush and we head home. That knot in my throat unties itself as we go, loosening with each familiar turn; passing my favorite coffee shop, the street corner where Lindsay and I used to set up our lemonade stand in the summer, the ice-skating rink where I spent too many birthday parties to count, and the sandwich shop my dad used to take me to every time we had a half-day of school.

Each piece of Rayou weaves itself together into a quilt of memories that warms me to my toes.

"What are your plans for tomorrow?" mom asks, her voice filling the quiet SUV.

"I need to unpack," I tell her. "I filled my duffle with most of my stuff, and I can have Lindsay bring what I forgot when she moves out this summer."

If she comes home, that is. I'm actually not sure if Lindsay will ever come back to Rayou. I wouldn't be surprised if she stays with one of her college friends in California between the school years.

"I want to talk about what this time home means tomorrow morning," mom says, glancing my way before slowing the car to make the next turn. It brings us to Olive Street and around the pot hole where I wrecked my bike when I was seven. I lean forward in anticipation of what I'll see next, my mom's words completely drifting away.

The seatbelt pulls against my chest when I rest my arms on the dash, blonde curls falling around my face and, with a breath lodged in my throat, I see it.

Home.

The little house with faded yellow siding sits back from the snow-covered street, a cloud of white blanketing the yard. The two-story home glows in the moonlight that seeps through the dark clouds above, and like all the other houses on this street, Christmas lights still stretch along the edge of the roof, the red and green bulbs reflecting against the white peaks of the house.

"You still have the lights up," I say, though I'm not all that surprised. When my mom doesn't respond right away, I look at her and see her studying me. "What?"

"You're acting like you can't believe the house exists," she says.

"I'm just glad to be home," I explain, leaning back into my seat as she maneuvers the SUV into the garage.

"Right, you just missed us so much. Homesickness," she says as the ignition dies, quoting my reasoning from this morning. She sounds skeptical, as if she's wondering if there is another reason for my return. One that probably has to do with how nothing in my life was chosen by me and I'm having a mid-life crisis at eighteen.

I'm already hopping out of the SUV and heading into the house, duffle draped on my shoulder, before she says anything more.

The garage opens to the mudroom. White tiles with blue accents fill the space. I kick off my leather boots and run for my room. The magnetic force tugging me there is too strong to ignore. Maybe I am surprised the home is here. Maybe I doubt my room will be too. I've been gone for so long, and the decision to come home was so sudden, it's hard to believe it's in front of me.

The kitchen and living room are a blur in their shadows, and I take the tan carpeted steps two at a time, the moonlight coming in through the glass on the front door illuminating my path. I'm down the hall in three steps, throwing open the door to my left, and then I freeze on the threshold, my hand on the doorframe to support me.

It's exactly how I left it, like no one has stepped foot in here since that day in August when I pulled the door closed behind me. My duffle slips off my shoulder, the carpet muting its *thump,* and my feet are heavy as I walk through the space. The closet to my left is pulled open, mostly bare shelves casting shadows over the few remaining shirts I didn't take with me. There's a long mirror on the door and my reflection in the glass makes my blonde curls almost appear white. I trail my fingers across the dresser on the far wall. The make-up bag I used to keep in my gym locker sits next to a pile of forgotten hair ties and a dish with stud earrings.

I bring my hand back to my side when I reach the bed, the white metal rung footboard resting against the edge of the dresser. Blush bedding is tucked neatly around the mattress, one less pillow than normal at the headboard. Left thrown over the edge of the bed is my cheer uniform, the black and gold fabric like a second skin to me. I trace the stitched *RH* on the skirt for Rayou High and I swear I can hear the chants I spent years reciting with the squad in the back of my head.

I look over my shoulder at the wall across from my bed and see my desk is a mess, like it always was. The white paint peels up around the edges where I hit it with the chair too many times. Acceptance letters to colleges I didn't choose are discarded in the bin beneath my desk, some of my final reports from high school stacked on the edge. Pictures of Lindsay and me in our cheer uniforms are pinned to the bulletin board above the desk, my gold cheer bow perched on the hook. There's a photo of mom, dad, and me at the beach last summer, one of me in my teal prom dress, and another with me in front of the Christmas tree when I was five.

Ever since I left Rayou in August, I've caught myself daydreaming about this moment when I would return home. Picturing the room I left behind vividly while my professors droned on in my morning lectures. I think everything is where it should be. That every piece of the life I left behind is here and perfect, but the pretty homecoming begins to fracture. A harsh light pierces through the cracks as I realize something is missing, and the room I daydreamed about isn't exactly what I see now. The back of my desk chair shouldn't be bare, the corner of my nightstand is missing that blue vase, there are empty spots on the bulletin board where pins still stick out, but no photo is pinned beneath them.

I take a step back, the wave of realization throwing me off balance.

The things that are missing—things I didn't realize I had left in the daydreams I had of this moment—they... They carry memories I'm not ready to relive.

As quickly as I ran to my room, I flee from it, back down the carpeted stairs and out the front door. The white washed wood of the porch groans beneath my steps. I pull my mustard coat tighter around me and suck down the freezing air, thankful for its bite that sends the dangerous memories away before they can take root.

Not tonight, Penny. We are not thinking about that tonight.

I curl my toes in my thick wool socks, missing the leather boots I didn't bother to put on. Careful to avoid the patches of snow that have drifted onto the planks of wood, I take a seat on the old porch swing, the chains creaking as I start to sway.

When my racing heart finally slows, I slump my shoulders back into the swing, letting those memories in my room go. I've almost forgotten about the missing photos, vase, and jacket when I hear the engine of a truck approaching from the left. Its headlights send two bright beams in front of it, the slushy snow on the road glittering in the light.

When my eyes catch on the red paint, on that rusted spot above the wheel on the passenger side, the fake calm all comes crashing down. The wave finally caps and pours over the shore, flooding me with the memories of *him*. Of his varsity jacket on my chair, the bouquet of marigolds he gave me on my birthday in the blue vase, the pictures of dates at the ice skating rink and photos he took of me when I was laughing or looking at the stars.

Christopher Samson drives by my house in that red pickup truck I would know anywhere. I can see his silhouette in the cabin, one hand on the wheel, the other propping his head up, elbow on the door. The way he always sits when he drives.

Maybe it's my imagination, but I swear the truck slows. The brake lights glow red for a second before he keeps driving. He takes the light with him, and all I'm left with are the memories of Christopher Samson, of us, and the break in my heart that stretches open in the moonlit porch.

Chapter 2

My steps are quiet on the carpeted stairs the next morning. Tired eyes strain to see against the morning sun that shimmers on the snow outside the windows. The watch on my wrist buzzes, reminding me of the text from my dad I left unanswered on my phone. There's a clattering of plates in the kitchen, and I let the sound guide me through the foyer, back toward the mudroom and garage at the rear of the house.

"Sleep well?" My mom's enthusiastic voice rings over her shoulder when she sees me shuffle into the room, plopping onto a cushioned barstool.

I mumble a generic response, causing her to freeze.

She scans me up and down, surely noticing my heavy eyelids, messy bun, grey sweatpants, and old cheer camp shirt. "What happened to the bubble of energy that sprinted to her room last night?" mom asks, looking back down at the eggs she's scrambling.

She saw her ex-boyfriend.

I shrug and say, "Dad wants me to call him." I hope my half-truth will suffice because it's still a storm cloud hanging over my head.

My mom huffs a laugh and scoops the eggs onto the two plates she set on the counter. "I bet he does." She slides the empty skillet off the burner and brings our plates to the bar I'm sitting at. The eggshell blue china is bright on the black granite. When she sees the distant look on my face, she adds, "Just tell him what you told me, Penny."

I take the plate from her and nod, acting like that advice solved everything for me. While this call with dad is daunting, it's not what's weighing me down. That unbearable weight comes from a hazel-eyed brunette who cracked my heart with just a peek of his silhouette in the cabin of his truck.

"So, let's talk about this time off from school," my mom says around a mouth full of eggs.

She leans her hip against the counter, choosing to stand while she eats. I lift my fork and scoop up the eggs, thankful for something to talk about, so I stop thinking about Christopher.

"Your dad's temporary placement in London doesn't end until July. So, it's you and me until then."

"Does that mean movies, cookie baking, and game nights?" I joke.

A light glitters in my mom's blue eyes at my propositions. "We'll see, but first, you'll run the errands, help with your grandmother on Fridays, and enroll in your fall classes."

I give her a sour expression, crinkling my lips and nose.

To which she responds, "This isn't a vacation for you, Penny." Her voice grows more serious, wiping my face clean of the silly expression.

"I know, I was just kidding," I say, but she shakes her head.

"I mean it, Penny. You can say you were homesick this time, but you need to solve this before August. Whatever is going on in your head needs to settle itself out before I'm flying with you to California on move-in day. You can't do this again."

"I know," I say again, a bite finding my voice. "I know I'm going back in August. I know what this time home means."

My mother pauses while she scrapes her plate clean, finishing her eggs. She turns, dumping the plate in the sink, and grabs a piece of paper off the counter, handing it to me. "Good. Then here's what I need you to do today."

The wheels of the royal blue SUV spray the slushy snow up the sides of the car when I pull away from the library, having dropped mom off for the day. Already we're back to sharing the car like we used to. The first thing on her list is groceries, so I head to the local market. The store is quiet today, nothing like the bustling supermarkets in California, and it doesn't take me nearly as long as I thought it would to get the items on her list.

Back at the house with the groceries put away, the clock on the stove glowing a neon *10:00 a.m.* in my face, I know it's time to call my dad. I was waiting so it would be in the afternoon for him, hoping to catch him when he's back at the hotel after the hours of meetings I'm sure he sat through today. I know if I called while he was working, I'd be getting salesman dad on the phone. Who would just tell me to call him back when he had more time to talk. I have a feeling this conversation can't be a quick hello and life-update.

Dragging my feet across the light hardwood floors, I pull my phone from my back pocket and plop down on the oversized white sofa. The fabric is soft and warm, thawing my cold limbs from bringing the groceries inside. With a deep breath, I click on his contact and call him. It rings twice before he picks up.

"Hello, this is Walton Wilson," he answers, clearly not looking at the caller ID. That's not a good sign. It means he's in a hurry.

"Hi, dad," I say, voice cracking through my tight throat.

"Penelope!" he says, and I hear recognition fill the sound of my name now that he knows it's me and not one of his customers. In the background, I can just make out the sound of some kind of string instrument accompanied by casual chatter.

"I can call back if this is a bad time."

"No, it's fine. Give me one second." I hear him press the phone to his chest, the fabric scratching the microphone. Faintly, he dismisses himself, and then his voice fills my ear once more. "Sorry, I was just finishing up dinner with the guys."

The guys are my dad's coworkers, who primarily live in Denver and often go on these business trips with him.

"I didn't mean to interrupt your dinner," I groan, rubbing a hand over my forehead. I hadn't even considered that.

"Interrupt? You just saved me from having to buy another round of drinks," he says, his tone oddly bright.

A hesitant laugh leaks through my parted lips, unsure of how to respond to him. I hear the ding of an elevator on his end and assume he's heading to his room now, having eaten dinner at the hotel restaurant.

"So," he says, silence hanging between us after the word.

"So," I copy, and after a beat, I hear him sigh.

"What's going on, Penelope?"

I bite my lip for a second and get my words organized. "I just wanted to come home. I needed a break." I cringe, knowing those were not the rehearsed words I wanted to say. That sounded childish.

There's a shuffling sound on the phone, and then I hear the door to his room click closed. "Transitioning to college can be hard," my dad says, catching me off guard with the empathy in his voice. "Your mom and I thought it would be easy for you since you had Lindsay there."

"I just missed home," I say, the same thing I've been saying for two days. "I just wanted a break. Time to breathe. I want to slow down the fact that everything around me is changing."

"I hear you, Penelope, I do," he says.

"You're not mad?" Tears have risen to my eyes, but I try to blink them away.

"Mad? No, of course not. I just want to make sure you're okay, Penny."

My chest collapses with relief. "I'm fine," I tell him, clutching to the saying that is so easy to speak, it's like breathing.

"You're obviously not," my dad says. "That's why you're at home instead of at Frostard."

He's right. I know he is. "I'm going back in the fall. Just taking a breather right now."

"You emailed your advisor?" my dad asks and I tell him that I sent all my emails yesterday while I waited to board the plane. We've been refunded for the spring semester and I outlined the classes I should take in the fall.

"I'm sorry I sprung this on you and mom. I know I usually don't do anything so rash," I say, apologizing for the first time at completely turning their lives upside down.

"We'll get through it, Penny. You know what you need. Your mom and I are just trying to do our best to help you," he says.

Our conversation drifts after that, talking about how his trip in London is going and if he's having any success with his sales pitches.

My dad sells industrial equipment and apparently, his boss thought they should expand business in London this year. I can't say I blame him. I'd kill for an excuse to go to London.

After a while, I finally hang up, feeling so much better after talking this through with him. I don't know why I was so worried in the first place. Maybe it's because I've never done something for myself. Usually my parents or Lindsay decide everything for me. I didn't know how he'd react to me making a decision for myself, especially something as drastic as taking a semester off from school. But he wasn't angry, quite the opposite actually. I'm glad for that, because now I don't have this guilt hanging over me that I've upset my parents. Now, I can actually use this time at home to get my head wrapped around the idea of returning to Frostard in the fall, so *this* doesn't happen again.

I lift my mom's list off the coffee table where I tossed it when I sat down on the couch and see the last thing she needs me to do is run some books by the high school. Just when I'm about to get up, my phone buzzes with another text from Lindsay.

Lindsay: Are you really not going to respond to me? Did I do something to upset you?

Oh, no! I forgot to text her back last night. With seeing Christopher drive by and then having this daunting call with my dad hanging over my head, I completely spaced. I open our messages and write her a quick reply.

Penny: I'm fine, Lindsay. Just staying home for the spring semester. I'll be back for our classes in the fall, and if you decide to come home for summer break, I'll see you then. I'm not mad at you, promise.

Lindsay: You aren't making any sense, Penny. Rayou is a dump. You can't throw away your spring semester. You'll never graduate

on time and you're missing out on all of the college fun!

My stomach twists at her words. Out of everyone, she's the only one who is resisting my decision. I try to tell myself that it's not personal, it's just who Lindsay is. She doesn't mean to insult me or my decision.

It's times like these where I begin to question why we ever became friends, but I'm quick to remind myself it's because I didn't have anyone else. We were both in cheer and in the same grade at a small school. I was someone who never told her no, and Lindsay loved that. She was someone who always seemed to have an answer for me, and I loved that. Or, I thought I did, until I opened my eyes and noticed how little she let me decide.

Penny: Lindsay, I'm not coming back. Turning off my phone while I'm home. I just need a break.

I do not, in fact, turn off my phone, but just mute the notifications from her. I need to clear my head and she's not helping. Her one text already has me doubting my decisions, inflicting this desire to please her and jump on the next plane back to California.

No, I'm staying in Rayou. I'm taking the break for myself. I'll make it up to Lindsay later.

With my phone now silent, though I'm sure still receiving messages from Lindsay, I stand up and head for the garage, swinging the car keys to the SUV around my finger.

Chapter 3

Two plastic bags filled with a variety of books hang heavy in my hands as I walk across the slippery school parking lot. My mom didn't have much to say when I stopped by the library to pick up the books. She didn't seem all that surprised when I told her about dad's reaction to me coming home for a few months. This leads me to believe that she may have called him and talked him down before I spoke to him. That makes his calm reaction a little more understandable. He already got all his complaints out of the way.

The orange brick building rises in front of me, a double story school that has icicles hanging from the roof, reflecting beams of sunlight into the air. It felt weird to park the SUV in the visitor's spot instead of my old parking space in the third row. Not that we were told where to park, but at a school as small as Rayou High, you just knew which spot belonged to you.

Careful not to slam the bags of books into the glass doors, I swing one open and shuffle in sideways. I stomp my brown leather boots on the rug, bouncing the clumps of snow off. Still, the shoes squeak beneath my feet as I walk down the white-tiled hall to the main office. Every few feet, a cluster of gold and black tiles are clumped together, decorating the narrow corridor. Above my head, along the ceiling, hangs the banners of this year's senior basketball players. Their season just started. I know that well enough, because I used to cheer at every single one of their games.

All of their faces are familiar to me, not only because they were just a grade below me, but because Christopher was their captain and friend. At the thought of him, my heart stutters and I tear my eyes away from the banners, wishing I hadn't let my mind drift to him so easily. Me coming home has nothing to do with him or what happened last summer.

Using my hip, I push against the door to the main office and enter, my breathing a bit uneven against the cold outside and the heavy bags of books. Ms. Nancy, the school secretary, is sitting behind the front desk, and her lips spread to reveal a toothy smile when she sees me.

"Penelope!" she exclaims. "Those are from your mother, right?"

I bend my elbows and rest the two bags on top of the desk, thankful to give my arms a break. "Yep, she wanted me to drop them off for the library." I'm almost positive my mom called ahead to let Ms. Nancy know I would be dropping off the books. I doubt she would have known my name otherwise. I wasn't the kind of student that spent much time in the main office.

"I'll get you a pass so you can take them to Ms. Yession. Go ahead and sign-in," Ms. Nancy says. She turns around in her office chair and begins digging through a box behind her, pulling out a piece of laminated cardstock on a string.

While she's untangling it from other matching passes, I write my name beneath the short list of visitors.

"Here you go, just bring this back before you leave." Ms. Nancy turns back to face me and I take the visitor's pass from her, hanging it around my neck.

"It shouldn't take too long," I say and pull the heavy bags of books back off the counter, using their weight to propel me toward the main doors.

The path to the school library isn't all that familiar to me. I could probably count the number of times I've been in there on two hands, and I bet each time was because I was dropping off books my mom donated from the Rayou Library to the school. They had a circulating agreement where we give them new books to put on their shelves, and then they bring us ones that haven't been checked out recently.

Mrs. Yession, the school librarian, has the door propped open for me, anticipating my arrival. "Hi Penelope!" she greets in a cheery voice that makes her wrinkling neck bob. "You can put those here," she says, patting the yellow counter, her rings clicking against the ceramic top.

The bags of books thump loudly when I set them down and I don't hold back my exhausted sigh. "Need me to take any back to my mom?" I ask breathlessly.

"No, I haven't had time to put a bag together. We just got back from our winter break last week," Mrs. Yession explains. She begins to pull the books out of the bag to examine the titles, but something causes her to pause, and her dark brown eyes look up at me. "Shouldn't you be back at school?"

My throat tightens at her question. "I'm taking the semester off," I say, my voice dropping to an almost whisper.

Her thin lips turn down, and she gives me a dismissive nod. "Tell your mom I said thanks," Mrs. Yession adds when I start to head back toward the hall.

I tell her I will and close the library door behind me. At this moment, the speakers in the ceiling above my head blare an obnoxious alarm, signaling the end of a class period. In a blink, the halls are filled with bodies. Students push past one another to get out of the classrooms, just to move into another one. I stick to the edges of the hall, but it's near impossible to walk against the current of bodies. So, I pause, letting them pass. The incoming freshman get the lockers by the library this year, so, many of the faces that surround me are unfamiliar, and I'm surprised by how young they look. Wasn't I just walking through these halls only nine months ago?

"Penelope Wilson, is that you?"

I spin around, instantly knowing the sound of Coach Violet's voice, my shoulders straightening from years of muscle memory. "Coach," I breathe my surprise.

She smiles so wide her green eyes squint, crinkling at the corners. With a clipboard in one hand, she spreads her arms wide, nearly knocking a short girl in the head. "It's so good to see you! What a surprise!"

I welcome her hug without hesitation, pressing my face into the slick material of her jacket. "Hi, Coach," I say, more confident with my words.

She pulls back first, grabbing my shoulder with a tight grip. "What are you doing here?"

"Dropping some books off for my mom," I say, nodding toward the library behind me.

"Have spring classes not started yet?" Coach Violet immediately asks the same thing that Mrs. Yession had.

"I'm taking the semester off," I say, repeating the explanation I had given to Mrs. Yession, but this time, the words are surer in my mouth.

"Really?" Coach asks, eyes squinting with curiosity.

"I wasn't transitioning well," I say, offering her a small piece of the truth. Coach Violet has known me since I was an awkward sixth-grader. Hundreds of hours spent together at cheer practices makes it easy for me to tell her this.

Her eyes soften at that and she releases her grip on my shoulders, standing taller in front of me. My ears strain to hear her next words above the sound of the bell overhead that signals the next hour of classes is beginning. A few tardy kids shuffle through the suddenly deserted halls and I hear the doors to classrooms click shut.

"Why don't you come by cheer practice tonight? I bet the team would love to see you," she says.

"Really?" I hadn't even thought about stopping by one of their practices. That all feels so behind me, but just thinking about the team has me longing for those nights again.

"Sure, we have the state tournament in March. I'd like to show you my plans for their routine and I know the team will be excited to see you," Coach Violet says, a smile returning to her green eyes.

"I'd love to!" I quickly exclaim. I never thought about coming back to visit the squad, but now that the opportunity has presented itself, it sounds like a great idea. I mean, would it really feel like home if I wasn't going to cheer practice? I don't think I'd even know how to be in Rayou without cheerleading.

"Great. Come back by the school this afternoon. Tonight's our first practice since we've been back from break."

"Okay, I'll be there," I say, a rush of purpose filling my veins. She tells me she'll see me then and dismisses herself to get to the gym before the boys start getting restless in her absence.

On my way out, I return the visitor's pass to Ms. Nancy and, as I'm about to leave, the sound of muffled voices drifting through the hall makes me pause. I glance over my shoulder, eyes naturally locking on the doors to the gymnasium at the other end of the corridor. I think back to the conversation I had with Coach Violet and decide it wouldn't hurt to just take a peek at the gym before coming back for practice tonight.

The gymnasium is like a second home to me. So many hours spent in there for cheer practice and basketball games. Right now, I'm almost as excited as I was to see my house last night. As I near the double doors, the sound of voices increases from the P.E. class on the other side. I stop outside the gym and lean against the door, peering through the small window. The fluorescent lights are bright overhead, the white rays glowing and reflecting off the polished wooden floor. On the other side, the boys' P.E. class is playing basketball, and the sight takes me aback.

I came down here because of my excitement for cheer practice tonight, but my mind gets pulled in an entirely different direction when I see the basketball game unfold in front of me. This gymnasium holds some of my most important memories; late nights with Lindsay, homecoming game victories, and it's also what brought Christopher and I together.

Two years ago—almost to the day—our worlds intersected. Standing in front of the gym causes that night to come back so vividly, and I live it all again. It was one of the first games after winter break, so the team was a bit rusty, and honestly, so was the squad. The Rayou Hawks were losing by a score that seemed impossible to come back from until Christopher completely lit up the gymnasium. I remember the way the court came alive every time he stepped foot on it, and he rallied that team back into a tied match. It was the most exciting game I've ever witnessed in the years I cheered at the high school.

We were on track to win that game until the other team targeted Christopher. Rayou Hawks were on the offensive, and one of the other team's defense members clearly wanted Christopher out of the game.

They lunged for the ball, snapping back their elbow and jamming it right in Christopher's face.

Goosebumps raise on my arms at the memory of how quiet the gym became when Christopher's neck snapped back, and he fell to the ground, colliding his head with a nasty crack on the wooden floor. The other team only received a minor penalty, but Christopher was pulled from the game. I remember his coaches had to carry him out of the gym and to the nurse's office, where the team's personal trainer was stationed.

That ended the first half of the game, which signaled our squad to perform our halftime show. It was an absolute disaster. I don't know if there was some bad karma placed over the gym that night, but at the highest toss of our routine, I was flipped in the air and missed the basket on the way down. I fractured my wrist and was scratched across my cheek by Trinity, who tried to catch me. I remember screaming from the shock of the pain in my wrist. It was one of the worst falls in my career. Coach Violet had me out of the gym and down to the nurse's office in a blur, and suddenly, the terrible karma that seemed to curse both the Rayou basketball team and cheer squad lifted when I entered that room and found Christopher.

"What happened to your face?" he asked when I closed the door behind me, his focus honing in on the terrible scratch from Trinity's nails.

"Elmhurst Tigers decided to unleash their mascot," I joked sourly and my black and gold cheer skirt swished as I walked across the room.

Christopher was sitting in the only chair against the wall, so I hopped up on the cot and sat at the edge, cradling my wrist in my lap against the pleats of my skirt. Of course, I already knew who Christopher was, but before that night, I can't recall ever having talked to him.

As soon as I sat down, Christopher stood and went to the cabinet that was left ajar. His heavy basketball shoes thudded against the tiled floor and then he began taking out wraps and band-aids.

"I'm surprised you're standing," I said, watching him carefully, since the last time I saw him, his coaches were carrying him off the court.

"I'm fine, just got a hell of a headache," he said, still pulling different items from the cabinet.

"You mean a concussion?" I inquired.

Christopher paused with his arms raised and looked at me. I mean, *really* looked at me for the first time ever, and I saw the caramel swirls in his eyes glow in the dim light of the nurse's office. "You're one to talk, you just got mauled by a tiger."

An easy laugh ricocheted from my chest at how he played off my earlier joke. I remember vaguely wondering when the last time I truly laughed like that was, and it was in that moment that I realized I wasn't pretending to be the polished cheerleader I'd been sculpted into. From the shock of the fall and the horrible pain radiating from both my wrist and my face, I'd forgotten to keep that mask on.

Christopher stepped away from the cabinet and came to stand in front of me, his hands full of different medical supplies.

"Is Suzy here?" I asked, mentioning the basketball team's personal trainer that Coach Violet wanted me to see.

"Just missed her," Christopher said as he dumped the wraps and bandages onto the cot beside me. "She went to go find some cheerleader that was dropped during the halftime show." He paused, looking up at me through his long, brown lashes and added, "That wouldn't be you, would it?"

"Guilty," I said, but my voice had grown thin in his proximity, the scent of coffee and pine folding around me in his presence.

"Technically, I don't think you're the guilty party in that accident," he said.

I scoffed and nodded. "You're right. Those sophomores need to get their act together."

The corner of Christopher's mouth tugged up in a loose smile that did dangerous things to my heart. In my entire high school career, I never had a boyfriend. I didn't do anything except train for cheer and work at the library with my mom.

When Christopher picked up a package of medical wipes and opened it, I narrowed my eyes. "What are you doing?"

His hazel eyes flipped up to meet mine. "I'm helping." He slipped the wipe from the package and paused. "Unless you don't want me to."

"It's not that," I stumbled over my words, seeing a wave of insult fill his eyes. "You just—" I shook my head, still a bit surprised by his gesture. "You don't have to."

Christopher shrugged and pressed the damp cloth to my cheek, instantly sending a jolting sting across my face. "Who knows how long Suzy will be until she realizes you came here," he said, gently wiping the cut on my face. "I don't mind, really. I've cleaned up my fair share of accidents."

I offered him a weak smile, knowing he was trying to distract me from the tingling pain scorching my cheek.

The gym doors in front of me rattle and I jump back, shattering the memory of that night with the wild basketball pass.

My chest cracks open, a horrible ache making me feel like I'm being turned inside out. I told myself last night that I wasn't going to think about him. *I can't do it right now.*

I spin around and stride for the exit of the school, trying to outrun the memory from that night, but I fail, and it continues flashing through my mind with my frantic steps.

Christopher had been so kind. He completely bandaged my face and wrapped my wrist. I never would have expected him to do that, but I really didn't know much about him except that he was the star of the basketball team.

"You're Christopher, right?" I asked when he'd finished and was placing the unused supplies back in the cabinet.

I felt awkward that we hadn't properly introduced ourselves before, though, thinking back on it, in a town as small as Rayou, that really wasn't necessary. I think I was actually just looking for a way to continue our conversation and make the exchange more personal.

He nodded, his brown waves loose around his face like they always were.

"I'm Penny," I added.

Christopher closed the cabinet and turned to look at me. He shifted his weight to rest his hip against the counter and a grin split his lips, those hazel eyes shimmering in the dim room like stars.

"I know."

Chapter 4

"**D**o you want to sit at the bar, or at the dining table?" I ask my mom as we walk in from the garage, kicking off our boots and unzipping our coats. I started making the spaghetti after getting home from the school so it'd be ready to eat once I brought her home from the library. After I escaped the high school and let the cold bite of winter suffocate my lungs, the memories of Christopher faded.

"Bar is fine," she says, sliding across the tile in her socks. "It's nice to come home to dinner already made," she adds, a bit teasing but also genuine appreciation hanging in her voice.

"Well, I don't want to be late to practice," I say, moving for the plates I left stacked on the counter, forks and napkins piled on top of them. I set our places at the bar that overlooks the sink and begin to ladle the spaghetti onto the blue china.

"Right, from your run-in with Coach Violet," Mom says, hoisting herself onto the tall barstool, and shaking parmesan cheese onto her spaghetti. She does the same to my plate as I put the pot back on the stove. I had briefed my mom on the encounter after picking her up from the library, and, I won't lie, the idea of visiting the squad during practice has me giddy.

As we eat, I hear about her day and the things she has to do tomorrow. Mom tells me she'll clean up dinner so I can get to the school a little early, and she gives me the keys to her SUV.

The drive to the school from my house is so familiar I could do it blindfolded, but then I couldn't watch the sun set against the snowcapped mountains that rise to the clouds on all sides of Rayou. The orange rays of sun are bright against their white peaks, and the light blue sky above looks like ice. The dash tells me it's a freezing 31°F right now, and I know it's only going to get colder. Some of our worst snows don't even happen until March.

Again, I park in the visitor's spot at the school and I turn the engine off, popping open the door and side-stepping a pile of slushy snow. Eager to get out of the dry, cold air, I race to the front doors and hurry inside. I didn't think I'd be visiting my high school twice on the first day home, but it oddly feels right. I study the cases of state awards on the wall as I walk toward the gymnasium. For being so small, Rayou has an impressive amount of plaques and trophies. Most are for our basketball team, but my eyes cast over them, trying not to think about the person they are tied to.

A bit further down is the case for cheerleading, something the school recently had to expand. Pride swells in my chest when I see the plaque we won at the state tournament last year. The dark wood is polished and makes the gold plate on the surface shine bright. COLORADO STATE CHEER TOURNAMENT is engraved in big letters with our ranking of third. Beneath the metal plate is a photo of last year's squad, Lindsay and me kneeling together in the center. We were the only seniors last year, and finishing third at the state tournament was a dream we never knew we could achieve. Before then, Rayou's cheer squad hadn't finished in the top ten in years. Since 1997, according to the plaque next to ours, claiming that year the squad took third as well. And there, in the back row, is Coach Violet. I've looked at this picture many times. Stood here with Coach and daydreamed about adding another to the trophy case, only to do just that last year.

"Ah, I thought I'd find you there."

I glance to the left and see Coach approaching me. Her thin, blonde hair is pulled into a knot at the top of her head.

"I don't think they actually put the plaque in the case until I had already graduated," I say, looking back into the trophy case. I remember Coach had it propped on her desk for the rest of the year, but it feels odd to see it with the other trophies. As if it's a reminder that this is history, something from the past that is over. A memory that other cheerleaders will walk up and talk about, crossing their fingers that they could do just as well as we had. Suddenly, the meaning of being here weighs heavily on my chest. That's what every member of the squad is doing *now*. That's what seeing me here will mean to them. *Maybe we can do it again.*

Coach reaches me and faces the array of plaques. "Weird to see your face in that case, isn't it, Penelope?"

"Very," I say through a sigh, having thought that exact thing. Maybe for the other members of the squad it isn't weird, the juniors, sophomores, and freshmen that stand on either side of Lindsay and me in the photograph, because they're still in school, still a part of the squad, still competing. They're still living in what is now my past.

"How's the team doing this year?" I ask, and in unison, Coach Violet and I turn to head toward the gym, always moving in sync like we did when I was in school.

"We're having a strong start to the season," she says, and I see her organizing her next words. "They've won a few local tournaments. We're just starting to learn our competition routine today, so it's hard to tell how they'll do at the state tournament, but I have good feeling." Coach Violet glances at my profile, the proud curve of her lips making me smile.

"That's promising," I say. "What are you planning for the routine?"

Coach Violet begins to walk me through her thoughts on the music selection and which members of the team she'll highlight in solos. I agree with almost all of her decisions. By my senior year of high school, I was as invested in planning our cheer routines as Coach was. I've always loved the challenge of designing a performance, of trying to put something together that will score high with the judges. She tells me about a new freshman flyer they recruited this year and that makes me laugh, knowing that story sounds too close to home. Before I can ask about the new member, Coach Violet pushes open the doors to the gym, the overhead lights bright compared to the dim hall.

When I step into the gymnasium—the smell of sweat and polish from the floor pinching my nose—I flinch at the cheer that erupts.

"Penny!"

The group of people who had been stretching in the center of the room screams and leaps up, racing toward me. I'm tackled with a blur of brown pony tails and warm arms. Above the overwhelming welcome, I hear Coach Violet laugh. When I'm released from the huddle of cheerleaders, I finally get to look at them. At all the teammates I've spent hours of my life training with, and it's like those nine months since graduation never happened. My heart swells, feeling full and beating happily for the first time in a long while. Being surrounded by them all—

Sammy, Trinity, Gale, Bryan, Lily, Rachel, Courtney, Mark, Bailey, Vicky, Hanna, Kelly—even the young girl at the back of the group who I don't recognize, makes me smile.

"They wanted to be here early to see you," Coach Violet says, explaining why they're already dressed and stretching. "Let Penelope take off her coat and breathe. Then, we'll get started," she adds, using her hands to wave them back into their stretching circle. Some of them reach out and squeeze my arm, giving me enormous smiles that reach deep into their eyes before heading away.

"How've you been?" Trinity asks, lingering with me. This year's sole senior, someone Lindsay and I prepared all throughout our senior year, is the team captain—a role Lindsay and I swore we'd share as a pair, but with only one senior this year, the responsibilities rest on her shoulders.

"Good," I tell her, and it doesn't feel as much of a lie as I thought it would. I am doing good now that I'm home. "Taking a break from school. This seems a lot more fun," I say playfully, letting my eyes flutter around the gymnasium, a place I know like a second home.

Coach Violet steps away and Trinity leans closer. "We're all really excited that you're here," she says, voice hushed. "I don't want the others to overhear, but I think we really have a chance to do just as well as last year."

That determination and competitiveness that used to live in me when I thought of the state tournament blooms in her eyes. "Maybe even better," I say, feeling a sense of excitement ignite in my veins.

Trinity's smile spreads wider, and she nods. "Maybe even better," she agrees before turning to join the rest of the squad in their series of stretches.

I unbutton the silver studs of my mustard coat and walk toward the bleachers, loving the feel of the gym floor beneath my boots, the way it sounds when the team takes off for their warm-up jog. The soles of their shoes squeak on the polished wood, and their voices travel in an echo into the deep corners of the room. I was so overwhelmed by their welcome that no threat of past memories of Christopher surface. My coat slides off my shoulders and I toss it onto the front row of the bleachers, taking a seat next to it while the team continues their warm-ups.

Sitting here and looking *at* them instead of being *with* them takes me aback for a second. It's not a bad feeling, but one that almost feels like an accomplishment. Like I put the work in, and now I'm on the other side of it.

It makes me think back to that day in sixth grade when I met Lindsay for the first time. I knew cheer tryouts had been the week before, but I didn't attend them. Back then, I had no interest in cheerleading, but that all changed on that Monday morning in September. Of course, I knew of Lindsay long before that day. There are only so many people in Rayou, especially in the same class as me, but we had never spoken more than a few exchanges during projects or group discussions.

I was sitting in the cafeteria at a long, black table. The chairs on either side empty like usual. Some kids who were in chorus sat a bit further down. On occasion, I engaged in their conversations, but normally, I stuck to myself and the stack of books I always had ready to dive into. That day, Lindsay plopped down next to me, no lunch in sight. I looked at the empty place on the table next to my tray, and then met her brown eyes, so bright they almost looked auburn. Clearly, she was not sitting here to eat with me.

"You're Penelope, right?" she asked and then popped a bubble with the gum she was chewing.

"Yeah," I said, still trying to figure out what was going on. I remember I looked over her shoulder to see if anyone else was watching whatever joke I thought she may be playing on me.

"Have you ever thought about joining the cheer team?"

I blinked at her, surely having heard her wrong. "No," I said, honestly.

"Would you want to be on the cheer team?" she asked, changing the direction of her question.

Again, I blinked at her and then shrugged. "I've never really thought about it—"

"You'd be a perfect flyer!" she said, interrupting me and tucking her gum behind her teeth. "We really need one and I think you could do the job."

Me, who had known absolutely nothing about cheerleading in sixth grade, asked, "Why?"

"Because, you're little!" she exclaimed, waving her hand up and down to emphasize that yes, I was small and had no muscle because I didn't partake in sports. "Flyers are the ones we throw in the air," she added, and I'm sure my eyes widened at the idea.

I don't remember much more about the conversation, except once I told Lindsay I'd go to their practice that afternoon, she walked away, leaving me alone in the cafeteria to wonder what in the world was about to happen to my life.

Suddenly, I went from being the quiet girl in sixth grade who just wanted to read her books, to being recruited as a flyer for the Rayou cheer team. All because I was little and didn't know how to decide for myself if it was something I really wanted to do. Odd, thinking back on the moment Lindsay and I met, I was already letting her decide things for me.

Granted, I am not the least bit upset with her decision. It gave me one of the best things I've ever called mine in my entire life. Cheer turned out to be exactly what I needed, and I love it more than anything else. I loved having a team of other girls and boys who wanted to be my friend, that I could rely on for anything. I loved having a place to go after school every day, and something to be a part of.

"Run them through the cheers for the game, Trinity," Coach Violet says, her voice shattering my train of thought and bringing me back to the present.

I see her approaching me, clipboard in hand, while the team lines up in two clumps, reciting the chants they say at the basketball games.

Coach sits next to me on the bleachers, placing her clipboard in front of me and says, "So, here's what I'm planning

Chapter 5

The winter air is sharp in my throat as I hurry across the parking lot. Moonlight casts itself atop the shimmery snow, faint footprints guiding my steps. On the other end of the parking lot, the sound of doors popping open and slamming shut chorus together as the squad heads home. It was a good first practice. I mostly oversaw the tumbling training while Coach started teaching the beginning of their state competition routine.

At first, it felt good to be back. There was a sense of belonging that filled my chest, but after two hours, that warmth turned heavy. It felt like I was being sucked back in time, thrown into the chaos and drama of high school. I didn't realize it before, but a lot of my time in cheerleading I associate with Christopher. We met when I was cheering at one of his basketball games. Being in that gym, while it reminds me of cheer, it also reminds me of him.

So maybe that's why I pause at the front of my car, why my eyes lift over the horizon of the parking lot and seek out the bench I know is tucked in the alcove of pines by the near the football field. My feet shuffle, not seeming to know which way to walk, until they straighten themselves out and I'm moving away from my car and toward the silhouette of the trees against the midnight sky.

The ground becomes uneven beneath my feet when I step off the parking pad and into the snow-covered grass, sinking up to my ankles. Some of the snow slips into my boots, but I ignore the bite of the cold and continue on. Behind the bleachers that overlook the football field, pine trees grow in tall clumps with lamp posts between them. Tonight, the lights are off, and my eyes strain to see through the shadows. I bend forward to access the trail and the moon's iridescent glow guides me through a cluster of pines, the needles soft on my cheeks and wet with snow. I run my hand along the trunks to guide me through the tight, small tunnel that is thick with the scent that reminds me of Christmas. When I reach the center clearing and can stand straight up, I see the bench and my heart peels open, though I completely expect the ache to come. I knew it would the second I stepped away from my car.

I hadn't put my gloves on when I left the school since I fully intended on getting in my car and leaving, so I pull them out now and use them to brush the snow off the bench. Only a dusting of snow covers its wooden planks, the trees above providing coverage to the winter world outside these branches. Here, the breeze isn't as frigid, but my breath still comes out in a small cloud.

I sit down, tucking the gloves back into my pocket. The motions are slow, like I'm moving against a strong current. When I lean back on the bench, my eyes drifting up the puzzle of branches in front of me, I'm transported back to that night with Christopher.

Though, then it was early August. Then, the evening buzzed with bugs and the air was sticky with humidity.

I sat on this bench that night, Christopher to my left, and broke his heart.

"Every time I bring this up, you go mute," I said, crossing my arms in a defensive stance, fully prepared for the argument that was about to commence.

Christopher's jaw tightened, chin balanced on his knotted knuckles, elbows digging into his knees. When he spoke, I was actually surprised. I really thought we were going to go through the silent treatment again. "Because I know once we talk about this, you're going to walk away and I will never see you again."

My stomach knotted, not wanting to admit that what he just claimed was probably going to happen. After a moment, I said, "But I'm still leaving in two weeks, whether we have this conversation or not."

"Why?" Christopher had blurted, turning to face me and throwing this hands wide. "Why do you have to leave at all?"

"Because I'm going to college. I start classes at Frostard," I fumbled for my explanation, voice raising with his.

"You don't even want to go to Frostard," he had countered, always knowing me better than I gave him credit for. "Lindsay wants to go to Frostard. That doesn't mean you have to go with her."

He had said as much to me the night I got the acceptance letter in the mail. I didn't even tell him I applied, because I honestly didn't remember sending in the application. Lindsay had filled in my form for me, though I sat beside her the entire time, moving in a haze while answering the essay questions and giving her my resume.

"It's too late to say these things, Christopher," I said, bringing my voice back down. "I'm enrolled in classes and I've taken out the loans. I'm going."

Again, Christopher's jaw tightened and defeat filled his eyes. I don't know why he thought he could change my mind. I told him the day I got the acceptance letter that I was going with Lindsay to college. He's known for months that I was leaving, and yet, he refused to talk to me about it. I don't think I realized, in all those quiet moments, he had been secretly hoping he could change my mind.

"So this is it?" he had said, and his voice was a whisper, one that still scrapes through my head. I had never heard him sound so broken in all the time we were together.

"We both said we didn't want to do long distance," I said with a shrug.

That defeat in his eyes chilled to what I can only assume was hatred. "No, *Lindsay* told you not to stay in a long distance relationship. That is not the same thing as *us* not wanting to try it."

The hair on my arms had raised at the edge in his voice. Christopher and Lindsay never liked each other, and that always made me upset because they were both so important to me. I think Christopher would have given Lindsay a chance if she wasn't always intervening in our relationship, stealing me away on date nights, telling me what I could or couldn't do that weekend, and this—deciding I shouldn't do a long distance relationship.

And I let her. I let her decide all of these things for me.

It makes me wonder if Christopher also hated me for not standing up to her. He probably saw me as a hypocrite. All the nights he had to listen to me complain about Lindsay and how much I hated doing some of the things she suggested, to just turn around and let her keep doing it day after day.

Until she dragged me all the way to California and planned out my entire life. I guess I finally drew the line, even if it's only for a few months. Just a break to get myself back together. I still think Frostard is a great school, and the degree I'm getting will help me find a good job. Hopefully, one at the same company my dad works for, and I'll have a successful life. It was just too much change, too big of a decision to not be my own choice, so I need this time to fully accept the path I'm on.

I remember after Christopher had said that, I turned away and stared at this exact twisting of tree branches. "So this is it," I said, each word sharp and heavy in my throat.

After a few minutes, Christopher stood up and ducked out of the alcove of trees. I haven't talked to him since. I went home and Lindsay was there, swaying on the porch swing, waiting for me to return.

"Did you finally do it?" she asked, her voice too bright for the dreary storm clouds hanging at the edges of my eyes.

All I did was nod, and then she grabbed my hand and took me upstairs. I sat on the edge of my bed while she removed every photo of Christopher and me from my bulletin board, took that blue vase off my nightstand, and removed the varsity jacket from the back of my chair, and shoved it all in a bag. She left after that, saying she'd give them back to Christopher for me, and once the door to my room closed behind her, the tears broke free.

Just like the single tear does now, the memories from that day still so raw. It tracks down my cheek, chilling in the cold.

Snow crunches behind me, and I nearly jump off the bench. I snap my head in the direction of sound and the air in my lungs is sucked free when he comes up behind the bench, his shadow casting over my face. I stare at him, my eyes wide and face paling.

Christopher Samson stands before me.

In the haunting silence, he sits down next to me, hazel eyes trained on the trees in front of us. I just blink, still not fully convinced he is really in front of me. The weak moonlight that finds its way through the protection of the pine needles makes his olive skin glow, catching on the loose waves of his chocolate brown hair. He leans back into the bench, placing his hands in his lap, and I see the camera he holds in his grasp. It's his favorite one, a gift from his parents that he got at the beginning of our senior year of high school.

"I thought I saw you last night," he says and I flinch at the sound of his voice, now confirming that he is truly sitting in front of me, that voice something my ears have been straining to hear for months. My heart lifts in my chest just at the sound of him.

"I thought you were going to stop," I say, my voice not nearly as strong as his. "I saw you drive by," I add, that moment from last night— though only mere seconds—has replayed in my head a hundred times today.

I don't know what I expect him to say next, but when he does speak, he finally pulls his eyes from the wall of pine needles and looks at me. "Why are you home, Penny?"

Words rush up my throat and collect there, unsure which to say first. I've wanted to call him too many times to count, to just tell him about my day, what I was struggling with. Now that he sits in front of me, I have too much to say, and I have no idea where to start. This oddly feels like that summer night all those months ago. Like these could be the moments that could have happened if he hadn't gotten up and walked away from me. If I hadn't gone right when he went left. My heart warms in my chest at the idea of him and me. The universe has brought us back to the spot where we ended everything, letting me change my mind. Letting me pick him.

"Don't tell me Lindsay's decided you should drop out," Christopher says, shattering my naïve thoughts.

I can't choose him. This is not the universe making our paths intersect. I have a life to live, a path I'm already on. Plus, I have no idea where *he's* at. When I left Christopher, he was preparing to take classes at the community college, but I have no idea what has happened in that time... or who he could be with now.

"No, she didn't," I say through the dam of words, finally sorting out what to say. "I just wanted to come home. I'm taking the semester off."

Christopher's hazel eyes glimmer in the moonlight, their brown depths scanning every inch of my face, concern swelling in them. "Are you okay, Penny?"

A pit in my stomach opens up. His voice is gentle and caring. He doesn't reach out and take my hand, but his words feel like a hug wrapping around my waist.

A shaky breath eases from my lungs. "I don't know," I admit, letting myself speak honestly. I always do with him. "It was just a lot of change and I lost my grip on everything. I need a break."

"Too many things decided for you?" He shifts his weight, cocking his head to the side. Nothing about his voice is condescending. He knows exactly how I feel when Lindsay becomes overwhelming.

"Yes." I nod and swallow through the knot of tears climbing my throat. I don't need to cry about the stress I was drowning in at Frostard. I've escaped that, now. "Except this time she isn't deciding how we do our hair for the game, or what prom dress I should wear. Now she's choosing my entire future. Her hands are around the pen, writing out how the rest of my life will be."

I shake my head and peer up at him through my blonde lashes thick with mascara. I know I'll see the look of *I told you* so before I even meet his gaze, and it's there, all over his face, but it's not as bitter as I thought it would be. It almost looks like he feels sorry for me and I think that might be worse.

Instead of voicing those thoughts, he clears his throat and looks back at the trees around us. "I wouldn't think this would be a place you'd want to come to."

I pull my bottom lip between my teeth, nerves about discussing our break up making my heartbeat falter. "Coach Violet asked me to come by practice tonight," I say, and add, "When I left the school, I was just kind of drawn here."

He gives me a soft nod of understanding and it raises a question in my mind now that the overwhelming shock of seeing him is fading.

"Why are *you* here?" I know Christopher too well to miss the twitch of his fingers around the camera in his lap. He's just as nervous as I am.

"Well, I know what it must look like," he says, his tone tilting up into forced humor.

The corners of my lips tug in a weak smile, seeing that he's trying to break the heavy tension between us. "You sure you're not just following me?" I tease, knowing that's what he was implying.

The whisper of a laugh leaks through his lips. "I promise, I'm not."

"I don't know, two nights in a row," I draw out and a stronger laugh escapes Christopher.

"There are only so many roads in Rayou," he says as his excuse. Christopher lifts his camera from his lap, letting my eyes catch on it before adding, "I came here to shoot a picture for an assignment."

Reality continues to seep through the branches around us, reminding me again that this isn't the memory of us talking on that summer night. Those people are gone, lost to our history. "How are your classes going? Do you like Rayou Community College?"

Christopher nods, shuffling his feet to stretch his legs out. "I do," he says. "I really like the photography classes they offer."

"That's good!" I let my excitement seep into my answer. I know how excited he was to take his love for photography and turn it into something he could make a living at. While Christopher's dream has always been a technical design school for photography, he had to settle with a couple of courses at the community college, but it looks like it's working for him. "I'm sure you're the best in the class," I add, and against the white moonlight, a pink blush heats his cheeks. I've been the muse for so many photo shoots, I know just how talented Christopher is.

"I don't know if I'd say that," he says, dismissing my compliment. "I guess I'll know by the end of the semester."

His last words are said more to himself than to me. "What do you mean?"

Christopher seems to realize that he spoke aloud and shrugs. "There's a pretty prestigious competition happening this semester at the college."

"And you're competing?" I ask, though I can assume I know the answer based on his earlier statement.

"Everyone in my photography class is required to," he says, glancing at me to see if he can read my facial reactions to this conversation. It feels oddly right to be sitting here and talking with him about his classes at Rayou Community College. "It's a portfolio competition," he explains. "You're supposed to put a collection of photos together that tell a story and evoke emotion. The prize is a secret, but it's supposed to be amazing."

I process his words, at first not realizing the meaning behind them. It sounds interesting, something pretty straight forward that I think he could excel at. But then I remember what brought this up. I had asked him why he was here and he told me he came to shoot a photo for a project. "The photo you came here to take," I say, pausing to catch my breath. "It's for the portfolio, isn't it?"

He never tears his hazel eyes from mine, and I see the emotions swelling in their brown depths. "Yes," he says, causing my heart to ache.

Because there is nowhere more emotional than this place. Than the bench where his heart shattered and everything we built and promised one another crumbled away.

Tears bloom at the edges of my eyes and I try to blink them back, thankful the frigid air helps to keep them from falling. The last thing I want to do is cry in front of him when it's my fault we broke up. "I can see why you'd choose to come here for that," I admit softly.

"It was the first place I thought of," he says, craning his neck back to look at the maze of pine needles overhead, though a part of me thinks I see his own tears glisten in the moonlight and he's trying to keep them from falling.

We're quiet for a moment, letting the sound of the tree branches brushing together fill the hollow space. Eventually, I ask, "What other photos are you planning?" Christopher drops his head to look at me when I add, "It's a portfolio competition, right? You'll need a few pages of pictures."

Christopher's shoulders lift as our conversation changes course. "I have some ideas for different stories I want to tell," he says, fingers fidgeting over the buttons on the camera. "I'll need to find someone to be in a few of them. They can't all be nature shots."

I let out a soft hum and nod, trying to understand the technical side of his project, but it's hard to focus when I can hardly believe he's sitting in front of me. I'm so lost in the way the shadows on his face sharpen his jaw, how his brown waves glisten in the moonlight, making me want to run my fingers through the soft strands I know so well, that I'm completely caught off guard when he asks, "You wouldn't be looking for a modeling job, would you?"

"What?" I blurt, locking my eyes on his and focusing on what he just asked me. "You want me to be in your portfolio?"

"Only if you have nothing better to do," he says, and I see him second guess the offer. "I'm sorry. That was weird of me to ask. We're not... We don't—"

"I can do it," I say, cutting him off.

When we were dating, we used to do photo shoots all the time. Photography was always Christopher's passion, and like any other hobby, it requires practice. He was learning what source of lighting was best, when the best time to shoot during the day was depending on if you were on the east or west side of town, how to catch the light in someone's hair, and how to make the camera focus on a face and not the world around them. I know why he is so quick to ask me, because that's what we did. And I don't know who else he could ask. I'm sure he has friends at the community college that would do it, but aren't they all competing for the same prize? You can't ask your competition to help you.

"It could be fun, and I really don't have anything else to do," I say.

His brown eyes are like glass marbles as they sweep across my features. "Are you sure?"

"Of course," I say, trying to make this arrangement sound more casual than it feels.

I do want to help him, and I always had a lot of fun doing the photo shoots when we were dating. Plus, besides my mom, Coach Violet, and the high school cheer members, I don't really have anyone left in Rayou to hang out with. I have a feeling running my mom's errands is going to get old pretty quick.

"Maybe it's the competitor in me," I say, sitting a bit taller. "I do love a good competition, and now I really want you to win."

After an unsure second, I see the corner of Christopher's mouth tug up. "Okay. Thanks, Penny. I can text you later and we can go over the different pictures I want to capture."

Just when I'm about to tell him that sounds good, I feel my phone buzz in my coat pocket. I reach inside, the screen illuminating the alcove of pine trees. "It's my mom," I say, reading the text she just sent. "I should have been home by now." I turn off the screen and slip the phone back into my pocket. When I look up, Christopher is still studying me with unsure hazel eyes and I see his fingers are still fidgeting on the camera buttons. "Oh, did you need me for this photo? I can tell my mom I'll be a few more minutes."

Christopher's eyes drop, and he brushes his tongue across his bottom lip. "Actually, I think the point of this photo is for the bench to be empty."

His words are ice that freeze around my heart, making my blood chill to my toes. "Oh," I say and can't hide the hurt that fills my voice. He looks up at me, an apology in his eyes, but I speak before he can voice it. He doesn't need to apologize for anything. "I understand," I say, rising to my feet. I pause and spin around, scanning the little alcove of trees. "I think you're right. The message you're trying to capture will come through better that way." I look at Christopher and force a smile to my lips, not wanting him to know how much pain still lingers from our breakup.

"This isn't going to be weird, is it?" he asks after a moment.

I shake my head, blonde curls falling in front of my shoulders. "No, it'll be fun. I know we haven't talked since... Since then," I say, shifting my feet in the snow, "but I'd really like to be a part of this."

What I want to say is that I miss him, miss our nights together, and the way he used to make me laugh. I bite my tongue to keep the words at bay because it's not fair of me to claim that. Maybe this is the least I could do for breaking his heart. Help him with his portfolio and receive this mysterious grand prize. After the mess I made of our relationship, breaking the trust and love he had for me, I should do a lot more, but this is a start.

"Okay," he says, his own small smile pulling at his lips. "I'll text you."

"Okay," I reply, taking a few steps toward the trail out of the cluster of pine trees. "Goodnight, Christopher," I add, looking back over my shoulder to see him still watching me.

"Goodnight, Penny."

By the time I get home, mom has already gone to bed. In the shadows of my bedroom, my phone illuminates with a text message. I'm about to flip it over and continue to get ready for bed when I see it's from Christopher, the tiny heart icon still by his name.

Christopher: I was thinking, maybe we could get breakfast tomorrow and go over the project. Meet me at the Snowcapped Diner at 8:00?

My thumbs hesitate over the keyboard. Snowcapped Diner. *Our place.* We used to get breakfast there every Monday before school because seniors started an hour later than everyone else. Honestly, a very weird thing to do, but when you go to a school as small as Rayou, we do a lot of things that are unique to us.

Once I'm able to push the memories back, I let him know I'll be there. Before closing out of the conversation and putting my phone down for the night, I click on his contact and erase the red heart.

Chapter 6

I'm reading the text from Christopher for the seventh time this morning when I hear my mom's steps creak outside my room, heading downstairs and toward the kitchen.

Snowcapped Diner? With Christopher?

My mind is buzzing with confusion. Part of me really thought I dreamt the entire conversation with him last night. But I didn't. I'm seriously about to get up and go get breakfast with my ex-boyfriend.

Before mom can get too far in her breakfast preparations this morning, I hurry and get ready. As I bound down the stairs, I pull my hair back into a messy ponytail. My golden crewneck hangs to my thighs, leaving yellow pieces of fuzz on my black leggings.

"Good morning," mom greets without looking, her focus inside the refrigerator.

"I'm going to get breakfast with Christopher."

I just blurt it out, like ripping off a band-aid. The door to the refrigerator rattles closed when she spins to face me.

"As in, Christopher Samson?"

"Yes," I say, though I know my voice holds no confidence.

Her lips purse together and I can tell she's thinking something, but keeping it locked inside. In her curious silence, I fill the void.

"I ran into him last night after cheer practice. He's participating in some photography contest at the community college and needs some help," I explain, trying to make this sound more nonchalant than it really is. "Can you drop me off at the Snowcapped Diner?" I ask, getting to the point of this conversation. With only the blue SUV between us, I'll need her to drop me off on her way to the library. I could walk to the diner from there, but it's on the way, and it seems silly to even think about hiding this from her. *Why would I?* I'm just helping him with his project, and my mom has always liked Christopher.

After a silent second of making me fidget, my mom says, "Sure." She draws out the word suspiciously and turns back to the fridge, pulling the stainless steel door open. "I'll make something for myself really quick and then we can go."

I know she wants to say much more than that, but she doesn't. I'm already struggling to keep my mind from reliving past memories with Christopher. I really don't want to talk about him with my mom. I turn around and head back upstairs to the bathroom, attempting to finish my morning routine and keep any second-guessing thoughts at bay.

Mom pulls up to the curb in front of the diner, tires spitting snow everywhere. The diner's metal sides are painted white and neon lights wrap around the edges of the roof. This morning, they're off, though I know in the afternoons they turn them on and vibrant blue and green rays light up the night. Above the galley style doors, the giant SNOWCAPPED DINER sign hangs half covered with snow. Three mountain peaks made of the same metal from the siding are tucked behind the letters. Off to the side of the diner, I see a corner of the parking lot and Christopher's red truck is in full view.

"Changing your mind?" mom asks, reminding me I need to get out of the car.

I take a breath and shake my head. "Nope. I'll come by the library when we're done," I say and reach for the handle, popping the door open.

"Have fun," she calls, and I swear the words drip with humor.

I swing the door closed behind me and climb over the snowdrift by the curb. I'm swallowed in a pocket of warm air once I enter the diner and the strong scent of coffee and syrup hits me so hard it grips my stomach. It might be my favorite smell in the entire world.

The diner is busy this morning. The sounds of cups clinking at the bar and plates stacking chorus together in a sort of buzz that makes my heart beat faster in my chest. I scan the diner and find Christopher easily. His height makes him hard to miss in any room, but the added glow of the sun coming through the window beside him puts Christopher in a spotlight.

It takes me a second before I realize he's sitting in *our* booth. The one we claimed after coming to the Snowcapped Diner became our routine senior year. I have to assume he picked it out intentionally. If I remember that's where we sat every Monday, surely he does too.

His dark brown hair falls over his face as he hunches forward to look at his phone. There's a soft voice in the back of my head that tells me I can still turn around. He hasn't seen me yet. I could leave. I quiet that voice and step forward, fingers working on the stud buttons of my coat.

My boots squeak as I cross the diner and slide into the booth. "Good morning," I say as a casual greeting. My coat falls off my shoulders and I tuck it into the seat beside me.

Christopher lifts his head, swiping his brown waves to the side, and when he looks at me, an easy smile finds his lips. "Good morning," he says, and he slides his phone into the pocket of his denim jacket. A thick, black sweatshirt hugs his form beneath the coat and I can barely see the hawk that is Rayou high school's mascot printed across the front.

I notice he has two portfolio books in the booth beside him, his camera balanced on top of them. Before I can ask about what he brought, a waitress walks up to our table, her blue dress swinging against the white apron. It's not Roxy, who I'm used to seeing in here every morning, and the traditionalist in me is saddened by that. The new server's nametag is shiny, with WILLIE carved on its metallic surface. She balances a round serving tray in her hand, two coffee cups on top of it.

"Now, he told me to get you a dark roast with creamer and honey. Swore up and down that's what you'd want, but if he's just lost his mind, I can get you something else."

I blink a few times, looking between her and Christopher. I don't know why I'm surprised he remembers my coffee order, after all the mornings we spent here, but it still catches me off guard. "That's perfect," I tell her and take the cup she hands to me.

"Oddest order I'll get this morning," she comments before handing Christopher his cup, which I know contains the lightest roast they have with caramel. "All right, and what will we be eating?" she continues, flipping open her pad of paper.

Christopher proceeds to order scrambled eggs with sausage, and as he speaks the words, the memory of them runs through my head, knowing that's what he would say. When our waitress turns to me, I know Christopher fully expects me to tell her I don't want anything. That

I'll just drink the coffee. He raises his eyebrows with surprise when I order a side of hash browns. The waitress flips her book closed and tells us it'll be right out before heading to another table.

"Hash browns?" Christopher immediately inquires. "At least your coffee order hasn't changed or else I'd look crazy."

"I think you probably still look crazy for even ordering it," I joke easily and lift the steaming cup to my lips, taking a careful sip of the coffee that tastes just as good as I remember it.

I know me actually ordering food for breakfast is almost as rare as me making my own decisions. I used to be overly self-conscious about everything I ate, being a cheerleader and all, but with that behind me, nothing is stopping me from enjoying some greasy potatoes. Nothing, and no one, I should amend, knowing Lindsay would lose her mind if she saw me right now. And not just because of what I ordered, but because of who sits across from me, his hazel eyes glowing in the morning light that seeps through the blinds on the window next to us, making them look like liquid fire.

I set the cup back down and break the silence, "So, do you want to tell me about this project?"

He nods and picks up the first portfolio I had noticed a second ago, placing it on the table and leaning his forearms against it. "So for the competition, I have to put together an array of photos that evoke emotion and tell a story. I have five different shots that I want to do," he says, and begins to walk me through his vision for the portfolio.

I'm not surprised the lookout spot is on his list of places to go. It's easily the most popular place in Rayou and will definitely produce gorgeous photos for his portfolio. He also wants to go to the local hot springs that Rayou is known for, find a valley in the mountains, and visit the ice rink.

"I thought we could also take some pictures at the library, if your mom wouldn't mind," he adds.

"Oh, I like that idea," I tell him as I continue sipping on my coffee, fully invested in the different photos he's laid out.

"I thought it would add some variety to the portfolio since everything else is outside," he says and I nod, agreeing. I never would have considered needing some variety in the selection of photos I'd submit in the competition, but I guess that's why he's the one pursuing a photography degree and not me.

"So, what's that?" I ask, nodding to the black binder that still rests beneath his arms.

He sits back, lifting his hands from its surface, and slides it across the table. "This is an example of a portfolio I put together for my classes last semester. It was an introduction assignment to help the professor to get to know us."

I nod as I flip open the cover and my eyes soak in the vibrant opening image of the WELCOME TO RAYOU sign. He caught it right at sunrise, the pink and orange rays streaming up behind the white-washed sign. It was taken at the end of summer, right when classes began, because there is no snow in sight. The cracked pavement that leads into Rayou is in full sight, grass flanking it on either side with marigolds blooming around the welcome sign.

Christopher's tan fingers balance at the page's edge, watching my reaction to the photo before turning it to the next display. He continues to flip through the portfolio while I take in each beautiful moment he's captured. It's like looking through the lens of a camera and seeing him on the other side, each image special to Christopher. There are a lot of pictures of the high school gymnasium, of shadows cast over the basketball hoop and a ball in mid-air. There are even pictures of pictures, a clever way to capture his love for photography. One of my favorites is a photo of him taking a picture of himself in the mirror. You can't see his face, just his chocolate brown hair behind the camera that hovers in front of his face. Because that's who Christopher is, a photographer.

The last photo in the album is the back of the Rayou welcome sign that says *COME AGAIN* in pretty cursive. This time, the photo of the sign was taken at sunset. Deep purple and red hues glow in the sky and reflect off the white sign.

The story he told, with capturing the welcome sign at sunrise and ending with the goodbye side at sunset, is so creative, so *him*. When he closes the portfolio, it feels like a rock sinks deep into my chest. That feeling of closure, of finality, is suffocating. If I had been the one turning the pages, I know I would have stopped one early, to avoid this feeling that always accompanies the ending of things. Maybe it's a superstition, a bad habit I can't break, but I hate this feeling in my stomach now. I reach for my coffee, taking a large drink, and hope the searing liquid warms the knot out of me.

"And what's that one?" I ask, after gushing about the first portfolio he's shown me.

Christopher's eyes drift down to the booth he sits on, seeing the second binder I'm staring at. "Oh, that's just another portfolio. I didn't mean to bring it in. I picked them up together by accident."

"Can I see it?" I ask and set the mug back on the table.

He sucks in the corner of his mouth, biting his lip hesitantly, and I feel as though I definitely shouldn't have asked that. Before I can dismiss my request, Christopher reaches for the black binder and places it on the table. "This is from the class trip we took last semester. We were supposed to capture the experience in a series of photos."

Again, he flips the cover of the portfolio open and I take in the photos. But this time, it's not the curious joy I had when looking at the last portfolio. This first image catches me by surprise, and my head clouds with confusion, thrown a bit off balance.

I study the moonlight in the picture, how it reflects off the clock surrounded by stone on Big Ben in London.

London.

"You went," I say weakly, and I honestly don't even mean to speak, but I can't help myself. I'm so surprised by what is in front of me, I don't think about locking my lips and keeping the thought inside.

"Like I said, it was a class trip. I didn't choose to go there," Christopher says, a hitch in his voice making my throat tighten. His long fingers are frozen on the page, not wanting to flip it, so I reach forward and turn it myself. A narrow street is captured on the next page, probably taken the same night as the previous photo. With each page I turn, each picture I see of Big Ben, the Tower Bridge, The House of Parliament, Buckingham Palace—

My breathing is weak, the air thick in my lungs. *London.* I can't believe he actually went.

When Christopher and I were dating, we always talked about taking a trip to London together. It was my dream—*is* my dream—to go there. We made a list on his phone of all the things we wanted to do, all the things he's now seen without me. I don't even get halfway through the pages when I can't look at it any longer, those thick emotions that surround memories with him making tears grow at the edges of my eyes. I don't know if I'm upset that he went without me, or if it's just the heartache that consumes me when I think of our past. Maybe it's a bit of both.

"Penny," he says my name when I've been quiet for too long.

I've kept my eyes down, begging the tears to pull back before I look at him. The portfolio is still open, the picture on display taken in a garden. There are four people captured in the image, two boys and two girls, pointing at something outside of the frame. I wonder if they're his classmates, because two of them have cameras hanging around their necks. Maybe one of them is a girl he replaced me with.

"These are great," I say, the words sounding like they are trying to break free. I speak so quickly, hoping to quite my thoughts from even suggesting that Christopher has moved on, but I'm not lying. The photos *do* look great. I just wish I hadn't seen them. I knew being around Christopher could be hard, but I may have underestimated the fact that I could handle it. "You never posted about the trip," I add, remembering that I never saw anything about it. I still follow Christopher on social media and see his rare posts, but never anything about London. I would have remembered that.

Though my eyes are still down on the portfolio, the tears finally disappearing, I see him shrug. He doesn't say anything, but I know what he is thinking. He didn't post anything because he didn't want me to know he had gone to London without me. I'm at a loss for words now, his silence the loudest thing in the diner, but our waitress is the saving grace, approaching the table with our plates. We snap out of the heavy moment that surrounds us and Christopher closes the portfolio. He slides it out of the way and I take my plate of hash browns, making a comment about how good the food smells. I'll say anything to drive our conversation away from his trip to London.

For the rest of breakfast, we never bring London back up, only talking about the current project he's working on and when we want to take the photos for the new portfolio. He asks if we can start with the photo at the lookout point tonight. I'm about to tell him that works for me when my phone buzzes on the tabletop, the screen lighting up with a notification from Coach Violet.

I blink, a bit stunned to see her name on my phone. It's been months since I've received texts from her about practices. My mind is still thrown a bit off, sitting in this diner with Christopher, seeing a text from Coach light up my phone. It's like my past and present are running in parallel and it's hard for me to remember which one I belong to. I pick up the phone and read her message, a smile pulling at my lips.

"Coach Violet wants me to be the assistant coach for the cheer team!" I say, turning my phone for Christopher to see, something I do completely out of instinct, because I'm so used to showing him everything that happened to me when we were dating.

"That's awesome, Penny," he says, eyes lighting up.

I turn the phone around, still reading the message she sent about how she got the idea after seeing me work with the squad last night. When I respond, accepting the offer with four exclamation points, I realize what this means; cheer practice every night, this time from the sidelines, coaching the squad for the state tournament. It'll be different, probably exhausting at first, but I really think it could be fun.

"So, can you still do the photo tonight?" Christopher asks, drawing my thoughts back to him.

"Oh," I say, running my schedule through my head. "Yeah, I'll be done with cheer practice at seven tonight."

"Want me to pick you up at the school?" he asks.

"Sure," I say, scraping together one last bite of hash browns and ketchup. As I chew, a thought comes to me that makes me pause. "Shouldn't you be in class today?" I ask after I swallow.

Christopher is wiping his fingers on a napkin, tossing it onto his plate when he says, "I don't have class on Tuesday or Thursday."

"That's nice," I say, slouching back into the leather booth now that

I'm full of hash browns.

"Saves me money on gas," he says with a shrug. He taps the face of his phone, the clock reading 9:15 a.m. "I do need to get going, though. Mom has me working with her on my off days."

I want to ask what she has him doing, knowing she's the principal at the high school, but I don't know if it's my place to ask him questions about things outside of the project. It's one thing for me to sit here and talk to him about his classes and the photos we're going to take, but it's another to ask about his family, about what he's doing in his personal life.

"Yeah, I need to get to the library. My mom probably has a stack of books a mile high for me to shelve," I say, working my way out of the booth. I grab my winter coat and pull it on, securing the buttons while Christopher and I head to the front of the diner.

The waitress asks if everything is on one ticket and I'm quick to tell her to split it, though I get the feeling Christopher fully intended to pay for my breakfast. Not that it would mean he's anything more than a nice guy. He wouldn't have done it to signify this as a date or that we are anything more than friends right now. If that, because I don't think friends feel this on edge with everything they or drown silently in past memories that still suffocate their minds. We pay at the register by the door and then brace ourselves for the winter morning.

The sun is bright today, working hard to melt the snow that still coats everything outside. What was a pristine blanket of snow on the road, is dirty slush now, trails of the melted stuff trickling down the street.

"Want me to drive you to the library?" Christopher asks.

I squint against the sunlight that's extra bright as it reflects off the snow. "That's okay. I was just going to walk. It's only around the block."

"Are you sure?" he asks, pulling his keys out of his pocket and swinging them around his finger.

I nod, digging my hands deeper into the pockets of my coat. "Yeah, there's still some more of Rayou I want to see." I give him a small smile that he returns.

"All right, I'll pick you up at the school tonight, then."

"I'll be ready at seven," I tell him again, taking steps toward the sidewalk that is hardly shoveled. He waves softly, just a slight raise of his hand, and then he turns for the parking lot, flipping his brown waves into his face and tucking his chin down against the cold. I watch him go, boots leaving prints on the slushy sidewalk until he pops open the red door and hoists himself into the driver's seat. I turn and head toward the library before he sees that I was watching him. I know that I'm going to see him tonight, but for some reason, I want to watch him for as long as I can, as if I may never see him again.

Maybe that's because I never thought I would after that day last summer. Maybe part of me still thinks I'm sleeping right now and none of these moments with him have been real. I surprise myself when that thought saddens me. I want this to be real. I want to be free from Frostard, coaching the cheer team with Coach Violet, and helping Christopher with his portfolio project. And for the first time in my entire life, I'm actually doing exactly what I want to do.

Chapter 7

WE GOT THAT TROJAN BEAT.
CAN YOU FEEL THE HEAT
WE GOT THAT TROJAN ROAR
FEEL THE RUMBLE IN THE FLOOR

The chorus of voices repeats the cheer three more times, each round a bit louder than the last. I stand on the sidelines of the court, nodding my head while the squad practices one of the many basketball chants we have. Now that basketball postseason is starting, the team has been reviewing the cheers they want to use at the games and even learning some new ones. I have to press my lips together to keep from saying the familiar words with them.

"Okay, let's get into the opening formation for our routine," Coach Violet announces, cutting off the repeated cheer.

The squad—dressed in casual shorts and t-shirts—rearranges themselves on the gym floor for the opening sequence I watched them learn yesterday. As they get into position, Coach Violet walks up to stand beside me.

"I'm really glad you accepted my offer to help with the team, Penny."

"Of course!" I tell her, that pep returning to my voice after only one night with the team. "I should be thanking you for giving me the opportunity. This..." I pause, gesturing around the gym and to the squad of boys and girls in front of me. "I've missed all of this so much."

"What I'd like to do, is split the routine in half, giving you the responsibility to teach part of the routine while I work on the other part. That way, we get this organized as fast as possible," Coach says, unclipping a piece of paper on her clipboard. She hands it to me, and I look over her notes and directions for the rest of the routine. She's handed me the group work, which includes the flyers. I'm not surprised, it's what I know best, but that's the hardest part of the routine, and it's what can make or break our scores. A weight falls on my chest. I don't want to mess this up. Before I can voice my doubt, Coach Violet signals for the squad to begin the routine and they perform the opening set we taught them yesterday.

While they rehearse, I study the paper Coach gave me and familiarize myself with what she's asking for. I even talk myself through it, moving my arms and feet in a sort of haze that helps me visualize the routine. When we split the squad in half, me taking the two flyers and six supporters, I try my best to put together the routine Coach has imagined in her head. We throw out mats and practice the various lifts, starting by simply simulating them on the ground. If you can't make the twist on your feet, there's no way you'll hit it in the air. I learn that the new flyer's name is Lillyanne, and can't help but be drawn to her every time we run a new part, going to her and giving her pointers. There's a sense of connection to her because she reminds me of myself.

It's the fastest two hours of my life. It's like I blinked and the entire practice was already over. I don't remember feeling that way when I was the one cheering, but I've barely taught the first two lifts when Coach calls us back together. The girls and boys are breathing heavily, sweat dampening their foreheads and necks, but breathy smiles bloom on their faces. The same joy that radiates from them takes root in my chest. There's something incredibly powerful about watching the routine be built from scratch, seeing the pieces come together that will represent the performance you take to the state competition. It plants a seed of hopeful thoughts and ambitious goals.

But underneath that joy, a rock is weighing heavy in my stomach. More than once, I looked over my shoulder, fully expecting to see Lindsay standing there. I caught a glimpse of myself in the screen of my phone, noticing my ponytail had fallen loose, and instantly fixed it. I tied my t-shirt into a crop, and rolled the hem of my shorts to make them hit my thighs the way Lindsay taught me. I even put on eyeliner, which I haven't worn since Christmas. Being back here, being with the squad, it's brought back my old habits. The ways I needed to be perfect. I was the flyer, the face of the cheer team for my entire high school career. I had to be the pretty face everyone expected from a cheerleader. When I did this every day of high school, I got used to it, not knowing any other way to carry myself, but now I'm exhausted. The bright voice and sometimes forced happiness has turned my throat raw, and I wasn't even the one cheering. I'm so lost in my own thoughts of just how much being here is molding me back into the girl I used to be, that I completely miss Coach Violet dismiss the team.

"Same time tomorrow?" she says, turning to me as the squad disperses.

"Yep!" I reply, tilting up the word in the way old-me would have.

As I walk across the gym, I pull out my phone and see a text message from Christopher saying that he's here. My heart dips and swoops back up at the sight of his name on my phone, and I silently scold myself. That can't happen every time he texts me, whether the feelings are there or not. I let him know that I'm going to change first. I packed a cream crewneck and dark skinny jeans in my old cheer duffle before coming to practice. There was no way I was wearing that in the gymnasium that rises thirty degrees the second the team starts running exercises, especially when I knew I'd be more a part of the practice today than last night.

Now in clothes more suitable for a winter photo shoot, I head out the front doors of the school and find Christopher's red truck the instant I'm outside. He's pulled up to the left of the doors, headlights pouring two rays of white light across the slushy parking lot. They're so bright I can't even see Christopher inside the cabin. Feeling like I'm in a spotlight, I hurry to the passenger side of the truck and pop open the door. I toss my duffle on the floor of the truck, and I step up into the seat, every movement so familiar to me I don't have to think about it.

I pull the door closed, a small shiver escaping me before l lean back in the seat and buckle up.

"Hi."

I glance up after clicking the buckle in place and meet Christopher's hazel eyes, the brown in them darker tonight. My breath stills in my throat. Seeing him, being in his truck, the way he's looking at me—like he also can't believe I'm in this seat again—has every inch of me warming. The rich scent of coffee fills my nose, the sweet and smoky aroma begging to release a million memories at the same time. I have never forgotten the smell of him, the smell that always lingers in this truck, even with no coffee in sight.

"Hello," I say, the word hitching as the pep from my cheer voice fades. I never have to use that with him. I sit up in the seat, nervous fingers finding the hair tie in my ponytail and pulling it loose.

Christopher blinks a few times, watching the strands of my blonde hair fall across my shoulders. Realizing he's supposed to be driving the truck, he shifts in his seat and his hands find the steering wheel.

"How was practice?" Christopher asks as he puts the truck into drive, slowly working his way across the slick parking lot and onto the main road. A song sputters from the radio in the dash. The signal isn't clear, though that's completely normal in Rayou.

"Good," I tell him with a sigh, suddenly very short with my words. The nerves that build in my stomach aren't the cautious and hesitant ones I thought I'd have. They are giddy and excited. I'm worried I might say the wrong thing and also anxious to catch him looking at me. It's the way I probably felt on our first date.

I shake my head and press a cold hand to my cheeks. I silently tell my heart to knock it off. My flushed face cools with my touch and my heart slows, coming back to the steady pattern I had this morning in the diner.

"Is the team going to win state this year?" he asks, and his voice carries a playful lift that has an easy smile blooming on my lips.

"That'd be awesome, wouldn't it?" I say, letting the daydream of being state champions fill my head. I tell Christopher about practice and working with the team, finally finding my voice now that the nerves have faded.

The truck weaves through the east side of Rayou and breaks away from the village, entering the thick pine forest that surrounds it. I keep my focus on the headlights guiding our path up the narrow road, stealing a few glances at Christopher while I talk.

I recognize the path we take, having been up to the lookout point many times before. The line of trees opens up, and, while the road continues to wind higher into the mountains, we turn off onto a rocky patch on the left.

"Gosh, I haven't been up here in months," I say, though I'm sure that is obvious. I haven't even been home for months.

Christopher parks the truck at the end of the patch of rock and says he'll leave it running while we take the photo so it'll stay warm. We reach for our doors in unison, pushing them open and letting the cold air bite our faces. Already I'm grateful the truck will be waiting to thaw the Colorado winter from my bones when we're finished.

The backdoor swings open and Christopher grabs his camera, using the strap to hang it around his neck, and we walk across the makeshift parking spots to the wooden platform that looms near the edge of a drop off. You can't see anything as you approach the platform, only the dark night sky speckled with stars and the mountain peaks in the distance. But when I climb the two short steps onto the wooden beams of the lookout point, the entirety of Rayou comes into view.

The air is already so cold it's thin in my lungs, but when I see my hometown below me, glowing as bright as a star atop a Christmas tree, I lose what little breath I have.

"Oh, wow," I sigh, crossing to the edge and leaning against the rickety banister. I had a sneak peek of this the other night when I came in on the bus, but that was nothing like the view I have now. Then, I was peering out a fogged window, trying to see it around the trees and street signs that lined the road. Now, I stand above the grid of streets lined with Christmas lights. Red and green and yellow flashes twist together into a patchwork that consumes the whole village. It's not as late as when I arrived on the bus. All the storefronts are illuminated tonight, cars driving by on the snowy roads below, but we are so high up, they are silent to me.

"This is my favorite spot in Rayou," I say, and out of the corner of my eye, I see Christopher step up to lean against the railing with me.

"Does it look different to you?" he asks.

I tear my eyes away from the village and look at him, seeing his eyes squint against the cold as he studies Rayou below us. "I think it looks more beautiful, but that's only because I've been gone. I got used to seeing it like this all my life."

He nods, understanding what I mean. "I think it looks smaller to me," he says, tilting his head to the side. "Like when I used to come up here in the summer on my bike as a kid, it felt like this gigantic city I got to explore."

I didn't know Christopher when he was little. I guess I knew of him, but we didn't even talk until our junior year of high school. I've heard his stories about being a kid though, and how he used to play little league baseball before he switched to basketball as he got older—and taller.

We're quiet for a moment, and the only sounds are the wind whistling through the pine needles around the lookout point and the soft sound of music coming from Christopher's truck. Standing up here and looking down on Rayou makes a heated anger bloom in my stomach. I wish I hadn't lost those six months at Frostard. Or at least, I wish it would have been my decision to leave. Seeing my hometown, glittering and gorgeous below me, makes me think of Lindsay and that dark dorm room I left her in. The cinderblock walls and drab tile floors. How did she convince me to spend Christmas there? With our tiny tree propped up in the windowsill, naked without ornaments or a tree topper.

That will forever be the worst Christmas of my life. There wasn't even a reason for us to stay, other than the fact that Lindsay didn't want to come back here. We were probably the only people on the planet ordering pizza on Christmas Eve, watching reruns of her favorite reality television show. She didn't even put on a Christmas movie or play music. The next morning we each exchanged a single gift, and that was as close as it came to feeling like Christmas.

"I know you're already aware of this, but I haven't actually said it aloud to anyone," I say, speaking over the frustration that makes me curl my fingers around the banister. Seeing Rayou, thinking of Lindsay and how much my life has spiraled, I finally tell him the truth, though it is not a secret. "I only went to Frostard because Lindsay told me to. She practically filled out the application and packed my bags for me herself."

I shift my weight and lean my hip into the wooden rails, looking at Christopher, who still watches the streets below us.

"Does that also mean you're admitting you let Lindsay end our relationship?" he asks so bluntly I have to force myself to run his words through my head a second time.

I've been quiet for too long, though I shouldn't be as surprised as I am to hear him ask that. Surely we've both been spending this time together thinking about the past. Christopher drops his head forward, brown hair falling into his face.

"I'm sorry, I shouldn't have said that," he apologizes through a sigh and lifts his head, locking his hazel eyes on me.

"I know why you said it," I admit, making my mouth work again. "But that's not true."

And it's not, because, for it to be true, for Lindsay to have been the reason our relationship ended, well... I would have had to actually let him go, and I know I haven't done that. It's why I catch myself checking my phone for a message from him, why I haven't dated anyone else, why

I'm so upset he went to London without me. Because I hate endings and, in my delusional brain, I never wanted to believe we were over.

Christopher doesn't understand that's what my words mean. I can see it on his face when he drops his eyes from mine, his chest falling. He thinks I mean that *I* chose to end the relationship, that it had nothing to do with Lindsay. He either thinks that, or believes I'm lying, but he certainly doesn't think I mean I still wish we were together. I still catch myself reacting as if we were dating. But maybe it's better he thinks those other things because me being home is temporary. I don't want to go through another heartbreak and goodbye. I don't want to see him hurt the way he did that day in August.

I don't think either of us knows what to say next. I catch Christopher's mouth open slightly, only for him to close it and try again a second later. Finally, he decides on circling back to where this conversation started. "Was there something I could have done to keep you from going with her?"

His hazel eyes meet mine once again. They glitter like they're damp with tears, but he's keeping them at bay. Perhaps it's just the reflection of Rayou below us that makes the auburn depths of his eyes ignite right now.

I shake my head, giving him my best guess, because at the time, I have no idea what could have swayed me. "I don't think so. But maybe I had to go to see how bad her control over me had gotten."

The air lightens around us. That comment he made about our relationship falling further away. "Trying to find the glass half-full mentality?" He says it through a grin that pulls at his lips, and I respond with a breathy laugh and a shrug.

"I guess so. But Frostard is a good school, and I'll get a good degree from there. I'm going back in the fall, but this time, it'll be on my terms."

Christopher's breath is shaking when he draws it in, making me nervous about what he's going to say. He takes a half step forward, close enough that our hands almost touch on the banister. "I'm proud of you for making the choice to come home, Penny."

Proud of me. No one has said that yet, but I don't think anyone else really understands just how much control I gave Lindsay. "Yeah, well, it was only one decision out of the hundreds I haven't made," I say softly, trying to remove some of the weight his honest words have left.

"It only takes one," he whispers, his breath clouding around his words. "Don't let this be the last time you do something for yourself."

He's too close to me. I can feel the heat of him radiating through the winter night, which only makes me want to lean into him more. I dip my head, breaking our eye contact, and take a step back. "I'll try to remember that," I say, again throwing humor between our serious moment. "Now, do you want to take this photo before I'm a popsicle?"

He laughs at that, reaching for the camera that still hangs around his neck. "Yeah. Just look down at the town and let me do all the work."

Chapter 8

I shift my focus to Rayou, watching the silent cars trudge through the slushy roads.

"Ready?" Christopher asks and I give him a thumbs up.

The camera clicks on and the first few shots are bright with the flash. I hear the camera behind me capture images and moments, catching me in a frame on its digital film. Out of the corner of my eye, I see Christopher drop to his knees, working to get a different angle. For the next series of pictures he takes, he keeps the flash off, probably to capture the lights of Rayou. While Christopher takes the photos, I study the city, toss my head to the side, and run my fingers through my hair. All things that come easy to me from the hundreds of photo shoots we've done in the past.

I snap my head back when a deep rumble fills my ears. Above, almost concealed in the night sky, a small plane soars through the stars, its white belly trying to camouflage with them. The red lights beneath its wings flash in time with the music that still leaks out of Christopher's truck, and I'm captivated by the sight of it, by the thought that sinks its claws into my mind.

What if I never left?

It's a question I know will always remain unanswered, because I'll never know what could have happened. But what if I never left, and Christopher and I were on that plane right now, heading to London like we always talked about doing? I still haven't shaken the thought of him going there without me, the portfolio I saw this morning at the forefront of my mind.

When the rapid clicking silences, I snap out of my drifting thoughts and turn around to face Christopher, leaning my back against the railing. "Well, did you get the perfect shot?" I ask, seeing that he's studying the small screen and pressing the buttons that let him preview the different photos.

He pauses, looking up at me and then down at the camera, then back at me and then down at the camera. His lips pull wide, a toothy smile peeking out. "Yeah, do you want to see?" he asks, already stepping forward to cross to me.

I hold up my hand and stop him. "No, I want to wait until it's finished," I say.

"You don't want to see any of the photos we take?" he asks and I shake my head.

"I'd rather you pick out the ones you want to use for the portfolio and I can enjoy the finished product," I say, shoving my hands into the pockets of my coat so my numb fingers can find some warmth. "Unless I look awful," I counter, seeing surprise and a bit of disappointment drop his features. I know he likes to show me the photos he takes, but it'll be better when it's all finished.

He shakes his head, clicking the camera off and letting it rest against his chest. "No, you look amazing," he says, and I catch his lips press together, probably thinking he shouldn't have said that.

"Well, if you got what you need," I prompt him and he moves past the slip of his compliment.

"Right, yeah, we can go. I'm freezing, which can only mean you're suffering from hypothermia right now," he teases, knowing I always think everything is ten times colder than he does. I'd pull out my coat in September when the fall winds bloom, whereas he could make it in shorts until November.

We walk together, down the platform and across the rocky makeshift parking lot, and get back into his truck. Instantly, the waiting warm air works at thawing my body. Christopher shifts into reverse and pulls back onto the road while I hold my hands in front of the air vents, begging the heat to come even faster.

"I had fun tonight," I say as the truck begins its descent toward Rayou.

"Yeah?"

I nod and rub my hands together. "It's been a long time since I've done something like this."

"You and Lindsay didn't go out all the time. Have the full college experience?" he inquires, and I hear the joking tone in his voice, but I think a part of him really wants to know what I was doing at Frostard.

"Lindsay did," I say, sitting back in the seat now that the last bit of cold has lifted from my hands. I shrug and add, "It's hard to go out and be around happy people when you're not happy."

He nods and presses on the brake, slowing at a stop sign, and turning left. "So, which photo do you want to do next? I'll be free again later this week."

"You don't have a certain order you want to take them in?"

His lips fold with his shrug. "Not really. You can pick."

I think about it for a moment and decide, "We can do the one at the library. I'm sure my mom will be excited to see you." I don't think the last part is necessarily true, but I know that she's definitely going to have questions about me hanging out with Christopher, and it may put her at ease to see him sooner rather than later.

"Does she know you're with me tonight?" he asks and I nod. I don't keep many secrets from my parents, and I never had to about Christopher. Both my mom and dad liked him enough to be lenient. Plus, in a small town, there weren't many places we'd go, anyway.

Now level with Rayou, the shops on either side of the road stand taller than me, welcoming us back into the village. The string lights illuminate the inside of the truck and I watch them shift and reflect off Christopher's face as we drive by. I wonder if he feels my eyes on him, but if he does, he doesn't turn to meet my gaze.

"Do you want to come by tomorrow?" I ask after a second, forgetting we were talking about the library photo and instead losing myself in the sight of him; his sharp jawline, muscled chest hidden beneath his denim jacket, and wavy brown hair.

He shifts his head to the side, now connecting our gazes for a split second before he looks back at the road. "I have class tomorrow. Can we do Thursday?"

"Sure," I say, knowing my schedule is flexible. "Before cheer practice would be best. That's when my mom has her shift and I'll already be at the library. Otherwise we'd have to deal with Sarah," I say, mentioning the other person who works at the library on the opposite shifts of my mom. She'd probably complain that the shuttering clicks from Christopher's camera were too loud for the library and we'd never get any photos taken.

Christopher makes another turn, taking us down Olive Street. I bite the inside of my cheek, a warmth blooming down my arms. I didn't even have to tell him where to turn to get to my house. I know that's not a crazy revelation—he drove by it just the other night and Rayou is so small everyone can get around on their own easily—but it still makes my heart swell at the idea of him driving me home, making myself fight that part of me that wants to pretend we're still living in the past. He stops at the bottom of the driveway, pulling up to the curb and putting the truck in park.

"Thanks for doing this, Penny," he says once the engine quiets. "Seriously, I know that you definitely didn't plan on helping me with my classwork when you chose to take a semester off from Frostard. It means a lot that you would do this." His eyes shimmer in the moonlight that casts shadows across his face.

I offer him a soft smile, and force my eyes to not drift down to his lips, to not think about kissing him like I would if this was a moment from our past. It's so easy to let those old habits back in, the muscle memory and instincts right at the surface once again. But I'm not living in the past, and when I reach for the door, leaning away from him and toward the cold winter night outside, my mind begins to adjust to how things are now, how things have changed.

"Like I said, I had fun tonight," I say, trying to dismiss his gratitude. I don't want him to know that I feel some sort of debt toward him, like I owe him this because I broke his heart. I push the door open wide and drop out of the truck, slinging my duffle bag over my shoulder. When I glance back, I add, "Plus, we do make a good team."

His lips spread in a grin and he nods. "We do, don't we?"

I tell him goodnight and swing the door shut, turning away from him and trudging up the driveway. I tuck my chin to my chest to keep the winter winds from wrapping their claws around me and beg the warmth from his truck to stay with me until I'm inside. As I go, I fully prepare myself for the millions of questions I'm sure my mom will have, and I feel my subconscious begin to count down the hours until I'll see Christopher again.

I managed to avoid my mom last night, slipping past her and up the stairs before she could ask me too many questions. Unfortunately, it won't be so easy this morning. When I come downstairs, another pair of leggings and a sweatshirt molding to my body, I see her waiting at the bar in the kitchen, a plate of eggs set for each of us.

"Good morning, Penny," she greets me brightly.

I tell her *good morning* and take my seat next to her. I get one bite down before the questions start coming.

"You saw Christopher twice in one day," she says the statement like it's an observation she's making about a piece of art.

"Yep," I say around my bite of eggs.

She lets out an amused hum and takes a drink from her glass of tea. "And it's because of some assignment he has for school?"

"That's right," I reply, knowing the bomb she's about to drop and that there's no avoiding it.

"And you're sure it's not because you still like him?"

There it is. The question I knew she was going to blurt out. I rest my fork on the side of my plate; the clink cutting through the quiet pause in our conversation.

"No, Mom," I groan out like any teenager would. "Christopher and I are just friends."

"You weren't just friends six months ago," she says under her breath.

There's a pinch in my heart that makes me stumble over my words. I know she doesn't say her words to hurt me. She's right. Six months ago, Christopher and I were definitely more than friends. "I know, but with college and life taking us in different directions, we aren't in a relationship anymore."

It's the same thing I told her the day I broke up with Christopher. She and my dad were both shocked that I had done it. They thought we'd try to do long distance, but I think they were also excited that I got to go away to college with no strings attached to home. I got to have a fresh start somewhere else. They probably anticipated it was coming, but I know they both liked Christopher and they knew how happy I was with him.

"So, you don't still like him?" mom asks.

Her question sounds different now. Before I heard it as if she was asking me if he and I were going to get back together. Now it sounds like she's wondering, even though I know I can't be with him, if my heart still skips a beat when I'm near him, if I still think about kissing him, reaching for his hand. If I fully expect to wake up to a text on my phone from him, telling me good morning like I used to every day.

I can't make the lie form on my tongue, so I only shake my head and pick up my fork once again. I don't know if she believes me, but she doesn't ask any more questions about Christopher and we finish our breakfast by talking about what our plans will be for today.

Chapter 9

S unlight leaks through the frosted windows of the library, coating the space in a warm glow that would make you believe it was the middle of July outside. I push the cart in front of me as I work my way through the maze of wooden bookcases, the little black wheels creaking under the weight.

The stack of books mom loaded onto it is dwindling as I find their homes among the other books. This is the job I always get when I help out at the library. She checks them in and I return them to their spots on the shelves. When I first started doing it, it would take me hours to find where each book went, and even though mom would definitely be faster than me, she'd let me take my time because I was always so excited to get to help. Like I had an adult job and I was doing something really cool. It's laughable now, but I really did enjoy every second if it.

I remember a few times I'd get it wrong, and place a few books out of order, and as we were leaving, mom would notice it was incorrect out of the corner of her eye and fix it. That always amazed me, that she knew these shelves so well, but now, so do I. Entire summers and late afternoons spent here have added up and now I'm just as quick as she is. Sometimes, we even race each other to see who can shelve the most books.

Today, though, I go at it alone because she's busy hosting the kindergarten class that's here on a field trip. Every few months, the school will bring the kids in for a day of story time and my mom usually ends up being the one reading the books. If they plan the day far enough in advance, they've had the author come in, and I always think that's amazing. That little Rayou could do that. It makes the world not seem so big.

That's how the rest of today goes, and most of the next. Cheer practice Wednesday night was productive, and on Thursday I get up to do it all again, but this time, I know Christopher will be by this afternoon. My breath caught this morning when I woke to a text from him. Not one saying good morning—like my stupid brain caught in the past thought it would—but just confirming that he could come by the library this afternoon for our photo shoot.

I shift my weight in the large, pea-green armchair I've been nestled in since I finished shelving for the day. The velvet fabric on the curved arms of the chair rubs against my black leggings as I swing my feet back and forth. My maroon sweatshirt is larger than what I normally wear. It swallows my hands that currently prop a book against my knees. The reading area in the library is right in the center of the space. There are couches and chairs split up by low sitting tables, the frosted windows at my back. Across from me, I see mom working at the desk by the entryway of the library.

I rein my eyes back to the book and continue reading. I started it yesterday and am almost finished. I've read nearly every book I'm interested in from this library after all the time I've spent here, but I've been gone for six months, and there are dozens of new releases I want to explore. One of the perks of working at a library is you never run out of things to read.

The pages under my right hand thin out as the time passes by, late afternoon turning into early evening. I can see the time change based on the color of the sunlight as it shines down on the cream pages of the book. Finally at the end of the story, I'm flying through the pages, feeling the adrenaline of the plot in my veins. The book started as a fairytale. The classic lower-class girl meets a prince and falls in love. Now, I'm completely invested as the plot reveals a curse, witches, and a beast that lives inside of the prince.

When the final page is between my fingers, my mind finally stills. I realize where I'm at in the book, and reach for the cover, pulling it closed and leaving the final page unread. I don't even think about doing it anymore, it's become second nature. My fingers tap on the dark cover of the book while my mind whirls around with the different possible endings. I try to decide what could be on that last page, but leave it unknown, leave the story unfinished so that I don't have to say goodbye to these characters or their adventure.

My eyes snap up at the sound of a soft chuckle. Christopher leans against the desk across the library, glowing hazel eyes watching me. My mom stands on the other side of the desk near him, shaking her head in my direction.

"Please don't tell me you still refuse to read the last page of a book," Christopher says, pushing up from the counter and crossing to me.

I rise to meet him halfway, placing the book back on the display table where I found it. "Maybe," I say, drawing out the word guiltily.

A shocked burst of air escapes him, making my cheeks redden.

"Penny, that's criminal!"

"I can't help it!" I whine defensively.

My eyes scan Christopher, taking in his light blue sweater, sleeves bunched up to his elbows, and the dark denim of his jeans. I catch him studying me too. His stare trains on my blonde curls that tumble from the half updo at the crown of my head.

His eyes come back to mine, and a thin breath escapes between his parted lips when he sees I've noticed him studying me. "You should really read the ends of those books. You're missing some of the best parts."

"Or worst," I say and step around him to approach my mom. The floorboards creak behind me as Christopher follows. "We're going to take a picture for his portfolio project," I tell her, though I had already mentioned that yesterday.

"Help yourself," she says, gesturing out to surrounding shelves. "It's good to see you, Christopher," she adds with a soft smile.

"You too, Mrs. Wilson," he says, being polite as ever, though I catch his hands reach for the camera that rests against his chest, hanging from a strap around his neck, and his nervous fingers fidget with the buttons.

I'd wondered if he was nervous about seeing my mom after everything that's happened. "We can start over here," I say, intervening so Christopher doesn't feel like he has to say anything else. I lead us away from the front of the library to a row of books near the back. Warm, amber rays from the setting sun stream through the window and shimmer in beams between the bookcase.

"Any ideas for how you want this picture to look?" I prompt him, and when I turn to face Christopher, I see his eyes dilating, sweeping across the space and imagining the perfect photo.

He comes to life and describes a variety of pictures he wants to capture. I start by walking along the books, trailing my fingers on their spines. Then I lean against the shelf with a book in hand. Most of the time I don't look at the camera. He just captures moments frozen in time, making sure nothing looks staged.

"Let me try a different angle," Christopher says, letting the camera hang around his neck. He walks up to where I'm currently leaning against the bookcase and pulls a stack of books free, setting them on the floor so he can see through to the row on the other side.

"Stay here." Christopher walks around the bookcase until he's on the other side, looking back at me through the hole he just created.

"How does it look?" I ask, repositioning myself so he can see me through the window he created in the bookshelf.

I hear the click of his camera go off and I know he's smiling based on how his words sound coming from his mouth. "Good, it changed the perception and depth of the photo."

A soft smile pulls at my lips. I love when he talks about the technical parts of taking a photo. It reminds me that this is more than a hobby for him. This is a passion, something he's practiced and researched for hours. There's another series of clicks and when the quiet returns, I glance over my shoulder, blonde curls swiping behind me. Christopher is looking through the pictures he just took on the small display, bits of dust rising in the window of space between us.

We're so deep in the library, that hardly anyone ventures down here. I can't remember the last time I came back here to shelve a book and I think that much is obvious from the accumulation of dust behind me on the wooden surfaces of the bookcase.

I don't know why I do it. Absolutely nothing in me tells me to do this, but it's happening before I can make it make sense. I suck in a breath and blow up the dust, blasting it towards Christopher. He fumbles back from the bookcase, swatting at the cloud that's exploded around him, coughing in surprise, and looking at me like I've lost my mind.

An enormous laugh breaks between my lips, throwing my head back in triumph.

"What the hell, Penny?" he says through his own laugh, no malice in those words. Christopher rubs his eyelids, wiping the itchy irritation from his skin. I dip out of sight before he can open his eyes and see me.

"Penny?" he questions, and I assume he's opened his eyes to see I've moved.

I bite my lip and let the child in me release itself. "*Boo!*" I jump back into his view and he flinches back, pink heat flushing his cheeks.

"Penny Wilson!" he yells, the familiar teasing tone finding his voice from when we used to goof around like this. He moves so fast he's around the bookcase before I realize I should run.

"Oops!" I call playfully, and then I take off running down to the other end of the hall, twisting and turning through the cases of books. Our feet ricochet off the hardwood floors, chorusing together with the sounds of our laughs, the two noises mixing into a harmony that my ears strain to remember forever.

He finally catches me at the rear of the library, having turned down the row I was heading to next. I abruptly stop to keep from running into him. My feet fumble back, but they collide with the wall of frosted windows behind me.

"Gotcha!" Christopher says, hands coming up to rest against the glass.

I'm still laughing, breathless giggles tumbling from my mouth. We're both breathing hard, chests rising and lowering with the rapid beats of our hearts. He hovers in front of me, pressing in so I can't get away. The air is warm and thick with his scent of coffee and pine. My lungs work hard to ease my breaths, but they ache for an entirely different reason now. It takes a minute, but the giddy energy that fueled us fizzles out.

"I want a rematch," I practically whisper. That playful side of me still wants the moment between us to linger, but my words don't carry the childish energy they should. Instead, they fall weak, like the notes of a song that don't hit their mark.

"I'd just win again," Christopher says, his words carrying the same off-key sound as my own. He drops his arms and stands straight up, giving me room to breathe and step away from the glass that's chilled my back through my maroon sweatshirt.

I reach for his camera, and when Christopher sees my hand moving toward him, I notice he freezes, becoming so still it's hard to believe he just chased me through the library. I don't know what he thinks I'm reaching for—his hand or the side of his face—but I cup his camera in my grasp and raise it so the weight of it is off of his neck. "Did you get the picture you need?"

Christopher takes the camera from me and goes through the options on the display. He's pressing the buttons for a long while, so long I have to wonder just how many he's taken. Finally, he stops, thumb hovering above the next button and that victorious tilt of his lips is enough to tell me that he likes the picture he's looking at. I've seen that expression enough times to know what it means without any words accompanying it.

"We have a winner," I assume.

His hazel eyes leap up from the camera to lock on mine, looking so deep into the light blue depths of my gaze it's like he's peering through me, through the window at my back. "You have no idea how much it means to me that you're helping me with this portfolio."

The corner of my mouth hitches up, and his mouth matches the movement. "This is most fun I've had in a long time," I tell him honestly, letting myself speak words that carry more weight than I think he realizes.

But he's Christopher, and he knows me better than anyone, and I should never doubt that he understands exactly what I mean. His lips part just a hair, and I can tell the next words he'll say will be gentle, but I never hear them.

My phone chimes from my back pocket, breaking the soft moment between us like a gunshot. I flinch so badly my heart is in my throat. Christopher takes a step back from me, also startled by the noise, and I mumble an apology as I reach for the phone.

"Oh, crap, I didn't even see what time it is," I curse through my ragged sigh. "Coach Violet wants me to pick up the charms she ordered for the team. We need to leave now." I look up and see that Christopher is already turning off his camera.

"Let's go, then. I got the photo for the portfolio. Are those the charms for the bracelets?" he asks as we turn and head toward the front of the library.

I nod, knowing I've told Christopher about them before. Every year, Coach Violet buys these charms for the squad that tie into the routine we are doing at the state tournament that year. I have four, for all the years I competed with the team in high school. Some of the girls put them on a chain bracelet or anklet. I liked to keep mine on the zippers of my backpack when I was in school. Now they dangle on the ring of my keys—a cat, star, tree, and snowflake—tinkling together, making a sound I've become so used to I hardly notice it.

"Yeah, we'll need to go by, Katie's Charms, but it's on the way."

"What's this year's charm?" Christopher asks.

I glance at him, watching his profile as the cases of books blur past us. "A heart."

Coach Violet and I hand out the heart charms at the end of practice, and the *oohs* and *ahs* from the squad are a sign of their approval. For all but one member, this is a charm they can add to their current collection, but for Lillyanne, it's her very first one, and her eyes light up when I give her the piece of metal shaped like a heart.

The charm is supposed to resemble the message of the state routine, and from what we've put together, I can recognize the connection and vision Coach has. Some people don't realize that a cheer routine can be more than just a series of captivating tricks. Only recently did we start forming stories into our routines, and it shows in the scores.

When we dismiss the team for the night, Coach Violet waves me across the gymnasium. I button up my coat, preparing to leave, and cross to her.

She's busying herself by jotting down some notes on her clipboard. I can't make out most of what it says, but I catch bits and pieces about how practice went today and the spots she wants us to polish at the next practice.

"What are your plans for tomorrow, Penny?" she asks when I reach her. She doesn't look up, still jotting down some final notes. "Since we don't have practice because of the Winter Wonderland dance," she adds, finally putting her pen to rest at the metal clasp on the top of the clipboard.

"I don't think I have anything planned," I tell her. Christopher and I haven't discussed when we want to do the next photo for his portfolio.

We both got distracted in the rush to get me to the school in time for practice.

"Would you be interested in chaperoning the dance? I know the school board is still looking for more volunteers." She turns her back to me to shove her clipboard into her black backpack and zip it closed.

"Sure," I blurt before even processing what she's asked me. I always do that whenever Coach Violet needs anything.

"Great!" she says, clearly excited at my quick acceptance. "It shouldn't be anything more than working the ticket counter and running the concession stand."

"Sounds easy enough," I say. "What time do I need to be here?"

"Doors open at seven, so try to get here a little before that." She picks up her bag and slings it over her shoulder. Her eyes widen, remembering something she needs to say. "Oh, and if you know anyone else who would be willing to help, bring them with you."

I tell her I will, but my mind is still processing what I've signed up for, and doesn't even register her last comment until I'm outside, trudging through the snow, seeking out the navy SUV with my mom behind the wheel.

She wants me to bring someone?

When I think about who I know that could chaperone the dance with me, the only person that comes to mind, that fills every crevice and overwhelms my thoughts, is the person who took me to that very dance my last two years of high school. Who stood beside me this time last year as we were crowned King and Queen at the Rayou Winter Wonderland dance.

That definitely crosses the terms of our agreement to only work on his portfolio. That's taking a step outside of the structure we have around our current friendship, and yet, I have the strangest urge to reach for my phone and call him because after this afternoon, with him chasing me through the bookcases in the library and the sounds of our laughter harmonizing against the vaulted ceilings, I want to spend more moments like that with him. I just want to spend more time with him in general. Any excuse I make up in my mind, and he's the one I'm thinking of, the one I'm trying to see.

So I'm not all that surprised that, once I'm alone in my room, I pull up Christopher's contact on my phone and dial his number. It rings a few times before his voice fills my ear. "Hello?"

I don't miss the surprise that weighs down his voice.

"Hi," I say, and press my back deeper into the stack of pillows at the head of my bed. I hadn't really planned on what I wanted to say to him once he answered the phone, and the second his voice fills my head, I go mute.

"What's up?" he asks in my void. His casual composure comes back and Christopher seamlessly transitions the conversation for me.

"What are your plans tomorrow night?" I ask, biting my bottom lip while I wait for his answer.

There's a pause on the line, and in the silence, I hear my heart beat in my ears. "Umm, I don't think I have anything planned," he finally says and my heart settles back in my chest. "Why?"

I take in a breath, feeling the need to prepare the words in my head. "Coach Violet asked me to chaperone the Winter Wonderland dance tomorrow and I'm supposed to bring someone to help."

He's quiet, and my pulse stutters, thumping more powerfully through each silent second. When he speaks, I swear I can hear the smile on his face. "Penny Wilson, are you asking me to the Winter Wonderland dance?"

"No!" I blurt, my cheeks heating so bright if my room wasn't coated in shadows from the night, I'd see they're cherry red. "Coach just said… They need more volunteers… If you can't do it," I stumble all over myself, an incoherent explanation trying to come out.

There's a soft laugh in my ear that stops my words. The hairs on my arms raise at the sound, just a whisper of the sound that surrounded me in the library this afternoon. "Sure, Penny, I can come help."

"Really?"

"Well, since my mom already asked me," he starts to say.

I mumble, "Of course," under my breath and close my eyes with embarrassment. His mom is the principal of the high school, of course she'd ask him to help at the dance.

"But I didn't tell her I'd do it," Christopher says, obviously hearing my words. "So, I guess that means I'm still going because of you."

I shake my head, though I know he can't see me. The whole ride home, I had been worried about this conversation. Excited to ask him, but nervous for his answer and if this would change how we're acting around each other. I like his company and having someone here in Rayou that I can see. And all that time I spent worrying, his mom had already asked him. He was already going, no matter what I said. My heart stills as that thought takes root in my head.

"If your mom asked you to volunteer at the dance, why did you tell me you didn't have any plans for tomorrow?"

"Well," he starts, but stops.

I try to fill his lingering silence. *Is he shaking his head? Biting his lip? Shrugging his narrow shoulders? Running a hand through his brown waves? Are they damp from his shower?*

He speaks again before my racing mind can continue on its spiral. "I guess I wanted to know what you needed first." His voice has changed, and it's a bit breathy now. "I didn't have to go to the dance."

The words he leaves unsaid are the loudest of all. That he would have skipped helping at the dance, would have told his mom no, if I had asked him to do anything else. The idea that he wants to spend time with me as much as I want to see him makes a small smile spread my lips.

"Then I guess I'll see you tomorrow," I say so softly it could almost be a whisper.

"Do you want me to pick you up?" he asks and I tell him I'll let him know after I talk to my mom about our schedule for the car tomorrow. After that, the conversation naturally dies away, and he tells me good night.

When I hang up the phone, laying in my bed watching the moonlight shift across the plaster ceiling of my bedroom, my mind begins to daydream about tomorrow. But it's not this year's Winter Wonderland dance that takes root in my imagination. It's last year's dance. My senior year that feels like a lifetime and seconds ago all at the same time.

Chapter 10

Milk sloshes into my glass as mom pours it from across the bar.

"So, the Winter Wonderland dance?" she asks.

I give her a *mhmm* through my mouthful of oatmeal. In a moment of hesitation, I had asked her if she wanted to chaperone with me on the drive home from cheer practice. As if she knew I was trying to find any excuse not to ask Christopher, she popped her lip up in a knowing grin and said she was working the night shift at the library today because she'd be busy this morning.

"Do you know what you're going to wear?"

The oatmeal burns a trail down my throat and into my stomach. "What do you mean? I'm not going to the dance, just chaperoning."

"I mean, did you bring something home with you that's nice enough to wear?" my mom asks, talking like she doesn't notice I'm already overanalyzing every second of this night.

The last couple of days, I've been living out of my duffle bag, too lazy to unpack the assortment of sweatshirts and leggings I brought home. "I guess not," I realize out loud. "What am I even supposed to wear? Why is this all so weird now that I'm not in high school?"

My mom laughs softly, her back to me as she puts the milk away. "Just find some jeans and a nice sweater. You can take the SUV and shop at Millie's this morning if you need to."

Jeans, okay yes, I have those. A sweater? Not a chance. When I packed at six in the morning the other day, I thought I'd be moping around on the couch in the living room watching reruns of my favorite television shows. The Winter Wonderland dance was the last thing on my mind at that moment.

I scrape the final bit of oatmeal out of my bowl, and drink the glass of milk mom poured me. "I can drop you off at the nursing home, and then go to Millie's. Once I'm done shopping I'll come by for lunch with grandma," I say, knowing we already had plans to go see my grandma this morning.

Friday visits to the Rayou Nursing home started a year ago when my grandpa died and my grandma decided she wanted to let go of the little house they shared outside of Denver. There were plenty of nursing homes available in the Denver area, but grandma wanted to be closer to mom and me, and so we moved her to the nursing home in Rayou and visit with her every Friday.

"Can I ask if Christopher will be at the dance tonight?" Mom asks, turning sharply to catch my reaction.

The now empty glass of milk clinks against the counter too loudly when I put it down. "No, you cannot," I say, slipping out of the barstool and retreating from the kitchen before she can ask me again. I hear her chuckle to herself as I go and can't fight the smile that spreads my lips.

The clothing racks inside of Millie's are crammed with shirts and pants, hangers pressed together so tightly it's almost impossible to even see what's being sold. It's been slow going for just over thirty minutes, peeling apart hangers, when I spot something promising.

Music chimes softly overhead and I hum along, falling back into my shopping routine easily. Lindsay and I have spent way too much time in this store, especially over summer breaks. My arms are heavy with contenders, a variety of colors and fabrics because I have absolutely no idea what I'm actually looking for.

Finally, after surveying every rack weighed down with sweaters, I walk to the back of the store and try on the options I pulled. I probably shouldn't even be this picky about what I'm going to wear tonight. I bet if I hadn't invited a certain boy to accompany me, I wouldn't be. Most of the options are cute and would be winners if I wasn't so in my head. Finally, nearly ten shirts later, I make my selection.

The grey sweater is cropped but hemmed nicely. It hits just above the black belt that encircles the waist of my dark denim jeans. In the dim light of the dressing room, it seems like a simple sweater, but when it hits the brighter lights near the cash registers, I see strands of silver placed throughout the cotton fabric. They shimmer like hidden gems. It's just enough to make me feel the right amount of casual and dressy. I shake my head as soon as the thought passes. *Why am I over analyzing this?*

I decide to purchase a few extra sweaters so I'm not just lounging in hoodies for the next couple of months, because I have no idea when I'll get the rest of my things from Frostard. I know I'm overreacting about the Winter Wonderland dance, but I still continue to get lost in daydreams about tonight and about what it will be like to be back in that school with Christopher.

A giant slurp thunders through the small common area of the nursing home when my grandma sucks down the little droplets of orange juice at the bottom of her glass for the third time. Finally, a nurse hears her signal of distress and comes by to refill my grandma's drink.

I offered to go get her a refill, but my grandma refused to let me do the nurse's job. "Penelope, you cannot do everyone else's tasks. She'll hear me eventually and come give me more juice."

Mom doesn't even bat her eyes at my grandma's behavior, and honestly, neither should I. Grandma has always been opinionated. Always wanting to judge people and test them. Growing up it was always: "Penelope, sit straighter or you'll have back problems when you're my age.", "Penelope, you can't be a cheerleader for the rest of your life.", or, "Penelope, your mother told me you already have a boyfriend. Don't waste your time with love at such a young age."

No matter what it was that I was doing, she had to give me her thoughts on it, and correct it because I always seemed to be living my life wrong.

"So, tell me again why you're not at that fancy college you showed me pictures of last time you were here," grandma says when the nurse walks away. Her eyes narrow in on my shoulders when I slouch back in my seat.

"She's just taking the semester off, mom," my mother says, coming to my rescue. I'm honestly getting tired of answering the question.

My grandma surprises me when she nods and says, "Well, you

should always do what's best for yourself."

The rest of our visit is nice, and for the most part, I don't get criticized for anything other than the fact that I don't use lotion enough. My grandma threatens to count the wrinkles on my hand the next time I come in, which honestly just results in an outburst of laughter from my mom and me. After that, we play some of my grandma's favorite card games and she even teaches me some new ones she's learned here.

My mom drops me off at the house before she goes in for her shift at the library, both of us eating a quick dinner together. I curl my blonde hair in large, loose waves, and put on minimal makeup.

I know I have a pair of silver hoop earrings somewhere in my room, but they're missing from the dish on my dresser. I sift through my drawers, searching for the tiny pieces of jewelry when my fingers brush on the glossy edge of a photograph. I pull the drawer out further, hitching it off its tracks and find a stack of old pictures I completely forgot about. These were on my bulletin board at one point, but I used to rotate them out frequently. The tops of them have a little hole pierced through the material where a push pin used to pinch it to the corkboard.

I prop myself on the edge of the bed, tucking my leg beneath me, and flip through the stack of photos. A lot of the ones on top are from Christmas my senior year. My eyes light up at the pictures from last year's state cheer tournament. There's a great moment of Lindsay and me crying and hugging, silver confetti frozen in the air above us.

When I slip that one behind the rest, my face falls. Eyes that were crinkled with my smile widen with surprise. The image is hard to see because it was taken in a dark gymnasium. My white dress hits just above my knees in a fluffy, tulle skirt. The bodice is an intricate, glittery lace. My right arm is around his shoulder, my left hand resting gently on his chest. The corsage he gave me is a mix of delicate white and pink roses.

Christopher looks so handsome in his black suit, the blush tie something I didn't even have to beg him to wear so we would match. His brown hair is pushed back with gel, the waves folding into the dark edges of the photo where the flash from the camera didn't reach. We both have easy smiles that reach our eyes, a moment of pure happiness caught here forever. On top of our heads are the crowns we'd won only seconds before this photo was taken. Mine is a small, silver tiara with blue gemstones. Christopher's is thicker, looking heavy on his head, but he tilts his chin back to keep it balanced. We each wear our gold and black sashes that read WINTER WONDERLAND COURT.

Tears fill the edges of my eyes with a mix of happiness and sorrow that confuses my heart. I toss the stack of photos back into the drawer, and, just when I'm about to slam it shut, I find the silver hoop earrings I was looking for. I pick the jewelry out, shove the drawer closed, and make myself move on like I never saw the photograph of Christopher and me.

I try to take my time so I lessen the amount of minutes spent pacing at the bottom of the steps while waiting for Christopher to arrive. When my phone finally lights up with a text from him, I've walked a trench in the floorboards. With my coat already on, I face the cold and crunch through the slushy snow to his truck. The sun has started setting behind the mountains that surround Rayou, tangerine streaks bright in the sky.

I pull open the red door of his truck and hop into the passenger seat. "Hello," I say, my breath fogging up the frigid air that snuck in with me.

Christopher pulls away from the side of the road and says, "I was going to get out and open the door for you, but I thought that may be taking this all a bit too far."

I flash my crystal blue eyes at him, noticing his pink cheeks from the cold are stretched tight from his wide smile. "Definitely too far," I

ht?" Christopher says, locking the money box and
arm.

ve the chance to answer him before one of the moms
ing me toward the concession stands. Up until now,
snacks or water, so she could handle the table on her
he wave of kids will come soon. I lose Christopher in
d assume someone else has stolen him for help

say, and settle into my seat. "Did your mom tell you anything specific about what we have to do tonight?"

Christopher reaches for the knob on the radio, turning down the music with a deep bass that he'd been listening to. "I think she wants us to work the ticket table when we first get there."

I nod, sending my hair tumbling in front of my face. With my profile blocked from his view, I let out a soft breath, releasing the nerves and excitement I had built up in my head about seeing him again and going to the Winter Wonderland dance together. When I've composed myself, I tuck my hair behind my ear and study him from the corner of my eye.

Christopher holds the wheel with his right hand, propping his left on the door like he always does. He's wearing his favorite denim jacket, rips down the front and the sleeves, and I can barely see the black t-shirt underneath. His jeans are as dark as his shirt, making the white tennis shoes seem extra bright.

"You look nice," he says, catching me off guard and I notice he's caught me looking at him.

"Thanks," I say, pulling my eyes back to the windshield. "So, what are our next steps for your portfolio project?"

"I was thinking about doing the photo at the hot springs next because I'll need to get permission from the resort owner to be on site," Christopher explains, flipping on his blinker to make the last turn onto the street with the high school.

"That one's going to be fun," I say.

Even though I've lived in Rayou my whole life, I've barely spent any time at the hot springs resort. It's what Rayou is known for, and any tourists that come by visit only for our award winning hot springs. I guess because of that, it always felt like the hot springs were there for people outside of Rayou.

When we get to the school, the parking lot isn't as crowded as I imagined it would be, but then I remember it's because the dance doesn't actually start until seven. It's still weird for me to be on the other side of everything.

Christopher finds a spot near the front doors, so I don't have to trudge through too much of the slushy mess on the sidewalk. As soon as we walk inside, a mom that's in charge of the volunteers strides up and gives Christopher and me last-minute decoration tasks. We work together to build an archway of string lights above the gymnasium doors, and set the table for collecting tickets next to it. All week long, the senior student council officers have been selling tickets, but we know some students will purchase them last-minute at the door. Christopher says he'll be in charge of the money box and I'll just take the prepaid tickets as they arrive.

"Did it feel weird the first time you walked back in here?" Christopher asks. I glance to my right to meet his gaze. We're leaning against the cinderblock wall behind the ticket table, arms crossed and waiting for the doors to open.

"Well, the first time I came back since graduation, I was bringing books to the library for my mom, so I didn't really take the time to look at it all again," I say. Odd how that feels like months ago when it was just the other day. "When I came back that night for cheer practice, though, it was very weird. Especially seeing my face in that trophy case."

Without having to say more, we both turn our heads to the left, looking at where the plaques and awards are displayed. Christopher is in there more times than most people. The basketball team has won the state tournament every year for the last four years. Hopefully, this year will be the fifth.

I don't add that everything is twice as weird now that he is standing

next to me. That le
through these halls,
the desks—

"Are you both rea
charge comes up unann
the best.

"No, we're fine for n

He hasn't even finishe
off to the next set of volunte
else, the doors at the front of
snow floating in with the line

Heels click against the po
Their dresses are pink and pur
They hand me their pre-paid tick
twinkling lights I just hung up.

Students continue to arrive by
themselves or taking pictures. The ta
grow to absorb, even though I kno
second they reach the dance floor.

After a while, the upperclassmen a
recognize. Some stop and chat with n
members of the cheer team show up toget
them all before the dance started. They
them, and while, at first it feels awkward,
ear while Christopher captures the moment

From there it's just a blur of people co
Their voices mix together into a chaotic rumb
door. After an hour passes, we assume most
coming are already here and we shut down the t

"Not so bad, rig
hooking it under his
I don't even ha
is behind us, usher
no one had needed
own, but I know t
the transition an
elsewhere.

Chapter 11

The night continues on until my feet begin to hurt from standing so long. I bounce between rolling up the sleeves of my sweater to man the popcorn machine to refilling the ice buckets. I give up on the pieces of hair that pull against their pins making my once tight braids, spread and droop against my fallen curls. When the night is nearly over, I only get one second of relief in a stranded folding chair behind the concession stands before Coach Violet finds me.

"There you are!" she exclaims.

I push to my feet, finding the little energy I have saved up, and ask what she needs. I'm relieved when she doesn't say they're out of ice, or that the popcorn needs buttered. Instead, she just waves me to follow her and we head toward the gymnasium. I've pretty much avoided the space all night. There's enough going on out here in the hall that I haven't needed to go inside.

When we walk under the strung lights, I'm swallowed by the dark, forcing my eyes to adjust to the neon flashing lights overhead. A mat is spread across the hardwood floor to keep it from scratching, and a sea of bodies crowd on top of it, dancing and laughing in clumps as the music pounds overhead. I struggle to keep track of Coach Violet as we walk around the edge of the gymnasium. My heart thuds hard in my chest with the beat of the music, shaking every cell in my body.

On the far side of the gym, the wall we now walk along, a wooden platform is set up with two set-piece thrones for the Winter Wonderland King and Queen. With everything that's been keeping me busy today, I hadn't even remembered the crowning. The song that's been shaking my mind senseless begins to fade and two spotlights ignite, making the gold painted thrones shimmer on the stage.

"All right, Penny. Stand here, I'll be right back," Coach Violet says, having to lean into my ear so I can hear here above the raised chatter from the students.

We've stopped next to another set of doors that opens up to the locker rooms. I wait beside them like she instructs, and my attention is pulled to the squeal of a microphone clicking on. Christopher's mom walks on stage, her black dress pants crisp against the blush sweater she's wearing. I haven't seen her all night. Not that I was avoiding her, but my feet shift at the sight of her, not wanting her to notice me. I have no idea how she feels about me or what she thinks of my decision to break up with her son before leaving for college.

Her voice fills the gymnasium as she begins the crowning ceremony. She first congratulates the basketball team for their win last night over Nerom high school, and then asks the court members to join her on stage. The door next to me swings open, and I step out of the way, just in time, as Coach Violet appears, propping it ajar. A soft theatrical song plays under the applause, and the spotlights swivel in my direction, not catching me in their beams but focusing on the line of girls and boys that say, and settle into my seat. "Did your mom tell you anything specific about what we have to do tonight?"

Christopher reaches for the knob on the radio, turning down the music with a deep bass that he'd been listening to. "I think she wants us to work the ticket table when we first get there."

I nod, sending my hair tumbling in front of my face. With my profile blocked from his view, I let out a soft breath, releasing the nerves and excitement I had built up in my head about seeing him again and going to the Winter Wonderland dance together. When I've composed myself, I tuck my hair behind my ear and study him from the corner of my eye.

Christopher holds the wheel with his right hand, propping his left on the door like he always does. He's wearing his favorite denim jacket, rips down the front and the sleeves, and I can barely see the black t-shirt underneath. His jeans are as dark as his shirt, making the white tennis shoes seem extra bright.

"You look nice," he says, catching me off guard and I notice he's caught me looking at him.

"Thanks," I say, pulling my eyes back to the windshield. "So, what are our next steps for your portfolio project?"

"I was thinking about doing the photo at the hot springs next because I'll need to get permission from the resort owner to be on site," Christopher explains, flipping on his blinker to make the last turn onto the street with the high school.

"That one's going to be fun," I say.

Even though I've lived in Rayou my whole life, I've barely spent any time at the hot springs resort. It's what Rayou is known for, and any tourists that come by visit only for our award winning hot springs. I guess because of that, it always felt like the hot springs were there for people outside of Rayou.

When we get to the school, the parking lot isn't as crowded as I imagined it would be, but then I remember it's because the dance doesn't actually start until seven. It's still weird for me to be on the other side of everything.

Christopher finds a spot near the front doors, so I don't have to trudge through too much of the slushy mess on the sidewalk. As soon as we walk inside, a mom that's in charge of the volunteers strides up and gives Christopher and me last-minute decoration tasks. We work together to build an archway of string lights above the gymnasium doors, and set the table for collecting tickets next to it. All week long, the senior student council officers have been selling tickets, but we know some students will purchase them last-minute at the door. Christopher says he'll be in charge of the money box and I'll just take the prepaid tickets as they arrive.

"Did it feel weird the first time you walked back in here?" Christopher asks. I glance to my right to meet his gaze. We're leaning against the cinderblock wall behind the ticket table, arms crossed and waiting for the doors to open.

"Well, the first time I came back since graduation, I was bringing books to the library for my mom, so I didn't really take the time to look at it all again," I say. Odd how that feels like months ago when it was just the other day. "When I came back that night for cheer practice, though, it was very weird. Especially seeing my face in that trophy case."

Without having to say more, we both turn our heads to the left, looking at where the plaques and awards are displayed. Christopher is in there more times than most people. The basketball team has won the state tournament every year for the last four years. Hopefully, this year will be the fifth.

I don't add that everything is twice as weird now that he is standing next to me. That less than a year ago, we were walking hand in hand through these halls, stealing kisses behind lockers, passing notes under the desks—

"Are you both ready? Do you need anything?" The mom that's in charge comes up unannounced and interrupts my thoughts. Probably for the best.

"No, we're fine for now, Ms. Turner," Christopher says.

He hasn't even finished speaking before she spins around and rushes off to the next set of volunteers. Before Christopher or I can say anything else, the doors at the front of the school are pulled open, spirals of loose snow floating in with the line of students arriving.

Heels click against the porcelain tiles as the first giddy girls arrive. Their dresses are pink and purple, hair curled and pinned beautifully. They hand me their pre-paid tickets and walk into the gym beneath the twinkling lights I just hung up.

Students continue to arrive by the handfuls, each group talking to themselves or taking pictures. The tapping of heels is something my ears grow to absorb, even though I know the girls will kick them off the second they reach the dance floor.

After a while, the upperclassmen arrive, and these are the students I recognize. Some stop and chat with me or Christopher. Most of the members of the cheer team show up together. Trinity hosted a dinner for them all before the dance started. They ask me to take a picture with them, and while, at first it feels awkward, I find myself grinning ear to ear while Christopher captures the moment with Trinity's phone.

From there it's just a blur of people coming and filling the gym. Their voices mix together into a chaotic rumble on the other side of the door. After an hour passes, we assume most of the students who are coming are already here and we shut down the ticket table.

"Not so bad, right?" Christopher says, locking the money box and hooking it under his arm.

I don't even have the chance to answer him before one of the moms is behind us, ushering me toward the concession stands. Up until now, no one had needed snacks or water, so she could handle the table on her own, but I know the wave of kids will come soon. I lose Christopher in the transition and assume someone else has stolen him for help elsewhere.

spread across the hardwood floor to keep it from scratching, and a sea of bodies crowd on top of it, dancing and laughing in clumps as the music pounds overhead. I struggle to keep track of Coach Violet as we walk around the edge of the gymnasium. My heart thuds hard in my chest with the beat of the music, shaking every cell in my body.

On the far side of the gym, the wall we now walk along, a wooden platform is set up with two set-piece thrones for the Winter Wonderland King and Queen. With everything that's been keeping me busy today, I hadn't even remembered the crowning. The song that's been shaking my mind senseless begins to fade and two spotlights ignite, making the gold painted thrones shimmer on the stage.

"All right, Penny. Stand here, I'll be right back," Coach Violet says, having to lean into my ear so I can hear here above the raised chatter from the students.

We've stopped next to another set of doors that opens up to the locker rooms. I wait beside them like she instructs, and my attention is pulled to the squeal of a microphone clicking on. Christopher's mom walks on stage, her black dress pants crisp against the blush sweater she's wearing. I haven't seen her all night. Not that I was avoiding her, but my feet shift at the sight of her, not wanting her to notice me. I have no idea how she feels about me or what she thinks of my decision to break up with her son before leaving for college.

Her voice fills the gymnasium as she begins the crowning ceremony. She first congratulates the basketball team for their win last night over Nerom high school, and then asks the court members to join her on stage. The door next to me swings open, and I step out of the way, just in time, as Coach Violet appears, propping it ajar. A soft theatrical song plays under the applause, and the spotlights swivel in my direction, not catching me in their beams but focusing on the line of girls and boys that

Chapter 11

T he night continues on until my feet begin to hurt from standing so long. I bounce between rolling up the sleeves of my sweater to man the popcorn machine to refilling the ice buckets. I give up on the pieces of hair that pull against their pins making my once tight braids, spread and droop against my fallen curls. When the night is nearly over, I only get one second of relief in a stranded folding chair behind the concession stands before Coach Violet finds me.

"There you are!" she exclaims.

I push to my feet, finding the little energy I have saved up, and ask what she needs. I'm relieved when she doesn't say they're out of ice, or that the popcorn needs buttered. Instead, she just waves me to follow her and we head toward the gymnasium. I've pretty much avoided the space all night. There's enough going on out here in the hall that I haven't needed to go inside.

When we walk under the strung lights, I'm swallowed by the dark, forcing my eyes to adjust to the neon flashing lights overhead. A mat is are beginning to exit the locker room. I know that is the staging room, where they gathered minutes ago to be given specific instructions on when and where to walk, what spot to stand in on stage, and then each girl was given a bouquet of flowers to carry.

There are four pairs from the senior class, and then one from every class below that, even though only seniors are eligible to be crowned. Trinity is among them, her wine-colored dress fitted to her slim figure. The bouquet they gave her is filled with white roses that look pristine against the fabric.

A senior basketball player walks beside her, and once everyone is out of the locker room, I can safely assume Trinity will win the crown. She's clearly the front runner, especially when the crowd's cheers raise an entire step in volume the moment she enters the small walkway between the locker room doors and the stage. I attest most of that to the cheer team since that's kind of what they do best. I'm glad I decided to come tonight, to be here to watch her. This is her moment, something I had happening to me just last year.

Once the parade of court members reaches the stage, they split apart, with girls on the left and boys on the right. Christopher's mom stands even further to the right with a sealed, golden envelope in her hands.

"And now it's time to name Rayou High's King and Queen," she says, speaking with her lips against the black mesh of the microphone. She breaks the seal with her perfectly manicured finger and unfolds the results. "Gentlemen first. Your Winter Wonderland King is…" she pauses for dramatic effect, then says, "Steve Haley."

There's a wave of natural applause as the senior boy steps forward. It's not the basketball player I thought would win, but a trumpet player from the marching band. I hear his friends whistling from the crowd and his cheeks heat to a bright red. I assume he also didn't think he was going to win based on the fact that he almost sits in the throne meant for the queen and the students erupt in laughter. I don't know much about Steve, except that he's the class clown and is always making people laugh. Part of me thinks he may have mixed up the thrones on purpose.

"Your Winter Wonderland Queen is," Christopher's mom says, pulling everyone's focus back to her, "Trinity Gillian."

Again, the crowd applauds, the cheer team screaming at the top of their lungs for her. I catch myself clapping without thinking to as I watch Trinity take her seat next to Steve.

"Now," Christopher's mom says, her voice carrying a tone that brings the applause to an abrupt stop. "Normally, we don't ask last year's Winter Wonderland King and Queen to come back for the crowning ceremony, but since they're both here—"

The rest of her words are lost beneath the beating of my heart. *She means me. She's talking about me.* My brain is trying to comprehend this thought when Coach Violet steps in front of me, a wide-eyed Christopher beside her.

"Finally found him," she huffs and then he's shoved beside me, his shoulder bumping my arm. "All you have to do is walk on stage and crown Trinity and Steve." Coach's eyes narrow as she looks at me. "Penelope, are you listening to me?"

Christopher must sense my nerves and confusion because he forces a calm mask over his surprised face. "Take my arm, Penny." His voice is soft, but it stands out to me amongst the loud crowd and bass-filled music. I let my eyes drift to him, locking on the dark browns that seem to pulse with the flashing lights. Christopher's arm is raised slightly, and I loop mine against the crook of his elbow, letting my fingers gently rest on his forearm.

"Please, help me in welcoming Penny Wilson and Christopher

Samson back to the stage." The words crackle through the speakers overhead, signaling our entrance.

Christopher takes the first step forward, tugging me with him until my mind can process I need to walk and my feet move on their own. As soon as I'm in the beam of white light, a wide smile plasters itself on my face. I hear the applause and even some of what the students say as we walk by, but their faces are masked to me by the spotlights. If it weren't for Christopher, and probably the fact that I've walked this path before, I wouldn't have a clue as to where I'm going. The toe of my boot hits the wooden stairs pressed to the front of the stage and I begin to ascend them, my grip on Christopher tightening. He lets me lean into him, his muscled arm taking my weight naturally.

Once we're on stage, his mom ushers us behind the thrones. A thin, silver tiara is pushed into my hands and I somehow know to place it on Trinity's head, while Christopher places the golden crown on Steve's head.

I step back from the new King and Queen, watching as the crowd claps and whistles for their newly crowned classmates, and then the music turns back up, a slow piano ballad bouncing around the gymnasium walls. Trinity and Steve rise from their thrones and carefully maneuver to the mat on the gym floor for their dance. Once her arms are around his neck and they've had a few minutes to themselves, all the eyes in the crowd turn up to Christopher and me. A heat blooms on my face under their focused stares, but I have no idea what they want from me.

"Do you think we're supposed to dance, too?" Christopher's voice startles me at my right and I look up at him.

"You think so?" I question.

"I don't know, we've never done this before," Christopher says.

His mom must overhear our conversation, because she appears

behind us and confirms just that. "You're supposed to join them."

I don't glance over my shoulder to meet her gaze, still slightly terrified of what I'll see if I do. Instead, I move down the stage with Christopher and we take our places on the dance floor. I face him and lift my arms to rest on his shoulders. His hands find my waist naturally, but there's a pocket of air between us that didn't exist last year.

We only get about two steps in before the rest of the students are pairing off and the small aisle that had been cleared for us to walk down is swallowed up by bodies. The kids press in on all sides of us until we're both forced to take a step forward, filling in the space that had been our barrier. Now my chest presses against his, warmth seeping through my silver sweater. The smell of coffee and pine fills my nose instantly, making my heart dip like it always does around him.

"I swear, I had no idea they were going to do this," Christopher says, making me focus on him instead of my thundering heart.

"How could you?" I ask before I remember who announced us. *His mom.* I never once thought Christopher was a part of orchestrating this. I had no reason to believe anything like this would even happen tonight. Rayou has never passed off the crowns before. I can only assume some of the volunteer moms thought it would be a cute idea after seeing us both show up to help. Maybe an even more ironic possibility is that fate simply lined all of this up.

"Don't worry, I won't step on your feet this time," I tell him, finally letting the last of my nervous energy go with the fading spotlights. Only the neon glow of the slowing strobe lights ignites the dark gymnasium, and I no longer have to bear the weight of everyone's judging stare.

Christopher laughs at my joke, and his chest shudders against mine, raising bumps across my arms. I lean into him, wanting to hold on to that vibration between us. My nose brushes his when I look up to meet his dark brown eyes, sending a jolt through me. It cuts his laugh short, making him draw in a sharp breath.

"If I remember correctly, it was *me* who stepped on *your* feet," Christopher says, and his words are almost lost in the breathiness of his voice.

"I had to limp around for three days," I pout playfully, this banter familiar to both of us.

"Oh, you were fine. You just wanted to get as many piggy-back rides out of me as you could," Christopher counters and I can't help the laugh that bursts from my parted lips.

"Excuse me? Are you saying I was using you to carry me around?" I say through my laugh.

His lips part in a gorgeous smile, white teeth bright in the dark gym. "We all know that's what you were doing."

"Was not," I say, though I know it most definitely was.

Christopher's arms tighten around my waist, pulling our chests closer, and he dips his head to rest his forehead against mine. "Penny Wilson, don't lie to me." His voice curls up, rumbling under the sound of the rising music.

"I would never," I say, forcing as much fake innocence into my words as possible, fighting a smile that's peeling my lips apart.

"I'll remember that," he says, the breath of his words brushing my cheek.

I soak in every inch of him that I can, because I have no idea when he'll ever hold me like this again. I memorize the pressure of his arms around my waist, how they hold me to him with a force that lets me glimpse the rapid beats of his heart through my sweater. I dial in on the warmth of his forehead as his soft skin meets mine. Christopher's brown waves fall in a curtain between us, brushing the sides of my face like whispers of a breeze. That intoxicating scent of roasted coffee beans and winter holds us in a cocoon.

My gaze drifts down from his dark eyes to the soft curve of his lips. "Christopher—"

I lose the rest of my words when the music suddenly changes from the slow melody to an electric guitar riff, sending the dancing bodies around us jumping and knocking everyone over. Christopher and I are bumped apart and I am suddenly very out of place on this dance floor. A strong hand finds mine through the wall of bodies and I see it's Christopher. He pulls me behind him as he parts a way through the crowd and heads straight for the exit of the gymnasium. When we burst through the doors beneath the archway of string lights, our laughs and friendly mannerisms have returned, leaving the energized moment behind, but still buzzing in my head.

One of the moms who we've worked with most of the night comes up to dismiss us. Now that the king and queen have been crowned, the dance will wrap up soon and the concession stand has already closed.

"Need me to take you home?" Christopher asks, his loud voice sounding off to my ears that had gotten used to straining to hear him above the music.

"If you don't mind," I say.

"Of course not." He gestures toward the front of the school and we walk side-by-side down the wide porcelain tiled hall.

Outside, snow has started to fall in thick flurries, the flakes the size of blueberries, cold and wet when they melt against my cheeks. We set off toward his truck, and I slide my boots across the sidewalk and through the slick slush. I try to stomp off as much snow as I can before leaping into the safety of the cabin.

The dim, yellow lights glow to life when Christopher gets in and starts the engine. After securing my seatbelt, I lean forward and press my hands to the vents, letting the air warm my skin. As Christopher backs the truck out of his parking spot, the overhead lights fade away and the dark shadows of the night wrap around us. Even though the walk to his car was short, the cold clings to me almost until my house is in view.

"Well, we survived the night," I say, breaking the silence I hadn't realized settled between us.

Christopher glances at me over his right arm that grips the steering wheel. "Yeah? Wasn't too much work?"

I shake my head, knocking bits of snow out of my hair. "It was actually fun. I'd rather do this than what I'm sure I would be doing at school."

"I had fun, too," Christopher says, and his voice softens.

I'm leaning so far to the left, my hands hover over the vents on Christopher's side of the truck, knowing they always spit out warm air the fastest. My arm brushes his, but after tonight, after that dance, I don't jolt away. I keep it pressed there, taking in the comfort from both the hot air in the truck and him. My blue eyes travel up his sleeve until I meet his sideways glance, dark eyes watching me intently, noticing how close I'm sitting to him.

"I'm glad you asked me to help you with your portfolio," I say, and pull my hands back from the vent, but keep my weight against the console between us. "I'm glad we're talking again."

"Me too," Christopher says with a bit of enthusiasm that brings me up short. "I hated the way we ended things. The last few months have been so…" He trails off as we pull up to the curb in front of my house.

"So quiet?" I fill in the words for him and he nods, that knot in his throat throbbing when he swallows.

Christopher reaches down and puts the truck in park, placing his arm against mine that still rests between us. My hand tilts back, thin fingers touching his coarse knuckles, and my heart thunders in my chest. The urge to intertwine our grasp clouds my head and makes me dizzy.

I lift my gaze to his, heart still pounding in my throat, and get lost in the way the moonlight shines through the windshield. It brushes his cheeks with a glow that makes my lungs close up at how breathtaking he is.

Christopher turns to face me and his eyes sweep over every part of my face. He takes in my bright blue eyes and messy blonde curls, looking at me like he *needs* me to breathe. When his hazel gaze drop to my mouth, his eyes glittering like stars against the dark sky, I suck in a short breath, lips freezing slightly apart.

He's going to kiss me.

I can see it on his face, the way he's tilted his head forward, eyes studying my mouth, his own lips parted with thin, short breaths escaping. And I don't pull away. I don't flinch back or break the moment. I raise my chin just an inch and *beg* him to close that distance.

Just kiss me, you fool. Do it.

Christopher slides his focus up my face to meet my wide eyes, and my heart sinks at the shadows that are forming, extinguishing the tiny stars that glimmered there. The perfect moment dissolves, the hot tension between us freezing over as he pulls away from me.

Rejection sparks in my stomach with an icy burn that rises up my throat when that pocket of air presses in between us. I gasp a bit for my breath, shocked at how quickly the moment turned. "I thought—"

"I'm sorry, I can't..." Christopher lets his words hang in the cabin of his truck, keeping his eyes on the shadows outside the windshield. "I can't hurt like that again."

There's a weight that Christopher carries in his gaze that refuses to meet mine and makes my stomach hit the floor when I realize what he means.

Christopher is afraid to kiss me because he fears I could break his heart all over again.

And I would, wouldn't I? Because what's between us isn't this magical second chance. This isn't where we make up and forget the breakup ever happened. Christopher doesn't trust me not to hurt him again. To let him get close to me and then pick up and walk away when I go back to Frostard in August. And how can I blame him? I *am* leaving in a few months and I *would* break his heart. I never should have let us get close again, never should have let him get this close to *kissing* me, when I know how it will end.

Tears rush to my eyes, guilt flooding my veins at what I almost let happen. At what I wanted to happen, without caring about how it would end for him in August. Lindsay may have encouraged me to break up with Christopher, but I'm the one who did it. I said the words and shattered his heart. I got up and left Rayou and everyone in it behind. I'm the reason those hazel eyes I love so much just filled with dark shadows when he remembered what *I* did to him.

My heart cracks open, making my breathing weak. I lean away from Christopher and reach for the door with fumbling fingers. I barely get out a *goodbye* before I close the door and race for the front porch, tears freezing against my cheeks as they fall.

Chapter 12

S aturday morning mom is waiting for me at the kitchen bar with two plates of stacked pancakes drenched in syrup.

"Hope you're hungry. I may have overdone it," she says, her voice softer than it normally is.

My heart pinches in my chest. I know that tone. It means she's well aware of the fact that I ran past her in tears last night and she waited until this morning to approach me about it.

I slide onto the barstool next to her, cutting off a bite of the chocolate chip pancakes. They melt in my mouth, the warmth of the fluffy texture spreading across my tongue. There's nothing better than Mom's chocolate chip pancakes.

"What'd they have you do at the dance last night?" Mom asks, taking a bite of her own breakfast.

It's an easy question, one that lets us transition into what she really wants to ask. I walk her through the night and all the things I did. But I know where this conversation is going, so I don't waste any time getting to the part she wants to discuss.

"I still like him, Mom," I say, placing my fork down in a puddle of sticky syrup. I know *like* wasn't the first word that wanted to jump out of my mouth, but it's what my brain decides on.

"Of course you do, Penny," she says, blue eyes softening to meet mine. "You and Christopher dated for almost two years."

"But the problem is..." I trail off and then try again. "What happened last night..." Again, words fail me, so I just blurt out what I'm trying to explain. "I hurt him, Mom. I broke his heart, and he doesn't trust me. Last night, he pulled back from me. I could see it on his face, the fear of us getting close again, because he's scared that I'll hurt him again."

I cried late into the night until I fell asleep, but still, fresh tears flood the edges of my eyes. She throws a comforting arm around my shoulder and pulls me into her side. I rest my head against hers and pinch my eyes closed, pulling back the pools of tears before they have a chance to escape.

"I never wanted to hurt him," I say so softy I don't think she hears me. "I just miss him."

A blank screen stares up at me as I check my phone for the fourth time tonight. Christopher hasn't called or texted since the Winter Wonderland dance. Not a word. At first I understood why. But now, Thursday night, six days of silence later, and I'm starting to get frustrated.

Clearly my phone is just as frustrated with me because it clicks off, the screen fading back to black. I shove it into my pocket and turn my focus to the section of the cheer team that I'm working with. I know why Christopher suddenly stopped talking to me, but it doesn't make the ache in my heart any less powerful.

Coach Violet dismisses us early from practice. A reward to the squad for a perfect run through of the material they've learned so far. I push through the front doors of the school, and struggle to suck down a breath against the bitter cold air. My fingers dig deeper into my coat pockets, searching for the keys to the SUV. Luckily, mom has been working the morning shift at the library every day this week, so I've been able to have the car in the afternoons to drive to the school.

I squint through the spirals of loose snow that are being blown off the roof of the school, and find the navy SUV where I left it, but my eyes catch on the red truck parked beside it, the headlights sending two beams of light in my direction.

Christopher.

I don't think there's any other reason he'd be at the school this late at night, so I don't have to question my movements as I cross the slippery parking lot to the passenger side. Before I reach the door, Christopher leans through the cabin and pops it open, causing the overhead lights to turn on. I climb inside, closing the door behind me, and speak before letting myself think. "You've been avoiding me."

"No," he quickly defends, running his hand through his brown waves.

I tilt my head and give him a look that lets him know I don't believe him. "I've been waiting on you to text me about the portfolio project."

"I know," he says, pausing to swallow against his tight throat. I hadn't realized how tense he was when I got in the truck, but now that I'm studying him in the fading cabin light, I see the muscles in his jaw are locked, fingers flexing into fists. "It's been a busy week. I had an exam yesterday and a lot on my mind."

He's quiet, letting me wonder what could be consuming his thoughts. I know for me, he's all I've thought about this week. That moment where we almost kissed... I replay it a million times a day, wondering what would have happened if I leaned in first, if I didn't notice the hurt in his eyes, if he wouldn't have let our past ruin what is happening now.

"I did reserve some time for us at the hot springs for next Tuesday," he adds, glancing at me with eyes that seem unsure of what he's saying. They reflect the last rays of light in the cabin before only the shine of the moon lets me see his shadowed face.

"What time?"

"After cheer, if that's okay with you." His words sound heavier than I think he intends them. Like he's asking if I still want to do the portfolio after everything that happened at the Winter Wonderland dance. After he's been clearly avoiding me all week, probably trying to wrap his head around what I'm also battling. These feelings aren't going away, and I'm planning to be home until August. That's seven months with Christopher in this town that drowns me with its memories. And every day I know I'll be fighting the want to be with him again. But right now, the heartbreak that will surely come in August is enough to keep me from crossing that bridge.

"Sure," I say with an easy shrug.

"I actually wanted to ask you something else," he says.

When he doesn't elaborate, I draw my eyes up to his, seeing that he's looking at me questioningly, like he's still considering if he should say what he's about to. I tilt my head to the side, resting it against the seat, and it's enough movement to bring his words out.

"Would you want to come with me to my photography lecture tomorrow morning?" He draws his bottom lip between his teeth, waiting for my response.

I process what he's asking, but am confused where the idea came from. "Really? You want me to come to your class?"

"Well, now that you say it out loud, it sounds like an awful idea," he says, the words coming out so fast they pile on top of each other. "Of course, the last thing you want to do right now is sit in a college lecture. This is your break from school—"

"I'll come," I say, interrupting him and his words cut off. "Are you sure it's okay that I tag along?"

"Yeah, Mr. Riley won't mind," Christopher says, his tense shoulders finally falling. "I just thought you might want to be on the other side of the portfolio project. See what I'm learning and how I can use it in the photos we take. A lot of the other people in the class have brought their friends."

I shift in my seat, pulling my blonde curls over my shoulder. "What time do you want to pick me up?"

Christopher's lips part, his answer hanging in the silence as he pauses, eyes sweeping over my face, catching on the way the moonlight makes my gaze shimmer. "You really want to come?" The question is soft, dripping with disbelief and surprise, and it makes my heart tug in my chest. It means something to him that I'm not only willing to do this, but I *want* to do it.

"What time are you picking me up," I ask again, the corner of my lips pulling up in a loose smile that he reflects.

"Seven sharp. Don't make me late," he teases, letting our easy humor filter through the serious air that floats between us.

"Should I bring anything?" I ask, sitting up from the seat and reaching for the door handle.

Christopher shakes his head and lets his hand rest on the gear shift between us. "I'll see you in the morning."

"See you in the morning," I repeat, popping open the door and dropping into a slushy pile of snow.

I trudge around the front of his truck, letting the headlights hit me with their harsh beams, and then climb inside the navy SUV.

Photography class. With Christopher.

I've never been to the Rayou Community College campus, let alone sat in one of their lectures. A bit of excitement seeps into my veins as I pull out of the parking lot, thinking about what I'll do tomorrow, and a heat flushes my face, my heart beating happily now that the agonizing silence in Christopher's absence is gone.

But beneath all of that, is a pit in my stomach that keeps trying to remind me of that kiss last Friday. Of the hurt that bloomed in Christopher's eyes because of what I did to him. He's spent the entire week trying to wrap his mind around the feelings that are reigniting in our hearts, but battling the truth that I'll be leaving again in August. I think we're both trying to fight to understand that this new friendship we've formed is living on borrowed time.

Chapter 13

A piercing honk breaks through the barrier around my mind while I load the dishwasher. My eyes lift, seeking out the frosted door at the front of the house. A cherry red blob is on the other side. Mom brings my focus to her, sitting at the bar, still finishing her breakfast.

"Is that Christopher?" she asks without turning around.

When I got home from cheer practice last night, she was already in her room and she came down late for breakfast today, so I haven't had the chance to tell her about my new plans.

"Yeah," I say, swinging the door of the dishwasher up. "I'm going with him to his photography lecture this morning."

My mom freezes with the spoon halfway to her mouth. White droplets of milk drip from the overflowed edges. "Really?"

I give her a hum for a response and reach for my mustard coat, sliding my arms inside and storing my phone in the pocket.

"Are you going to come by the nursing home later?"

My feet pause as I round the bar. Right, it's Friday. "I'll have Christopher drop me off when we get out of his class," I say, trying to make it sound like I planned to do that from the beginning, when in reality all I've thought about since I set foot in Rayou is the brunette boy waiting for me outside.

The response I get from my mom tells me she sees right through my quick cover. "I can't be there until 1:00 this afternoon anyway, so there's no rush. Tell Christopher I say hello." She adds the last bit as my feet unfreeze and I continue on toward the front door.

Once outside, the early morning air burns my lungs, the below freezing temperatures still trying to hold on from nighttime. The snow crunches beneath my brown leather boots as I stumble down the slight hill in the front yard. Behind me, a deep channel forms where I've walked. The snow sticks to my boots even after I try to stomp off as much as I can, and a small pile forms beneath my seat when I hop into the truck, letting the already warm cabin thaw my fingers.

"Good morning," Christopher says, an easy grin on his face. There's no sign of the nervous and tense boy from last night. Today, he's all confidence and jokes like normal.

My eyes drop to his hands where a to-go coffee cup glows on display. "Is that for me?" I ask, letting the last of the cold air out of my lungs before taking in the warmth.

"Dark roast with creamer and honey." Christopher recites my Snowcapped Diner order from memory and extends the coffee cup to me.

"Thank you!" I reach with gracious fingers, brushing his as I take it.

"Well, it's the least I could do after inviting you to a college lecture at seven in the morning on a Friday," Christopher says through his easy grin.

"Now I'm ready to learn all I need to know about photography," I claim as I take a small sip of the piping hot coffee.

Christopher barks a laugh at that and pulls the truck back onto the road. "I don't think one morning lecture is going to teach you all of that."

I lean back in the seat, turning my head so it rests against the soft material. The joke I've told in many variations builds on my tongue, my lips smiling in anticipation. Christopher glances sideways at me, feeling my gaze on him.

"Surely there's not that much to know. It's only taking pictures," I say teasingly.

"Only taking pictures?" he says, defensive of his passion. It's an easy banter that bounces between us like old times, helping to ease us into the day ahead.

As we drive, I watch the homes that line the street pass by and we make our way south from Rayou and toward the Community College. Christopher drives the route easily, probably something that is engrained in him already. I reach for the radio, turning on one of the few stations we get out here in the mountains of Colorado, and let the easy melodies fill the space between us. I ask Christopher some questions about his classes from last semester, letting him do most of the talking while I drink my coffee.

"So what's the plan for after?" I ask. My eyes are closed now, resting my head back on the seat and letting the sun streaming through the window confuse me into thinking it could be summer outside. We bump across some train tracks and I'm jostled in my seat.

"After Community College?"

"Mhmm," I hum. Even though Christopher and I dated for nearly two years, he never had a plan for the future besides classes at the community college. Now that he's enrolled, I wonder if he's decided what the next step will be.

The silence that fills the cabin of the truck makes the beats in the song on the radio seem louder. I crack my left eye open and study Christopher. His right hand grips the steering wheel a bit tighter, muscles in his arm stretching the denim of the jacket he's wearing. Christopher dampens his lips, still in thought. Finally he says, "If I could do whatever I want, I'd transfer to Rhode Island School of Design after another year at Rayou."

"Rhode Island?" I echo and he nods.

"I've been researching the best school for photography and it's at the top of my list. Right now, it's my dream school," Christopher says, slowing the truck to make a sharp turn near a sign that reads WELCOME TO RAYOU COMMUNITY COLLEGE.

"So why do you talk about it like it's not an actual option?" I ask, sitting up straighter in my seat to fix my blonde curls that had matted together.

"Because it's expensive," Christopher says, and the words sound like something he's probably repeated to himself multiple times.

"Like how expensive?" I ask.

"Like so expensive it's not worth discussing." Christopher twists the wheel to the left and the truck bumps along into the parking lot. For a Friday morning, the campus is fairly empty. I assume most people don't want to come in on a Friday if they don't have to. We find a spot right at the front of the parking lot, the expansive school spreading out in front of us. Christopher must catch my widened eyes scanning the massive size of the building because he says, "Haven't been here before?"

I shake my head. I know some of my classmates from high school took early college classes here last summer before leaving for their universities, but I wasn't one of them. The black cinderblock building is long, snaking around the parking lot with different wings. There's a metal enclosed bridge that stretches across an entire lot of cars, connecting to a second building on the other side.

"It's a lot bigger than I thought it would be," I admit.

We climb out of the truck, and I follow Christopher toward the double doors nearest us. He taps his black cloth wallet to a card reader and I hear the doors unlock, allowing us to enter. Inside, the floors are a gold and grey checkered porcelain tile, and my boots squeak as we walk. As far as I can see, we are the only two in the building, though soft conversations drift out of some of the rooms along the hallway. We take a right and Christopher stops outside a door at the end, pulling it open for us. Inside, wooden desks spread the length of the room, five rows deep. It's about a third of the size of the lecture halls I'm used to at Frostard.

Six other students already sit in the classroom. Four fill the front row, each of them giving Christopher a half-wave when we enter. I follow him to the left side of the room and we fill two seats side-by-side. Other people trickle in over the next few minutes, and just as my phone lights up saying it's 8:00 a.m., the door clicks shut and a tall man with a thick, brown beard walks to the front of the classroom. He's wearing jeans and a faded red t-shirt, whatever it used to say lost to time. I have to assume he had a jacket on at one point and walked here from his office, but I'm not so sure when the flopping sound of his flip-flops rings against the tiled floor, toes red from the snow.

"Class," he greets, tossing a satchel that hung around his neck onto the table at the front of the room.

"Happy Friday, Mr. Riley," one of the guys in the front row speaks up, leaning back in his chair and tilting his voice up playfully.

"That it is Billy, that it is," Mr. Riley responds without even glancing at Billy.

Instead, the professor digs through his satchel and pulls out his laptop, reaching for the HDMI cord to project his screen for everyone in the class to see. It's only now that the man's brown eyes lift and scan the faces in the room. They meet mine almost instantly, knowing I'm someone new. His stare lingers a minute longer until I begin to fidget and tuck my blonde curls behind my ear. Mr. Riley's eyes flip to Christopher and then back to me. I think he may call me out, and I'm about two seconds from blaming this on Christopher who swore his professor wouldn't mind, when the corner of Mr. Riley's mouth twitches up and his gaze moves to his laptop.

"Today we're starting our chapter on shadows," he says, jumping into the lecture.

I glance at Christopher, knowing he must have seen the exchange between the three of us and the tops of his cheeks are a light pink, the barest hint of a blush. After a second, he meets my sideways glance and smiles softly before he turns his focus back to the front of the room. The look from Mr. Riley lingers with me as I lean back in my seat and I let my roaming mind filter my thoughts and Mr. Riley's lecture for the next hour.

Chapter 14

When the lecture is over, Christopher says he wants to stay after to ask Mr. Riley about the exam he took on Wednesday. I pull on my heavy wool coat and hover near the front of the room while the rest of the students file out.

Christopher walks up to Mr. Riley and the professor's smile widens, clamping a hand on Christopher's shoulder and giving him a light shake. It's a gesture family or friends would make. I nearly choke on the idea of the professors at Frostard doing that to one of their students. I bet none of them even knew my name.

Their words aren't spoken loud enough for me to hear, but by the smiles and nods, I assume Christopher did well on the exam. I'm still watching the two of them when they both turn to look in my direction, clearly talking about me. My lips curl in a small smile, but a nervous pinch takes root in my stomach, spreading through me when they both walk toward me.

"So, you're the famous Penny Wilson," Mr. Riley says as a way of greeting.

Wide-eyed, I look between him and Christopher. "Umm—"

"I told him you were helping me with the portfolio," Christopher cuts in. "I wanted to be sure you could be in the pictures even though you're not a student, here."

"Oh," I say with a sigh, though I'm not sure if that's really what Mr. Riley means. The glimmer in his smiling eyes tells me he's finding something about this humorous.

"I've liked some of the photos Christopher's shown me," Mr. Riley says, stuffing his hands into the pockets of his jeans. Even though I've been watching Mr. Riley lecture for an hour, his appearance still shocks me. Especially the sandals in February. All of my professors wore ironed business attire to class every day. "You may have a calling in this industry."

"Definitely not," I say. "Christopher does all the work. They wouldn't look nearly as good if he wasn't the one behind the camera."

"That's not entirely true." Christopher tries to stay humble, but it's most definitely true.

"I really enjoyed your lecture," I say, turning my gaze back to Mr. Riley. "I didn't think I'd find myself back in a classroom this soon, but this was much more interesting than the Business Ethics course I was supposed to take this semester."

"Yeah, Christopher said something about you taking a semester off." Mr. Riley shifts his weight so I have his full attention now, eyes narrowing curiously.

I just nod and say, "I'll be back at Frostard in the fall."

"Frostard, huh?" Mr. Riley says thoughtfully. "You know, I actually took a semester off from college when I was studying at the University of Colorado."

"Really?" I inquire, a small gasp escaping me.

Mr. Riley nods, his relaxed smile meeting his eyes. "It was the best decision I ever made."

I study Mr. Riley, still surprised by what he's told me. "Most people think less of me since I've come home," I admit, remembering the judgement that hung in Ms. Yession's eyes when I delivered those books to the school library.

"Well, if it makes a difference, I think quite highly of you, Ms. Wilson. It takes a lot of courage to not only acknowledge that something needs to change, but to make the effort to do just that."

His praise makes my chest lift, and the fact that he understands exactly what I'm going through only solidifies the comfort warming my veins.

After a moment Mr. Riley adds, "You're welcome in my class anytime, Penny." He takes a step back from us, giving a departing nod before turning and heading to his desk at the front of the room to collect his laptop.

"Want to grab some lunch before I take you back?" Christopher asks.

It only startles me for a second, his question sounding a lot like he's asking me out on a date, but I brush it off. That's definitely not what he is asking, and I agree to get some food. I follow Christopher back through the halls of Rayou Community College until we get to the bridge I had seen earlier.

"There are food options on both sides," he says, stopping next to a small directory at the base of the staircase that lists out the different stalls serving food on either side of the bridge.

"What's your favorite?" I ask, knowing he must already have somewhere he likes to eat.

Christopher considers it for a minute before looking up the stairs toward the bridge. "I really like this sandwich shop on the other side."

"Then sandwiches it is," I say, moving to side-step a group of students coming down the stairs.

We climb the metal steps and cross the bridge, the noon sun shining through the windows on the landing. It makes everything glow in an orange hue. Beneath us, cars are parked across the dirty snow-covered pavement. I look out both sides of windows, the Colorado mountains climbing around the school with tall, snowcapped peaks.

"Honestly, this is ten times prettier than California," I say as we reach the other side of the bridge and descend the stairs.

"Really?" Christopher inquires and I nod.

"I mean, don't get me wrong, Frostard's campus is beautiful, but it's right in the middle of this industrial part of the city. I didn't step foot off of the campus the entire time I was there."

"Yeah, the mountains just have something about them," Christopher says, both of us glancing over our shoulders and out the windows. "Now, tell me if we have better food than Frostard, too," he adds, nudging me playfully.

An easy smile spreads across my face as we walk up to the stall for the sandwich shop Christopher recommended. I let him go first so I can watch what he orders and have a bit more time with the menu.

Christopher orders a pizza sub with marinara and meatballs. I go the safer route and just order a turkey sandwich. I watch the lady behind the counter make the sandwich and I tell her what toppings to add. Once I reach the register and pull out my wallet, I ask how much it's going to be.

"He actually already paid for yours," she says, looking over my shoulder. I turn in that direction and see Christopher sitting at a table in the center of the eating area. My stomach mixes with *swoops* and *drops* and I'm not sure what I'm thinking. I tell myself again that this isn't a date, but he bought my meal. I wish he wouldn't have done that, but it was also really nice. Confused with a spinning head and a fluttering heart, I pick up my sandwich and join Christopher at the wooden table.

"You didn't have to do that," I say, taking my seat across from him.

"Sure I did. I just made you sit through an hour lecture on shadows in photography. It's the least I could do," he says, taking a bite of his sandwich and dripping marinara all over the paper basket. It makes a small giggle build in my throat and I shake my head.

"You didn't make me go. I went willingly, and I did have fun," I say again.

Christopher chews his bite while studying me and when he swallows he says, "Does that mean you'd be interested in coming to more of them?"

My eyes lift from him as I consider the idea, and they trail around the room, taking in the details of Rayou Community College. This is definitely not where I pictured spending my time, but I, oddly, do want to come back. Maybe it's because Christopher is here, or that it's a change in my schedule.

I bring my gaze back to his, seeing that he's still waiting for my answer. My lips pull up in a smirk, a smart remark forming on my tongue. "I guess that depends how good this sandwich is."

"Try the lift again," Coach Violet's voice rings through the gym Tuesday afternoon, breaking through the cheer the squad is reciting. They freeze, startled by her interruption, and then begin shifting backward through the routine to go back to the lift Coach is talking about.

My watch vibrates and I twist my wrist to see a notification from Christopher. It's a text message letting me know he's sitting in the parking lot, ready to take us to the hot springs for our photo shoot. I don't realize a smile splits my lips until my cheeks pinch.

After lunch on Friday, I did agree to attend more of his photography lectures. I claimed it was because that was the best turkey sandwich I'd ever eaten, but the truth is, spending time with him seems to be the only thing I want to do. My second lecture with Mr. Riley was yesterday, and he didn't seem surprised to see I was there again.

The squeak of tennis shoes on the gym floor pulls me out of my head. I shift my weight and cross my arms, eyes now focused on the team's movements to see what we can polish before the state tournament. We've taught them the entire routine, now it's time to perfect it.

Which is why Coach is having them run the lift again. It's obviously our weakest moment in the routine. The squad splits into the three groups of four members. Each perform a lift and they look to Coach and me for some direction.

"With or without music, Coach?" I ask, her phone that's connected to the Bluetooth speaker in my hand.

"Without," she says, and I nod at the squad to continue without the beat to accompany them.

It goes without saying that this means they need to count out their steps. Trinity starts off by counting them in and then the rest of the team joins her, snapping together in unison. They go through a few tumbling moves and jumps before clustering together and the three flyers take their positions in the center of the groups, placing their right feet into pockets formed by hands, and up they go.

I catch myself nodding along, mouthing the beats with them. I can't help but see myself in the routine, knowing exactly how it would feel to be in their place. I cringe when the three flyers rise out of sync, one after another, instead of all at once. The weakest of the group is the freshman flyer, Lillyanne. She just lacks the confidence that comes from years of being thrown in the air. I know before the team even does the toss, that Coach will have them run it again. She may even single out Lillyanne. Her knees are weak, causing both of her legs to tremble beneath her weight, but her arms are strong, snapping through the sharp movements before coming together in a thunderous clap that signals the toss. Together, the three flyers are thrown in the air, performing a double twist. My eyes dilate as I focus on each movement, the tuck of their arms, the cross of their ankles, how their center of gravity rotates through the air. While the flyers go up in the toss together, they come down out of sync, again one after the other. Lillyanne being the last.

She falls toward the basket of arms that waits to catch her, and in the process, over corrects her twist, hitting the catch on her side instead of her back, The two members in charge of making the catch lose her, their arms buckling under the force and the entire cluster tumbles together, a mass of bodies hitting the floor hard.

"Dammit, Lillyanne!" Rachel, the spotter for her cluster, screams, pushing to her feet.

"I'm sorry," the freshman flyer quickly apologizes, still sitting in the huddle of other bodies, clutching her wrist to her chest.

"Maybe if you'd pass on those chocolate chip cookies every day at lunch, we could catch you," Rachel snaps and the gym falls silent.

My cheeks flush with heat, anger and shock thickening my blood. A latch on a door in my mind rips open. Moments from my past that I'd subconsciously forgot about leak into my head because I've been Lillyanne. I was the sixth grader that Lindsay brought to cheer practice, that was sculpted into a flyer. I was already small enough, but Lindsay made sure I stayed that way, taking the chocolate milk off my lunch tray and replacing it with apple juice, giving any birthday treats we got in class to the boys we thought were cute. She woke me up at 5:30 a.m. on the weekends to go on runs, even when I had to layer three sweatshirts on to keep warm, even when my toes turned blue in my shoes and I was screaming at her to leave me alone.

"What are you going to do if we can't lift you, Penny?" she yelled in my face. "We don't need another spotter, or a tumbler. We have all the other positions filled. You're the flyer, Penny. If you can't fly, you're cut."

Then I'd start running again, breathing hard through the sobs that turned to icicles on my cheeks in the colder months because I didn't want to lose cheer. I didn't want to lose her as my friend. Or maybe I wanted those things because she told me to want them.

In the gymnasium, Coach Violet's voice is muffled as she scolds Rachel, probably making her apologize to Lillyanne, but I can't focus on anything in front of me, too consumed with everything living *inside* of me. The trauma I so carefully ignored because cheer was over, because it didn't matter if the squad could throw me in the air floods through me. I'd fixed my diet, let myself fill my body out the way it was meant to be, but all of those delicately crafted walls tumble at Rachel's remark, and now Lindsay is back in my head, yelling at me for ordering those hash browns the other day, for eating the bread of my turkey sandwich at lunch on Friday—

I'm going to be sick. My fingers tremble so badly that Coach Violet's phone slips from my grasp and clatters on the glossy gym floor. The team's heads turn in my direction, stares studying me, and through the cloud in my mind I hear their concern, my discomfort visible.

I stumble back from them, turning to find the bathroom because the bile in my throat keeps rising, burning and twisting my stomach. I think I mumble some parting words before I leave and the gym doors rattle shut behind me, but when I look in the direction of the bathroom, my heart stutters. Instead, I spin to the left and run for the exit at the front of the school. My lungs close inside of me, begging for air that isn't thick with guilt and memories of those awful nights with Lindsay in the school bathroom, my fingers in my mouth—

I gasp, struggling to breathe, to rip my mind from the grip the past has on it. Tears bloom in my eyes and they bite my cheeks as I burst into the cold night. I only make it past the sidewalk when my legs give out and I collapse into a pile of dirty snow, chilling my exposed skin instantly. The shorts I wear are no protection to the elements. I hug my bare arms around my stomach and scream, curling forward as my body continues to lose control to the trauma in my head.

Make it stop. Please make it stop.

But Lindsay's voice persists above it all, and now it's more than the diet. It's about skipping this semester, letting myself fall behind everyone else, letting go of the plans she so carefully crafted for us.

Warm hands grip my arms, like the sun shining beams on a lost soul. "Penny, are you okay? What happened?"

His voice fractures the trauma, letting me see through it. My head snaps up, eyes searching and finding his in the night. Christopher kneels before me, denim jeans soaking in the snow beneath us. My breathing is still erratic, coming out in pants that never fill my lungs.

"Take me home, please." It's all I can get out before the fractured split closes and Lindsay's voice is there again, the hold on my throat tightening and closing off my air.

The next ten minutes are a blur of Christopher pulling me to my feet, practically carrying me to the truck, and then speeding through the narrow streets and up my driveway. We're stumbling across the front porch when the next wave of agony hits, making me roll forward and hug myself tighter.

Christopher rings the doorbell, and then pounds on the front door until my mom is there, her eyes as wide as the full moon overhead.

"I don't know what happened," Christopher quickly tells her. "She just ran out of the school and collapsed. I can't get her to talk to me. I don't know what to do—"

"It's okay," she interrupts him, arms reaching out for me. "I'll take it from here."

I'm pulled into my mother's embrace, through the front door of my house. I vaguely hear my mother tell Christopher goodnight and then the panic attack pulls me into its black void.

Chapter 15

S oft fur brushes my cheek, subtle and comforting. My eyes are closed, but I can sense the room around me. My entire body is warm, like the flames of a fire wrapping around me. Something sweet fills my nose, the scent wafting through the room. The mattress I'm lying on dips when someone sits next to me, thin fingers running through my hair.

I let each of these moments fill the void in my head until I slowly open my eyes. Baby blue material meets my line of sight, the furry pillow pressed against my face the first thing I see. On the night stand in front of me is a cup of hot chocolate, the source of the sweet smell. I blink through heavy eyelids, each movement forced and stiff.

I turn my gaze to the right and my mother's blonde hair comes into focus, bright against the beams of moonlight seeping through my drawn curtains. A heated blanket is tucked around me, like I'm a human burrito, the hot coils warming every inch of my body. Mom's hand comes back to the crown of my head and she lets her fingers run through my blonde hair once more. I know she sees I'm awake, but I don't want to say anything that would fracture this moment. I want to lie here and let her comfort me like she did when I was little and forget about what happened tonight.

I think my mom may understand that because we continue to sit in this bubble for a couple more minutes before she asks, "How are you feeling, Penny?"

"Better than I did," I tell her honestly. Not even a breath of cold air remains in my lungs, my stomach settled and my lungs relaxed.

"What happened?" She draws her hand back, letting my hair fall free from her fingers. My mom's blue eyes are thick with worry, and I know she isn't going to let me claim some made up excuse.

But I don't want to do that. I've kept the things Lindsay did a secret from her, let her believe every second at cheer was amazing, and never let her know how much I was struggling. If it weren't for Rachel bringing all those memories back to the surface, I don't know if my mom would ever know about this. I thought that part of my past didn't bother me anymore, but I was wrong.

I push myself up to lean my back against the headboard and reach for the cup of hot chocolate, taking a small sip while the words form on my tongue.

"Something happened at cheer tonight that brought up some bad memories," I say, and already the words are hard to get out. "There are things I've never told you about that happened when I was on the squad."

When I meet her gaze again, her eyes are filled with the same deep concern, but they've widened, waiting for me to continue. I look back down at my cup of hot chocolate, but I don't think I can stomach it with what I'm about to say, with those echoed comments from Lindsay still in my head telling me that if I drink this, I'll have to run an extra mile tomorrow. With trembling fingers, I put the mug back on my nightstand and bring my arms around my waist.

Tears build in my eyes as I lift them to meet my mother's gaze. "Lindsay used to tell me if I gained any weight, I'd be cut from the squad."

"What?" she breathes, and my tears break loose.

I nod, hugging my arms around me tighter and I tell her everything that happened when I was in high school. I tell her about the awful diet I was on, the intense exercising, and the nights in the bathroom. To my mom, to someone I never confided in about how I felt, she never knew the difference. She thought I just wasn't hungry. That Lindsay and I went on the runs because we wanted to. I never made myself throw up at home. I only did it in the school bathroom so there would be no evidence, no reason for her to ask questions.

My mom crawls into bed next to me and pulls me into her arms, letting me rest my head on her shoulder and cry until the room settles in a quiet hush.

"Penny Wilson, you are beautiful," my mom says, her words gentle and hushed.

Another silent tear rolls down my cheek and I swallow through my tight throat. I have never felt more torn from my own body than I do right now. "I wish I would have told you sooner," I admit.

"I wish you would have, too," she says honestly. "What you did was wrong, Penny. That isn't how you love yourself."

I nod against her head. "I know, Mom. It hasn't been a problem since I graduated. I thought I was past all of it. I *am* past all of it," I correct, because I don't plan on spiraling back into those unhealthy habits. But the memories of them still haunt me. They still make me sick and send me into a panic.

"But something happened tonight that reminded you of it," my mom says, her arms tightening around my shoulder.

We're quiet for a second while the moment from tonight replays in my head. "They dropped the flyer," I explain. "And Rachel said it was because of what she ate." Bile rises in my throat at the thought of the exchange.

My mom knows who Rachel is. Being a junior on the cheer team means we spent two seasons together. "She should be kicked off the squad for saying such a thing," my mom surprises me with the anger that blooms in her voice. "That's a horrible thing to say."

In the silence that follows my mother's comment, I'm sure she's imagining me in Lillyanne's place. I've had my fair share of falls at cheer practice. So many, in fact, I don't even fear it anymore. Now she's seeing those memories in a new light, seeing all the nights I came home crying from a fall and understanding I was crying because I hated my body, blamed myself for not being small enough, fearing if I didn't lose another five pounds I'd be cut from the cheer team.

I sit up from my mother, stretching my neck and easing full breaths into my weak lungs. My eyes lift to the full-length mirror that hangs on the back of my closet door and my reflection meets my gaze. Blonde curls stick to my damp cheeks, falling in a mess of knots around my narrow shoulders. The tight shirt that's cropped at my waist lets my judgmental eyes skim every inch of my body.

I can't remember the last time I looked in a mirror and hated what looked back at me. Probably the morning of graduation when Lindsay told me I'd put on too much weight since our cheer season ended. I worked so hard to leave this negativity in the past, but it all came crumbling down in one night.

My mom shifts next to me, her gaze also going toward the mirror across from us. Again she says, "You're beautiful, Penny."

"I wish I felt that way." The words are hollow, scraping out of my raw throat and tears threaten to form once more.

The bed suddenly shifts as my mom crawls over me and stands upright. "I'll be right back," she says, an energy finding her voice that surprises me. She practically runs from my room. Her footsteps sound through the upper level of the house, heading into her room at the other end of the hallway. When she resurfaces in the doorway, her arms are overflowing with rolls of wrapping paper.

"What's that for?" I gawk, feeling that weight on my chest lighten at the sight of the shiny paper and the confident smile on my mother's face.

She doesn't answer right away, and instead drops the wrapping paper into a pile on the floor, moving to find a pair of scissors and some tape from my desk. "Pick a roll of paper," she says, pointing to the pile with the scissors in her hand.

I slip from the bed, my feet sinking into the soft carpet of my bedroom, and pick up the first roll that catches my eyes. It's a red and white stripped paper that resembles a candy cane. The moonlight catches on the glitter in the red stripes, making it look like it's moving in my hand.

"Unroll it and hold it over the mirror," my mom says.

I crinkle my eyes, confused at what she's asking. I twist the roll of wrapping paper in my hand until the strip is as long as the mirror. I step toward the reflective glass; the girl staring back at me, making the heavy weight in my chest return. My eyes catch on my thighs and how they rub together now, how my face is fuller than in my senior yearbook photo.

"Cover the mirror, Penny." My mom comes to stand beside me, laying her hand on my shoulder.

I lift the sparkling paper up to the mirror, covering the reflection, and my breath comes back to me instantly. Now I understand what she's doing, and the immediate relief it brings causes a whole new wave of tears to spring to my eyes.

While I hold the paper to the mirror, my mom tapes the corner and uses the scissors to trim it down until it's a perfect fit. When I step back, a pretty rectangle of glitter infused wrapping paper stares back, emitting so much Christmas joy I can't help but smile at it and at what I can't see anymore.

"Now, grab another roll and let's go to the bathroom," she says, already heading for the door.

"Wait," I stop her. "You want to cover every mirror in the house?"

"Every single one," she says, not letting her words falter for even a second.

"That's crazy—"

"It's not," she cuts me off, coming back to stand right in front of me, our eyes at the same level. "You're my daughter and I'm not going to have you feeling this way if I can prevent it. You don't need a mirror to tell you what I already know, what I want you to know. You are beautiful, Penny, whether the cheer team can throw you or not. Beauty is about so much more than what a mirror shows you. What happened tonight could happen again if we just shrug our shoulders and say it's in the past, when it clearly isn't. I want to help you heal from those memories, Penny. This is how you start healing, by learning to live as *you* and not what shines back in the mirror."

A lump forms in my throat while she talks, the truth in her words burning inside of me. I do want to heal. I don't want to have another night like this one. My gaze naturally flips to the mirror on my closet door, and when I see the Christmas paper shining back, no sign of the girl Lindsay was trying to form, the girl who I never really wanted to be, the knot in my throat unravels.

"We don't have to do all the mirrors," I say, turning back to my mom. "Just ones I use. You don't have to cover the ones in your bathroom."

My mother's lips curl into a sad smile, eyes filling with something I don't understand at first. "I could use some healing too," she says softly. "I can be my own worst critic." Her smile grows fuller when she says her next words, "We're doing this together, Penny. You aren't facing any of this alone."

I don't know who moves first, but we pull each other into a tight hug, the tightest we've ever shared, and my body begins to piece itself back together.

"I love you, mom," I say into her short, blonde hair.

She presses a hand to my back and says, "I love you too, Penny."

When we pull apart, I lean down and pick up another roll of wrapping paper. "It's going to look like Christmas threw up in our house," I say, my voice filling with a joking tone that makes my mom laugh.

"What's wrong with that?" she says with a shrug.

We move through the house together, picking a different paper for each mirror. She even plays Christmas music while we work and neither of us can keep from singing along. To anyone else, I bet we look insane, screaming every word to *Deck The Halls* while taping wrapping paper over the mirrors.

The bathroom looks like a Christmas tree farm, the paper almost completely green with the deep shades of all the pine needles. We choose one with metallic ornaments for the decorative mirror in the hall. My mom puts the paper covered in snowflakes over the mirror in her bedroom, coordinating it with the one in her bathroom by selecting the snowman wrapping paper. It's in this moment that I realize how Christmas-crazy we are to own so many rolls of wrapping paper, but I'm thankful for it now.

When we're done, the house looks like Christmas presents have been hung all over the walls. The melody of *Jingle Bells* rings through the foyer as I spin around, taking in the shimmering paper and vibrant colors. Mom stands next to me, an empty roll of tape dangling in her fingers with the scissors.

"If your dad could see this," she says through a tired laugh.

"He'd lose his mind," I agree, and we both smile at the idea. I step closer to my mom, leaning against her and resting my head atop hers. "Thanks, mom." The words feel small, but I don't know how else to express just how grateful I am for her and what she's trying to do for me.

She loops an arm around my waist and pulls me closer to her, twisting her head to kiss my forehead. "In a way, this can be how we celebrate our Christmas." Her voice is soft, and she's probably remembering my empty place at the dinner table on Christmas Eve, the quiet that hung in the house on Christmas morning.

"Not coming home for Christmas was the biggest mistake I ever made," I say with the shake of my head. "I don't know why I let Lindsay talk me into that."

"We all do things we regret, Penny," she says, trying to keep the weight of the guilt from forming in my chest. "What matters is how you correct those mistakes."

My mom's words filter through the house and we stand together, not speaking. Instead, I let what she says take root in my heart, knowing the list of things I let Lindsay control that I now regret is endless.

So, how am I going to fix them?

I suppose only time will tell, but since I made that decision to board the plane over two weeks ago, a sense of confidence has followed every decision I've made since then. I'm choosing my own path now. Everything I'm doing now, I chose to do. Maybe these are the first steps to correcting those mistakes. Maybe these are my first steps in my own shoes, marking the path I'll travel.

Chapter 16

My mom and I spend the night in the living room with *It's a Wonderful Life* playing until we're both asleep on the couch. When I wake up Wednesday morning, the smell of bacon makes my mouth water. I stumble off the couch and rub my eyes as I walk down the narrow hall to the kitchen. A soft giggle vibrates in my throat when I hear my mom humming *Jingle Bells* over the sizzling skillet.

"Good morning," I sing cheerfully and she snaps her gaze over her shoulder, surprised by my sudden appearance.

"Oh, look who's up," she teases, sliding the pan off the hot burner.

I pull myself up onto a barstool, reach for the jug of orange juice that she removed from the fridge, and carefully fill the two glasses set before me.

"You look like you're feeling better," she says, coming over to slide a piece of bacon onto my plate with the eggs.

I notice she's made enough bacon for each of us to have three pieces, so I reach into the pan before she walks away and grab two more crunchy strips. "Much better," I say through a bite of the salty sensation. It's only slightly true, because my heart still aches in my chest, my eyes puffy and tired from all the tears I cried. The oval mirror that hangs next to the entrance to the mudroom catches the corner of my eye, its reindeer print wrapping paper peeling a smile across my face.

"So, are you going to class with Christopher today?" Mom asks, sliding onto the barstool next to me.

The crispy bacon falls from my hand. I reach for my phone—greasy finger prints smudging the screen as I check the time. "It's too late," I say, that optimistic energy that filled my chest seconds ago thinning out.

"Probably for the best," Mom offers. "I think you could use a day off from everything outside these walls."

When I go to turn off the screen of my phone, I notice a red light in the corner, indicating unanswered text messages. I bite the inside of my cheek, some internal barrier wanting me to leave them unread, to wait just a bit longer before looking at what lays beyond this little Christmas bubble Mom and I built last night. I click the screen off and place it face down on the counter. "Are you going into the library today?"

"I can call Sarah and see if she can cover. She may want the extra hours anyway," mom offers, licking the grease off her fingers.

I shrug and say, "I'd be okay by myself if you need to go in. I still have to unpack."

"Penny, you've been home for over two weeks," my mother scolds, and it eases a laugh out of me.

"Perfect time to actually unpack," I decide.

Mom agrees to go into the library just for a half day and says she'll pick up something from the Snowcapped Diner for us for lunch. When she leaves, and I've finished cleaning up the breakfast mess, I head toward my room. With each wrapped mirror I pass, my smile grows wider and the weight on my shoulders gets lighter. It seemed so silly last night, but now that I see the bright red and green wrapping paper in the daylight, I realize how ingenious it really is. I even reach out and run my finger across the gloss candy-cane paper that covers the mirror on my closet before flopping onto the mattress.

I stare at the ceiling, tracing the raised, rough plaster paths with my eyes while my foot taps against the duffle bag on the floor. It's nearly empty now that I've been home for eighteen days, so the idea that I would spend any time unpacking the last few things inside is silly. I just didn't want my mom to feel like she needed to change all her plans for today. She already did so much for me last night. I can hardly believe I told her everything and that she reacted the way she did.

My phone slips deeper into my pocket when I shift my weight, reminding me of its presence. Now, the curiosity of what messages are on my phone outweighs my desire to ignore the world outside of these walls. I slip it into my hand and hold it above my face, illuminating the screen and opening my text messages.

There's one from Coach Violet asking if I'm okay and that she wants me to call her when I have a moment. A pang of guilt blooms in my chest. I shouldn't have run out of practice with no explanation to Coach. She was probably worried all night about where I went and what happened to me. I click on her name and select her number.

It rings four times before I realize it's during school hours and end up leaving her a message apologizing for running out of practice. Some easy lie slips from my lips that I wasn't feeling well and that guilt only grows. Team code to never rat to the coach about what your teammates do outside of practice keeps the truth from coming out.

After I hang up, I go back to my text messages and see that

Christopher sent me six text messages last night. I read the line of grey bubbles over and over, each carrying a phrase that makes my heart swell. He asked if I was feeling any better, told me not to worry about the photo shoot—that we'd reschedule with the hot springs resort, asked again what happened at cheer to upset me, and then told me to call him I if I needed anything.

The memories before the panic attack faded last night are still a bit fuzzy. I know he was the one who found me in the parking lot and he brought me home. His distant voice in the cabin of the truck is still muffled to me, but I can hear the break of his voice, how his wide eyes searched my face, how he took my hand and squeezed it the entire time just to let me know that he was there even when I couldn't get words to form.

I look at the time on my phone and know that his class is about to start, but I may be able to catch him before he goes in, so I click his name and let my phone dial his number.

It only rings once before his voice fills my ears.

"Penny."

"Hi Christopher."

There's a short pause, the broken sound of my voice lingering between us before he responds. "Are you okay?"

He sounds hesitant to ask the question, but I'm glad he does. "Better than I was last night," I say, the tone of my voice turning more conversational. "I know your class starts soon, but I just wanted to let you know that I'm okay and thank you for bringing me home last night."

"You don't have to thank me, Penny."

"I do," I say. "I ruined our plans for the hot springs photo shoot and you most definitely did not agree to hauling a crying girl through the school parking lot." I try to make it sound like a joke, but it just sharpens the ache in my chest. I can't believe I broke down like that in front of him. He's seen me cry before—plenty of times, actually, because I wear my emotions on my sleeve—but that was when we were dating. That was when he knew everything I was thinking, was at the center of my entire world.

"Seriously, Penny, I don't care about the photo shoot, I'm just worried about you." The hollow crack in his voice splits open the pain in my chest, warming me and lessening the ache.

"We can reschedule the photo, right?" I ask, though he said as much in one of his previous text messages.

"Whenever works for you," he says.

My eyes drift over the ceiling of my room, but I have no idea when I'm going to feel like leaving this house. Right now, I just feel like curling up under the fuzziest blanket I can find and drinking hot chocolate.

"We can try for Saturday," I offer and Christopher says he'll call the resort this afternoon. "I should probably let you go. I want to keep Mr. Riley in my good graces," I say, and there's a muffled laugh on his end of the phone.

"All right. I'll talk to you later?" Christopher asks.

I tell him we will and hang up the phone, letting the silence of the house fill the space his voice was. I imagine him getting out of his truck in the paved parking lot and walking through the double glass doors on the wing with the photography classrooms. The checkered floor is vivid in my head and I picture Christopher sitting in the same desk on the left of the room, the chair to his right empty. That's where I would sit if I were there. My lip twitches with a sad smile, because I actually do wish I was there.

My foot still absent-mindedly taps the edge of my duffle, and my ankle gets wrapped in the woven strap, the bag tugging back. I prop myself up on my elbows and survey the room, my laundry basket now overflowing with dirty clothes, the last few remaining shirts peeking out of my bag.

I guess now is as good a time as any to finally empty the duffel bag and put it away. Even though I've been home for over two weeks, when I fold the duffle and tuck it onto the shelf in my closet, something feels final about me being here, making it official. I'm not attending Frostard this spring. I'm falling an entire semester behind everyone else. There won't be any classes for me to sit through no exams, essays, or projects. I'm not going to see Lindsay again for who knows how long.

I'm back in Rayou, I've seen Christopher almost as much as I've seen my own mother, every mirror in my house is covered with Christmas wrapping paper, and I am most definitely not the same Penny that left six months ago.

The smile that spreads my lips only grows at that thought.

By Thursday night, I know exactly how many planks of wood stretch from the stairs to the edge of the kitchen where the floor changes to a white tile. I know how many of those tiles are full squares, and how many are triangles at the edges of the room. In other words, I need out of this house.

Mom snores softly beside me on the couch, her feet propped up on my legs, while she spreads out across the cushions. I wiggle my phone out from under my thigh and the bright screen floods light through the dim living room. My thumbs move across the screen on their own as I pull up my text messages with Christopher. Since I called him yesterday morning, the last ones in our chat are his from Tuesday night.

Penelope: Hey.

Simple enough.

Christopher: You're up late.

Christopher's response comes through almost immediately, and I'm not sure I like how that makes my heart dip in my chest.

Penelope: So are you.

I respond teasingly and I wonder if he can hear my voice in his head as if I spoke the words, like I can do with his messages. The three dots immediately appear at the bottom corner of the screen, but then they disappear, and then reappear a moment later.

Christopher: What's up?

My thumbs hover over the keyboard, and my mind can't help but think about what Christopher had typed and then deleted. *Maybe it was nothing. Maybe he just misspelt something?* Yes, he misspelt something in his two word text. I roll my eyes at myself and then type out my message before I let the pause in our conversation last too long.

Penelope: I'm looking for a ride to my photography class tomorrow morning. Think you can take me?

Christopher: Your photography class?

His response causes me to laugh, just a weak breath that splits my lips.

Penelope: If you can't take me...

Christopher immediately responds.

Christopher: I'll pick you up at seven.

Chapter 17

The hot air billowing out of Christopher's dash surrounds me like a warm hug when I pull myself into the passenger seat Friday morning. I get out a breathy hello, my words fogging up from the cold outside. Once I click my seatbelt into place, I meet Christopher's watchful eyes and I realize how timid he is. Both hands grip the wheel, hazel eyes wide as they survey me. He's trying to figure out how he's supposed to act after literally scraping me off the school parking lot Tuesday night.

Something flashes in his eyes, and it looks like a forced glimmer, the corner of his mouth pulling too sharp. "Ready for class?" he tries to tease, but his voice isn't the confident tone I'm used to.

I nod and tuck my blonde curls behind my ear. Christopher pulls away from the curb and heads for the southern part of Rayou. I settle back into the fabric seat, letting the warm air thaw the memory of the cold from my skin. As we drive and I watch the houses roll past in a blur, I organize my words in my head. I don't know if Christopher can tell that's what I'm doing, but he doesn't force a conversation and waits for me to speak first.

Rayou falls behind us and we're twisting and turning through the evergreen forest between the town and the community college. Here, the snow is more untouched and the pure white powder glistens under the early morning rays. It hangs heavy on the branches, weighing them down into arches over the road. I know the snow could be here until April, but I still get lost in seeing it so pristine, so frozen on the other side of the window.

The tires skid through a patch of slush when Christopher slams on the break, throwing me forward against my seatbelt. A ringing alarm signaling the lowering of railroad gates breaks the fragile silence we are sitting in, and candy cane striped arms block the road. I can feel the train through the rumble in the ground before I see it.

"Damn thing gets me every Friday, I swear," Christopher says, but his tone isn't bothered. He reaches down and puts the truck in park, knowing the length of the train before it even reaches us. The black bars of the pilot break through the tunnel of trees and the train streams past like a stampede plowing ahead.

Like the anxiety I had hidden so well exploding through my veins Tuesday night.

The rattle of the tracks fills the cabin of Christopher's truck, offering some noise to fill the tense silence I'm finally ready to break. I look at Christopher, resting my head against the seat and say, "About Tuesday."

He meets my gaze, giving me his full attention while we wait for the train to pass.

"They dropped the flyer," I say, never looking away from his hazel eyes. "Rachel made a comment about her weight, and it just made all those…"

"Those times from high school come back," Christopher finishes for me.

I press my lips together and nod once. Christopher is no stranger to what I went through. He knows everything that Lindsay said to me, what she made me do to stay the weight I was. And I know that's one of the many reasons he's always disliked her. I protected Lindsay when I shouldn't have, and I forced Christopher to let me handle the situation. I never let him confront Lindsay or have anyone else intervene. Which resulted in me continuing to suffer until my senior season was over.

I only allowed Christopher be my support on the nights it was too much to bear alone. Christopher is the reason none of that broke me beyond repair. He's the reason I was able to put it behind me after graduation. We spent the entire summer leading up to college helping me find a way to love my body the way I always should have. But then we broke up, I went to college with Lindsay, and the shattered girl from high school never became whole.

"I didn't realize I was still hurting from that until everything came crashing down," I whisper and one of my blonde curls falls into my face.

Christopher reaches out a hand, pushing the piece of hair behind my ear, and he lets his touch linger on my cheek, pressing his warm palm flush to my skin. My breath pauses in my throat, everything but those hazel eyes fading away. He licks his lips, words forming on his tongue. "Penny, you are the most beautiful girl in the entire world." His thumb rubs across the top of my cheek, leaving a trail of warmth in its wake. "I know we aren't dating, and you're not my girlfriend anymore, but it's true."

My breath is thin, working against the rapid thumping of my heart. I don't know how to respond to that because he's right, we aren't dating, and he shouldn't be saying these things to me. Just like I shouldn't still get lost in the amber hues that curl in his eyes and are enhanced by the sunlight. I shouldn't love the way his brown waves curl around his face, or catch myself counting the faint freckles on his cheeks, or daydream about what it would feel like to have his arms around me again, for his lips to be on mine.

"I know you always told me you wanted to handle the situation with Lindsay, but I hate that never intervened," Christopher says.

I reach up to where his hand still rests against my cheek and I curl my fingers around his touch, wishing he didn't have the weight of that guilt on his chest.

"I just wish you could see what I see," he adds. His bottom lip trembles on his shaking breath, and I think his eyes dampen with tears.

"Tell me what you see," I say with a soft squeeze on his hand.

His eyes flicker across my face, taking me in before he speaks. "I see eyes as blue as the sky, filled with a navy as rich as the deepest depths of the ocean. Cheeks that blush when I make silly jokes." He pauses, the corner of his lip pulling up as a heat rises in my face. "Just like they are right now."

I tilt my head into his hand, and the smile that forms is natural. His eyes catch on the pull of my lips and I know that's what he'll say next.

"I see a smile that makes my breath catch," Christopher continues. "A silent laugh held behind lips I still think about kissing."

His hazel eyes lift back up to meet my gaze and he takes in another breath, moving on as if he didn't just say what he did. "I see the girl who cheered the loudest at my basketball games, and that had nothing to do with her being a cheerleader. I see someone who has been my best friend for two years, who used to hold my heart in the palm of her hand, who I'd do literally anything for."

Christopher's voice drops off, barely audible over the thunderous train. "I see *you*, Penny," he adds after a moment. "Every time I look at you, that is what I see."

My heart beats so hard in my chest, it aches, rapidly trying to even itself out, but Christopher has always had that ability. His words always go straight to my heart. I let my hand fall from his that still cups my cheek and shake my head softly.

"Nothing about you needs to change, Penny," he says, his voice breathy. "Not the way you smile, the color of your hair, the way you tap your foot when you're thinking, how you bite your lip when your nervous." Christopher dips his head forward just an inch, and his next words go straight to my dropping stomach. "And definitely not your weight. You are perfect. You are Penny and I..." His eyes dilate, the blacks swelling over the hazel swirls. The words that get caught in his throat still manage to grip my heart. I know he won't speak them, though. That fear that kept him from kissing me the night of the Winter Wonderland dance is still there, knowing that he is walking a fragile line to keep from having his heart broken again.

"I wouldn't change a thing about you," he says, the words fumbling in place of the ones he was going to say. His hand falls from my face, and even though the truck is circulating with warm air, a coldness spreads where his touch is now absent.

"You see all of that?" I try to tease him, but I sound awestruck, still processing everything he just told me.

"That and so much more." His half smile is sad, and I wonder if the words he just left unsaid are weighing in his chest.

I open my mouth to respond, but the screeching whistle of the train interrupts me and the last wheels rumble by, the crossing arms raising and their signal ringing out. Christopher only waits a second, taking me in with his sweeping gaze, before he puts the truck in drive and continues on our route for the community college. We bounce across the train tracks, and I shift in my seat until I face forward. In the review mirror, I watch the tracks get smaller, that spot we were parked like a frozen bubble I wish we could stay in forever because for those few minutes, it felt like Christopher and I were the only people in the world. He said words I know he never would have spoken if we were surrounded by the reality of our situation.

When I can no longer see the slushy pavement in the review mirror, I turn my gaze to Christopher, who meets it for a second before he looks back at the road. "Thank you, Christopher," I say, letting every ounce of my appreciation into those words. He has no idea what he's been for me, how he's saved me time and time again.

He glances at me and notices the easy smile that pulls at my lips. His previous words echo through my head at the tug on my face, especially when his hazel eyes drop to my mouth. *I see a smile that makes my breath catch. A silent laugh held behind lips I still think about kissing.*

My entire chest swells, and the uneasy breath I take parts my lips.

"You're going to make me crash this truck," he mumbles, pulling his eyes back to the road.

I know he means it as a joke, trying to play off the heavy truth he spoke, but now that I know what he thinks when I smile, when his eyes drift to my lips, I can't pretend that's not what's happening. He may be the one behind the wheel, but I'm the one who would drive him off the road, and I can't help but think that his truck isn't the only thing we'd wreck.

This time we're spending together is dangerous, sending us down a bumpy road. Our relationship is this truck, his hands guiding what we are, and my restless heart pulling us both off the edge, because if we're not careful, that's exactly what we're going to do. We're going to wreck this fragile friendship and shatter each other in the process.

My boots squeak against the tile floor, ricocheting down the empty hallways of Rayou Community College. Christopher walks beside me, but he no longer needs to lead me to Mr. Riley's classroom. Now the path is mapped in my head, these halls familiar to me.

When we enter, the classmates I've grown to recognize turn and wave to Christopher and me. I find my seat and a grin pulls at my lips when I refer to it as my own. Mr. Riley comes in shortly after, his sandals slapping the floor with each step, and a stack of papers is tucked under his arm. I barely have my coat off before he's already addressing the class, telling everyone to get out a pen or pencil. For the past visits, I've just observed Mr. Riley lecture about using shadows in photography, but it looks like he's going to have the class do an assignment today.

Once he connects his laptop to the projector, Mr. Riley walks through the desks, placing a piece of paper on each of them. He walks down the aisle between mine and Christopher's desk, pausing in front of us.

"Christopher," he says, snapping the paper through the air for Christopher to take. His brown eyes under bushy brows swivel to me and he offers me the final piece of paper. "I printed an extra in case you want to participate, Ms. Wilson."

I instinctively take the page. Seeming satisfied with my decision, Mr. Riley turns around and returns to the front of the classroom. He explains what he'd like us to do for the assignment and my eyes follow along with the instructions on the page. Out of my peripheral, Christopher leans across the aisle, and a black pen clatters on the top of my desk. I look at him, catching the toothy grin that spreads his lips, before he faces the front of the classroom. I pick up the pen Christopher gave me, twirl in between my fingers, and continue to listen to Mr. Riley's final instructions.

My eyes drift across the room—the tiled floors, walls close enough that only a few rows of desks fit, faces of other students who are more familiar to me than anyone from my lectures at Frostard—and a warmth blooms in my chest. It spreads through my whole body, this sense of belonging consuming me. In the six months I spent at Frostard, not once did I ever feel like this. Like I was supposed to be there, like I was surrounded by people who knew me, who would wave when I entered the classroom or want to get lunch afterward. Somehow, I've found all of that after a few days at Rayou Community College.

Chapter 18

The fabrics of the various swimsuits deep in my dresser drawer slip between my fingers. I pull out the red bikini I had since returned to the drawer after our first attempt of the hot springs photo was interrupted, and hold it out in front of me, trying to remember the last time I wore it. Probably last summer when we took a vacation to the beach. A giddy energy follows the idea of wearing a swimsuit in February, but that's the point of the hot springs. After I change into the stretchy material, I instinctively step in front of the mirror on my closet door. My breath catches in my throat when candy-cane wrapping paper looks back at me.

I look down at myself and then back at the covered mirror. A moment like this is precisely why my mom and I covered these mirrors. The anxiety attack over my weight is still so raw, that seeing myself in a swimsuit could have sent me down another spiral, because I probably would have found something in the reflection I didn't like, something that the past me would have cried over, but not today. The swimsuit fits me, and I feel good in it. It's not too tight, I can move comfortably, and I like it. That should be reason enough to wear it. Nothing in that mirror would have told me that. I reach for the door of my closet and slide it out of the way, pulling on a yellow sweatshirt and a dark denim jeans over the swimsuit. I don't want to freeze until I absolutely have to.

My phone buzzes on my nightstand, and the illuminated screen tells me that Christopher is outside. I pull my hair back into a low ponytail and grab my phone, taking the carpeted steps two at a time.

"I'm leaving!" I holler through the house as I pull my brown leather boots on.

"Hold on," my mom calls from the dining room. As I finish buttoning my coat, she appears in the narrow hall along the staircase, money pinched between her fingers. "Lunch is on me. You and Christopher have fun, today."

"Oh, you don't have to do that," I start to say, but she extends her arm to me.

"Take it, Penny. You've been helping out at the library, you earned this." Her small smile meets her blue eyes, shimmering in the sun that seeps through the frosted glass on the front door.

I do as she says and take the money, thanking her before I open the door and brace for the cold. I curse under my breath as I crunch through the ankle deep, freshly fallen snow. A cold front blew in last night, the air so dry and frigid it scratches my throat and tears bloom in my eyes.

"You had to pick the coldest day of the year for the hot springs photo," I complain when I close the door of Christopher's truck behind me, giving him a dramatic sigh that makes him laugh.

"Technically I picked Tuesday," he teases gently, pulling the truck back onto the street.

"Oh, okay, okay," I groan, waving him off and relieved we are keeping the moment from Tuesday light. He is right, though. If it wasn't for my untimely panic attack after cheer practice, we would have already done this photo.

Christopher turns his blinker on and slows at the stop sign at the end of my street. "I actually think the photos will look better in the daytime than they would have that night," Christopher says.

"You don't think it will break up the other night photos?" I shift my weight forward, leaning as close as I can to the vents pumping out warm air.

"Not with this overcast," he comments, drawing both of our eyes up to the thick grey clouds overhead.

The only light getting through is a hazy glow that makes the world look as frozen as the temperature suggests it is. "If it starts snowing," I mumble beneath my breath, afraid to even speak something like that out loud.

"Better hope the water's warm," Christopher says through a laugh he's trying to bite back. His hazel eyes glow with humor when he glances my way and I shake my head, my own loose laugh seeping out.

The snow on the road sprays along the sides of Christopher's truck as he slows and turns into the parking lot of the Snowcapped Diner, our pitstop before the hot springs resort. I try not to lose myself in the skips of my heart as we walk in, side-by-side, and gravitate to our booth, the once foreign waitress becoming more familiar. Christopher's hazel eyes give the only hint that he may be thinking the same things as me. They shift with shadows of our past, trying to keep them separate from the present.

My teeth are clattering so hard I've given myself a headache. "Are we ready yet?" I ask, raising my voice to be heard over the bustling wind that howls across the valley with the hot springs. Christopher leans over the tripod he's setting the camera on top of and says, "Almost," as his fingers continue twisting the lens and adjusting the lighting settings on the camera.

I wiggle my toes in my leather boots, trying to keep the blood flowing in them. I've created a narrow trench in the snow that's drifted on top of the concrete decks around the hot springs. The Rayou resort has a total of five and they spread around the property behind me. I glance over my shoulder and a small whimper escapes my tight throat at the sight of the glowing windows of the resort from the warm fire inside. It's designed to look like a log cabin, but towers nearly five stories tall, making it the most immaculate log cabin I've ever seen.

"Okay, ready," Christopher declares, standing up. "Let's take some out here with the resort behind you first."

I nod sharply and attempt to shake out the cold. I'm still buttoned from my knees to my throat in my mustard coat, but the winter air has found its way to my bones. Christopher begins taking pictures of me walking around the edge of the hot springs and the steam that billows off the crystal blue surface curls around my shoulders. I smile to myself, just imagining how these photos will look in the end. I know the steam was an added challenge, which is why Christopher brought his tripod and adjusted the camera settings before the shoot so that we could keep as many variables constant, but it's going to be worth it in the end. These are probably my favorite pictures we've taken.

As I walk and change my angle, Christopher turns the handle on his tripod to follow me. Sometimes we get the thick, evergreen forest behind me, and others we center in front of the resort. When he decides we have enough around the hot springs, he adjusts the height of the tripod to get a better angle at the same level as the water and I work on wiggling my cold feet from my boots.

With the side of my shoe, I create a little path across the concrete, clearing as much snow as I can so I don't get frostbite on my feet, and then set aside my boots and socks. "You better be ready," I call to Christopher. My steps are uneven and awkward from the cold as I navigate the narrow path in the snow to the edge of the pool. I can't resist the steaming water beneath me, and I dip each of my feet inside, sighing at the instant relief from the cold. But when I place them back on the concrete, a chill latches onto them, inching its way up my legs.

I hop from foot to foot and tug on the buttons of my coat with numb fingers. The heavy wool loosens from my shoulders and slips off with the next burst of frigid wind. I shudder so hard it reaches my bones. I fold my coat and set it on the small patch of concrete I cleared at the edge of the hot spring and my cold fingers find the hem of my sweatshirt, but they freeze, and not from the icy air.

"Are you ready, Penny?" Christopher asks from behind me where the camera is set up.

I lick my lips and urge my fingers to move, but they curl into the fabric, like the knot forming in my throat. The scene from cheerleading practice last week comes back to me, but instead of Lillyanne falling through the air, it's me, and it's Lindsay—not Rachel—who screams at me when the squad can't make the catch. The swimsuit under my shirt becomes too tight, the fabric burning against my skin. I can't... I can't show that much of my body. A nausea rises in my throat, and tears bloom in my eyes. This is all too soon from the anxiety attack on Tuesday. We shouldn't have done this photo today. My breaths shorten, making the rhythm of my heart turn erratic and I hug my arms around my waist, trying to settle myself before I lose control like I did the other night.

"Christopher... I don't think..." I try to speak through my uneven breaths, and when I look over my shoulder at Christopher, I see him watching me, trying to understand what's changed between the teasing moments between us two seconds ago, and the breaking girl in front of him.

I turn back to face the hot spring and try to silence the hateful words in my head. I want to do this. I want to be able to take these photos and feel confident about my body without the memory of the broken girl getting in the way, but when I curl my fingers around the hem of my shirt again, they freeze and twist into the yellow fabric, unable to cross that line.

I take a step back and am about to tell Christopher that I can't do this photo today when he's suddenly behind me. Actually, he's running into me and scooping me up into his arms. I have a second to process the fact that Christopher picks me up, before he jumps over the threshold of the pool and I scream as we launch through the steam-filled air.

I have enough sense to hold my breath as we hit the water and my skin prickles with the heat that replaces the cold. When we hit the water, Christopher's grasp on me loosens, and I kick through water, nearing the surface. When I break through, my lungs ache for air and I release the gasp that consumed me.

"Christopher!" I shriek, turning to find him behind me, brushing back his soaked brown curls. "What the hell?" But no anger is in my voice, instead a cackling laugh bubbles over and every bit of anxiety that had chocked me two seconds ago vanishes.

The hot spring is shallower than I thought, and I'm able to walk across the bottom on the very tips of my toes. I close the distance between Christopher and me until my bare foot finds his tennis shoes attached to his feet. That's when the heavy weight of my now sopping wet sweatshirt registers to me, my jeans weighing me down into the water.

"You looked like you needed a push," Christopher jokes, white teeth grinning wide.

I can't even deny it, because he's right. "What about the photo?" I ask, an apology ready to follow, because it seems like I've completely messed up our plans for this photo shoot. Christopher lifts his wrist from the water, the face of his water-proof watch glowing.

"Smile," he says. Christopher taps the screen of his watch, and there's a soft flash that comes from the camera still balanced on the tripod.

"I thought I ruined the shoot," I say.

Christopher reaches for my hand under the water and his warm fingers tangle with mine. "You didn't ruin anything, Penny. I was jealous you got to warm up in the hot spring, anyway." He shrugs like it isn't that big of a deal and he releases my hand.

I wish he understood just how much he means to me and what he did just now… Jumping into the hot spring and pulling me with him fully clothed was crazy, and somehow incredibly romantic, and very Christopher. He extinguished that anxiety that weighed me down like it was nothing. He saved today and saved me from the haunted memories in my head.

"I don't know anything about being on this side of the camera," Christopher says, drawing my focus back to him and I see a nervous twitch lift the corner of his smile.

"Can you set that camera on a timed loop?" I ask, taking steps away from Christopher and toward the shallower end of the hot spring. I get to where my shoulders are above the water before I stop, the cold air outside trying to latch on.

Christopher faces his watch upward and begins taping through the settings. Another flash erupts from the camera and Christopher nods. "Set to take a photo every fifteen seconds," he says, looking back at me.

I bite the inside of my cheek, my brain already counting the seconds from the last flash, and when I think enough time has passed, I crash my hands through the water, sending an enormous wave across the steaming surface and drenching Christopher who had followed me into the shallow end. The camera erupts with another bright light just as the water hits Christopher in the face. I fall back laughing, letting the warm water lap over my shoulders.

Christopher wipes his eyes, and blinks at me, shock radiating in the ambers swirls. "Oh, is that how you want to do this?" Christopher says, amusement dripping from the words, and I know I started something I'll probably regret later.

Just as the camera is about to take another photo, Christopher uses both of his arms to pull in a wave of water that towers above me and slaps me right in the face. I cough through the fresh water and laugh, declaring a full on splash war to commence. The steam from the hot water seems to thicken, curling around us and putting Christopher in a haze. Waves of water ripple back and forth between us as I catch the dim flash of the camera out of my peripheral.

I'm laughing so hard my lungs ache, the taste of winter strong in my mouth. With every splash, Christopher works his way closer to me, reaching for my wrists to keep me from returning the fire. For a minute, I'm able to slip free of his grasp and continue to back away from him.

Christopher's teeth are spread in a wide grin, his deep laugh warming me almost as much as the water. I gasp when my back hits the edge of the pool and I realize I have no where left to go. I turn around, planting my hands on the snow-covered concrete, fully intending on jumping out of the pool to escape him, but Christopher is on me before I can work up the courage to do it.

"Gotcha!" he exclaims victoriously, encircling his arms around my waist. He pulls my back to his chest and twirls me away from the wall, creating a mini whirlpool around us.

I'm overcome by giddy giggles, and I tilt my head back onto his shoulder. Christopher's lips are by my ear, his laugh crawling across my skin. I can't believe only minutes ago I was in tears and on the verge of a breakdown, and now my cheeks hurt from smiling and I feel like I'm the happiest I've felt in months.

When Christopher releases me, I spin free of his grasp and get sucked under the shallow water. It moves around me as I pop back up, my blonde ponytail pulled almost completely out, weighed down with water and slipping over my shoulder.

"I think that makes me the winner," Christopher says, arms crossed at the crest of the rippling pool that's trying to settle in the wake of our splashing war.

"I don't know, you probably cheated," I joke and shrug.

"Cheated?" he gasps, clearly offended that I would ever imply such a thing, and it causes another laugh to rip from my weak lungs. My heart is beating like wings in my chest, racing from the adrenaline, and the weight of exhaustion is just around the corner, my arms already stiffening.

White light flashes through the steam, reminding me again that the camera is still taking photos. "I think the real winner should be who made the biggest splash," I offer, drawing my focus to the fading flash. "And that would make the camera the judge."

"You won't believe me when I tell you I won because you're not looking at the photos until we finish," Christopher says, sinking down so his shoulders are in the water. He drifts away from me and toward the deeper end where we jumped in.

I follow him across the pool, the water slipping past and I have to kick hard to swim against my soaked clothes. "Then I guess we can't name a winner until the portfolio project is over."

Christopher reaches up and grasps the edge of the pool with his hands, holding on even though I think he can probably touch the bottom. My toes struggle to keep my head above water, so I place both of my arms on the concrete deck. They're so heavy they *splat* with water. I rest my head on my crossed forearms and let my legs float up behind me, anchoring myself to the edge of the pool.

"Winner gets a free meal at Snowcapped Diner next time we go," I offer, looking at Christopher from where I lay my head against my arms.

He moves to do the same, crossing his arms on the concrete edge and laying his head in the twist of them to look at me. "Deal," he says, his smile still true, but clearly tired.

We stay like that for a few seconds, just staring at the other through the steam from the hot spring. Beads of water trail the sides of Christopher's face and I watch them glisten against the flash of the camera that's capturing this moment.

"I'm oddly very glad you threw me in the pool," I say, breaking our silence.

If Christopher wasn't already exhausted, the pull on his lips would widen, but I still see the smile grow in his eyes. "So am I," he says. "I'm also glad I came to the high school that night and found you on that bench," he adds, dropping his voice to a whisper that chills my skin—or maybe that's the melting snow beneath my arms and the frigid air trying to break the barrier of the hot spring.

"Me too," I whisper, hardly any sound coming from my moving lips because I'm too afraid to ruin this moment. A swelling sense of belonging takes root in my chest, and when I look at Christopher, everything else fades away. Frostard, Lindsay, the cheer team, my anxiety, all of it. The camera flashes a few more times as we stare at each other in silence, before my fingers begin to go numb from the cold.

Christopher must feel it too because he lifts his head first and pushes off the wall with his feet, floating back to the shallow end of the pool where the steps we should have used rise out of the water. "You don't think they'll mind us sopping wet in their lobby, do you?" Christopher asks sarcastically, and he glances over his shoulder at the resort behind us.

"I've been dreaming about sitting in front of that fireplace since we got here," I say, and swim toward the steps.

Christopher twists his wrist to look at his watch and turns the camera off. The steady pattern of flashes that had filled my vision makes me feel off balance in their absence. "On three?" he asks, locking his hazel eyes with mine.

I follow the path from the hot springs to the pool room they said we could use and nod. Granted, that was when they thought Christopher was staying out of the pool and I was having my picture taken in a swimsuit. Not two teenagers absolutely drenched in their clothes after taking part in a splashing war.

Christopher counts down, and we trudge up the steps. Our idea to run fails us the moment we have to stand against the weight of our wet clothes. Winter wraps its fingers around every inch of me. The cold air is sharp in my throat when I gasp, and my feet are instantly numb the second they hit the snow-covered concrete.

Christopher's hand finds mine in our movements and we hurry for the warmth of the poolroom, leaving the hot springs behind us. But unlike the other photos we've taken, we bring the moments—the light-hearted banter, the laughter, the smiles, and honesty—with us instead of leaving them frozen in a memory on his camera. It happens because of our changing relationship and it makes Christopher and me that much closer.

Chapter 19

"Hot chocolate?" Christopher stands over me, the porcelain mug in his grasp looking like a million dollars right now.

I reach up with both hands, and the warmth from the delicious sensation tugs on my numb fingers. I know I should sip it slowly, but I burn my entire mouth on my first attempt to drink it. Christopher sits next to me on the stone ledge of the fireplace, a matching mug in his hands.

The fuzzy, white robe the resort staff lent me works hard to thaw my frigid bones, and with the help of the crackling fire at my back, I'm able to stop shivering like a wet dog. I steal a glance at Christopher, who also wears a fluffy robe, and giggle. His hazel eyes catch on me with a playful glare and my laugh only grows.

"You're never going to let me live this down," Christopher says beneath his breath, and he takes a sip from his hot chocolate.

I bite the inside of my cheek through my smile. "I'm tempted to learn how your camera works, just so I can capture the sight of you in that robe forever," I tease and my eyes drift across the pool room to where his camera leans against the corner on its tripod, my coat and boots on the chair next to it.

I was nervous about what the resort staff would say when Christopher and I ran in, sopping wet in our clothes. I struggled to find the right words to explain that mess, but I never had to say anything. Apparently, we had drawn the attention of every staff member in the resort with our splashing war, and they had warmed robes ready for us to change into the second we got in the poolroom. One of the maids even brought in Christopher's camera and my other things. To avoid hypothermia, we changed into the spa's robes while the hotel staff took our clothes to dry them. We're lucky it's not tourist season, and we live in Rayou, Colorado, where the population is only a couple thousand. This is the most exciting thing they've seen in weeks.

"Are you saying I look ridiculous in this robe?" Christopher gawks and my eyes widen, thinking he's being serious with that question.

"Have you seen yourself?" I ask, my own eyes trailing over him, but he owns every inch of the white, fuzzy fabric, even if the sight makes me laugh.

"Actually, I haven't, but I'm afraid if I do, I may lose what little confidence I still have left," Christopher says, and nudges my shoulder.

That temptation to go for his camera rises again, if only so he could see how truly ridiculous he looks in the robe, but the idea of leaving the protection of the fire keeps me from standing. Instead, I lean over and slip Christopher's phone out of his pocket, swiping left to bring up the phone's camera.

"Here, now you can remember this forever," I tease and hold the camera out in front of us, the screen reflecting back our faces. Christopher doesn't shift away from the camera's sight. In fact, he leans closer to me, his damp, brown curls brushing the side of my face, and I tap the screen, capturing the image of us grinning into the camera, hot chocolate in hand. When I bring the phone back down, my heart stutters, beating out of sync when I realize what I just did and what I'm looking at now.

A picture of me and Christopher. Something we haven't done since we broke up in August, and something that happened so naturally, felt so easy, it turns my fluttering heart into a painful clench.

"See, I don't look that bad," Christopher says, slipping the phone from my hand as my fingers loosen around it.

I'm not sure if he just doesn't feel the same sinking feeling that's flooding my chest, or if he's doing a better job at hiding it, but he's able to keep the same, loose conversational tone that we've had all day and it helps me to push the pang of sorrow away. My eyes drift over the screen of his phone, the photo I took still on display, and I realize I can't even argue with him. I mean, the sight of him in that robe is still a shock, but his damp skin is glistening in the firelight behind us, hazel eyes looking alive with caramels swirls, and his smile steals my breath from my already weak lungs.

He's as attractive in that robe as he was in his basketball uniform, and it makes a fire bloom inside of me. I feel Christopher's gaze on the side of my face when I'm quiet for too long and I wonder if he can see the racing beats of my heart. I put a pocket of space between us and lean closer to the fire. "I guess I've seen you in worse," I say, and though I try to pull at that playful banter we always have, the tremble in my voice surely doesn't go unnoticed.

"Well, that's true," Christopher says, turning off his phone and returning it to the pocket of his robe.

I slurp another sip of hot chocolate, careful to blow on it first this time, and feel my body warm as it trails deep into my stomach.

"Like the time I had to wear the mascot uniform," he adds, and I almost spit out my hot chocolate.

"Oh my God!" I say with a laugh so loud it fills the room. "That was hilarious!"

Christopher is shaking his head, but laughing too. He had sprained his finger and couldn't play basketball for two weeks, so his coach made him wear the school's mascot uniform to the games. I went from dating the number one basketball player to *Henry the Hawk*. I still remember the first night he wore the bird uniform, leading the basketball team into the gym at a full sprint, arms extended with brown feathered wings. I didn't even know it was him until he finished his grand entrance, circling the entire gymnasium, and the basketball players branched off to begin their warm-ups.

I was standing in the front row of our cheer formation on the sidelines, and Christopher stopped right in front of me. The girls around me giggled as he mirrored my movements, and just when I was getting weirded out that this giant hawk was in my face, Christopher popped the mask off, revealing his brown curls and hazel eyes, and he kissed me in front of the entire gymnasium full of people.

Our laughs soften, and I wonder if his mind drifted to that same memory. It leaves a warms sensation around my heart that raises bumps down my arms, but as I lift the cup of hot chocolate to take another sip, I try to attest that feeling to the drink.

A few moments later, the resort staff returns with our now dry clothes and Christopher and I change, flooding them with thanks and apologizes, though I really don't think they minded. The sun sinks behind the mountains encircling Rayou as Christopher drives me home. My head rolls against the headrest of the seat as the truck bumps along the street.

Christopher finds one of the few stations on the radio that spits out clear music and hums along, one hand on the wheel, the other balanced on the door.

"How many photos do we have left?" I ask, my voice sharp against his soft humming.

Christopher taps the rhythm from the song into the door. "Two, I think."

I try to ignore the dip in my heart and nod. "What do you want to do next?" My eyes drift to his profile, watching the silver beams of moonlight glow across his face, the still damp brown strands of his hair shimmering. My breath is thin, hardly filling my lungs when I take him in and I curl my fingers into clamped fists to keep from reaching out to him.

Christopher seems to be thinking through his upcoming schedule, and when he feels my stare on the side of his face, he glances my way. I get just a peek at the amber in his hazel eyes under the silver light. "I actually have exams for like, the next three weeks."

Some internal calendar in my head registers his words. "Oh, midterms?"

He nods, shifting his weight in his seat. "Instead of having them all the same week, my professors spread them out over three weeks. So, I'll be pretty tied up for a while. We could pick the photos back up afterward."

My mind stores his words, but my thoughts have drifted now that Christopher has made me think of my own schedule. "The state tournament is in two weeks," I say the words, and have to repeat them again before I register what I'm saying. "The state tournament is in *two* weeks."

"Is the squad ready?" Christopher asks, seeing the anxiety that always comes with competition on my face.

"I don't know," I admit. "I haven't been back to practice since Tuesday." Coach Violet hasn't even texted me after that brief message Wednesday morning. I slip my phone out of my pocket and confirm that I've heard nothing from her.

"Are you going to go back on Monday?" Christopher asks, glancing at me and then pulling his eyes back to the road.

"Coach hasn't texted me," I say my worries aloud.

"She was probably just giving you space, Penny," Christopher offers, his voice softening.

I swallow through the forming knot in my throat. "I guess I'll stop by practice Monday and see if she still wants me to help."

"Do *you* still want to help?"

His question draws my eyes back up to him, his lips pressed into a thin line.

"After what happened on Tuesday, do you really want to go back to that environment?" His eyes meet mine for a moment before he slows the truck at a stoplight.

I hadn't even considered not going back. I know where his concern is coming from, but I still love cheerleading. I'm still committed to the team and I want them to win the state tournament. And for the first time since Rachel's outburst on Tuesday, a thought blooms in my head that I can't silence now.

I want to see things on the Rayou cheer squad *change*. The things that go unnoticed by coach Violet, things that happen behind closed doors—or in bathroom stalls—I want to change that. I can't do that by running away from it and putting it in the past I try to never think about.

"Am I stupid to think that I could change the way the cheer team functions?" I ask, voicing my thoughts. "I want to confront Rachel and tell her what she did was wrong. There should be a consequence to her actions, so things like that stop happening. I want to help the team understand a healthy diet, and exercise that is good for their bodies." I lick my lips and shrug. "Am I stupid for wanting to keep what happened to me from happening to someone like Lillyanne?"

Christopher's warm hand moves to rest on my knee, a soft squeeze accompanying the gesture. My eyes connect with his, the red glow on his face shifting to green with the changing streetlight, but the truck sits idle. His hazel eyes are locked on mine, wide and full of their caramel color. "That isn't stupid, Penny. That's a great idea."

"You think so?"

He nods, swiping his thumb across the fabric of my jeans, leaving a trail of goosebumps beneath the denim. "You should talk to Coach Violet, and you should make that change."

Christopher pulls his hand back, seeming to just now realize the light turned green and thankfully, the streets of Rayou are empty. The truck begins to move again, but the idea of bringing a big change to the Rayou cheer team comes with us, still flexing in my head and giving me no other choice but to seriously consider the idea.

"I think I'll do it," I decide, speaking more to myself than to Christopher, but I catch the pull at the corner of his mouth, a small smile forming there.

In the seconds that follow our conversation, the song on the radio switches and Christopher changes the rhythm he's tapping into the door, his soft humming filling the truck once more.

I don't know if it's from the frigid weather, exhaustion from the entirety of the photo shoot, or the hot chocolate, but my eyes grow heavy as we drive and my lids pull closed. I let my other senses drift through the cabin of Christopher's truck, soaking in the smell of pine and coffee that clings to him, the sound of his humming making my skin vibrate with its beautiful tone, and the feeling of the cloth seat beneath me, my body practically formed to its shape after all the time I've spent in here. And for a moment, Christopher and I aren't doing this portfolio project together, we haven't been reunited after six months of loneliness. It's like that time never passed, like he's driving me home after a basketball game or dinner at the Snowcapped Diner. He's still mine, and I never made the mistake of breaking his heart.

I would give anything to live in this moment for the rest of my life.

Chapter 20

The squeaking of tennis shoes on the polished gymnasium floor reaches me as I enter the foyer of the school. My face flushes with heat against the brisk late-February air, nervous fingers curling into fists inside the pockets of my mustard coat. The school is dim, moonlight casting a beam for me to follow until the overhead lights in the gymnasium take over. I know I'm late to practice. I've missed nearly the entire rehearsal, but it took me longer than I thought it would to get up to courage to come here.

When I step into the gymnasium, I see that the squad is running laps, which can't be a good thing. Immediately, I recognize Rachel's absence, and just when I'm about to assume the worst, she enters from the locker room, dragging a cloth laundry bag behind her. I find Coach Violet sitting on the bottom row of bleachers, her nose nearly grazing the clipboard she's studying. I mean to walk to her quietly and not interrupt practice, but once the squad sees me, their pace slows, stunned feet jolting to a halt. In the absence of the sound of their running, Coach Violet looks up and her green eyes find me. A hesitant smile reaches for the corners of her lips as she stands. She seems to remember the squad stopped running and snaps her attention to them. "Get going. You still have six more laps."

Her voice echoes through the gym and there's a murmured response from the team before they start running again. I can't help but let my gaze linger with Rachel on the sidelines, but when Coach reaches me, her cautious hand guides me out of gym and back into the shadowed hallway.

"I didn't know you'd be coming by today," Coach Violet says. "Are you feeling better?"

I remember my short lie in the voicemail I left her, claiming to have been sick on Tuesday. Still, I nod, and that's not because of the lie. I am feeling better, and a desire to bring a change to the Rayou cheer team fuels life to a fire inside of me. "I wasn't completely honest with you, Coach," I say, studying how her green eyes don't seem all that surprised. I take in a deep breath to steady my racing heart, and finally, I tell Coach the truth about what happens outside of practice on the Rayou cheer squad.

"Why would you use a short shutter speed?" I ask, reading the question from the stack of index cards Christopher gave me. I look up and watch him, waiting for his response.

Christopher hangs upside-down off the side of his bed, his cheeks flushing with all the blood running to his head. A pencil is pinched between his lips while his fingers tap against the navy rug across the floor of his bedroom. He reaches up and removes the pencil, the answer finally reaching him. "To let more light into photos taken at night or in the dark."

Christopher's hazel eyes meet my gaze, waiting for me to confirm if he's correct or not. "Right again," I say, flipping the card to the back of the pile and realizing we're at the front of the stack again. "That's all of them," I say, stretching to place them on the long wooden table that sits in the center of his room. I shift my weight, sinking deeper into the blue beanbag, and turn my eyes up to the ceiling. "You got every single one correct, twice. I think you're ready for the exam."

"Let's go through art history one more time," Christopher says, rolling off the bed and to his feet. He crosses the room to where his black desk sits beneath the window on the second floor, picking up another stack of flash cards.

"I thought you said your art history exam wasn't until next week," I say.

"It isn't, but it's my worst class and I have to get an *A* on the exam to keep my grade up," he explains, handing me the index cards. Christopher sits on the edge of the low table in front of me, legs stretched out to rest next to mine that barely reach the floor from the enormous beanbag.

I shuffle through the flash cards, making sure to mix them up so he's not just memorizing the order of the answers. "I should be charging you by the question," I tease, the snapping of the fifty art history cards only solidifying my point.

His soft laugh makes bumps raise on my arms beneath the thick, grey Frostard crewneck. "You're the one who offered to help me study," Christopher reminds me.

I press my lips together and hope my blush isn't visible in the dim yellow light from his desk lamp. The only alternative was going home after cheer practice for the next three weeks and not seeing Christopher, and the idea of being here with him was much more appealing. Ever since

I started helping him with this portfolio project, I've been trying to spend as much time as I can with him. I want to tell myself it's because he's the only one in Rayou that I used to hang out with, that I don't have any friends in the entire town because they're all on college campuses spread across the country, but I know I'd only be lying to myself. The way my heart beats out of sync when I catch his eyes looking at me through his long, brown lashes, is proof enough that I am still head over heels for Christopher Samson.

"Well, that was before I knew just how many flashcards you planned on having me read," I say through the pull on my lips.

"Door's right there if you've changed your mind," Christopher says, his response quick and only intended to poke fun at me.

I roll my eyes. "And live with the guilt of you getting a *B* on your art history final?" I say sarcastically. "I could *never.*"

His laugh is stronger now, the corners of his eyes creasing. Christopher nudges me with his foot and says, "Then get to it before I forget everything I just forced myself to memorize."

I shake my head playfully, blonde curls tumbling in front of my shoulders and start reading the questions off the cards again.

This is how I spend almost every night after cheer practice for the rest of the week. Of course, Christopher continues to get the majority of the questions right. He aces his first exam that Thursday, and we celebrate with milkshakes from the Snowcapped Diner.

The tension at cheer practice lessens as the days since Rachel's outburst pass. The night I told Coach Violet about what happened to me when I was on the cheer team is still raw, keeping her sensitive to how she acts around me, but I expected that. I couldn't get the story out with dry eyes, tears rushing down my cheeks only seconds into my explanation. It was a long night but I'm glad I told her, and now we are making sure things like that aren't occurring anymore on the cheer team.

Coach Violet approached the entire squad the next day, telling them of the consequences they would face if she found out any of them were pressuring each other and threatening their positions on the team. While she didn't tell the team that *I'm* the one who told her about how these things come out behind closed doors, I could sense the heated glances my way knew well enough where this lecture from Coach was coming from.

It didn't help that before I told Coach anything, she had already removed Rachel from the squad for the rest of the season. I hadn't realized Coach already punished her, but now the sight of her with the laundry bag full of our spare uniforms makes sense. She's been tasked with errands from Coach, and is still expected to attend the state tournament, but she's not allowed to perform. Rachel has to go and watch everyone else perform without her, and the rest of the squad has to learn the changes to the routine.

Coach has even set up monthly meetings with each member individually as a way to check in, to give them a safe place to let her know if there are any concerns on the team. I don't know if this will fix everything, but it's a start. It's more than I had when I was on the cheer team, and I can't help but wonder where I would be if I ever had that opportunity to come clean to Coach Violet all those years ago.

"Are you nervous about the state tournament?" Christopher asks Sunday night when he takes the set of flashcards we just finished from my hands.

I shrug and say, "I'm not the one competing."

Christopher glances at me over his shoulder, eyes narrowing suspiciously. "It doesn't matter if you're the one being thrown in the air or not. I know how you work, Penny." He turns back to his desk and ties a rubber band around the index cards, adding, "You're probably more nervous than all the members on the team combined."

"They're just not ready," I groan, giving in to the nerves Christopher already knows I'm trying to ignore. It's Sunday night, meaning state is less than a week away.

"You still have a few more practices," he says, crossing the room to plop on the beanbag next to me. I rise and fall with the velvety material and settle against his side.

"We need at least another month," I say, and Christopher gives me a breathy laugh.

"Relax, Penny, they'll do fine," he says, drawing his words out in a soothing tone. He reaches for my knee, squeezing it reassuringly, the gesture too easy for him to make and I don't even second guess the warmth that spreads from his touch.

"You're going to be okay without me this week?" I ask, mostly teasing, but there's a pinch of realness in my question.

"I'll manage," he says, a loose, half smile pulling at his lips. "You said you wanted to help the following week, though, right?" His question hangs in the air between us, his breath stilling in his throat, giving me just a glimpse of how much he wants me to be here.

"Of course," I say, resting my head back on the beanbag. It's why I even offered to come over this weekend, because I knew I'd be at cheer every evening this week. We're extending our practices an entire two hours in hopes to polish off the routine before Friday. "What exams do you have the week after?"

"Calculus and Mr. Riley's midterm" he says with as much disgust as his voice can muster aimed toward the first class he mentioned.

"Ohhh," I say, drawing out my word and ending it with a laugh. "That's going to be rough."

Christopher nods and throws his hands in the air, letting them flop back down on the beanbag and bumping my leg. "I don't even need to know Calculus for the field I'm going into."

"I don't know," I tease through my teeth. "You may need to calculate some crazy angle for a photo—"

"Shut up, Penny," Christopher says, elbowing me in the side.

When our laughter quiets, we sit together on the navy beanbag in silence, our gazes on the ceiling. Christopher's hand rests against mine, the backs of our fingers brushing each other. My heart pauses, the idea of moving my hand into his, taking his fingers and intertwining them with my own, flooding through my brain.

I know Christopher and I are over. I know I broke his heart, and he doesn't want to get close to me in that way. That much was clear the night of the Winter Wonderland dance, but I still want him in the ways where he used to be mine. I can't help but want to kiss him when he smiles, run my fingers through his brown waves when the wind blows them across his face.

On their own, my fingers shift, moving against the back of Christopher's soft hand, and I hold my breath, completely unsure of how he will react. He could ignore that I moved at all, pretend my hand isn't waiting for him to hold it. He could even pull away, put more space between us and keep himself on the other side of the wall he built when I broke his heart. I keep my eyes trained on the ceiling, not daring to move an inch. In my peripheral, I see that Christopher hasn't moved either, gaze still staring up. My heart beats so hard the sound of it pounds in my ears as I hold my breath.

After a second, Christopher's hand slips away and drops beneath my own, coming flush with my palm. His long fingers spread mine, weaving our grasp together. I close my hand around his and hold on tight, afraid that if I let go, I'll lose him forever.

The hot air in my throat releases in a steady stream, pulling my heart back to even beats. Again, I keep my eyes trained on the ceiling, because if I move, if I look at Christopher and acknowledge that he's holding my hand, I'm afraid it'll scare him back across the wall he built to protect his heart.

Him holding my hand means nothing. Friends can hold hands. This isn't us getting back together. This isn't him telling me that he still has feelings for me. I'm acting like I'm a naïve teenage girl all over again, getting butterflies in my chest just because he's *holding my hand*. And even though this changes nothing, means absolutely nothing...

In this moment, it means everything.

Chapter 21

T he air is thick with perfume and I nearly choke as I climb the steps of the bus on Friday morning. Giddy chatter filters down the aisle as the girls help each other with their hair and the three boys on the squad bounce between tasks that are thrown out.

"Hand me another bobby pin!"

"I need my cheer bow."

"Have you seen Trinity?"

"I'm right here."

I flop down in one of the front seats, the cracked leather rubbing against the leggings that are trying to keep my legs warm. It's too early to have this kind of energy, but I can't deny that it is a bit infectious, even at five in the morning. Today is the first day of the state tournament, and while we're almost guaranteed to qualify for finals, I know the squad is still nervous to perform in prelims today.

Coach Violet comes onto the bus after me and quiets the squad. "Let's take roll call," she says, not an ounce of exhaustion in her voice.

Coach goes down the list, calling out each name with a cheery *here* following each one. "All right, we're all here." She snaps her binder closed and turns around to say something to the bus driver. I unzip my duffle bag and wiggle out my pink, fuzzy blanket, wrapping it around my shoulders to keep the cold, wet window from reaching me. The bus lurches forward, and Coach sits in the seat across the aisle, going over a stack of papers on her clipboard. They look like registration forms for the tournament.

I settle back into my seat, letting my head bounce against the leather back, and hope the deep sleep my alarm ripped me from can find me once again. The bus weaves through the empty streets of Rayou, but when it turns onto Main Street, I sit straight up and press my face to the window. Outside, two trucks with tall arms used to reach powerlines are stretched around the large evergreen tree that grows in the center of town. Now that it's March, Rayou is finally taking down its Christmas decorations. I only see a second more of the men working early in the morning to unwind the garland and lights from the snow-covered branches before the bus makes another turn and moves toward the north end of town.

If it weren't for the jumble of nerves clouding my mind about the state cheer tournament, I'm sure my heart would sink at the sight of all the Christmas cheer being packed away, though it honestly is about time. I'm glad I got to see it at all, even if it was only for a little over a month. I pull back from the window, and try to settle my anxious thoughts. It's nearly a six hour drive to Denver where the state tournament is being held. That's plenty of time to sleep and help keep my mind from losing itself to the nerves that have already threatened to bloom.

Just when my eyelids grow heavy, my breathing slowing, my phone buzzes against my hand that's stuffed inside my jacket pocket. I slip it out, letting the phone glow to life, bright in the dim bus, and see

Christopher's name flash across the screen.

Christopher: Good luck today at the tournament! I'll be cheering for you all the way from my Art History final.

My smile is easy, forming before I even finish reading the text. I reply and remind him one of the facts he kept missing on his flashcards. The screen clicks off and I slide the phone back into my pocket, letting my eyes close again and this time, give in to sleep.

The sweat on my palms makes my hands slip between each other, and I think I'm going to be sick. How is it that I'm more nervous now than I was when I was on the team?

"Okay, squeeze together!" the photographer hollers, using his hands to visually wave the team together. Rachel—who was awkwardly removed from the team photo—and Coach Violet try to help him arrange all the girls in the frame.

Even from outside the performance space, I can hear the cheering crowd, the distant rumble of the music that accompanies the team currently performing. The Rayou cheer squad chatters amongst themselves, nerves and excitement fueling the air and the photographer has to repeat himself twice before they finally get into a formation that fits in front of the black backdrop. The gold on their uniform shimmers beneath the hall lights, outlined crisply by the black triangular pattern on the skirt. The giant *RH* for Rayou High School is worn proudly on each of their chests.

For a second, when he tells them all to smile and their conversations fall quiet, the racing heart in my chest pauses, admiring the smiling faces staring at the camera and the importance of this moment for the team. I have this same photo from the last four years in my memory box at home. Eyes glistening with hope, smiles so large they dimple their cheeks. It's no wonder they make every squad get their state competition picture taken before they perform. That way, everyone is still happy. Who'd want to buy a photo where everyone is crying because they didn't hit their marks or got disqualified?

The shutter erupts on the camera, capturing the kids in their pose. The photographer straightens, quickly glancing at the screen to make sure he has one where everyone's eyes are open. Simply seeing the camera has my mind drifting to Christopher. To the sweet text message he sent this morning and the moment from the other night when he held my hand. My heart starts racing for an entirely different reason now, but it's short lived as the sounds of the cheer competition filter back to me.

Once we get the thumbs up from the photographer, we're dismissed and told to enter the performance waiting area. A state official is at the door guiding the team inside, and Coach Violet and I branch off to the coaches section, giving our last minute encouraging words and hugs. Rachel finds her seat among the other spectators in front of us.

"Penny, you look like you're about to pass out," Coach Violet says, her voice low as we find our seats.

The school performing before us is just wrapping up, waving and smiling in their final formation while the audience goes crazy. I can't decide if I'm glad I wasn't able to watch their performance or if I want to know exactly what we're up against. For prelims, we're only the second school to perform, a complete nightmare after driving six hours. Whoever organized this schedule clearly didn't take travel time into account, but the team got ready on the bus and we basically walked right into our warm-ups, leaving very little free time to let our minds wander.

"Thank you, Corinsville Cheer," a booming voice crackles through the speakers overhead and the team on the floor dismounts, waving and throwing their fists in the air as they exit the performance space. "Next, we welcome Rayou Cheer to the floor."

Coach and I are on our feet in seconds, clapping and cheering as the squad skips out of the entryway and onto the mats. The other coaches around us give encouraging applause, and our excitement filters into the surrounding audience. Rayou is too small of a school to bring together a student section at the state cheer tournament, but we've started to make our name known here with an impressive third place finish last year. The other teams recognize us, and I know we're one of the favorites to dethrone the two teams who always take first or second every year.

The applause die down and Coach Violet and I sit, balancing on the edge of our seats, eyes trained on the floor, on the black and gold uniforms, and I don't even blink as the performance begins. Not when Trinity counts them in, or when they explode into our school chant, each word crisp and clear through the performance space. The music comes in next, signaling the tumbling sequences and jumps. I try to catch every detail, focusing on Vicky's toe touch and Sammy's back walkover. The impressive series of backhand springs leading into a back tuck from Gale, Mark, and Bryan go over well, like we knew they would. The other girls in the crowd scream when the three boys stick their landing, lining up perfectly for our first pyramid. Here the music cuts for another chant, pom-poms being picked up as the formation takes shape and I catch myself mouthing the words with them. Our final set of counts begins when the music fades back in and the pom-poms are left littered at the front of the mat.

The lifts.

I hold my breath as Vicky and Hanna cartwheel into place. Courtney and Bailey perform a series of jumps to draw the crowds eye away from our flyers as they get into place. As soon as they land their pike, the boys throw the flyers up, a perfect switch over, and catch each of their feet in the palms of their hands. Screams and gasps filter through my focus, and I only let myself have a second to breathe, to enjoy the small success of them doing the lift, because I know the hardest part is still ahead.

The three flyers land the first flip perfectly, jumping from one set of hands to another, their knees tucked to their chests and then coming out of the tight ball to hit their pose. The last eight counts pound in my head, and my eyes focus in on Lillyanne. On the swing of her arms, the bend in her knees, and then the throw. There's series of impressive twists into the catch, a perfect basket built by the foundation. I can't help the scream that passes my lips, arms flying in the air with obnoxious claps as the team hits their final pose, one flyer left at the top of the hold with the rest of the squad standing or kneeling around her foundation.

Perfect.

They were *perfect*.

Everyone in the room is on their feet, and for a moment, I forget that this was only the qualifiers for finals. The relief in my chest is short lived when I remember they have to do it all again tomorrow, but I relish in the brief moment of success, of cheering for the team I know has put hours into getting to this very moment.

The next day, I'm standing shoulder to shoulder in the foyer of the Denver Civic Center, the Rayou cheer team surrounding me and Coach Violet, as the other hopeful cheer squads cram in around us, waiting for the tournament officials to post the list of teams that have qualified for finals.

I know we'll get through. The team was perfect yesterday, but I still clasp my hands and hold them to my chest, my breaths thin with anticipation. Dressed in their yellow and black training suits, the team links hands as two state tournament workers enter the foyer, posters in hand. There's a total of five, one for each division. We're already stationed the furthest to the left so we'll be right in front of the 2A posting, and as the list nears, time slows, making the moments in my past where I stood right here mold with the present.

They pin the corners of the rolled poster up first and, at the same time, unclip the document, letting it unroll to reveal the list of qualifying names. My eyes fly down the poster, reading the seven teams who qualified in the 2A division, and I exhale when I see a large *R* printed at the bottom.

Rayou High School is written in thick, black sharpie ink, not only saying we qualified for finals, but we're also performing last. In my opinion, that's the best time to perform. No matter what, the team will finish in the top seven!

I flinch at the explosion of screams around me; the team noticing what I just understood. I'm sure they felt as confident as I did with their performance yesterday, but it's still incredible to see your school's name on that poster.

As the foyer clears out—teams either going to get into uniform or pack up their hotel rooms—I pull out my phone, the text messages between Christopher and me from last night coming right up.

Penelope: WE QUALIFIED FOR FINALS!!!

I send the text without any hesitation, knowing he asked me to let him know the night before. He also told me that he felt really good about his Art History exam, giving complete credit for his success to me.

Christopher: I knew you would! Congratulations!

Penelope: But now we have to perform again

Christopher: They're going to do amazing, Penny.

"You coming, Penelope?"

I look up from my phone and see that Coach Violet is watching me, slipping her own phone back into her pocket.

I nod, tucking mine away, and we trail behind our skipping team toward the hotel that's connected to the Civic Center to get ready for finals. We'll have about two hours until our warm-up slot, and then another thirty minutes until performance time, and each second is going to be agonizing.

Chapter 22

While performing last means we will be the final team the judges see before they decide rankings, it also means I'm not able to watch any of the other teams we're competing against. I still can't decide if that's a good thing. I did see every team except for Corinsville yesterday. Some squads do two routines, though. One for qualifiers and one for finals. Coach and I didn't see the point of doing that since the judges change and it took us every second leading up to the state tournament to perfect this routine. I couldn't imagine teaching them a second, but there's a sense of strategy there and I've seen it work well in the past.

"*MARK!*" Rachel screams, snapping my focus back to the team. "You can't forget to be here for the jump!"

"I'm sorry. Yes, I know. I'll get it right," Mark rambles, his voice quivering with nerves. This is his second year on the squad, and as a sophomore he still has a lot to learn about cheer.

"Let's go back eight counts," Coach Violet says, keeping her tone calm. "Rachel, you need to rein it in," Coach adds as a warning.

The squad huffs out nervous breaths and resets. When they go through that section again, Mark hits his spot and the jump is perfect. Yet no relief follows, because I know how many things can go wrong in a final performance. It doesn't matter if you do it right a hundred times before, anything could change in that last performance.

"And lastly, let's welcome Rayou Cheer back to the floor!" The announcer's voice booms overhead, and the stands go wild.

Coach Violet and I stand in the coach's section, but today, our cheers are mute, soft claps in comparison to the enthusiasm we had yesterday. Now I'm too nervous to scream, knowing I might throw up if I do.

The gold and black uniforms of our squad glitter as they run onto the dark mats, waving and beaming wide smiles toward the audience. I don't know how they do it—how I did it for so many years—but they look *fearless*, and confident, as if they've already won.

I want to focus on the performance, count each step, make sure each arm is straight, each jump is crisp, the tumbling tight, and the toss elegant, but my mind is on overload. Their cheer is muffled against my racing heart, the moments fly by and blur in my frantic eyes, and for the first half of their performance I forget to breathe.

It goes by so fast, over before I even have a chance to slow my nervous heart, but they hit every mark as far as I can tell. For a minute, it was nice to just watch them, to enjoy the performance and not look at the technical analysis of every step they took. The season ends today, whether we win or lose. This is the last time they perform this year. For Trinity, it'll be the last time she ever performs. It doesn't matter if I catch every little detail and critique the performance, because the season's ending.

When Bryan hits the final lift, bringing Kelly up into the landing position above his head, the rest of the team hits either their standing or kneeling positions. The cheers from the audience make the stands rumble beneath my feet. I knew we were the crowd's favorite, everyone wanting to root for a team to come in and dethrone last year's champion and runner-up, but even this surprises me.

When the squad hits their final pose, freezing for the applause, it finally feels like fresh air floods my lungs, and I join in, screaming and clapping like a fool. Coach Violet throws her arm around my shoulders, squeezing me into a hug.

I catch the spotlights glisten against tears that streak Trinity's face, her final performance now over, and I know exactly how she feels right now.

The moments that pass after that are a blur. All of the coaches are ushered down to the floor to be with their teams. The squads sit in clumps around the performance mats to await the awards ceremony. The judges deliberate for nearly an hour, and in that time we take pictures, some with tear-streaked cheeks and others with open mouthed laughs. The overhead speakers blast the latest pop music and everyone is singing and dancing, mingling with the other competitors. The audience filters in and out of the stands. Some of them heading for the bathroom before the winners are announced, and others stopping by the concession stands. I thought the nerves might resurface while we wait, but I know there's nothing more we can do. There's simply no point in worrying, so I enjoy every second, grateful that I'm even here at all. Last year was supposed to be the last time I experienced the state cheer tournament. I never thought I'd stand on these mats again, look up into the stadium seating against the spotlights. I can't thank Coach Violet enough for letting me be a part of this.

A hush falls over the performance room when three state officials walk across the mats, standing behind the table that is piled high with medals, plaques, and trophies.

"That never fails to silence a room," one of the officials says, stepping behind the clear podium with a black microphone in his hand. His soft laugh helps to keep the air from becoming overly thick with tension, but I can still feel it bubbling in the people around me as teammates reach for each other's hands and hopeful eyes focus on the glimmering awards.

They start by naming the winners in the individual categories. We're too small of a school to enter in most of them since the competitors aren't divided by program size like in the group division. As the surface of the table becomes more visible, the medals and plaques beginning to dwindle, I know we're coming down to the final awards for the night.

Next, the man moves into the awards for the group performance. While these categories don't receive any kind of physical award, he still names the top performing school in most of the criteria sections. Rayou takes best tumbling, best audience engagement, and best synchronization. It's good, better than last year when we only took first in two categories. I try to determine scores in my head based on who wins the other categories, but I know it isn't possible. I have no idea by how many points we were ahead, or how we ranked in the categories that are left unannounced.

"Now, for the overall group performance," he says, clearing his throat and making the speakers overhead crackle. "Out of a perfect score of 100, in fifth place, with a score of 70, the team from Kaleburg High School."

Applause chorus together as the team dressed in blue and green uniforms stands, coming down to receive their small plaque, and then taking their spot at the edge of the mat once more.

"In fourth place, with 77 points, the team from Parevalley High School."

I swallow against the tightening knot in my throat, wrapping my arms around my waist. This is it. Top three. No matter what, we'll at least do as good as last year, but the fire heating my cheeks, making a sweat break on my forehead, wants to win. It's us, Corinsville, and Silverton, the same top three teams from the previous year. I bite the inside of my cheek, trying to ignore the voice inside my head saying that Corinsville and Silverton have been the top two teams for going on seven years, that we'll never break through their streak.

"In third place, with 81 points…" the announcer pauses, bringing the paper he's been reading off of closer to his face. He lowers it, black eyes raising to meet the bright spotlights. "The team from Silverton."

My jaw comes unhinged, air tumbling from my lungs. *We placed in the top two…*

Or we didn't place at all.

That thought has me snapping my mouth closed and squeezing my arms even tighter around my waist. *Please, call Rayou. Please, call Rayou.*

"In second place," the announcer continues once the Silverton cheer squad has moved back off the mats. "With a score of 91…"

91. My eyes widen at the thought. Last year's champion only scored an 89. We only scored a 72 as the third place finisher.

"The team from…" the announcers draws out the silence until my aching lungs can hardly take the strain. "Rayou High School."

My tight lungs deflate, but a smile spreads across my face, tears rushing to my eyes. Tears of joy and celebration. *Second!* This is the best the school has *ever* scored. Coach Violet and I are clapping so loud our hands turn bright red, and the members of the squad run and skip toward the awards table. Silver medals are draped around each of their necks and Trinity takes the large, second place plaque, nearly double the size of the third place one we received last year.

I know the team wanted to win. I did too, but second place is no small achievement. It's school history, and I am so proud of them.

The squad comes back to our spot on the mat, tears streaking their faces, but accompanied by big smiles.

"And your cheer state champion," the male announcer continues when a hush falls across the stadium, "taking first place by one point..."

One point?

A gasp goes through the air in unison from every single person in the arena.

"Corinsville Cheer!"

I nod, completely expecting them to take first, as they always do. Coach nudges my shoulder and I turn my gaze to her, letting the sight of the other team's swaying uniforms and screams fade.

"One point," she says, though I read her lips more than I hear her over the cheers.

A smile pulls at my own mouth, knowing exactly what she means. We were that close to winning. That isn't a technical problem, nothing that we could have done better. One point is judge's preference. "That's going to be us, next year," I say through my grin, a matching one appearing on her face.

Coach Violet throws an arm around my shoulder, pulling me into her side. "You bet it is."

In this moment, I take in every ounce of happiness radiating around me. I don't think about the fact that this time next year I'll be in my third semester at Frostard. I won't be here to see the team take first, and even though Coach and I are talking like I will be, I know I won't be.

The award ceremony closes soon after that, and all the members of the team move in small clumps, taking pictures with the plaque and their medals. I watch it all from the sidelines, still smiling so big my cheeks hurt. It's like watching a movie, and I force every second of it to memory.

"Can you believe Corinsville only won by one point?" A deep voice filters through the chatter as someone steps up beside me.

My breath stills in my throat when I snap my head to the left, locking my gaze on his hazel eyes. "Christopher?" I gasp and my heart explodes at his sudden appearance.

"Surprise!" he says, throwing his arms wide and I wrap mine around his neck without a second thought. He closes the hug, squeezing me so tight against his chest I mold to his shape. "They did so well, Penny," he says into my hair.

Tears of shock and pure happiness bloom in my eyes. I squeeze the hug a second more before stepping back from him. "You saw them perform?" I ask, trying to process his words. "What are you doing here?"

"I drove up this morning. You think I'd miss this?" he says through his grin, stuffing his hands into the pockets of his worn jeans.

There's a hint of regret that makes the end of his words dip. I remember during my senior year he couldn't come to watch the state tournament because the basketball team had sectionals. I vaguely think about the fact that they probably do again this year, and even though Christopher has no ties to the team anymore, it means something to me that he had today free and chose to come here.

"Christopher Samson," Coach Violet says, walking up behind me. "Didn't expect to see you here, today."

His easy smile only grows, reaching his eyes. "You know I'm still the team's biggest fan," he says, though his hazel gaze never leaves mine.

She huffs a soft laugh, and my stomach twists at the meaning in those words.

Me. He means he's still *my* biggest fan. It's something he always used to say.

"I'm taking the team out for dinner," Coach says. "You can join us if you want."

Christopher accepts the invitation, and Coach tells me I can ride back with Christopher if I want, probably knowing I'd prefer that to the bus, anyway. The crowd in the performance space begins to thin as the spectators leave and the other teams filter out. Coach Violet steps away to wrap up the photo taking and get the team to head toward the bus.

"I can't believe you came all this way," I say, my voice soft.

"It isn't that far," he says with a shrug.

"Yes it is. It's a six hour drive for a couple hours at a cheer tournament."

Christopher's wide grin sinks into a small smile through his pressed lips. He sucks in a deep breath through his nose and takes a step forward, closing the space between us until I'm surrounded by the warmth radiating from him. "It was a six hour drive to watch you make school history. To be able to be a part of this moment with you. I wouldn't have missed this, Penny."

The swelling in my chest is nearly overwhelming, making it hard for me to breathe or form words. When he does things like this… When he makes me feel like I am the only person in the entire world, that he would do anything for me… It makes me want to kick myself for ever breaking up with him. There's no denying it. I still have feelings for Christopher. Part of me thinks that him being here is just him being a good friend. We have built a sort of friendship around his portfolio project and me attending his classes with him. But I can't help but think he may also be here because he still likes me. *Could he?* After all the pain I brought him last year, could Christopher still want to be with me in that way?

The spotlights that ignite the stadium in a florescent glow make the caramel swirls in his eyes shimmer, and I think I see it. For a second, he looks at me the way he did the night of the Winter Wonderland dance, the way he did when we were dating, when he would kiss me or tell me he loved me. But when he blinks, the glimmer fades and he fills the pause in our conversation. "Plus, after all the finals you helped me study for and the portfolio, this seems like the least I could do."

I latch on to the light excuse and try to compose my racing heart. "I suppose so," I say playfully and let the moment lift, the air becoming breathable again.

What Christopher is saying could be true. He could have felt obligated to do this for me after everything I've done for him. But I can't shake the sight of that shimmer in his eyes, the way his voice curled around his words tenderly. Christopher can claim he's here because he's a good friend, but I'm starting to wonder if there's something more going on here.

The question is, will Christopher want to risk everything to take that chance with me again?

Chapter 23

The crisp smell of coffee fills the air, tickling my nose as Willie places a second cup of coffee on the table. Dark roast with creamer and honey, just how I like it. Christopher scrapes the last bit of his eggs from his plate, and the sound makes me cringe, bumps trailing up my arms.

It's the Monday following the big, cheer weekend, and honestly, I'm still buzzing from the tournament. I haven't processed that I no longer get to spend my afternoons in the school gymnasium quite yet. I bet my mom will want to fill that time with shelving books at the library. Or maybe Christopher and I can wrap up this portfolio project soon, not that I want it to end, but I don't think I have to worry about us drifting apart again once it's finished. I have a feeling we'll find another reason to hang out, or at least, I hope we do.

"So, just Calculus and Mr. Riley's midterms left?" I ask while I blow across the top of my piping hot cup of coffee.

Christopher nods, wiping his mouth and settling back in the cherry red booth. "Calculus is Thursday night and Mr. Riley's is bright and early on Friday morning."

"So, do you want to postpone portfolio photos until next week?" I ask, sipping carefully on the coffee that makes my bones tingle all the way to my toes.

Christopher clears his throat and leans forward, driving both elbows onto the table. "Actually, that's what I wanted to talk about this morning."

I freeze with the scorching cup pressed against my lips, and only when it starts to burn do I move to place it back on the table. Something in Christopher has shifted, making the air heavy with a serious weight.

His mouth opens, words hanging there in silence, and his eyes flip across my face. Finally, after blinking a few times and closing and reopening his mouth, Christopher speaks.

"What are your plans for next week?"

My eyes narrow instantly. "Plans?" I ask cautiously, still feeling like a glass doll he's about to drop.

He licks his lips, hazel eyes looking out the window at the snow-covered street, before drifting back to me. "Would you want to go on a spring break trip with me?"

Now I'm the one whose mouth falls open, blinking while I process his words. He wasn't preparing himself to deliver bad news, he was nervous to ask me to go on a trip with him. Like a teenage boy asking a girl on a date for the first time.

"Should I not have asked?" Christopher says, misinterpreting my shocked face.

"I'd love to come!" I say, blowing out the stiff air that makes my lungs ache. "I just wasn't prepared for that," I clarify.

Christopher gives me a weak smile that says he's not too sure my excitement is genuine. "Seriously, if you don't want to come, you don't have to. Just, everyone else is bringing someone…" He trails off and runs his hand through his brown waves, the long sleeve of his black hoodie pulling up his forearm.

"Where are we going?" I inquire.

"One of my classmates has a cabin near Denver," he says with a shrug. "It's really low-key, just going to stay there for a week. Really, if you don't want to come—"

"Who's going?" I ask, interrupting him so he doesn't uninvite me once again.

Christopher's hazel eyes drift back to the window, making the hairs on my arms stand beneath my white sweater. "Billy and Paul," he says, keeping his voice short and bringing his gaze back to mine. His cheeks have a pink blush slowly warming beneath the surface.

"And they are?"

"Classmates," he says. "You've seen them in Mr. Riley's room. They usually sit in the front."

It only takes me a second to remember the lanky boy that spoke the first day I sat in Mr. Riley's classroom. He was always trying to pair with the shorter student that sits next to him for the in class work. I assume that must be Paul.

I remember Christopher saying that everyone going on the trip is bringing someone. Which explains why he's asking me to go, but now I'm curious why he's suddenly being so short with me. Almost like he's embarrassed about something that's being left unsaid.

"Who are they bringing?" I ask, and his hazel eyes lock on mine. "You said everyone was bringing someone."

His lips part as he takes in a thin breath and he says, "Their girlfriends."

My stomach hits the floor as the blush on Christopher's cheeks deepens. "Oh," I say without thinking.

"But obviously we'd go as just friends," Christopher fumbles, shifting his weight in the booth.

Just friends.

The words leaving his mouth make my heart crack, that ache now filling my entire body. I know Christopher and I aren't dating, but to hear him say those words... It's like he's shattered my blind heart that has clearly been ignoring the fact that our relationship isn't what it used to be. That part of me has been happy just relishing in our moments together, the times he makes me laugh and sends butterflies exploding in my chest. Now his nervous mannerisms make sense. He knows what I would think when I found out everyone else is bringing the person they are dating.

"Yeah, of course," I rush the words out, feeling my own cheeks begin to heat. My eyes had drifted down to the empty plates on the table, but after I take a steadying breath, I bring them up to meet his hazel orbs. "I still want to come," I say softly.

"I don't want this to make things weird," Christopher says, his own voice softening, the tense nerves loosening. "You were just the first person I thought of when they asked me to bring someone, and I thought it'd be fun." He's looking at me through his lashes, head dipped forward so his brown waves frame his face, brushing across the edges of his cheeks.

The corner of my mouth pulls up, offering him a small smile. "When do we leave?"

"Well, that depends," Christopher says, shifting his weight and making the leather booth squeak. "Billy got permission to take his mom's van so we could all ride together." He pauses, licking his lips before adding with the tilt of his head, "Or you and I can take my truck and drive separate."

I scan his face, trying to read what his expression means, what the tilt of his head signifies, why he'd even offer to take his truck if there was room in the van. Maybe he wants to spend more time alone with me?

"I think my mom will be more likely to approve if you're driving," I say as a safe medium. While that's true, I also don't want Christopher to think that I don't want to ride with his friends.

Christopher nods, latching on to my excuse. "I thought so," he says, and his easy smile returns, settling our conversation. "I'll pick you up after my exam?"

The words to accept his offer rush to the tip of my tongue, but I make myself wait a second longer to really analyze this. I'll be gone for a week, stuck in a cabin tucked away in the mountains. I can't change my mind once I go, and Christopher will now be my only way home. I left Frostard to come to Rayou and spend some time with my mom, to figure out how I'm going to get in control of my life. Instead, all I've done is sign on as an assistant cheer coach and help my ex-boyfriend with his portfolio project.

And now I'm about to run away for a week-long trip with Christopher and a bunch of his friends.

This isn't what I came back to Rayou to do… *Or is it?* Is this new life… This new freedom I've found myself in exactly what I came home to find?

Christopher's hazel eyes watch me, the caramel swirls seeing each passing second I spend reevaluating the offer. I think he's holding his breath, and when I speak, his shoulders drop with relief.

"I'll bring the snacks."

"Mom, have you seen my beanie?" I yell from my room, hoping my voice reaches her in the kitchen.

"In the mudroom!" she hollers back.

I'm running behind schedule. Christopher is going to be here any second and I'm not even packed yet. I spin around to race out of my bedroom and flinch at the sight of my reflection in the mirror on my closet door. I'm still getting used the paper being gone. After the state cheer tournament ended and I returned to Rayou to see all of the Christmas decorations were gone in town, the colorful paper started to feel a bit out of place. Now the only remanence of Christmas are the lights still strung on the house. Those will remain up until warmer days come and my dad returns from London.

Since cheer is over and I bounced back from that awful night in February, I'm ready to test the waters and uncover the mirrors. Mom and I spent the week taking off the wrapping paper one mirror at a time, only doing the one in my room last night.

Still frozen in my room with my eyes locked on the mirror, I take in my long, blonde ponytail. The fuzzy maroon sweater making it glow in the early morning sun that streams in the window behind me. I take a steadying breath, and then I'm able to move again, remembering the tight timeline I'm on. I hurry out of my room, down the stairs, and through the narrow hall by the kitchen.

"I don't know why you waited until now to pack," my mom scolds me as I slip by and disappear into the mudroom.

It's not that I waited until now to pack. I just didn't know *what* to pack. I've had everything I own in that duffle bag and then back in my closet so many times I hardly know what actually ended up in there this morning. I snatch the black beanie off the third hook and jog back up to my room, breathing hard when I make it to the top of the stairs. The duffle sits open on my bed, a mound of clothes rising above the edges. I toss the beanie inside and tug the bag closed, having to lean all my weight against it to get the zipper to start moving. After wrestling with it for a moment, the duffle bag closes, and I toss it on the floor, collapsing in its place on the bed, just to have my watch vibrate with a message from Christopher saying he's here.

I let out an exhausted sigh, but excitement and adrenaline flood my veins, and I'm back on my feet in a second, slinging the bag over my shoulder. I tuck my coat under my arm, safely securing my phone in the band of my leggings before stomping down the stairs.

"He's here!" I call out behind me and my mom rounds the bar in the kitchen, coming to say goodbye.

"You packed your toothbrush?" she inquires, and I let out a breathy laugh.

"Yes, mom, I packed my toothbrush."

"And deodorant?"

"Yes, I got everything I need," I say as I finish shoving my feet into my ankle high leather boots and I turn to look at her.

"What about the cookies we made for the drive?"

My pulse pauses, remembering that I did tell Christopher I'd bring snacks for the trip. Mom and I stayed up last night to finish them. "No, I forgot—"

Mom brings the hand that had been tucked behind her back into view, the bag of cookies in her grasp. "Here you go."

I take them and sigh, feeling like I've finally checked everything off my packing list. "Mom, I'm going to be fine," I say when I see her face has paled, blue eyes wide. I didn't realize she was nervous about me going. She seemed fine with it all week.

"I know, I know," she says, and pulls me into her chest, squeezing a quick hug around me. "Just be careful and send me lots of updates."

I squeeze her back and when she releases me, I tell her that I will. Mom reaches for the door handle, opening it for me. The frigid winter air bites my arms, cutting straight through my maroon sweater. I'm about to make a run for Christopher's truck, trying to get out of the cold as fast as possible, when my mom says, "And Penny…"

I pause on the edge of the porch, glancing back over my shoulder to see my mom in the doorway, her thin blonde hair blowing back around her face, "Yeah, mom?"

Her smile is tight, thin lips spreading on her face, and I watch her crystal eyes drift over my shoulder to the red beacon of warmth behind me. She pulls her focus back to me and says, "Don't forget to take some pictures and have fun."

My teeth clatter through my wide smile. "I will," I say, my feet moving again. "I'll see you in a week, Mom!"

"I love you!" she yells out after me.

"Love you, too!" I say over my shoulder, letting my words travel back to her on the gust of a winter breeze that robs my lungs of air.

When I reach Christopher's truck, I have to stomp off the excess snow from my boots and I throw my coat and duffle bag in the back seat before pulling myself up into the front. The warmth is short-lived when I realize Christopher is rolling down the passenger side window.

"Bye, Mrs. Wilson!" he calls up to my mom, and I look back at my house, the ghost of Christmas lights peaking beneath the slushy snow on the roof, and see my mom is watching us from the porch, arms crossed as she leans against the banister.

"Drive safe, Christopher," she says, waving at us while Christopher rolls the window back up and puts the truck into drive.

"Ready?" he asks and his wheels spit up slushy snow as he pulls onto the road.

I sigh back into my seat, the nerves and excitement at going on this trip finally settling down. "Ready." I rest my head on its side, studying the profile of his face with the golden morning rays of sun lighting up his features. "How'd your last exam go?"

His lips spread in an easy grin. "Aced it," he says with a shrug. "Mr. Riley's class is my favorite, so I'm not surprised."

"Me either," I tell him and turn to face the windshield. "Want to pick up food for the road to celebrate?"

Just as I finish asking the question, Christopher turns on his blinker, slowing down to turn into the drive through of one of the few fast-food restaurants in Rayou. "Already ahead of you," he says.

The conversation bounces naturally between us, the thrill of a trip and the easiness of being with him making the cabin of the truck my favorite place right now. Rayou falls behind us as thick pine forests close in on either side of the road, masking us in a tunnel of green. We both just made part of this drive last weekend to get to Denver for the state tournament, so the scenery is uneventful for the first six hours. Traffic picks up around the city and we play an alphabet game to fill the time stuck in the lines of cars, calling out different signs that start with whatever letter in the game we're on.

"Olive Garden!" Christopher snaps, pointing across the dash to the restaurant sign to my right. "Okay, you're P."

I scan the upcoming signs, looking for something that starts with the letter P. While I'm looking, I ask, "How's the portfolio coming together?"

Christopher shifts his weight, taking the wheel with his left hand so he can reach for his soda in the center cupholder. "Good," he says before slurping out the last drops. "You're going to really like it when it's finished."

"Do you have a favorite photo yet?" I ask, shaking the ice around in my cup.

Christopher's hazel eyes darken while he thinks about it. After a minute, he looks at me and says, "Can they all be my favorite?"

"No!" I quickly groan with a soft laugh. "Have you decided what story you're telling yet?"

The cars in front of us begin to move again, so Christopher lifts up on the brake, easing the truck forward before we all stop once more. "I don't know, maybe? I guess I do have a favorite photo, but I don't want to tell you it until you've seen the whole project first."

I nod and say, "I can understand that." The truck falls quiet with the exception of the soft music that spits out of the dash, and I go back to reading the signs in the distance.

"Have you registered for your fall classes yet?" Christopher asks, surprising me a bit with his question.

I haven't thought much about my return to Frostard. "I know what I need to take," I say, and I know my voice dips, giving away how unenthusiastic I am about college. "I still have to register, though."

Christopher hums softly, saying, "You'll probably need to do that soon."

"April, I think," I say, and can't ignore the heavy rock that's landed in my stomach. That's only two weeks away. I take in a deep breath and try to ease my tightening lungs. But I don't go back for over three months. I need to remind myself of that, because that is much more manageable. I'll be ready then.

"What about you? Have you registered for your classes?" I ask, pulling my gaze away from the busy streets running beneath the interstate and look at Christopher who's still studying me.

"I met with an advisor this week to lay them out," he says. "I'll still be at Rayou Community College. At least one more year, anyway."

I bite my lip to keep from asking what he'll do after that, because I know he probably doesn't want to talk about Rhode Island School of Design and how he'd never be able to afford his dream school. I'm sure he has some other plan in place, but it's not his first choice, and that's what will upset him.

Instead of letting our conversation darken with that topic, I say, "Will you have another class with Mr. Riley?" Christopher nods and without thinking, I add, "Well, maybe I can come to a few lectures."

Christopher snaps his head toward me, wide eyes leaving the idle lane of traffic for a moment, and I realize the mistake I've made. The stiff air I was trying to avoid settles heavy in my chest.

"You know, when I'm home from Frostard on breaks," I stumble to add, but I think I just make things worse. I shouldn't have said anything at all and I bite my tongue so hard a metallic taste fills my mouth. I not only mentioned that I'd be back at Frostard in the fall, but that, somehow, Christopher and I are still going to be friends, still going to be this close even though I'm going to leave again.

I turn my face toward the side window so Christopher can't see the heat that streaks my cheeks because, when I mentioned visiting his lectures with Mr. Riley, I wasn't picturing a few days with Christopher when I'm home from breaks. I pictured me with him *every* day like we are now, with myself in Rayou, working at the library with my mom on the weekends, and helping coach the cheer team in the afternoons.

"You could if you wanted," Christopher says, trying to save the conversation I just blew up.

I nod, still biting my tongue to keep from saying anything else that will make this whole conversation worse. That rock in my stomach has dissolved into a nauseous wave because the truth of what I'm doing, talking about going back to Frostard, is me paving a path toward a future I don't want.

This entire time I told myself I was just taking a break, that I'd go back to Frostard in the fall.

But for the first time, I think I've realized that maybe Frostard isn't where I want to be.

I flip my blonde curls over my shoulder, turning my gaze back to the boy behind the wheel, slurping his soda for every last drop.

Christopher is what I want.

Daydreams of what my life could be like if I made this move permanent flood my head and warm the ache in my chest. It's a crazy thought, one that will probably fade when I'm out of this truck and we put some distance between us, but I let myself entertain the idea a moment longer.

My line of sight shifts from Christopher to a giant sign, glowing off the interstate. "Party City!" I call out, pointing across the cabin so fast I almost hit Christopher in the face.

His hazel eyes follow my finger for a second before letting out an exaggerated sigh. "About time," he groans and suddenly flips on his blinker, guiding the truck to our right and across the tight lanes of traffic.

"Q for Qdoba," he says, nodding at the list of food options on the sign. "Can we get dinner now?"

I gawk at him and let out a throaty laugh. He'd already found his letter and was just waiting for me to say mine so we could get out of this traffic.

"You're ridiculous," I tease him.

"No, I'm hungry," he counters, and his wide smile returns.

As if on cue, his stomach growls so loud it fills the entire cabin, causing a cackling laugh to explode from both of our mouths and the two of us ease back into the warm energy that wrapped around us for the last six hours before he brought up college. We stop for dinner, getting a refill on drinks, and eat the biggest burritos I've ever seen.

It doesn't faze me when Christopher pulls out his phone, saying he wants to document the whole trip, and we take some photos in the booth at Qdoba, the enormous burritos held up to our faces for comparison, and I laugh so hard my stomach hurts. With Christopher, there's never a shortage of smiles or laughs. And there's most definitely never a shortage of pictures and memories being made. Memories I know I'll never forget.

Chapter 24

Christopher's soft humming fills my ears as I slowly leave sleep. I know I dozed off somewhere after Denver, when we had another hour left of the drive. I blame the carb-filled burrito.

When I crack my eyelids open, the inky black passenger window comes into view, my cheek pressed into the coarse cloth seat. I shift a bit, pulling the sleeves of my crewneck down over my hands, and just when I'm about to let my heavy eyelids close once again, a wet droplet appears on the glass.

My eyes widen, focusing in on the pane of glass and the world around me sharpens into view, fully pushing my grogginess aside. Drops of water bloop across the glass, shimmering from the lights on the dash against the night backdrop. For a second, I think it's raining until I realize it's *snow*, melting on contact with the truck.

I sit up from the seat, blonde curls shifting down my back, and gasp when I see out the windshield. "It's snowing!" I say my thoughts aloud.

"Look who's awake," Christopher says, his voice cracking with an edge that makes me realize how off his humming was. It wasn't relaxed or at ease. It was forced and shook with nerves.

It's not just snowing flurries, it's a complete powder storm.

Thick whips of white slam against the hood of the truck, the wind so loud its howls cut through the truck, making the hairs on my arm stand. Now I notice the truck struggling to pave a way through the covered road, gripping and sliding through the thick layer of white.

"When did this start?" I ask, searching for my phone that fell between the seat and the center console while I slept.

"About thirty minutes ago," he says. Christopher's knuckles are white as he grips the steering wheel, the muscles in his arms flexing with the strain of keeping the truck on the road, guiding it down faint tracks that probably came from his friends who were driving ahead of us.

"How much further?" My fingers finally connect with the cold case of my phone and I slip it free, opening up a blank screen that lets me know I have no service. "Shit," I curse, clicking the phone off and running a hand through my hair.

"Just a few more miles," Christopher says.

I slump back into the seat, my body relaxing just a bit. At least we're not far. I've ridden in this truck through more than one snow storm.

"No service?" Christopher lets his wide eyes glance at my black screen for a second.

I shake my head just as the truck's wheels lose their grip and we slide to the right. A shocked squeal escapes my closing lungs, nails digging into my palms and Christopher turns the steering wheel to the left, hard. The truck finds some traction and corrects itself, barely missing the tree branches full of pine needles reaching for us.

I blow the stiff breath out of my nose, and Christopher gives me a weak laugh. "Think of it this way," he says, and his voice shakes even though I know he's trying to keep it steady. "I'm sure there are worse places than my truck to get caught in a snowstorm."

I snap my blue eyes to him with a glare that could cut glass. "Don't even give the universe the idea," I tell him. "Just get us to the cabin."

We bump over another patch of clumped snow and the back end of the truck pulls us right and left. "Easy enough," Christopher says, and we break out of the thick trees and into a clearing.

It's hard to see against the glowing headlights that struggle to pierce through the thick snowfall, but when I make out a flickering light on the other side of the windows of the cabin ahead, my heart finally starts beating again.

"Oh, thank God," Christopher sighs heavily, audibly showing the relief that's filling my chest. He maneuvers the truck through the thick snow and slides to a stop next to a black van that is just as crookedly parked as we are.

"Should I be nervous?" I ask, nose pressed against the chilled glass of the passenger side window. A curtain on the window beside the door flutters, someone having just walked away from it.

"About what?" Christopher asks and I pull my gaze to him.

"About meeting your friends," I say.

Christopher gives me a tired smile. "You don't need to be nervous, Penny."

I press my lips together, not convinced. When Christopher turns the ignition off, pulling the keys free, I know I don't have any other choice. I pop the door of the truck open, ice that formed while we drove trying to freeze it shut.

When I jump down from the passenger seat, I sink past my ankles and am instantly surrounded by a brutal wind, blasting snow against my exposed skin and sucking all the warmth from my body. With shivering movements, Christopher and I pull our duffle bags and coats from the back seat, slinging them over our arms.

Christopher leads the way, and I hurry alongside him for the cabin. It's so cold and dark that I don't see most of it. Wooden steps creak beneath our feet as we climb the porch. Bits of charcoal colored wood peeking out where the snow has blown away. Someone inside pulls the front door open and I follow Christopher through the entrance, stomping our boots off on the welcome mat and latching onto the warmth.

"You made it!" a nasally voice exclaims.

I wipe the blonde strands of hair that were blown wild out of my face, and see the lanky boy—Billy—from Mr. Riley's film class appear beside Christopher, laying a hand on his shoulder.

"Yeah, no one mentioned a snow storm would be hitting tonight," Christopher huffs.

"That's every night in Colorado," a girl says, and I find her leaning against an impressive wooden post that stands in the center of the room. Her dark brown skin glows with the light from the fire in the living room.

Now inside, I take in the space; dark wood floors beneath my feet and a small kitchen to the left. The living room makes up the rest of the space, cream colored couches forming a U around the magnificent stone fireplace, a loud pop coming from the real fire inside.

Who I assume is Paul lounges on the love seat. His feet are propped up on the stone coffee table, and a redhead girl with freckled cheeks lays her feet across his lap, her head resting on the arm closest to the fire.

"Penny, this is Billy and Paul," Christopher says, finally filling the quiet that fell over the cabin.

"So, we officially meet the mysterious girl from class," Paul says, his voice as smooth as his black hair that is slicked back from his forehead, so much gel in it, each piece is pronounced.

"And this is Maggie," Christopher continues, pointing to the redhead laying with Paul, who I can safely assume is his girlfriend. "And Janay," Christopher finishes, gesturing to the girl who still leans against the center post. Billy drifts to her side and throws an arm over her shoulder.

I offer a soft wave and know the heat blooming on my cheeks isn't from the fireplace. I knew that Christopher and I would be the only pair here not dating, but I didn't expect to be this exposed to it. "It's nice to meet you all," I say. "Thanks for letting me tag along."

Everyone but Janay smiles at that and tells me they're glad I came. But Janay's eyes narrow a hair, her gaze sweeping me up and down, from head to toe.

I shift my weight, wet boots squeaking on the wooden floors. Billy's eyes widen, realizing he should take on the host's responsibility. "Here, let me show you where you guys can put your stuff," he says, noticing I'm still buckling beneath the weight of my duffle.

Christopher and I follow him across the living room toward a door that blends into the rough logs that stack together to form the walls. Billy reaches for the brass knob, pushing it open. "Paul and I already took the rooms upstairs, but you guys can have the one down here."

My feet freeze in the threshold of the room, causing Christopher to stumble back from me. "Wait," the word fumbles from my mouth, my brain processing what he just said.

"This is the only room left?" Christopher asks, forming my worries on his tongue faster than I can.

"Yeah," Billy says with a shrug, but I don't miss the tug on the corner of his lips, the way his eyes seem to light up at the obvious tension in the air.

The bastard set us up.

My mouth fills with an imaginary sand, words failing me right now. I glance back at Christopher, but his steel gaze is on Billy, who I'm sure knows of our past. If these people are Christopher's best friends, they must know about me, about how I broke his heart, and how we definitely came on this trip as just friends.

I've read enough of the romance books in the Rayou Library to know exactly what's going on here. Billy's trying to corner us into the same room, some kind of shove to get Christopher and me back together.

"Well," Christopher huffs, finally releasing his glare and letting his eyes drift toward the living room. "Good thing the couches look comfortable."

An icy air follows his words, reality settling back between us. My cheeks burn so hot it's hard to believe a snow storm is overtaking the world outside these walls. All of Christopher's friends look at me, the tension in the air suffocating, and I'm so embarrassed Billy has put us in this situation that it takes me a moment to speak.

"Wait... What?" The words rush past my numb lips. "No, you should take the room—"

"It's fine, Penny," Christopher interrupts.

"But you drove all day—"

"It doesn't matter. Seriously, I don't care." Christopher turns his back to Billy and me with his final words. He tosses his duffle bag to the side of one of the open couches and flops across it, letting his feet hang over the armrest.

Billy still leans against the doorframe, and I meet his chocolate brown eyes studying me. I bite my tongue to keep from spitting out some rude comment. Billy knows well enough that Christopher and I came here as friends, and that makes this all that much worse. Because if he really does know about our past, about how badly I hurt Christopher,

Billy would know exactly what this would do to his friend. That pisses me off more than the fact that Christopher would rather sleep on the couch than just share the room with me.

Afraid of what I might say, I step inside the room and close the door behind me, letting the rattle of it in the wooden frame be my answer.

I walk to the bed in the right corner, and sink onto the edge of the mattress, the black quilt rough beneath my touch. Darkness cloaks the room, making it seem like I've crawled inside my own little hole where I can hide the embarrassment that's choking my lungs. I let the duffle hit the floor, looking like it's on display from the beam of moonlight that glows across the wooden beams.

Outside the room, I hear a muffled conversation start, and I let out a deep sigh. I knew I shouldn't have come here. The second that Christopher told me the other guys were bringing their girlfriends, I knew this would be awkward. Christopher and I are just getting to a position where being friends is natural, not forced. Our relationship is already fragile, and I fear this trip could shatter everything we've worked so hard to put back together.

Chapter 25

The tone of the phone ringing in my ear fills the quiet room. Thank goodness the cabin has better signal than the road leading in. I only have to wait a second before my mom answers.

"Hi Penny," she says, voice bright.

"Hey mom," I say, and cringe when the words crack in my throat. She doesn't seem to notice that I'm upset and asks what I'm doing. "I just wanted to let you know we made it. The snow is coming down pretty heavy right now."

I pause and listen to the repetitive tapping of it hitting the window that rattles from the harsh wind. That sound means there's some ice in the mix.

"Have you checked the radar yet?" Mom asks, filling the silence I let linger for too long. I tell her I haven't, but before I can finish speaking, she's already pulled it up on her laptop. "Oh, Penny, you're lucky you made it when you did."

"That bad?"

"Mhmm," she says, and I can tell she's processing something she's seeing on her computer screen. "It's not going to let up for a while. They're saying it could be up to seven inches."

I sigh back into the wall beside the bed and twirl a piece of my blonde hair around my finger. "Good thing we aren't planning on leaving anytime soon," I offer, but it also solidifies the fact that I'm stuck here. For a second, I almost considered asking Christopher if he wanted to leave rather than be trapped here where everything seems to be balancing on a fragile line.

My mom asks if we thought to bring food and I recall that Christopher said Billy and Paul were supposed to pick up groceries on the way here, courtesy of Billy's mom. She tells me to have fun and I don't let her know about how we've already started this trip on the wrong foot. The conversation is short, and the silence of the room is palpable after I hang up.

I turned on the lights and started unpacking before I thought to call her, so my duffle lays unzipped on the floor. Most of the clothes are already pulled out and hung up in the small closet in the corner of the room that is packed with a pile of blankets.

I hop up from the bed and scoop my toiletry bag into my hand while I slide across the wooden floorboards in my fuzzy socks to the connected bathroom. It's been recently remodeled, with a white vanity and marbled granite. The walls are a pale blue that brings out the hints of color on the tile in the shower. I unzip the toiletry bag and hang it on a hook across from the toilet, working to unpack the things I brought.

After I've wasted just about as much time as I can, I take in a steadying breath and finally move to leave the room. It's been at least an hour since we arrived, and when I open the door, I see Billy, Paul,

Maggie, and Janay have all filtered out of the living room. Overhead, the floorboards squeak and their conversation softly travels down to the lower level. I guess they've started unpacking as well.

The living room is dark, all the lights flipped off, besides the glow coming from the fireplace, the occasional pop of a log shifting filling the room with a soft sound that keeps the uncomfortable silence away. Christopher is laying across the smaller couch to the right of the fireplace, his head propped against the armrest, in almost the identical position he was in when I last saw him. His arm is draped under his head, and when I step near him, I see his hazel eyes are trained on the flickering flames, the glow shifting against his caramel swirls, making them look alive.

"Hey." My voice is soft, almost covered by the harsh gust of wind that shakes the shutters outside.

Christopher tips his head back, snapping his eyes to me. The neutral mask that was on his face shifts, a weak smile growing. "Hey."

I move toward the fire, crossing my arms and letting the warmth radiate across my body. The fuzzy sweater molds to my shoulders and absorbs every bit of heat it can. Even though it's not all that cold in here, the sounds of the snow storm outside still make my teeth chatter.

"Get unpacked?" Christopher asks after a second.

I drop my arms and turn to him. "Yeah," I say as I cross to sit on the floor beside the couch he's lying on. The red and black checkered rug that runs beneath the couches and the coffee table is thick. Christopher offers to sit up, but I make myself comfortable on the floor. At the right height to look into the fire over the stone coffee table.

"You can have the room if you want," I offer, and look at Christopher, our faces level now. "Really, this was your spring break, you shouldn't stay on the couch."

To my surprise, Christopher laughs softly. "Seriously, Penny, it's not a big deal. I don't mind."

I twist my lips in a defeated pout. I don't really know what to say to that. "The cabin's nice," I offer instead, deciding to just ease the conversation in a different direction.

Christopher hums a response and then adds, "Have you seen the storm cell overhead?"

"I just got off the phone with my mom. She said it was bad."

Christopher slides his phone from where it's tucked between the cushions and shows me the radar.

I suck in a harsh breath through my teeth and shake my head. "That's not good."

"Nope," he says, clicking his phone off and tucking it back at his side. "I'm sorry about that whole awkward arrival," he says after a minute.

"It's fine. You didn't know," I say, and catch his lingering stare out of my peripheral. At least, I don't think he knew.

He shakes his head as confirmation, turning his gaze back to the fire when a large log shifts, sending sparks up the chimney. "If you're not comfortable here—"

"I'm fine, Christopher," I interrupt him. "I think this is still going to be a fun trip."

"Yeah?" He looks at me questioningly, not sure if I'm telling the truth.

I smile, the corners of my mouth pulling my cheeks. "Yeah," I say and nudge the couch cushion he's lying on.

We sit like this for a while, just enjoying each other's company and watching the mesmerizing flicker of the flames in the fire.

"Who wants to make some s'mores?" Billy's nasally voice travels through the house. The wooden steps groan beneath his heavy steps and Paul trails behind him.

Christopher raises himself up on his elbows and looks over the back of the couch in the direction of the stairs, meeting Billy's wide smile when he hits the landing. "Umm, in case you didn't know, we're in the middle of a snowstorm," Christopher says.

"In case you didn't know," Billy mocks, taking his naturally nasally voice up another octave.

"Obviously, Chris," Paul teases, and I watch the two boys round the kitchen counter and begin to sift through the grocery bags that were left by the pantry. They begin to sort the food, putting away things like cans of chicken noodle soup, bread, and peanut butter, but setting the marshmallows, graham crackers, and chocolate to the side.

Christopher looks back at me and pops up an eyebrow up, asking the silent question of curiosity. I shrug in response, and push myself to my feet, sliding across the wooden floors to take a seat at one of the barstools. Christopher comes to stand behind me, resting his crossed arms on the back of my chair.

"Okay, so how do you plan on making s'mores?" Christopher questions the boys as they finish putting away our groceries for the week.

"Have you ever made s'mores in the microwave?" Billy asks, and he begins to tear some paper towels free.

"Ohh," Christopher sighs his acknowledgment. "Of course."

"Ohh, of course," Paul repeats sarcastically and playfully palms his forehead.

I let out a soft giggle, caught up in their exchanges.

"Penny, would you like one?" Billy asks, pausing with two graham crackers open over a napkin.

"Sure," I say and watch as he assembles a line of three down the counter. He pops them all in the microwave at the same time and starts the timer.

"Look at us, already making s'mores and having fun," Billy says as he hoists himself up to sit on the counter. "No snow storm is going to ruin this spring break." His voice holds an apologetic tone and I wonder if he feels bad about the earlier confrontation he orchestrated.

Paul and Christopher nod, agreeing to that, and when the microwave timer goes off, Paul hands them out to each of us. We take our s'mores to the living room and spread out. The three boys fill the couches, and I find my spot back on the floor next to the couch, preferring the proximity to the fireplace. That's when an idea dawns on me.

"Why don't we just make the s'mores in the fireplace?" I look across the stone coffee table to where Billy and Paul sit on the other two couches, mouths full of chocolate and marshmallow goo, graham cracker crumbs on their lips.

Billy snaps and points a finger at me. "Genius!" he says around his full mouth and he hops over the back of the couch, jogging to where we left the s'mores ingredients in the kitchen.

I eat the microwave one that Billy made, not even hiding the approving moan that vibrates in my throat at the velvety chocolate mixed with the sweet, fluffy marshmallow. I can't remember the last time I made a s'more.

We find some marshmallow roasting sticks in a closet downstairs and sit on pillows in front of the fireplace, taking turns building s'mores for each other. Billy and Paul tell us their girlfriends are already getting ready for bed, but I hang out with the three boys for a moment, letting the easy conversation about how their exams went filter between us. We stay clear of talking about mine and Christopher's and relationship, and the awkward air doesn't return, the sounds of the crackling logs filling the space.

When 10:00 p.m. comes and goes—and I've already eaten three s'mores and a handful of marshmallows—I can hardly keep my eyes open. I decide to turn in for the night and barely have the covers pulled over my shoulders before I drift to sleep, the long trip taking every bit of energy out of me. With the accompanied soft tapping from the snowstorm outside, it's easy to let the repetitive lullaby pull me to sleep, my stomach full and happy with s'mores.

Chapter 26

Against Billy's optimism about not letting this snow ruin our spring break, I think the odds aren't in his favor. The next morning I rise to soft beams of sun, setting the wooden walls aglow in my room. When I reach for my phone, I learn that it's past nine in the morning, and when my feet hit the floor, they instantly freeze like icicles. That's when I notice my breath is coming out in small clouds and, as the thick comforter falls from my shoulders, a chill instantly seeps through the crewneck and leggings I fell asleep in.

I reach for the drawer of the nightstand and free a pair of fuzzy socks, rescuing my already numbing toes from the cold. I rub my hands up and down my arms, trying to cause some friction in hopes of holding on to the warmth from the bed. Instantly, I know something is wrong.

The bedroom door creaks loudly, signaling my exit, and it takes everything in me not to leap over the couch and place myself directly in front of the crackling fire. Maggie and Janay already sit on the floor in front of it, and when they look up to see me, Maggie pats the space next

the stone edge of the fireplace. Goosebumps bloom under my

when Christopher's arm brushes mine, and not just because of

ll that clings to him.

illy hops off of the counter top, his socked feet padding toward the

g room. "Mom said no one can come out until the storm has passed."

h the five of us already packed around the fireplace, Billy balances

the edge of the coffee table.

"The fire is helping," Janay offers and I do agree, now that I'm out

f my isol— bedroom, I am more comfortable than before.

n of blankets in the closet in my room," I say.

let his snow storm ruin anything," Paul

kicks Billy playfully in the

to her.

"Billy says the heater isn't working," M[...]
beside her, my back to the orange flames. [...]
enough to burn, but I don't shift away.

I find Billy sitting on the island in the kitchen[...]
and forth with his phone pressed against his ear. "Wh[...]
I ask through my chattering teeth.

"His mom," Janay says. "I think she's going to call so[...]
take a look at the unit."

I nod and my eyes drift toward the blinding white[...]
windows. My heart sinks in my frozen chest when [...]
of snow and ice coming down against th[...]
outside.

It's *still* snow[...]

to her.

"Billy says the heater isn't working," Maggie says as I take a seat beside her, my back to the orange flames. The heat is almost strong enough to burn, but I don't shift away.

I find Billy sitting on the island in the kitchen, feet swinging back and forth with his phone pressed against his ear. "Who's he talking to?" I ask through my chattering teeth.

"His mom," Janay says. "I think she's going to call someone to come take a look at the unit."

I nod and my eyes drift toward the blinding white world outside the windows. My heart sinks in my frozen chest when I hear the pelting mix of snow and ice coming down against the glass, the wind howling outside.

It's *still* snowing.

The front door flies open and two bundles of winter coats come stumbling in, a blast of snow dusting the floor around them. The shorter one on the right rips his stocking cap from his head, and I see that it's Paul.

"Make room!" he calls, sliding on the snow that's falling in clumps from his boots. His jacket swishes with his arms as he walks across the living room and plops down on the other side of Maggie. I look back toward the door, seeing Christopher removing his snowy layers before joining us by the fire.

"It's still coming down out there," Christopher says through deep breaths.

"At least five inches already," Paul adds, using his toe of one boot against the heel of the other to pop them off.

Christopher sits next to me, and his shoulders sink with relief when the fire begins to thaw his body. He extends his arms behind him, leaning back on the stone edge of the fireplace. Goosebumps bloom under my sweater when Christopher's arm brushes mine, and not just because of the chill that clings to him.

Billy hops off of the counter top, his socked feet padding toward the living room. "Mom said no one can come out until the storm has passed." With the five of us already packed around the fireplace, Billy balances on the edge of the coffee table.

"The fire is helping," Janay offers and I do agree, now that I'm out of my isolated bedroom, I am more comfortable than before.

"There are a ton of blankets in the closet in my room," I say.

"See, Billy, still not going to let this snow storm ruin anything," Paul says, a half grin spreading on his face and he kicks Billy playfully in the foot.

Billy nods and claps his hands together. "All right. I officially declare today board game day by the fire."

We all let out small whistles and hoops of agreement. I push to my feet and pull out every blanket I can find in my room. The others discover even more in a chest in the corner of the living room. We spread out the thick grey ones on top of the rug in between the couches to make a comfortable padding for us to sit on top of around the coffee table. Billy brings out a pile of board games that towers over his head.

"Damn," Paul whistles when he notices the stack of colorful boxes, some I haven't seen since I was little. "Your family like board games?"

Billy drops them next to the couch and dusts off his hands. "Obviously," he says through a weak smile. "So, what should we play first?"

Spirits stay high through the morning. We start at the top of the stack of board games and work our way down. Christopher sits next to me on the mat of blankets with Billy and Janay across from us and Maggie and Paul to our left. In hopes of staying warm, Christopher drapes a large, heavy blanket around our shoulders, and I lean into his side, my fingers fumbling over his every once in a while. If it weren't so cold in the cabin, this proximity would feel awkward. Or maybe my stupid heart and all those confusing feelings for Christopher just wants a reason to be close to him. To cuddle under a fluffy blanket like the other couples are doing.

If Christopher finds it odd, he doesn't say, and instead, pulls me closer to his side, his hand running up and down my back in soothing strokes that thaws any chill trying to take root. When Paul rattles off one of his *many* dumb jokes, Christopher laughs into my shoulder, and his breath tickles my skin.

The day goes by and the cabin is filled with cheers of victory and accusations of cheaters, which is just followed by more laughter. The games vary from cards to tokens on a board to questions and trivia.

I finally get the grand tour of the cabin, including a peak at the hot tub outside on the porch. It has a rustic charm that I love, especially with all the natural wood. Maggie and I make an enormous pot of chicken noodle soup for lunch, and the games continue with warm bellies. Between her and Janay, Maggie has been the most welcoming to me. I had a weird feeling about Janay when I first arrived, and I haven't forgotten the way she surveyed me like she needed to be cautious in my presence.

The pile of wood next to the fireplace continues to dwindle and we draw straws for who has to venture out to the shed to get more of the dry storage Billy's family keeps. My heart plummets when I pull one of the short straws, but Christopher slips it out from between my fingers and goes in my place, telling me I can make it up to him with more chicken noodle soup.

But when the sun begins to set, a deep purple filling the sky, and the snow is still coming down in heavy flurries, the bright energy in the room begins to darken. After checking the radar for the tenth time today, Paul reports that the last of the snow should be blowing through in the next hour or two.

Our unfinished game of cards lays scattered across the coffee table, and we no longer feel like playing after hours have already been spent on other games. Janay has the ingenious idea to find the hot chocolate, and she makes enough for everyone.

We find our seats around the coffee table on the living room floor once more, each holding a mug of hot chocolate filled to the brim. All things considered, we've actually managed to stay warm.

"This reminds me of that day it stormed in London," Janay says when she lowers her mug from her lips, her dark-skinned fingers tight around the porcelain cup.

Paul, who's leaning back against the couch with his knees pulled to his chest, scoffs a laugh. "When Billy made us play charades for four hours straight?"

Maggie lets out a sarcastic groan and they all laugh, the memory fresh to them. The couch shifts behind me with Christopher's deep laugh, and I know this is a joke amongst friends, something that I obviously wasn't a part of. But that's not why my stomach opens into a deep void. It's the fact that they're talking about *London*. About that trip from the portfolio I saw weeks ago when I sat in the Snowcapped Diner with Christopher. I'd almost forgotten it was even real, but Janay's words are a cold reminder.

"You guys were on the London trip, too?" I ask, interrupting their chorus of laughter. My voice quivers just a hair, not enough for the others to notice the emotion rising there, but I'm sure Christopher doesn't miss it.

Paul nods, twisting his mug of hot chocolate in his hands. "Yeah, Mr. Riley taught a different class last semester that we were all in," he says and Maggie and Janay nod.

"We're both studying film, so some of our classes crossover," Maggie explains.

When I had looked through Christopher's portfolio of the trip to London, it had been brief, but I recall a photo that was taken in the garden, two boys and two girls captured in the frame. That must have been them. Even though I've known that Christopher made that trip without me, disappointment builds in my throat like I'm hearing it for the first time again. That was supposed to be *our* trip. Something we daydreamed about together and created lists on his phone of places we wanted to visit.

"Paul and I actually started dating at the end of the trip," Maggie adds, still telling me about the story.

"Which left poor Christopher as our only single friend," Billy teases and they laugh lightly, the weight of me sitting beside Christopher not registering to them.

"Not that we didn't try to find him someone," Paul boasts, and my blood stills as understanding filters through my already clouded thoughts.

"Oh, right!" Billy says, tagging on to what Paul had begun to say. "Cynthia was head over heels about you."

"Do you still talk to her?" Janay asks, drawing all of our eyes to Christopher.

For the first time since we started talking about London, I look at him. His hazel eyes are dark, their gaze angled at the cards spread across the stone coffee table. "Nah, we didn't even exchange numbers," he says with a shrug, a muscle in his throat bobbing when he swallows after he speaks.

"That's a lie," Maggie huffs. "No way after *that* night did you not get her number."

My stare never leaves his profile, watching how his eyes fill with a caramel-colored storm cloud, his jaw locking with grinded teeth. He clearly doesn't want to talk about this, and I don't think it's because he doesn't want to relive this memory. I think it's because I'm sitting right next to him while his friends imply he hooked up with some girl he met in London. Their school trip would have been in the fall... He moved on that quickly? He flew across the ocean and hooked up with Cynthia after we'd only been broken up for a couple of weeks?

I don't like that jealousy heats my cheeks, that the sweet hot chocolate turns bitter in my mouth. *I* broke up with *him*. He had every right to go and do that. I could have done the same, but the second I think that, I know it's not true. I never stopped thinking of Christopher, and my heart definitely never stopped beating for him, longing for his presence.

In the drawing silence, Janay and Maggie's gazes shift to me, finally understanding why Christopher seems so uncomfortable.

"She was hot, Christopher," Paul says, nudging his friend's foot underneath the table, oblivious to the heated tension growing in the living room. "You definitely messed that up." His words only turn my stomach more and tears threaten to bloom.

Maggie elbows Paul, not so subtly, in the side, stopping him from making this any worse.

"Hot chocolate refill?" Janay says, clearing her throat and abruptly standing up.

"I think we need more firewood," I mumble, placing my mug on the coffee table and pushing to my feet.

"I can get it—"

"No, I'm already up," I speak over Christopher.

I try to keep my motions smooth and not sprint for the exit, but I *do* want to run from the scene around me. Before I break down or say something I can't take back. With sharp movements, pull my mustard coat on and lace up my leather boots. I actually welcome the blast of frozen air that bites my nose when I face the outside world.

Each step I take feels like my body is trying to outrun my racing heart, to clear the cabin and get as far away as I can before the tears are released. There's a small path through the deep snow leading across the wooden porch and the yard to the storage shed where the others have walked earlier today. I make it to the bottom of the porch and before I have to stop, needing to lean against the frame for support while I force down an icy breath of air. Snow continues to fall, but the flurries are thin, just a few flakes drifting on the soft breeze, the harsh winds having passed. They land in my hair, sticking to the blonde strands. My heart is still clenched in my chest, their words loud in my head. I reach up to massage the spot beneath my throat and grip the collar of my coat as tears fill my eyes.

Christopher moved on that fast?

He found someone else to fill my place? I know I shouldn't be upset, but I can't help it. The waves of pain washing over me are out of my control, but at the end of the day, I can only blame myself. I did this. I left him. I broke his heart.

A single tear breaks free, its streak pinching my cheek and freezing instantly. The bite that follows sends the rest of my tears reseeding, my eyes clearing. I take in a few deep breaths, squeeze my arms around myself, and then continue to trudge through the snow-covered yard.

I can't blame Christopher for how he chose to heal himself after what I did, and I definitely can't make a scene about it now.

By the time I return to the cabin, arms filled with logs and bits of bark and dirt clinging to my coat, I've let everything about the London trip slip from my mind. I've pushed it aside, and I force a wide grin on my face. Stomping off my boots, I find the five of them still sitting around the coffee table in the living room, their hushed conversation silencing. No doubt they were talking about me. Maybe Christopher was even yelling at them for telling me about Cynthia. Even though this is probably true, I ignore it, pretending I don't even seem to notice the tense air that still lingers.

"I come bearing good news," I say, my voice singing the words as cheerfully as my fake persona can manage. I let my gaze linger with Christopher's, naturally drawn to his hazel eyes, wide with concern, surveying me and over analyzing my appearance. He's clearly worried about how I'm reacting to learning about Cynthia, but I don't let any of my distress show. Instead, I release the stack of dry logs next to the fireplace and dust of my hands, turning to look at the rest of our group.

"Well, spit it out," Paul says, waving his hands dramatically.

My cold fingers travel to the buttons of my coat, working to pop them each undone. With a wide smile I say, "The snow is finally letting up."

Chapter 27

When I roll onto my side Sunday morning, a soft rattling by my ear startles me, eyes breaking open. The black sheers that hang in front of the window drift on a soft current coming from the floor vent. My hand snaps out, a sigh of relief curling like the hot air between my fingers.

The heater is back on.

I stumble from the bed and get ready for the day, walking out into the living room to find Maggie and Janay in swimming suits in the kitchen.

"I know they turned the heat on, but it's not *that* hot in here," I tease them, drawing their gazes up from their coffee mugs to me.

"We're about to go check out the hot tub!" Maggie says, rinsing out her empty mug in the sink. "Want to join us?"

My jaw hangs slightly ajar. *Seriously?* In the middle of February, after the biggest snow storm I've seen in a couple of years, they want to get in the hot tub?

"Billy turned it on for us already," Janay says, thinking my hesitation lies in the wrong place.

Truly, I don't particularly want to sit in the hot tub with them. I didn't even know to bring a swimsuit, but when I state that as my excuse, Maggie is quick to tell me she has an extra one and thinks we'll be about the same size. I feel this pressure to do what Janay and Maggie want because they're Christopher's friends. I want them to like me, and they're nice enough to let me tag along during their spring break.

Maggie returns to the kitchen with a navy colored one piece and I change into it. It's a bit big on me, the fabric around my stomach loose, but Janay tightens the shoulder straps and I pull my blonde hair into a high ponytail, picking up the blue polk-a-dot towel they found for me.

"I suggest we run," Janay says, rocking up onto her toes and back down to her heels by the front door. She peers through the window beside it, locating the hot tub on the deck to the left. "Ready?" She reaches for the handle, ripping the door open and disappearing into the blinding sun outside.

Needles prick every inch of my exposed skin when the winter air blasts inside the cabin. Maggie and I let out a squeal and we hurry after her, trying to stay on the path Billy must have shoveled across the deck. Bits of snow left behind bite my feet and I'm practically shoving Maggie up the steps of the hot tub, throwing myself into the warm water.

"Oh my gosh," Maggie sighs with relief and I mimic the sound. Steam coils up from the water, and I instantly thaw.

"Okay, *this* is a spring break," Janay says with a soft laugh, finding a seat in front of one of the jets, resting her head back on the edge of the hot tub.

Maggie and I agree, finding our own corners to sit in. I admit it's nice; the warm water and the incredible view of the snowcapped mountains that tower around the cabin. The world is pure white in every direction, the freshly fallen snow absolutely breathtaking. Evergreen needles try to break up the white, the pine trees thick and full in this area of the mountains. But my body feels too exposed, even in the one-piece swimsuit. That part of me that's self-conscious is still a raw scar, discomfort spreading through my chest.

The three of us are quiet, letting the soft hum of the hot tub and the bubbling jets fill the steamy air. I close my eyes and try to give in to the idea of just relaxing in the hot tub. Every muscle in my body unclenches with the hot water, and I try to make myself comfortable, to enjoy this like Maggie and Janay so easily do.

"3…2…1!" A voice that sounds like Billy's rings out in the distance. I crack open an eye and see that Maggie and Janay haven't shifted at all, eyes still closed, and acting as if they didn't just hear that.

"Incoming!" Paul screams, the sound traveling from beneath the porch.

"What are they doing?" I question, shifting in the hot tub to kneel on the seat so I can see over the railing.

Maggie and Janay show no interest and say, "Whatever boys do after it snows."

I peer over the inch of snow piled on the banister and an excited gasp escapes me. Christopher, Paul, and Billy are spread across the front yard, three giant mounds of snow packed together near them. The ground that was perfectly untouched last night, has been demolished. That pristine, glittery snow is now trampled through with footsteps and trenches.

"A snowball fight!" I say through my wide smile, snapping my head around to see Maggie and Janay.

They still sit in their respective corners, eyes closed and breathing slow.

"Of course," Janay says with a snicker. "Absolute fools. It's way too cold for that."

Maggie nods her head in agreement and my chest deflates a bit.

I think it's a great idea. My gaze turns back to the battlefield just in time to see Christopher get hit in the face, the snowball exploding in a cloud of white and a laugh bursts from my lungs.

That looks like more fun than sitting in the hot tub.

Paul dives behind his fort—the smallest of the three—and narrowly avoids Billy's snowball. The three boys laugh and continue to run around the yard, breaking every few minutes to build up their stock of ammo. I watch them for a moment longer and then make up my mind.

The whole reason I left Frostard was to get some control over my life. I wanted to make the decisions for myself, to choose what I wanted. Since that day I flew across the country in January, I've only been with my mom, Christopher, or the cheer team. I haven't been with girls my age, with any friends or teenagers that I had to engage with. This spring break trip is the first time I've been social in months, and I immediately went back to my old ways of letting others decide what I should do, folding to their decisions because it's easier than voicing my own opinion.

The realization makes my stomach flip and gives me the push I need to move. I walk across the hot tub, reach for my towel, and brace myself for the cold air.

"Where are you going?" Maggie asks, finally opening her eyes at the ripple of the water against my movements.

I ring my hands in the soft fabric, and I'm surprised how easy the words come out, how simple it really is to just say what I want, and go do it.

"I'm joining the snowball fight," I say and stand. The second the cold tries to penetrate the warm steam of the hot tub, I wrap the towel around my shoulders and run for the door.

Once inside, I quickly change, pulling on my fleece lined leggings and two sweatshirts for double protection because I don't want to ruin my nice coat. I layer on the fuzzy socks, having to relace my leather boots to give my padded feet extra room. I only have my leather gloves and I know they will do little in the snow, but it's better than nothing.

I slip from the house, the cold air just barely infiltrating through my winter clothes, and run across the porch, down the snow-covered steps, and into the front yard.

"Intruder!" Billy hollers, the first to notice me, and I scream as a snowball flies inches from my face.

I dive behind one of the shallow piles of snow created from one of the boys digging a trench in the yard. My leggings instantly absorb the cold, and a chill creeps up my legs. My hands work fast, scooping up the snow and packing it together. I make three snowballs and jump up, readying myself to fire at the boys. They're expecting me, but their eyes still widen when I come out from behind my small pile of snow, charging toward them to close the distance. Billy turns around to grab from his stack of ammo. The first snowball I throw hits Paul square in the chest, and he drops to his knees to try and return the attack. While Paul is packing his snow, I throw another at Billy, hitting him in the back. He whips around, hurling a snowball in my direction. I side step it easily, and sprint to find my last snowball's target, *Christopher*.

I scream when he comes out of nowhere, suddenly right behind me. His muscled arms wrap around my waist, and he shoves me forward, making us both topple into a large snowdrift. Christopher falls on top of me, his chest against my back, and my face hits the snow.

"Intruder detained!" he yells.

I twist beneath him so I can peer up at his hazel eyes and the wind blows the snow out of my hair. His smile is wide, all teeth, as he straddles me, keeping me pinned in the snow. My leggings dampen, letting the cold through the fabric, but I don't notice it. All I see is Christopher's beaming face above mine, the sun making him glow. The pressure of his legs on either side of me causes my heart to skip, and his weight and warmth above me is something I know I've missed.

"This is a very serious snowball fight that you just interrupted," he says, eyes surveying the makeshift snow gear I threw on.

"Yeah, well, sorry I didn't bother waiting for an invitation," I say with an easy grin.

His eyes narrow, creases forming at their corners. "I didn't realize you'd want to join."

I pull my arms out of the snowdrift from beneath me and lean up, pressing in even closer to Christopher so my nose brushes his. I point a gloved finger at him, resting it on his chest. "You looked like you could use some help."

He laughs at that, a breathy sound that shakes his chest and brings our proximity closer. "Are you wanting to team up?"

I shrug, and, finally unable to ignore the bite of the cold on my rear, I say, "If it means you'll help me up before my butt freezes, then yes."

Christopher's hazel eyes glitter and he stands up, offering me a hand to pull me from the snowdrift. As I dust my leggings off, Christopher turns to face Billy and Paul. "Change of plans. Penny's joining."

Billy and Paul immediately catch on to our motives. "You're just going to team up against us," they pout, seeing the numbers shift out of their favor.

"See if Maggie and Janay will come down," Christopher offers and I scoff.

"Don't bother. They are both very comfortable in the hot tub." I tell them.

Billy and Paul share a glance before the corners of their mouths pull up in mischievous smiles. They turn their backs to us, running across the yard and toward the porch, scooping up handfuls of snow and packing them into snowballs.

"What are they doing?" I ask, my voice tilting up with concern.

Christopher shakes his head, taking a hesitant step backward. "Something I'm sure they'll regret," he says with an unsure laugh. "Come on, let's build up our fort."

I fall back with Christopher to where his makeshift shield of snow is packed together. We work to extend the wall, so we both fit behind it, and begin creating a stash of snowballs. Just when I begin to register the cold and wet snow seeping through my leather gloves, a high pitch shrill splits the air. Christopher and I snap our heads up in the direction of the hot tub where Paul and Billy are throwing snowballs at Maggie and Janay.

"Oh, they didn't," I say between my teeth.

"Billy!" Janay screams, standing in the hot tub to peer over the railing, just as her boyfriend throws another ball of snow at her, impacting right on her exposed shoulder. She squeals from the cold shock and drops back into the water.

"Come join the snowball fight!" Billy calls up to her and Maggie.

"We don't want to take part in your silly game," Maggie sings the insult bravely, standing at the railing.

Paul pulls his elbow back, snowball loaded in his hand and ready to fire at Maggie.

"Don't you dare throw that up here," she warns him, pointing a red-polished finger at him.

"Then you better get down here," he says, shifting the position of his arm further back as a threat. "You're either on my team in this snowball fight or you're against me."

"I'm not in the game," Maggie reminds him.

"You are now," Paul says with a grin.

Billy picks up another snowball and mirrors Paul's stance just as Janay cautiously looks over the railing, this time only letting her head come above the wooden post.

"It's a couples' snowball fight, you have to join," Billy explains and Maggie and Janay lift their gazes to find Christopher and me behind our fort.

I busy myself with packing another snowball, trying to ignore the fact that Billy just implied Christopher and me are a couple. I glance to my right, seeing if Christopher caught Billy's words. His face shows no signs of hearing him, and he keeps his focus on the pyramid of snowballs he's building.

"It'll be fun, Jay," Billy adds, using his girlfriend's nickname.

"But it's cold," Maggie groans, a shiver already creeping up her exposed arms.

"Then put some clothes on!" Paul says. "You have until the count of three or you become the enemy," he threatens. "One…"

"Paul don't you dare—"

"Two…" Billy echoes.

The two girls look at each other, hesitantly biting their lips and wanting to call the boys' bluff. I know they shouldn't because I've already been at the receiving end of their aim.

"Three!" Billy and Paul yell together, and they release their snowballs, hitting Janay and Maggie each in the face. The girls let out a screech so high-pitched birds take flight in the neighboring trees. They stumble from the railing and fall back into the hot tub, causing water to splash over the edges. A laugh catches in my throat and Christopher loses it, falling back on his butt from the billowing laughter that erupts. I subconsciously put the sound to memory so I can always relive this moment.

Billy and Paul reach down, picking up more snowballs, and the two boys unleash all their ammo on the hot tub, landing dozens of snowballs in the pool of hot water that must be chilling now.

After a minute, Maggie's white towel flies in the air, her form of a surrender. "Okay, okay!" she yells, and when she stands back up at the railing, she drapes the towel over her shoulders, her red hair soaked. "We'll join your stupid snowball fight."

Billy and Paul let out a victorious whoop and high five, retreating to their own forts to prepare for the snowball fight that's about to commence amongst all of us.

I look down at the stock of snowballs Christopher and I created and feel good about our chances. "I can keep making snowballs if you want to throw them," I say and he nods, liking the strategy.

A few minutes later, Janay and Maggie come stumbling down the porch steps, their clothes layered on like mine, fuzzy headbands holding their damp hair back and warming their ears.

"All right, let's get this started," Janay says, waving her hand with dismissal, but I catch the grin that's trying to hide on her face and she crouches behind Billy's fort.

"Losers have to bring in firewood for the rest of the week!" Billy calls out from behind his fort, setting the stakes. He counts down from five, and then the battle commences.

Christopher pops up first, immediately choosing to target Paul, which—to my surprise—is who Billy also targets. As Christopher throws the snowballs from our stock, I create the replacements, packing the cold snow together, letting the clouds of breath rise up to warm my nose.

The fight goes on for at least thirty minutes, maybe even closer to an hour. There's screaming and laughing. Paul manages to hit me square in the face when I peek over the barrier of our fort and Christopher unleashes a whole armful of packed snow on him, threatening him to try that again. It brings a laugh out of all of us, but it warms my heart, spreading across my freezing skin.

After I've made what feels like a hundred snowballs, I can't ignore the sharp pain that has found my hands, now trembling from the cold. Christopher continues to fire away, and when he notices our stash of snowballs is diminishing faster than before, he stops, turning to see me cradling my hands to my chest.

"Sorry, my hands are freezing," I say through chattering teeth.

Christopher drops below the fort, sliding in the snow to crouch next to me. "Let me see them," he says, his breath clouding in the air.

I hold out my leather-gloved hands and he takes them in his. Christopher unzips his heavy, black winter coat—clearly packing better than I did for the winter weather—and pulls my hands to his chest, the soft fabric of his sweatshirt meeting my covered fingers. Instantly, the warmth that he has stored inside his coat seeps into my cold fingers, and I sigh with the relief it brings.

"Better?" he asks.

"Much," I breathe.

Christopher shifts his weight so he can rest on his hip and stay below the top of our fort. He presses in closer to me, and I know my icy fingers have to be spreading a chill across his chest, but he leans in closer, letting his warmth escape and drape over me. The familiar scent of coffee and pine follows, filling my nose and making my head start to spin.

"Do you think we're winning," I ask, wanting his opinion.

"Well, we're definitely not losing," he says, and we both laugh at that, knowing Paul and Maggie have taken a beating, their fort practically demolished the last time I looked. Our laughter vibrates between us, bringing our chests together, and my cheek brushes Christopher's. His skin is cold, but it still sends sparks racing across my face at the gentle touch. My breath catches, and I hear Christopher's own breathing slow.

Still holding my hands to his chest, cradling my arms against him, my face *so* close to his, I look up, peering through my lashes to find his hazel eyes. The dark browns and caramels are so vivid against the white backdrop of the world around us, shimmering in the beams of sunlight, glittering like the freshly fallen snow.

His gaze trails down my face, finding my lips, and every muscle in my body freezes, because if I even so much as breathe, our lips will meet. Christopher looks back up at my eyes, the question hanging there in his mesmerizing stare. *Should I kiss her?*

I almost close the space and forget about reality because the prickling sensation of anticipation is nearly suffocating, but I don't take that step. Even though I know we aren't dating, and I'm supposed to go back to Frostard in August, none of that registers to me in this moment. None of it matters anymore, because my *want* for Christopher has grown so strong, it pulses with my stuttering heart.

What does cause me to fall back from him, putting that frigid pocket of air between our bodies, is the thought of *Cynthia*. Of the girl in London, the one he spent that trip with when it should have been me.

I hate that the idea makes me jealous. It breaks my heart and makes me feel replaceable in his eyes, even though I gave him no reason not to replace me. On the contrary, actually, I told him to do it. I ended our relationship and I walked away from him.

Christopher shifts his weight, fingers loosening on my hands, and he lets me fall away from his chest as I move to put space between us. I have to look away from him, not wanting him to see the tears that are trying to bloom at the edges of my eyes, because I *want* to kiss him. I want everything with him to be the way it was before I ever went to Frostard, but unfortunately, I can't take that time back. I can't undo the conversation we had inside the alcove of pine trees on the school grounds that late-August night. And I can't stomach the idea that Christopher could replace me so fast with another girl. A girl he met in London nonetheless.

The space behind the snow fort has grown tense, and I'm honestly not sure what we'd do if that silence lingered. Luckily for us, Paul and Maggie scream out their surrender, accepting defeat, and ending the snowball fight. When Christopher and I stand up, walking separate ways out of the fort, it feels like something more than the snowball fight just ended.

Any thought of a second chance with each other just crumbled like the snowballs, coming to rest on the frigid ground.

Chapter 28

L ast night was the longest of my life. The boys decided they wanted to make a fire outside and have s'mores, even though us girls voted on just making them in the living room. The entire time we sat around the fire—Billy with his arm around Janay, Paul holding Maggie to his chest—Christopher and I sat a good foot from each other. That wall of ice only grew thicker as the day continued. I know the others noticed how tense we were acting. That distance wasn't something that had been there before I found out about Cynthia.

When I come out of my room this morning, Christopher is folding the excessive amount of blankets we used when the heater wasn't working, piling them high in the corner.

"Good morning," I say softly, my feet unsure if I should walk up to him or stay on course for the kitchen.

He looks over his shoulders, standing tall and throwing his brown waves back from his face. Christopher's smile is soft, and he says, "Morning. The others have a proposition for you." He rocks his head back, signaling toward the front door where I find Janay and Maggie lacing up their boots.

"Are we going somewhere?" I ask, crossing to them and tucking my hands inside the front pocket of my cherry red sweatshirt.

They stand up, dressed like we may be having a second snowball fight, and while it was fun yesterday, the idea isn't as appealing right now.

"Have you ever been to Estes Park?" Maggie asks, reaching back to free her red hair that got tucked inside her collar.

"I think so. When I was younger," I offer, though I don't remember much about it.

"Oh, it's gorgeous, Penny! Billy said he'd drive us there and we could do some hiking," Maggie nearly squeals with delight.

Janay must notice my surprised expression because she speaks my thoughts before I can form the words. "No, apparently the woods around the cabin aren't good enough to hike in." Her tone is sarcastic, obviously thinking this idea is a little silly. It's the first time I've felt Janay and I have agreed on something, and I'm hoping that means she's warming up to me.

"It's not the same!" Maggie protests. "Seriously, you'll understand once we get there."

"Okay, okay," I say, stopping her before she dives into a long explanation where she tries to convince me to go. "It sounds like fun. Let me put something warmer on and we can leave."

After I add a thick sweater beneath my sweatshirt and pull on a second layer of fuzzy socks, I lace up my leather boots and we all pile into the van Billy drove. Paul takes the passenger seat, yelling, "*SHOTGUN!*" before he even makes it to the bottom of the staircase. I climb to the very back, knowing Maggie and Janay probably want the center seats and Christopher joins me, still leaving that pocket of air from yesterday between us.

Billy puts the van in drive, slipping and sliding along hastily shoveled snow-covered path, but once we get down the long driveway, the main roads are clear and our journey to Estes Park commences. The GPS navigates the way, claiming it's only a thirty-minute drive.

"So, should we resume our sing-a-long?" Paul asks.

"NO!" Maggie groans so loud, and she snaps her head back, colliding it with the headrest.

"Please don't, Paul. We entertained it for the last hour of our drive on Friday, but it's too soon," Janay says.

"What was he playing?" I ask, and the two girls flip their heads back at me, faces grimacing in warning to not ask.

"See, Penny wants to listen to it," Paul says, completely misinterpreting my interest. He picks up his phone and, to my surprise, a classic Broadway musical soundtrack shuffles through the radio.

"Oh, Paul," Maggie complains, but Paul reaches for the volume on the radio and turns it up so loud my head pulses with the beat.

And then Paul begins to *sing*, belting out every word for the next thirty minutes.

When we drive past the park attendant windows, I understand what Maggie was talking about. Estes park is absolutely breathtaking. The mountain peaks stretch so high on either side of us that I have to press my face to the window to see their tops.

"Turn here," Maggie instructs, pointing to a side-road that branches off to the left. The map the park ranger gave us is grasped tightly in her hands as she tries to make some sense of the twisty trails and random icons printed on the creased paper. I'd never know what trails were worth hiking, but she says she has a favorite one her family always uses.

The road narrows, just two lanes that barely fit on the shoulder of the mountain, and we climb higher and higher through the snow-covered peaks. We're one of the few cars I see, probably the only people stupid enough to come up here right after a snowstorm.

After another ten minutes, Maggie finally points out a small parking lot to our left, signaling the beginning of a trail.

"Pull in here!" Her foot taps excitedly on the floor of the car and Billy barely brings it to rest before she's sliding back the side door and leaping onto the slippery pavement.

I pull on my leather gloves that I had stashed in my sweatshirt pocket and climb out of the van behind her. I've lived in Colorado my entire life. The mountains are literally my backyard. I'm as used to seeing them as people in the Midwest are to seeing cornfields, but there's something different about the peaks in Estes Park. The air feels cleaner here, fresh and full of nature. The woods are loud with birds and wildlife we can't see, and the cold doesn't even bother me. Even the snow is prettier, the sun shimmering against its pristine cover on the world.

"Okay, Maggie, you're the expert. Lead the way," Paul says, extending his hand for her to take it.

She doesn't hesitate, intertwining her fingers with his, and heads toward the bright yellow post that indicates the start of the trail. Janay and Billy follow behind them and Christopher and I bring up the rear. Immediately, we're swallowed between the thick pine trees, the smell so strong it tickles my nose. I thought it'd be harder to hike after all the snowfall, but there's a steady trail put down by travelers and volunteers that passed through before us.

For a while, the trail is spacious, but the further we go, the narrower it gets. Eventually, we have to form a single file line to continue the hike, and still, the branches from the neighboring trees brush our shoulders, snow floating to the ground as we pass. Above, the sky is a clear, bright blue, and even though the sun is shining brightly, it's deceiving when no warmth reaches us. But we're staying active and I haven't noticed the cold other than in my toes.

The hike takes about twenty-five minutes, and since I'm the second to last in line—only ahead of Christopher—I use Maggie's large gasp as a sign that we've made it.

I clear the line of pines, coming to the lookout point on the trail, and echo Maggie's shock. An enormous waterfall towers overhead, but the stream is frozen, white ice caught in mid-fall.

"Take my picture, Paul!" Maggie squeals, tossing her phone to her boyfriend and running up to the partially covered wooden post that keeps hikers from going over the edge and into the crater below.

"That's incredible," Christopher's words are breathed through small pants from the hike, coming to rest beside me.

My eyes trail over his flushed cheeks, the rosy red bright in the winter backdrop, his chocolate brown hair pushed back with flakes of snow hanging onto the ends. When he feels my stare on his profile, he turns to look at me, and I pull my gaze back to the waterfall, still amazed at how it appears to be stuck in the flow of rushing water. It looks like a picture; the moment caught in time for everyone to enjoy.

"Should we take a photo here for the portfolio?" I ask, though I know we didn't plan to include something like this.

Christopher thinks it's a great idea, and my chest warms a bit at an easy conversation returning to us. Once Maggie and Janay take a handful of photos to sort through for their social media accounts, Christopher pulls out his phone, wishing he'd thought to bring his professional camera, and we find the best angle with the waterfall. Christopher takes a few photos while I twist and turn, trying different positions and expressions.

Paul and Billy study us from the side of the trail. I know they're participating in the portfolio contest, too, but neither of them have mentioned it to me. I wonder if they're getting ideas from watching us take pictures for Christopher's portfolio. Now that Christopher and I have claimed this spot for his project, I don't think they'd want to use the same scenery since they are competing against each other. The competitor in me wants to ask them about their portfolios, if only to get a better idea of what we're up against.

"I think I got it," Christopher says, interrupting my train of thought.

He stands up from where he had been kneeling in a patch of snow, his thumb swiping across the screen of his phone to review the photos he took. Like always, I don't ask to see them, wanting to wait until the end to review all the photos laid out together.

"How are your portfolios coming along?" I raise the question, angling my head to where Paul and Billy stand.

A grin splits Paul's face and he shakes his head. He must know exactly what I'm trying to do. "Not happening, Penny."

I give him my best scowl and he laughs.

"He won't even tell me about it," Christopher says as he slips his phone back into his pocket.

"Didn't realize you were so competitive," I say, still trying to loosen some details out of him.

"Come on, Penny. Surely you got that from our snowball fight." Paul nudges Billy with his shoulder, hoping his friend agrees.

"Except you lost the snowball fight, just like you're going to lose the portfolio contest." Billy flings the remark so quickly it takes Paul by surprise.

"Oh, is that so?" Paul boast and the two continue to bicker about who they think will win the contest.

I give up on getting any real information out of them and turn to face the waterfall once more. Leaning against the wooden railing, I let myself get lost in the beauty of Estes Park. Pine trees grow along the rocky sides of the mountain, the rush of frozen water streaming between them.

My breath catches in my throat when a thought seeps into my mind, chilling that part of my heart that had begun to thaw.

I see myself in the waterfall in front of me. My life at Frostard felt like I was spiraling out of control. Like I was the rushing water streaming over the edge and losing my grasp on my life because I let Lindsay dictate everything for me.

But then I came home to Rayou, and it's as if my life hit pause, the roaring water freezing in mid-fall. I'm caught in a frozen descent, just buying time before reality melts the dreamworld I'm living in, and my life continues to tumble out from beneath me, control slipping from my grasp once more.

Returning to Frostard in the fall feels like thawing the waterfall, like letting go of the perfect balance I've found here in Rayou, and for the first time since I came home, I admit to myself that I don't want to go back to Frostard. *Ever.*

I don't want my waterfall to thaw.

"Come on!" Maggie's squeal pulls my gaze from the picture-perfect moment and I see she's pulling Janay along the trail where it twists back into the surrounding woods. I didn't realize there was more to the hike.

"Isn't this the end?" Paul asks and Maggie shakes her head, sending pieces of her red ponytail free.

"You have to see it from the top!" she says.

We all exchange a glance, knowing *from the top* means a steep climb and my already worked muscles want to protest. Still, we follow her down the trail and begin the ascent. As tall as the waterfall appeared, the hike to the top isn't all that long. The path was carved well, so we can take the fastest route. The hardest part is going up the snowy trail, but the hikers who came before us did a good job of clearing the trail down to the dark earth below.

When the ground levels beneath my feet, muddy earth turning into grey stone, my legs wobble, relief filling the muscles at the change in incline. My eyes had been trained on my feet, carefully watching where I was stepping, making sure I didn't twist my ankle or stumble back into Christopher.

So, when we reach flat ground and I look up for the first time, the world almost falls out from under me, my feet shifting back when I realize how high we are. Thankfully, Christopher is behind me, and he throws up an arm to keep me upright. He doesn't say anything. It's just an instinct, and his touch lingers after I've regained my balance, both of our focus turning to the whimsical world around us. We're higher than the surrounding peaks, and are looking down at the valley of snow-covered channels. Branches from the nearby pine trees hang heavy under the weight of the snow, making the white coating look like waves of water, pulling and curving the sides of the mountain like perfect strokes of paint.

"Well, was it worth it?" Maggie asks, surveying all of our shocked faces.

Paul mutters something that makes Maggie's smile only grow. Probably admitting that this view, this moment, was most definitely worth the climb. Maggie and Paul walk away from the edge, following the frozen stream along the mountaintop. Janay has Billy take more pictures of her, posing like she's standing on top of the world. I'm too afraid to walk around up here. This high up has my head spinning and I don't feel all that balanced. I lower myself onto a large boulder that protrudes from the rocky ground, the snow having blown off its surface. I'm welcomed with a subtle warmth that clings to the rock from soaking in the beaming sun above.

Christopher joins me on the rock, pulling his knees to his chest. We sit side-by-side in silence, just observing Estes Park from above, getting lost in the actual winter wonderland that stretches out beneath our feet.

"Are you okay, Penny?" Christopher's words are so soft, they feel like flurries of snow, cold on my skin.

I press my lips in a thin line, contemplating which words I'll choose to say. My gaze stays trained on the pristine world at my feet, watching the branches bend and bob under the weight of the snow.

"What happened with Cynthia?" I ask, sidestepping Christopher's original question, because this is what I really want to know, and it's at the root of what Christopher was getting at, anyway.

His gaze is heavy on my profile, and I fight the urge to meet his stare, to look into those caramel eyes, because I know tears would fill my own.

"Oh my God, Penny, is that why you're giving me the cold shoulder?" Christopher asks, dropping his voice as a serious tone grows in it.

At his shocked proclamation, my eyes deceive me, glancing at his surprised face, mouth hanging ajar. I look away and nod, swallowing against the lump that's growing in my throat.

Christopher looks back over the edge of the mountain, running a frustrated hand through his brown waves. "Nothing happened with

Cynthia," he says, and he pulls his knees closer to his chest. "I didn't realize you cared when the others mentioned her."

I stop myself from blurting that, of course, I care, because I know I shouldn't. Christopher and I aren't dating, and we haven't even talked about being with other people.

"Maggie made it sound like more than nothing happened," I say, not believing Christopher's quick denial. My throat continues to close in on itself, the thought of Cynthia and Christopher in London threatening to suffocate me.

"Penny, look at me." Warm fingers curl around my elbow, squeezing gently.

Tears bloom at the edges of my eyes, making Christopher blurry in my peripheral. I hadn't noticed he'd turned to face me, tucking his right foot onto the rock. I release the tight breath in my lungs, shaking with it as the air flows from me. My eyes drift and meet Christopher's wide gaze, sweeping over my face and seeing all the emotions I'm trying to bottle up and push down.

"I promise you, nothing happened with Cynthia," Christopher says again, and he looks desperate to make me believe him. His grip tightens on my elbow, trying to give it a reassuring squeeze. "I was an absolute wreck in London," he continues, explaining the trip to me. "I couldn't even breathe in that city and not think about you."

Restless butterflies bloom in my chest at his words, soft and muffled by the ache in my lungs, but they try to take flight nonetheless.

Christopher dampens his lips, dropping his gaze from mine for a second while he collects his words, obviously nervous about what he's trying to say. "You and I were supposed to go to London together, and everything there made me think about *you*. Cynthia was a bartender who helped me get back to my hotel room after I had one too many drinks."

His voice is raspy, scratching on the confession, and my ears strain to hear him.

For as long as I've known Christopher, he has never drank alcohol. He avoided it at parties and turned it down anytime someone offered him a glass. The ache in my chest cracks with my heart, now seeing his trip to London in a new light, and for the first time, I get a glimpse at the heartbroken boy I left behind when I went to Frostard.

His eyes are filled with pain as he looks at me. At the person who broke that heart, who caused him all that suffering. I'm the reason he was at the bar that night, why he had one too many drinks.

"I'm sorry, Christopher," I whisper, the tears that welled in my eyes breaking free in large streaks down my cheeks. I have more I want to say, a bigger apology that's been building up every day since I've been home. I owe him so much more than a simple *I'm sorry* after what I did to him.

With his free hand, he reaches up, cupping my cheek and rubbing the tears away with his thumb. "You don't need to apologize, Penny," he whispers, the pain receding in his hazel eyes. "I was mad for a long time, but I understand why you left."

My mouth feels numb, because he doesn't understand at all. I *shouldn't* have left. I never should have broke up with him. I should have been right here. I want to tell him that, but I stop myself, because what would that do? Just reopen old wound and make him realize all that suffering was for nothing? Is it better to just let him stay healed?

"The others had no idea how drunk I was that night," Christopher says when the silence lingers for too long, going back to his story and letting his hand fall from my cheek.

I feel like an idiot for letting the idea of Cynthia affect me. I've spent the last two days overwhelmed with jealousy and hurt when there was no reason to be. I realize why his other friends think something happened between him and Cynthia, because she had helped him back to his room, but they don't the know the real story. I think that makes it that much worse, because Christopher would rather his friends believe he hooked up with a random bartender in London then know he was still heartbroken over the girl who left him for college in California.

The pit in my stomach opens up when I think back to the snowball fight yesterday, to the moment when Christopher almost kissed me, and I pulled away because of something that wasn't even an issue. *What if that was our moment?* What if that was the one chance Christopher was willing to take on me and I ruined it because I really thought he had moved on from me so quickly?

Through the ache in my chest, I feel the warmth of hope grow, that Christopher could still have feelings for me. That he could still want to be together after everything that has happened.

"I should have asked about it sooner," I admit aloud. "I didn't mean to close you out."

"If you had told me it was bothering you, I would have explained," Christopher says.

I rub my eyes, pushing tears away and forcing a rough laugh through my trembling throat. "It seems so silly now," I admit through the shaky breath and the air between us lightens.

Christopher shifts his weight, wrapping his arm around my shoulders, and I lean into his side, resting my head against his. "It's okay," he says, running his hand up and down my forearm.

We sit like that for a minute, and with the winter landscape around us, it's easy to imagine us sitting inside of a snow globe, lost in our own little paradise. Christopher's warmth spreads across my sweatshirt, the scent of coffee and pine thick in the air around him. With his arm around me, my head on his shoulder, it's the closest embrace we've shared in months. It's the closest moment to the way things used to be, and I feel that hope continue to swell inside of me, fully believing that Christopher and I could get back together.

"Penny," Christopher prompts through a sigh. His chest falls, his arm tightening around my shoulders.

"Yeah, Christopher?" I ask, and the anticipation of his next words makes my skin tingle. He's quiet for too long, and I glance up at him through my lashes.

His head is angled, gaze watching me, his mouth ajar. The caramel swirls around the chocolate brown irises sweep across my face. When my blue eyes meet his stare, he blinks, pulling his focus back to the world around us. His throat bobs when he swallows, and he finally responds.

"I'm really glad we're friends."

Even in his arms, a chill slides across my skin, making my stomach sink. I thought he may have been thinking the same as me—that maybe we still have a chance to be together, to try again. *Friends* indicates something completely different. It's a wall drawn in the sand, put up brick by brick that keeps our relationship from becoming anything more than what it's been for the past month.

"Me too," I say, hoping he attests the crack in my voice to the cold burst of wind that just blew up over the edge of the mountain, flipping stray pieces of my blonde hair around my face.

It's true, I am glad that Christopher and I are friends. Not talking to him for six months was unbearable, but my heart wants so much more than a friendship with Christopher. It squeezes in my chest, hurt and defeat heavy in my lungs. Maybe it's time I let the idea of Christopher and me go. The foolish hope is just that, *foolish*. Maybe now, after seven months of being broken up, I should finally let him go.

Chapter 29

T he hike back to the van is fast, far easier going down the terrain than it was coming up, except for Billy, who continuously slips and falls on his butt. I think he slides down the trail more than he walks. The ride back to the cabin is quiet, Paul being outvoted on his musical playlist. We have a chicken noodle soup feast, and after an entire day out in the snowy mountain peaks, it's the perfect dinner.

We all drink hot chocolate in the living room and play a few rounds of cards, filling the cabin with the sounds of our laughter and the crackling fire. Janay and Maggie post the pictures they took at Estes park online and we add each other on social media, though I don't know if I'll ever see them again after this week. I hope I do. They only live one town over, but I have to remind myself that they're Christopher's friends, but then again, I guess that's all I am to Christopher too.

Just another one of his friends.

Hiking through the snow-packed trails wore all of us out, and we all turn in by ten, saying tomorrow will be a lazy day to make up for all the energy Maggie made us exert. She rolls her eyes at that and again says it was worth it, and I agree with her.

Inside the small bedroom downstairs, I change into a pair of cotton shorts and an oversized black crewneck that hangs to my knees, making it look like a dress. I get ready for bed, tying my damp hair from my shower up into a bun on the top of my head, and brush my teeth. I scroll through the different social media apps on my phone for a minute, seeing that Maggie posted another photo, swearing in the caption that this will be the last one. I smile at that and like her post. I click the phone off shortly after that and place it face down on the nightstand, letting it charge while I sleep.

Except I don't sleep. I toss and turn and rearrange the pillows a dozen times, but sleep still doesn't come. This is the only reason I hear the soft rattle outside of my room near midnight. I sit up and look at the wooden door, glowing in a beam of moonlight, thinking I may have lost my mind. Another patter of glasses clinking together rings out, confirming that someone is definitely awake.

I think about laying back down and ignoring it, but curiosity wins out. I throw back the covers and walk across the floor beams, cold beneath my bare feet. When I pull the door open, peering out into the dark cabin—the only light coming from the dying fire—I find Christopher standing in the kitchen over the sink that's spitting out water. His brown hair a mess, cascading in wild brown ripples around his face. In his hand is a mug that had held hot chocolate earlier in the night, now filled with soapy water.

Christopher is doing dishes at midnight.

The door creaks on its hinges when I lean against the doorframe and Christopher snaps his gaze up, peering over the sink and finding me in the shadows of the cabin.

"Did I wake you?" he asks, and his voice sounds rough.

I shake my head and push my hip off the doorframe. "No," I say, striding through the cabin to lean against the bar across from him. Up close, I see the bags beneath his eyes. "Could you not sleep either?" My gaze travels over my shoulder, looking at the pillow on the couch, his cotton white blanket thrown over the back cushions.

"Nope," he says with a sigh. Christopher turns off the sink and reaches for a towel, working meticulously to dry off the mug.

"And these dishes needed to be washed at midnight?" I tease him, a grin finding my tired face.

Christopher gives me a small smile and shrugs. "Someone has to clean them, and I wasn't sleeping, anyway."

"Are you planning to dust the mantel next?"

His warm eyes peer up at me through his lashes, hearing the teasing tone in my voice. "Maybe," he jokes through a toothy smile.

I laugh at that, shaking my head. "Well, if housework is what you want to do, I guess I could help."

"Not tired?" Christopher turns the mug over, setting it next to the other five he has already cleaned.

"Surprisingly, no," I say, and since I know sleep won't find me right now, I might as well do something other than lay in that bed and think about all the ways I've messed up my life. "Maybe doing some of this stuff will help," I add with a shrug.

"Okay," Christopher agrees, his gaze sweeping through the house to survey what he wants to tackle next. "We could put those blankets back," he offers, pointing to the enormous pile we used the day the heater stopped working.

Christopher and I walk through the house to where he stacked them up and each take a handful. I lead Christopher into my guest bedroom and toward the closet in the corner where I originally found them. We toss the pile on the floor and I pull the door open, shifting some of the clothes I hung up to the side so the blankets fit.

"You know what…" Christopher trails off and I look back to see him curiously studying the pile of blankets at our feet.

I stand straighter, a few pieces of my wet hair falling from my bun. "What?" I question, drawing his eyes back to me, a mischievous glint in them.

"We should build a giant fort made out of blankets," he says, the idea bursting past his lips fearlessly.

I blink a few times, looking down at the blankets and then back at Christopher who waits for my response. "Wait, you mean right now?"

"Why not?" Christopher asks, picking up one of the folded blankets to unravel it and examine its size. "Haven't you ever wanted to make one?"

"When I was five," I tease, but a childish sort of energy has ignited in my veins and I'd be lying if I said I didn't like the idea.

Christopher's arms drop, the blanket flopping at his knees. His face falls into a pout and says, "Penny, don't be a party-pooper. Build a fort with me."

I have to bite my lip to stop the smile that wants to grow, but Christopher sees it anyway and tosses me the blanket. I snatch it out of the air, pulling it to my chest. "Fine, but you have to help me take it down," I offer.

"Deal," he agrees and begins to walk around the room, plotting out the best places to secure the blankets.

We work together to tuck and tie the blankets around the edges of the room. The furniture in here isn't very tall, so the fort only stands to my shoulders. Christopher knots the corners of blankets together to make the ceiling of the fort bigger. While he works on the construction of the blankets, I work on the interior of our fort. Picking out the heaviest and softest blankets to spread across the wooden floor. I pull the lamp off the nightstand and tuck it inside of the blanket wall. I toss the pillows from my bed onto the floor and grab additional ones from the living room to act as seats in our fort.

When we're done, we stand with our backs against the wall by the door, admiring the pattern of blankets balancing in the air, tied to bedposts and tucked in doorjambs. Granted, now I can't open the door to my bathroom without collapsing the entire fort, but it is pretty magnificent. The blankets look like a patchwork of waves spreading across the room, hanging like curtains at the front, creating a tent-like slit for the opening. The glow from the lamp inside, makes it appear magical, like something out of a fairytale.

"Should we check it out?" Christopher asks.

"If it falls on me…" I start to tease and Christopher nudges me forward lightly. I drop to my knees and crawl through the opening flap of the tent. The warm, yellow light fills my eyes, taking the place of the shadowy night outside the fort. The blankets are soft beneath my knees and I move to the left side so Christopher can come in beside me.

He's taller than I am, so he has to duck his head a bit further, leaning on his hip and forearm once he's inside. I sit on my knees, taking in the warm bubble of golden light, until I look at Christopher, and then the sight of him pulls my entire focus, making everything around us fade away. His hazel eyes are like liquid gold, bright and child-like, filled with awe as he looks up at the roof of our fort.

He drops his gaze to meet my stare and I ask, "Does it meet your expectations?"

His eyes sweep across me, taking in my blonde bun with stray pieces of hair framing my face and my crystal blue eyes. My breathing stutters when his focus trails down to my lips and goosebumps raise on my arms.

"Surpassed them," he says softly.

In the tight space, Christopher suddenly feels much closer to me, and a group of nervous butterflies flutters in my stomach. I shift under his surveying gaze, reaching for one of the pillows and fluffing it out. "Want to see a surprise?" I ask, noticing he's still watching me.

His eyes narrow a bit, confused. "What do you mean, *surprise?*"

"Lay down," I say, tossing the pillow I'd been fluffing next to its pair at the head of the fort, just to the left of the lamp.

Christopher is already practically laying down to fit inside the fort, so he just rolls onto his back, propping his arm under his head. I lay next to him, my shoulder brushing his and I have to swallow through the breath that catches in my throat. I can't deny the feelings that are still there, the way Christopher sends my heart racing in my chest, a blush flushing my cheeks, but our conversation from on top of the mountain in Estes Park is still fresh in my mind.

I'm really glad we're friends.

"What am I looking at?" Christopher asks, breaking my train of thought. We both stare at the roof of the blanket fort, glowing with the warm light of the lamp.

"Turn off the lamp," I say, tilting my head to look at Christopher.

He studies me out of the corner of his eye before reaching over and twisting the lamp off. In seconds, the fort is swallowed in complete darkness. Even though I can't see Christopher, I can hear his breathing, the sound of it catching in his throat and growing shallow. His arm brushes against mine and my heart erupts at the whisper of his warm skin against me.

"I'm waiting, Penny," Christopher says, his voice breathy.

I squeeze my eyes shut, even though the room is in complete darkness, and tell myself to get it together. I force in a deep breath, making my lungs ache, but my heart steadies itself. I need the thoughts in my head to quiet, because what I'm thinking about doing right now... Alone with Christopher in the dark... It's definitely not something *friends* would do.

I reach for the little black remote I tucked under the blankets that cover the floor and press the top button. The twinkling Christmas lights I found in the closet come to life above our heads, woven through the different sheets and blankets that Christopher tied together.

They glow bright and then fade in a slow rhythm like little shimmering stars. Christopher comes back into view in the soft light, his profile where my eyes are naturally pulled to, not even wanting to look at the twinkling sky overhead. I see the light shift in his wide eyes, their soft, white glow reflecting on his skin, casting shadows along his jaw.

"What do you think?" I whisper.

Christopher turns his head to look at me over the side of his pillow, and again his eyes sweep every inch of my face, surely seeing the lights in my eyes as I see them in his. "It's beautiful," he says softly, eyes never once leaving mine.

My stomach tightens, a burst of warmth spreading through my body because his words feel like they're directed at *me*. With the flickering lights overhead, the air takes on an electric buzz, a sense of energy flowing between the two of us that warns me to rein in my drifting thoughts once more.

"I lied this morning," Christopher says suddenly, catching me by surprise and my mind pulls out of the hazy cloud it was about to get lost in.

"What?" I question, drawing my brows together.

Christopher dampens his lips, lips my mind keeps begging me to kiss, to lean into, to feel their gentle touch again—

"I'm not glad we're friends."

My breath catches in my lungs at his confession, an ache now filling the corners of my chest that had been buzzing with warmth. "You're not?" The words are broken, hurt inching up my throat.

Christopher moves, turning up onto his hip and propping himself with his forearm. He shakes his head, now looking down at me. "No," he says through a heavy sigh, eyes wide with deep brown swirls.

My throat bobs, feeling him slipping from me, dreading what he's about to say. I knew us being friends was farfetched. We have too much past between us. I've seen the way he hurts when I'm near, the way our breakup still haunts him. I thought we were past that, past the awkward silences and stiff looks that made up the beginning of our friendship when I first came home to Rayou.

Christopher reaches forward with his left hand, his fingers finding a piece of my blonde hair that had fallen from my bun, now soft and dry. His eyes follow his fingers and he twists the single curl, gently tucking it back behind my ear.

I hold my breath through each passing second, afraid to do anything in this moment.

Christopher's hand lingers at the side of my face, the tips of his fingers hot against my skin, a trail of warmth spreading in their wake as he traces my jawline. He brings his eyes back to mine, noticing how frozen I am, waiting for him to say or do something. I take in every inch of him hovering over me. The chocolate waves that frame his sharp face, cascading in beautiful strands that look darker in the dim light. His hazel eyes are more brown than normal, like dark storms swirling and sucking in the glittering lights overhead. His lips are parted, silent breaths making his chest rise and fall.

Christopher is as I always remember him. Gorgeous, taking my breath away with every glance. My heart belongs to him. It always has and I fear it always will.

His fingers spread over my cheek, his palm now cupping the side of my face. "I'm not glad we're friends," he says again, his next breath shaking and my skin prickles at the nerves I find in his eyes. "Because I want to be so much more."

My heart pauses in my chest, that ache that weighed me down evaporating. "More?" I question, doubting what he just said, thinking I must be misunderstanding him.

"What I want to do right now," his voice continues to shake, and I realize it's not just nerves that cling to his words, but fear. "Friends wouldn't do."

A heat blooms across my skin, making the spot below my stomach twist. I prop myself up on my elbows, bringing my face to his, closing that distance so his scent of coffee and pine fills my nose.

Christopher has completely changed the direction I thought he was going with his statement, and my heart begins to beat again, racing and skipping irregularly in my chest, but I've been in this moment before. More times than I can count, Christopher and I have found ourselves at this crossroad, but this time I won't run away.

I softly press my forehead to his, my chest rising and falling quickly, because I'm scared too. I don't know what this means for us, but I know that I want Christopher to be a part of my life for as long as I live.

When my forehead meets his, Christopher sucks in a sharp breath, his hand sliding back to the nape of my neck. His touch anchors me to him, strong and familiar, and it makes my next words easier to say.

"I'm not turning away this time, Christopher," I whisper, and he shudders against me when I say his name. I close my eyes, the lids fluttering shut on their own, and I let us balance in this embrace, my lips a mere breath from his, but I don't close that distance.

That is Christopher's step to take. *I broke his heart.* I am the one who put that fear in his chest. It has to be his decision to make this jump.

We stay like this for a second, and I fall very still, laying myself and my feelings bare to him. He knows what I want, but his next moves will confirm what it is *he* wants.

When he lifts his forehead from mine, pulling back, my heart sinks in my chest, disappointment welling in my throat, until a soft kiss meets my cheek.

My eyes snap open. It's so gentle, just a whispered breath, and it startles me. Christopher's eyes are silver-lined with tears, shimming in the pretend stars above. His gaze drifts down to my lips that are parted with surprise, and I see the shift in his hazel irises, the caramel swirls coming out, and I know he's going to kiss me. He doesn't pull away like he did in his truck after the Winter Wonderland dance. He doesn't give in to the fear that's been holding him back.

Christopher leans in, takes the jump, and presses his lips to mine.

They're soft and warm, and even though this isn't our first kiss, it feels like it could be, because something is different this time. The raw emotions hanging in the air around us energize the moment, making my skin warm and my heart pound in my chest. I reach up, placing my hand at the side of his face, and I curl my fingers into his brown waves.

As I kiss him, I pull him closer to me. His body shifts, long legs intertwining with mine, and our exposed skin is hot, sending sparks behind my closed eyelids. I lay back onto the pillow, Christopher's chest on top of mine, and the weight of his body fully presses against me. The kiss that started gentle grows surer, our mouths moving together, remembering the other. His tongue meets mine and I nearly fall apart right then. To be this close to him again, to be able to *kiss* him, feel him on me, awakens that part of me that I tried to close the door to, the part of my heart that has always beat for him, and I'm overwhelmed with a sense of desire that makes my head spin. It's like being in a drought for years, and he is my first drink of water.

I'm not sure who pulls back first. We may both do it at the same time, our breathing hard, lungs begging for more air. His hand slips out from behind my head, and his feather-light touch trails my arm until it comes to rest against my hip.

Christopher's eyes never waver from my own. "Penny." He says my name through his rough breathing and a chill sparks across my entire body. He swallows against his racing heart to force out his next words. "I'm scared."

His confession makes my pulse slow, pulling some reality back into our small blanket fort. My hand still cups his face, and I brush my thumb over his cheek. "I am too," I whisper, being completely honest with him. The unknown terrifies me, and there is nothing more unknown than the future, especially anything relating to me and Christopher.

"I want every piece of you, Penny. Right now, I want all of you," he says, biting his lip while his next words process. "But I don't want to lose you again. I can't—"

He locks his eyes on mine, leaving his final words unsaid, but my head races to fill them. *I can't lose you. I can't go through that pain again.*

"You're not going to lose me," I say, and even though I have no idea how I can ensure that, I do know that I don't want to leave him. I never want to spend another day without his charming smile, without hearing the sound of his deep laugh, feeling his arms around my waist. I don't know what tomorrow, or next week, or next month holds for me, but I know that I want Christopher to be by my side through it all, and I will do anything to make that possible.

Christopher dips his head, pressing one long and hard kiss to my lips. His hand slips below the hem of my sweatshirt, his warm palm pressing into the skin at my waist. He pulls his lips from mine, looking at me with glossy hazel eyes. "Don't break my heart again, Penny."

The sting of tears threatens the edges of my own eyes, and my breath shakes in my trembling throat at seeing him so emotional and open with me. I slide my hand down from his cheek and press it to his chest, the fabric of his shirt soft. My touch rests there, right above the heart he's offering to me once more. His pulse is concerning, the thumping of his heart hard against my hand, but I know my own mirrors the thunderous beats.

My eyelids flutter up so I can look at him when I speak my next words, hoping he can see the truth in them, and let his fear go.

"I promise, I won't," I say, again not knowing how I can possibly keep that promise to him, but knowing with every inch of my body that I will try my hardest to do so. "Christopher, I—"

His lips are back on mine, cutting me off before I can get the rest of my words out. It's a short and quick kiss, and when he pulls back, his words rush from his mouth. "Penelope Wilson, I love you."

A warm blush burns my cheeks that are pulled tight with my widening smile. "I wanted to say it first," I pout lightly, the tears that built in my eyes releasing with my smile.

"I know," Christopher says, the corner of his mouth tugging up, "But you said it first last time."

I think back to that night two years ago that started all of this. He's right, I had told him I loved him first that time around. The funny thing is, I never stopped loving him, even during all those months apart, but this still feels like a new beginning. Like everything we're doing is for the first time all over again.

I tilt my head back, offering him a quick kiss and I let him have his moment. I look into his hazel eyes, eyes I'd know anywhere, eyes that I've memorized, mapping out where the caramel swirls meet the deepest browns. "I love you too, Christopher."

We move in sync, bringing our mouths back together, and Christopher shifts his weight until he rests on top of me, a leg on either side, and his hands begin to roam my body. His fingers work slowly, tracing my curves and climbing my waist. It's as if he's taking in every inch of me, every part of me he used to touch, and remembering the way I feel. We reach for the hems of our shirts at the same time, separating the kiss for only a second, before resuming with his bare chest against mine.

I trace his spine with my fingers, and run my hands down the muscles in his arms. I love the way they flex beneath my touch, so much strength, and yet his hands are gentle on me. He makes me shiver and that space below my stomach swoops at the pressure of him against me.

When his mouth breaks from mine, he moves to leave a trail of kisses down my neck, my back instinctively arching, pressing me into him.

"I'm going to make up for every second we spent apart," Christopher promises against my shoulder before pressing another kiss to my hot skin.

I shift beneath him, my body swelling at what he means by those words, thinking about all that time we lost. Without a doubt in my mind, I know leaving Frostard in January was the best decision I've ever made.

It may be the only decision I've ever made for myself, but it was the best, and I know I don't have a single regret, especially since it brought me back to Christopher. Back to the boy I love, who resides in my every waking thought and is the reason I smile every day. To the boy who has saved me more times than I can count, who has always loved me for who I am, and has never given up on me.

I lift my hands away from his shoulders, letting his kisses travel further down my body and find the small remote above my head.

Christopher looks up at me through his lashes, a gorgeous smile spreading his lips wide, making my heart erupt. I slide my thumb over the button, and at the dip of his chin, turn off the lights.

Chapter 30

The sunlight barely reaches us, the beams warming the other sides of the blankets that crisscross overhead. My pillow is soft beneath my cheek, and I let my eyelids flutter closed again, not wanting to get up. Christopher must feel me stir, because the arm that's draped over my waist tightens, pulling my bare back into his warm chest. His chin tucks in against my shoulder and he sighs into me, making my heart stutter in my chest.

Last night hardly feels real. The fact that Christopher is laying behind me is also hard to grasp. I twist in his embrace so that I'm facing him, my nose brushing his as I turn. Christopher's sleepy eyes look me over, that same unbelieving feeling lingering with him. After everything we've been through, we've found our way back to each other, back to where we were always supposed to be.

"Morning," I say, nudging his nose with mine.

His smile grows, skin glowing in the dim light. "Good morning," he says.

Christopher drops his chin and presses his lips to mine, unable to keep himself from closing that distance. I think he means it to be a quick embrace, something sweet, but at the touch of his warm mouth to mine, a liquid fire turns in my blood, desire waking in my veins. I kiss him back, that gentle touch now a passionate exchange and when we break apart, I can tell both of our breathing has grown weak.

"We don't have to get up, right?" Christopher asks, moving his hand to brush a stray piece of my hair out of my face.

I'm about to confirm his thought, wanting to do nothing more than lay here with him, but the growl of my stomach interrupts me, having a mind of its own.

"Or maybe we get some breakfast," Christopher offers instead, a sleepy grin tugging at his lips.

"And then we can come back to our fort," I tack on, wanting to stay hidden in here with him forever. What lies on the other side of these blanket walls still scares me. Reality is cruel, and I know it has the power to break whatever fragile relationship Christopher and I are building. We sit up, finding the clothes we'd discarded last night. When Christopher reaches for his black t-shirt, I see the muscles in his back pull and stretch along his shoulders and arms, rippling with the strength that held me last night.

"It's not polite to stare, Penny," Christopher taunts over his shoulder, and he must feel my gaze lingering on him.

I snap my hoodie at him, hitting him on the side of his head playful. "Oh, shut up," I grumble and pull the warm fabric over my head, hugging the soft material to me in the absence of Christopher's arms.

I follow him from the tent, crawling and then standing once we're on the other side. I'm a bit disappointed by the look of the fort in the daylight, not nearly as magical as it had seemed last night. Christopher's hand finds mine, his fingers intertwining with my own and he squeezes, his gaze on me and not our fort.

I look from the patchwork of blankets to his loving stare, realizing I don't really care that it isn't as magnificent as I had thought it was, because it's still ours. It's where our hearts found each other again.

With my hand in his, I reach for the door, pulling it open and stepping out into the living room.

Four pairs of wide eyes instantly lock with mine, then drift to Christopher.

Billy, Paul, Maggie, and Janay sit on the couch facing the bedroom door, coffee mugs in their hands.

Christopher and I freeze like deer in headlights, like a child caught doing something they weren't supposed to do. Reality splashes cold against my face. Everything about the trip and the portfolio and his friends comes back to us so fast it shocks us into frozen statues.

For a moment, we all balance in this bubble of surprise, and every muscle in my body grows stiff, unsure of what to do because all of this with Christopher feels too fragile. Like one more step could bring it crashing down.

"It's about time," Paul says, shattering the silence and raising his porcelain mug in a toast.

A surprised laugh bursts from my lungs, the air I'd locked inside rushing out. And suddenly, everything in me relaxes. The air warms, the flickering fire reaching me, and I'm no longer scared of what's going to happen next. Christopher leans over, pressing a kiss to my cheek and his hand squeezes mine.

"You got that right," he mutters, pulling me alongside him as we make our way to the kitchen.

I look over my shoulder at his friends, who all share the wide smile that Paul wears, raising their coffee mugs in a toast to that.

Christopher and I grab our own mugs for coffee, and I do my best to recreate the drink I get from the Snowcapped Diner, but it's not nearly as good as when they make it. We join his friends in the living room, taking our place on the small couch that faces the fireplace. I tuck my feet up onto the cushion, leaning into Christopher's side easily, his arm draping over my shoulders.

We talk about what we want to do for the day, and for our remaining time here at the cabin. Maggie and Janay demand they get at least one day to enjoy the hot tub without being bombarded with snowballs. Billy and Paul agree on one condition. The boys get to take the van and have their own day trip. Billy doesn't disclose many details, but it seems like he has a destination in mind. Really, I just want to spend my time with Christopher, to make up for all that time we lost. But it seems like I'll be getting a hot tub day with Maggie and Janay.

After our discussion, Christopher, Billy, and Paul go to get ready for whatever adventure Billy has planned. I stay by the fire, sipping on my coffee and letting my mind wander back to last night. To Christopher and me hidden in our blanket fort, what we did and what it means for us moving forward.

Two strong arms loop around my shoulders from behind the couch, and Christopher leans forward, pressing the side of his face to mine. "Hey," he says, and at the single word, the second I hear his voice, my stomach does somersaults. "If you don't want me to go with them, I can stay here."

I glance at him, only seeing his profile. I think Christopher may want me to tell him to stay, to give him an excuse to spend the whole day with me, because I can tell he wants to make up for that lost time too.

"Christopher!" Billy calls from the porch, the wooden front door swung open. "Let's go!"

I laugh at his timing and Christopher's head falls forward, his arms tightening around my shoulders. "It's okay. As long as I get you all day tomorrow, I guess I can let you go," I say, my hand finding his forearm to give him a reassuring squeeze.

He groans, the sound muffled in the back of the couch. "Penny, you're supposed to tell me to stay."

I laugh again and pinch his arm, causing him to unwrap himself from me. "I can't ruin Billy's plan. He seems awfully excited."

"That's the problem," Christopher sighs, but he makes his way around the couches and toward the door, picking up his denim jacket and pulling it on over his sweatshirt, the material tight against his broad shoulders. "I'll see you later."

I curl deeper into the couch and nod as I bring my coffee mug back to my lips. "Can't wait to hear all about it," I call as he leaves.

The cabin is quiet and I turn my gaze to the dying fire, letting the crackling sound of the embers fill the hole that Christopher's absence leaves. I'm only alone for a second before the wooden staircase creaks beneath Maggie and Janay's steps. They bound down the stairs, turning on the handrail, and stride toward the living room.

"We need to talk," Janay says, and the hairs on my arms raise at the sharpness in her voice.

"About?" I prompt her, bouncing my eyes between Janay and Maggie.

Both girls are in their swimsuits, towels tied around their chests, and they flop down on the couch across from me.

"About Christopher," Maggie says, and her voice is her usual soft tone, giving me hope that I may not be in the middle of an interrogation. She reaches for a piece of her red hair and twirls it around her finger, almost looking nervous about what they're about to say.

"What about Christopher?"

"About how you better not break his heart again." Janay's words are almost like a slap, and I flinch at their impact.

"Janay," Maggie hisses, nudging her with her shoulder. Maggie brings her bright blue eyes back to me, obviously seeing the effect of Janay's words on my face. She sighs back into the couch and lets that strand of her hair fall free. "Penny, we were with Christopher in London," she says, her words dropping with sadness. "He was an absolute disaster."

My heart clenches in my chest at the thought, and I feel every ounce of blame Janay and Maggie are pushing on my shoulders, but of course, it *is* my fault. I am completely responsible for every ounce of pain I inflicted on Christopher. He didn't think they noticed how distraught he was in London, but he was wrong.

"It's taken him a long time to get back to the guy you see now," Janay cuts in, her tone still sharp, but she's lowered her voice, no longer boasting her words. "We just—" She presses her lips together, eyes surveying me from head to toe, much like she did the night I entered the cabin at the beginning of spring break. Now I understand why she was so distant from me then. Because I hurt her friend and she doesn't know if she can trust me.

"We just don't want to see him get hurt again," Maggie finishes for Janay.

I swallow through the knot in my throat and finally speak, feeling the pause in their confrontation as my time to respond. "I don't either."

Maggie and Janay study me very closely, and I can tell they're trying to decide if they believe me, if they can trust me not to hurt Christopher again. I look back at the fire just as one of the burning logs shifts, sending a storm of sparks erupting from the embers. "Can I tell you something?" I turn to the two girls, seeing their trained eyes haven't left me. "But you can't tell Christopher."

They look between themselves, a sense of worry flickering in their eyes. Without speaking to each other, they turn to me and lean forward, elbows on their knees. "What?" Janay prompts me.

I lick my lips, tightening my fingers around the mug. I've been thinking about this for weeks now, maybe not knowingly, but ever since Christopher took me to the Rayou Community College campus, the idea has been floating around in my head.

"I know what I want now," I say, breaking the tense air that fell in my silence. "When I broke up with Christopher last summer and went to Frostard, I had no idea where my life was going. I didn't even care enough to figure it out for myself and instead, let my friend, Lindsay, dictate everything I did."

Janay gives me a hum that tells me to continue with where I'm taking this.

"But now I know. I love Christopher. I always have, and I'm not going to break his heart again." My voice begins to tremble, an overwhelming wave of emotions washing over me because everything is about to change. I have my life gripped in my hands, and I'm finally making the decisions. "I'm not going to leave again." My gaze had drifted down to my coffee, but now I pull it back up to look at Janay and Maggie. "I'm going to enroll in classes at Rayou Community College."

After I tell them about my intentions to stay in Rayou for the time being, their mood instantly changes. I think they realize just how serious I am about being in a relationship with Christopher. That I would move my life back to Rayou so we wouldn't have the issue of long distance again.

I hold back the fact that Christopher is only a small percentage of the reason why I want to leave Frostard. I'm making the change for myself and the life I want to live. Rayou is home. It's where my family is. The things that matter most to me are here, and I truly have no idea what degree I even want to get. My only idea for the future is getting a job at my dad's sales company, but maybe that's not what is best for me either. Will this decision put me behind all of my other peers? Yes, but there's nothing wrong with that. Life isn't a race, it's an experience, and if there's anything this spur-of-the-moment trip home has taught me, it's that I'm ready to experience it for myself instead of seeing it through someone else's eyes.

Doubt tries to weigh me down, but Janay and Maggie are so excited when I tell them, it immediately makes me more confident about my decision. They are a bit confused why I don't want Christopher to know, until I explain that I want to make sure it's official before I tell him. I know he's going to be so happy to find out that I'm not leaving, that this relationship has the possibility to be something real.

There's a lot that has to happen before I'll feel comfortable letting Christopher know. First of all, I have to tell my parents, convince them that this is the best decision for me, and then I have to try and transfer my classes, make sure there's room in the courses I'll take at Rayou, figure out what classes I need to enroll—

My brain stops there because just thinking about everything I have to do to make this happen is exhausting.

Maggie and Janay promise me it'll be an easy transition, and they give me the contact information for an advisor at the community college. They even walk me through the website and locate all the forms I'll need.

After all their help, how could I not grant them a girl's day in the hot tub?

While we soak in the warm water, steam curling around us, they share stories from their time at Rayou Community College, what they are excited about for next year, and even discuss some of the general classes we might take together. It feels good to finally make decisions for myself and be surrounded by people who support them. I can tell that these moments are the beginning of our friendship. That Maggie, Janay and I are about to have an awesome year at Rayou Community College, and I am going to have friends that support me. I'm even finding myself wishing I didn't have to wait until August to start classes.

When the boys return from their mystery adventure, it's late and we are already inside, showered, and in pajamas on the couch with a romantic comedy playing on the television mounted above the fireplace. The boys join us, each couple taking a couch. Billy even makes some popcorn. I curl up next to Christopher, one of the heavy blankets that had made up the floor of our fort wrapped around us. I ended up taking the fort down this morning because I needed to get into my bathroom. It was a little sad to see it go, but the memory of it will stay with me for a long time.

"What did you do today?" I whisper, keeping my voice below the movie.

Christopher turns his head to whisper in my ear, his words traveling along the side of my face. "Billy says I'm not allowed to tell you."

I pull back a bit, looking into his glossy hazel eyes that make me catch my breath every time I stare into them. "Why not?" I ask.

The corner of Christopher's mouth tugs up. "Does it matter? The entire time I was gone, I just kept wishing I was right here."

My heart thuds out of sync in my chest, and I almost let that charming answer make me forget my question, almost let that compliment distract me. "Not falling for that. Tell me," I whisper a bit louder.

"I'm being honest, Penny," Christopher says as his grin pulls wider. "We went ziplining."

"*Ziplining*?" I gasp, my hushed voice forgotten, and everyone in the living room looks at me.

"Christopher!" Billy groans "You weren't supposed to tell anyone."

"He didn't even make it ten minutes," Paul adds on.

"You went ziplining?" Janay questions, obviously jealous she wasn't invited.

The rest of them erupt in conversation, questions and stories bouncing between Janay and Maggie with Billy and Paul, but my eyes still rest on Christopher, his focus never drifting, his gaze still glimmering from the forgotten movie on the television screen. His lips pull in a smile I'm dying to kiss.

"So, what did *you* do today?" Christopher asks, our conversation falling below the other's.

Now it's my turn to grin at him, so big dimples form on my cheeks. "Can't tell you," I tease with the roles reversed.

His jaw drops playfully, and he tries to get me to tell him, and eventually, I do. I tell him about the hot tub and cleaning up the bedroom. I tell him about the other two movies Maggie, Janay, and I have already watched today, but I don't tell him about my plan to transfer to Rayou Community College. I'll keep that secret for a little while longer.

Chapter 31

The next day, Christopher and I do an impromptu photo shoot around the cabin. It's my idea to capture our time here and use it in the portfolio. The point of the competition is to take pictures that evoke emotion, and right now, this isolated haven we've been living in holds my heart.

We start on the porch, Christopher liking the way the dark logs of the cabin contrast to the white snow. I pose and walk around in my mustard coat and leather boots. We take some really impressive action shots where I blow a handful of snow at the camera, and Christopher thinks they'll go over well with technical points. After that, we venture into the neighboring woods and find a frozen pond to take the last of our pictures.

The photo shoot is fun, and will definitely add to his portfolio, but I think his real motive was to find time for us to be alone. Christopher sits on a fallen tree at the edge of the frozen pond, the snow from a few days ago already melted from its rotting bark. He pats the spot next to him and I sit, extending my legs in front of me and crossing my feet at my ankles.

"Still don't want to see the pictures?" Christopher asks, holding his camera close to his face to keep the glare off the display screen.

"Nope," I click, shaking my head once, flipping my blonde curls wildly around my shoulders. I catch a smile tug at Christopher's lips as he examines a picture and the temptation to sneak a peek grows, but I stay strong and turn my gaze to the branches of pine needles overhead.

"If you insist," he sings, clicking off the camera and hanging it around his neck. The birds chirping in the neighboring trees fill the space between us and, after a moment, Christopher says, "Are you ready to go back to Rayou?"

"No," I answer so fast Christopher barely has his mouth closed.

"You like it up here at the cabin?"

"I like it away from reality," I correct, my words carrying the bite of honesty.

"What do you mean?" Christopher asks, though I'm sure he can figure it out.

I take in a deep breath, the cold air burning my lungs. "It's just," I start to say through my exhale, "who we are up here... I'm scared that's not who we'll be back in Rayou. In reality, where life will take over again." I turn and meet Christopher's hazel eyes studying me.

He reaches for my hand, linking his gloved fingers with mine. "This isn't going to change when we leave on Saturday." He leans closer to me, pressing his forehead to my temple. "I promise, Penny. The way I feel now has nothing to do with being away from reality."

"I just don't want you to change your mind about us because a lot of it is unknown, and whenever we leave, all those problems become real again." The words race from my mouth, and my pulse picks up, but when Christopher's grip on my hand tightens, my anxiety quiets.

"We're not moving backward again, Penny. I swear, nothing back in Rayou is going to change my mind." His voice quivers, that emotion peeking through. He's desperate for me to believe him and I think it's because the idea of us moving backward is scarier to him than taking the risk to be together again.

I turn to face him, pressing my forehead to his. "Promise?" I whisper.

"I promise." Christopher's lips meet mine, sealing our words with a kiss that heats my cheeks and makes my heart leap into my throat.

His lips are warm despite the cold around us, and I lean into them, moving my mouth against his, that blush now heating me from head to toe. Christopher's hand is on my hip, tugging me up from the log. I follow his touch, rotating myself so I settle on his lap, a leg on either side of him.

"I love you, Penny," He mutters against my mouth and through our heated kiss.

I run both of my hands through his brown waves, soft and thick. "I love you, too," I breathe, and then I bring our kiss back together, opening my mouth to him.

His muscles are flexed beneath me, strong hands on my waist and gliding up my back, and despite the warmth radiating from him, I shiver at his touch. Everything about Christopher sends my mind spiraling away, and even though we dated for nearly two years, the last three days with him have felt like an entirely different kind of love. I get lost in every inch of him; his scent of coffee and pine that makes me dizzy, the taste of him on my lips, his strong body against mine. Everything about our relationship is more passionate this time, the sense of desire stronger, the need to kiss him intoxicating.

Because we both know what it's like to lose the other.

When Christopher's hands slide along my thighs, I suck in a gasp of frigid air, our hot breaths fogging around us. His laugh at my reaction is soft, the sound vibrating his chest against mine that's rising and falls rapidly, having taken off the second he touched me, like a shock of electricity lives on those fingertips.

The noon sun is bright overhead, peering through the opening in the trees around the pond and making Christopher's skin glow, his hazel eyes swirling with caramel streaks. It only lasts a second, this pause in our moment where I just look at him, absolutely amazed that he's really here, that we've somehow put our relationship back together, and then my stomach starts to sink, that joy settling into fear that the boy I'm looking at, the one I gave my heart to, could be gone at any minute. That life could swing in and destroy everything we've put back together.

I curl my fingers into the front of his denim jacket and pull him to me, pressing my lips back to his. A hunger fills my veins that comes with this fear, that this could be our last kiss. The last time he looks at me, runs his hands through my blonde curls, cups my cheeks, tells me he loves me—

I hate endings. More than anything in the entire world, and if Christopher and I were a book, I know the story well. I'd read the ending once before, and it broke every piece of me. As his familiar lips move against mine, hands I know well squeezing my thighs, trailing my curves, I know I've been here before, I've lived these pages with him already. It feels like I'm rereading our story, but this time, I won't read the last page.

We leave the cabin that Saturday, embarking on our long drive back to Rayou, and just like Christopher promised, nothing changes between him and me. We play our alphabet game on the way home, stopping for food and taking pictures on each of our phones. He reaches over and lets his hand linger on my knee while he drives, his thumb moving in sweeping circles that calm me instantly.

On our way home to Rayou, Mr. Riley emails his students saying their Monday class will be canceled, actually giving them another day of spring break. Apparently, Mr. Riley's flight from Bora Bora got delayed. I want to be surprised that Mr. Riley would go all that way for Spring Break, but then I remember the professor walking in with sandals that first day I sat in his class at the beginning of February, and I realize that nothing he does could really surprise me anymore. Since Christopher has Monday off, we decide we want to do our ice skating photo for the portfolio, but it makes my heart skip when Christopher calls it a date.

Mom is excited to see me when Christopher drops me off in the afternoon until she sees all the laundry I brought back with me. The second the door swings shut behind me, my mom asks the question I knew was coming.

"So, are you and Christopher still just friends?"

I don't know how she knows, but immediately she dials in on the fact that something is different. I think she may have seen me kiss him goodbye in his truck, but either way, I tell her the truth. "We're actually dating again, I think," I say, dragging my duffle behind me as I head for the laundry room.

"You don't say," she sings with sarcastic surprise.

It gets a tired laugh out of me and I shrug. "Yeah, yeah," I groan playfully. I unzip my duffle and begin to shovel the clothes out of the bag and into the washing machine. Mom walks up to the laundry room, resting her hip against the doorframe, and my skin prickles at the feeling of her stare on me. After I've piled half the clothes in the machine, I stand up and look at her, meeting the bright blue eyes we share. "What?"

My mom shrugs, but it looks forced, like she's trying to put emphasis on the fact that what she's about to say doesn't really matter, even though it does. "I'm just wondering what this is going to mean for Frostard."

I reach for the detergent, giving myself an excuse to drop her sweeping gaze. I could tell her what my plans really are. That I want to enroll at Rayou Community College. I need to tell her, but after the week at the cabin, and the exhausting drive back, I don't think I have the energy to do it right now. I bite the inside of my cheek and shrug. "I don't know, yet," I lie.

I pour the detergent in and start the washing machine, letting a few quiet moments pass before I bring my gaze to hers. My mom studies me with crystal blue eyes that threaten to shatter the lie I just told her, to try and dig deeper and see what I'm really thinking. She must understand that today isn't the day I want to discuss the complexities of Christopher and me getting back together, and her narrow eyes lift, letting go of the interrogation she was debating about having.

"I've got your favorite meal in the oven," she says brightly, pushing her hip off of the doorframe and spinning toward the kitchen.

I tell myself that I can figure out transferring to Rayou Community College on a different day. I want to make sure I have all the research done before I approach my mom and dad about the plan, and I definitely want to shower and sleep in my own bed before going down that road. I follow my mom into the kitchen where the unmistakable smell of lasagna fills the room, making my stomach growl on entry.

We fill our plates and sit at the bar, that last bit of tension in the air seeping away when my mom changes the conversation. "So, did you take any pictures on the trip?"

A smile fills my face at the thought of all the moments I captured, and I pull my phone out of my pocket. While we eat our dinner, I show her all the pictures I took at the cabin and the day we hiked at Estes Park. I tell her about Billy and Paul and how they are in Christopher's photography class. She loves the picture Janay, Maggie, and I took together this morning on the porch before we left and I tell her about them too. I relive some of my favorite moments from this past week, sharing stories of the snowball fight. My mom soaks up the details, letting me go on and on about what an amazing week it was.

"I'm really glad you had a good time, Penny," my mom says, pushing her empty plate forward so she can cross her arms and lean against the bar. My mom tilts her head to look at me, short blonde hair falling over her left shoulder. "After everything you've been through recently, I'm so happy you had a good time."

I think I see tears fill the edges of her eyes, but before I can tell, she stands, wrapping an arm around my shoulder and kisses me on the top of my head.

"You deserve to be happy, Penny."

Mom pulls back, reaching for our plates and rounds the counter to rinse them off in the sink. I let her words warm my chest, and the nerves that flood my veins at the idea of telling her about transferring to Rayou Community College lift just a bit.

Chapter 32

"P enny!" My mom's voice travels up to my room, trailing behind the ringing doorbell. "Christopher is here!"

I curse beneath my breath when the hair elastic snaps and hits my wrist. "Be down in a minute!" I yell back, holding my hair up with my left hand while I dig through the drawer on the bathroom vanity for another hair tie.

My mom thought it would be nice to invite Christopher over for breakfast today since Mr. Riley's class was canceled. I wanted to be ready when Christopher got here so I could be a buffer between him and my mom. Who knows what kind of questions she's going to ask him about our break up and how we got back together?

Another elastic band connects with my fingers and I pull it from the drawer, securing my ponytail at the top of my head. I take a second to survey my reflection, the pink sweater a thick knit that emphasizes the soft blush on my cheeks, nearly reaching the corners of my blue eyes. My black leggings are a neutral choice, perfect for our date at the ice skating rink this afternoon. It's the last photo we plan to take for the portfolio, but something feels different about this moment, since we're no longer getting together to work on something for Christopher's class, but to go out as a couple. I grab my phone off the nightstand and bound down the stairs, my fuzzy socks muting my steps.

"*Mmm*," I hum the second I turn down the narrow hall leading to the kitchen, the sweet aroma of syrup and pancakes filling the house.

Christopher sits in the barstool at the counter, my mother pulling a plate of sausage from the microwave.

"Has Penny seen that?" my mom asks, obviously directing her question to Christopher who leans back on the barstool comfortably.

"Seen what?" I ask, entering the kitchen and climbing onto the barstool next to Christopher.

His hand finds my knee under the counter and he squeezes as a welcome, giving me a small smile. His hazel eyes look me over like he hasn't seen me in weeks. I know the blush on my cheeks only brightens, but it's hard to care when he looks at me like that.

"The photos he's using in the portfolio," my mom says, answering my question and bringing the plate of sausage to us.

"Oh, no, I don't want to see them until it's finished," I say, plopping two sausage links onto my plate.

"Really?" mom asks, letting Christopher take two sausage links as well. "Okay, I won't spoil the surprise," she says, her eyes catching Christopher's, a smile shimmering in them.

"You showed her?" I ask and Christopher nods toward his phone on the counter.

"I wanted her opinion on which ones I should include," he explains.

"If the judges don't select your portfolio, the contest is rigged," my mom says, pointing her spatula at Christopher as she approaches us with a tower of pancakes.

I agree with her, even though I haven't seen any of the photos, and Christopher tells us we're both biased. Which we are. We eat our breakfast, the conversation light and easy, not at all confrontational like I thought it would be.

"What are your plans for the day?" my mom asks while rinsing her plate off in the sink.

"We're going to the school to help Christopher's mom in the office," I say, hopping down from the barstool to retrieve my brown leather boots from the mudroom.

I try and hide the nervous bob in my throat when I mention Christopher's mom. Every time I try to think about talking to either of his parents about how I broke up with him in August, but am back together with him now, I break out in a clammy sweat.

The mound of laundry I had from spring break still sits piled up in a basket, but at least it's clean. I hear my mom ask Christopher how his family is doing while I slip my shoes on and grab my winter coat from its hook as I go back into the kitchen.

"Do you need any help at the library?" I ask.

My mom stands up, pulling the dishwasher door closed. "If you have nothing better to do, I could use some extra hands. It might also include lunch. Not that I'm bribing you," she says, the corner of her mouth pulling up in an easy smile.

I laugh at that and Christopher and I tell her we'll stop by on our way to the ice-skating rink. "Ready to go?" I ask Christopher and he nods, standing up and thanking my mom for breakfast. She brushes off his gratitude and tells us to have a good time. Christopher grabs his jean jacket off the barstool and shoves his arms into the sleeves as we make our way to the front of the house.

"Drive careful!" Mom calls from the kitchen, letting us know it got below freezing last night, and all the slushy snow that was trying to melt may have turned into ice.

"Bye Mom!" I call back, finishing with the buttons on my coat.

I reach for the handle of the front door and pull it open. My eyes lift to a tall brunette standing on the porch, her hand frozen in the air, hovering by the doorbell. My body locks up with shock and Christopher nearly knocks me over.

Lindsay Bradley stands on my front porch. Childhood best friend, Lindsay. Cheerleading co-captain, Lindsay. Frostard roommate, Lindsay.

Her brown eyes lift from my shocked face to find Christopher behind me and her gaze widens, an ugly laugh crackling through the still moment.

"Shut the front door!" she gawks, dropping her stare to me. Her eyes glance at my actual front door and she shakes her head once, long, pin-straight brown hair falling around her shoulders. "No, seriously," she barks through another sharp laugh. "Shut the front door and let's try this again, because there is no way your ex-boyfriend is standing behind you like we've just time traveled back to senior year."

"What are you doing here?" I ask, my voice weak with my thinning breaths.

Her eyes darken and her nose scrunches with hurt. "What am I doing here?" she repeats, the words like daggers. She lifts her perfectly manicured hand and warps it around the strap of her purse that hangs on her shoulder, a rosy pink that matches her winter coat. "No *Hey Lindsay*, or a hug, or *I've missed you*?"

The shock on my brain begins to thaw now that I've registered Lindsay is standing on my porch, and I realize how bizarre this must look to her. "Sorry, I'm just surprised to see you," I say.

"Well, maybe if you'd answer your phone," she shoots and I bite the inside of my cheek, remembering that I silenced her number when I got to Rayou and completely forgot about it. "I came here to see what the hell happened to you," she continues, eyes that could cut steel lifting back to Christopher. "I thought you may need a rescue plan to get you back to California."

"No saving needed," I mutter softly, crossing my arms as the cold wind begins to twirl beneath my coat.

"I beg to differ," she counters and my stomach sinks at the thought of disappointing her, of Lindsay not being satisfied with me.

The air grows stiff between us, Christopher and I staring at Lindsay, her judgmental gaze sweeping up and down. Finally, I break the silence and glance back to Christopher, his chest brushing my back in a blanket of warmth that makes me strong enough to say these words. "You should go. I'll call you later."

His hazel eyes look into my blue stare, like he's seeing through me and into my mind, like he could telepathically talk to me and ask me if I'm sure I want to be alone with Lindsay right now.

Lindsay breaks his stare by stepping to the side of my door, the porch creaking beneath her white furry boots, and opening a clear path for Christopher to leave. He swallows, tight throat bobbing, and I can see the fear in him that's rising in my chest. After a second, Christopher steps around me, dragging his hand across my waist. The touch is as light as a feather, and he descends the steps of the porch, making his way to his red truck parked at the end of my driveway, Lindsay's white sedan is parked behind him. I watch Christopher go for a moment longer, tracing the tracks he leaves in his wake on the slushy snow across the front yard.

"Well, are you going to let me in?" Lindsay asks, stepping back in front of the doorway that I'm blocking.

My lips press together as I look back at Lindsay and I think I may be sick. Christopher swore to me that nothing in Rayou would change his mind about being with me, that nothing here could ruin what we had rebuilt. Except, now the person who instigated our original break up is not only in Rayou, but is standing on my front porch.

Chapter 33

L indsay stands rooted on snow-covered boards and I lean against the doorframe, watching her for a minute. Her brown eyes judge me in every way they can, and I know she's waiting for me to tell her why I left Frostard all those weeks ago. I should be honest with her. Let her know exactly what she's done to me. What I *let* her do to me, a voice in the back of my head corrects.

I open my mouth, letting the cold air bite my tongue, but the words stay frozen inside. A thought occurs to me that keeps me from bringing everything with her to the surface. *Lindsay is going to leave.* She's going to have to go back to Frostard for her classes. Maybe it would be better to leave it unsaid, to let her think everything is fine, and then she'll leave and it will all go back to normal. Christopher and I will be just as we were before I opened this front door.

"I was homesick, Lindsay," I say. "I missed Rayou, and I missed my family. You may not understand that. I know you were having fun at Frostard, but I was distracted. I couldn't focus on my classes and I really questioned why I was there at all." I pause, waiting for her to say something, but her lips are pressed together, eyes still trained on me. I wonder if she can tell I'm holding back most of my truth. "I'm sorry, Lindsay. I didn't mean to take it out on you. I just knew I needed a break, and I left."

"That's absolutely ridiculous, Penny," Lindsay huffs. "But you have to do what's best for you."

I'm surprised by her words and how quick she accepts my half-truth.

"I wish you would've at least texted me back," Lindsay adds, and a pang of guilt pierces my heart, chilling my veins with the icy breeze.

"I know, I should have. I'm sorry," I apologize again. "I got home, life took over again, and I blocked everything out. You know what being in a small town is like."

Lindsay scoffs at that, knowing exactly what living in a small town can do to someone. How the world outside its limits ceases to exist once you've stepped inside of it. That's the beauty of a small town, in my opinion, but it's also one of the many things Lindsay hates about Rayou.

"Well, the plan was to come here, save you, and bring you back to California with me. I guess that's not the case anymore."

"No, it's not. I'm not going back with you, Lindsay. I couldn't even get into my classes now if I wanted to. The semester is half over," I say, my excuses rambling together in a way that will make it clear to Lindsay there is no way she's taking me from Rayou. Not after what's happened between me and Christopher.

"Well, I guess that means I'm spending spring break in Rayou," she says with a groan, and my heart drops.

"You're going to stay here for a week?" I say, and don't do a great job at hiding my disappointment. Now that I know she's on break from Frostard, her sudden appearance makes sense.

Lindsay shrugs, brown eyes studying me like she's trying to figure out why I wouldn't want her to stay. She's supposed to be my best friend, and I'm treating her like someone I haven't talked to in years. "Maybe only for a couple of days."

"You should spend some of it with your family," I say, trying to rein in my shock at learning about how long she'll be in Rayou. I remind myself that a few days will be over before I know it, and I focus on the part of her visit that ends with her departure.

"On the list of things I plan to do," she says, rolling her eyes.

I look at her in disbelief. I don't know how we've been friends for this long when what she wants is the complete opposite of what makes me happy. I was dying to see my family, and Lindsay is acting like it's a burden for her to spend a few days with hers, but she's here and I don't want to fight with her. I hate confrontation and I hate anything that makes Lindsay mad at me, so I pull all of my frustration towards her back in and, at least for the days that Lindsay is here, it'll be as it was when we were in high school. Best friends, as if all those moments she tore my life apart never happened.

"Do you want to go to the Snowcapped Diner?" I ask, trying to steer Lindsay and me away from having a serious conversation right now, because I don't know if I'll actually be able to keep the truth in. "I have some other things planned for the day, but we could catch up this morning."

Lindsay scrunches her nose at that, disgust clear on her face. She turns on her heels, spinning in the snow on the porch, and makes her way down the steps. "I guess I could go for some coffee. I wouldn't eat anything from that greasy shoebox."

My stomach flips at her words, the pancakes I had for breakfast unsettling. I bite the inside of my cheek and keep back my words. This is the Lindsay I know. The one who judges everything I love, but she's leaving soon. For a few days she'll be here, and then she'll be gone. I can hold back my words for that long. A metallic taste fills my mouth, reminding me to move and to unclench my jaw.

I pull the front door closed behind me and follow Lindsay across the yard, heading for her white sedan. As I walk, watching Lindsay's straight brown hair swing from shoulder to shoulder, my mind works in franticly to keep my anxiety at bay. I keep telling myself that, for a few days, I can pretend. For a few days, Lindsay can be my best friend again and then she'll be gone. Everything will go back to the way it's supposed to be. This isn't going to be another time where Lindsay manipulates my life. We aren't going to repeat the past. She's here, she's gone, and Christopher and I will be just fine. *Everything will be just fine.*

But no matter how many times I say it, how many times I try to make my anxiety quiet, I can't help but think I'm wrong. Everything is about to change, and nothing will be fine again.

Lindsay drives us to the Snowcapped Diner and the small shops of downtown Rayou pass in a blur. I can't help but see the difference between the two of us based on our reactions to arriving in Rayou. I had been awestruck by the small town and in love with the twinkling lights that were on display. Lindsay hardly gives the old buildings that line the street a second glance.

"You missed the Christmas lights," I say, knowing they took them down on the first of March.

Lindsay huffs out a half-laugh. "That's okay," she says.

We pull into the parking lot, finding a spot that's clear of snow and walk into the diner. There are a few empty seats at the bar that overlook the kitchen and we each claim one. Willie walks up, greeting me with a smile.

"Hey Penny, your usual?" she asks and I catch her eyes drift to Lindsay, knowing she's not who I usually come to the Snowcapped Diner with. I can see the question in her gaze, asking where Christopher is.

Lindsay's side glance meets mine and I know she's evaluating me. Judging the fact that I've definitely been here since I've been home, because this waitress knows my order and my name. I ignore Lindsay's glance and meet the waitress's eyes. "Yep, dark roast with honey and creamer," I tell her.

The waitress nods and looks at Lindsay. "What would you like?"

"Your darkest coffee with non-fat milk and two pumps of sugar-free vanilla syrup," Lindsay says, flipping her long, brown hair over her shoulder.

I can tell the waitress wants to laugh at her and claim that this isn't a Starbucks, but she meets my strong glance and somehow knows not to question Lindsay.

"Sure thing," the waitress says, turning on her heels to head back to the kitchen.

"So, what have you been doing?" Lindsay asks, pivoting on her swiveling stool to look at me.

It's a loaded question. Does she really want to know? Perhaps. Maybe she also wants to critique me. To tell me I've been spending my time incorrectly. Sweat breaks out on my brow. This could be where I make the mistake of letting the true nature of my visit expose itself. I have to choose my words carefully because if she gets under my skin, I really don't know what I'll say right now.

"Helping my mom at the library," I say first. An easy answer, something I've done for years and years with Lindsay. She nods, waiting for the rest of my story. I've been here for two months. *What have I been doing?* I lick my lips and I wonder if she notices my nervous glances. "Coach Violet asked me to help with the cheer team," I blurt.

Lindsay's eyes widen, leaning forward in her seat. Now I've piqued her interest. Of course, I can talk about cheer! That's easy. Lindsay looks at me, a million questions swimming in her brown gaze. "You helped with the cheer team? Tell me about it!"

So, I do. I tell her about how Coach Violet saw me in the hallway when I took some books to the school library, how she asked me to come by practice that night. I tell Lindsay that I was basically the assistant coach this year, and that I got to work with our team.

"I saw the picture Trinity posted with the plaque," Lindsay gasps, now remembering that she had seen it on social media.

"I know," I say, my grin widening. "They got second at state!"

Lindsay lets out an excited squeal that definitely draws eyes to us. "That's amazing! Too bad they broke our record, though," she says, nudging my foot with hers.

I look at her, the tension between us now lifting as if it was never there to begin with. The conversation bounces smoothly between us because cheer is easy. Cheer is something we both love. When the waitress comes back with our coffees, she slides them across the bar. Lindsay and I pick them up and drink without breaking the flow of our words.

"I think I'm jealous of *you*." Lindsay sighs back into her barstool.

"Really?" I question. I hadn't expected that from her. She's jealous of me and what I am doing?

Lindsay nods. "I miss cheer so much," she says, honesty dripping from her words.

It's something we talked about a lot at the beginning of our time at Frostard. Wondering what the squad was doing, what we'd be doing if we were still in high school. I know how much Lindsay loves cheer and I know how much she would've loved to help coach the team this year.

"Maybe, while you're here, we can stop by and see them. They're still doing basketball games," I say.

Lindsay's features brighten a little. "So what do you want to do today?" Lindsay asks.

I'm just about to tell her she can decide, because that's what I always used to do. I suck in those words for two reasons. One, I don't let Lindsay decide things for me anymore, and two, because, "I already have plans, actually," I tell her, the words harder to say than I thought they would be in my head.

Lindsay looks at me, waiting. "Are you going to invite me to do them with you?" she asks teasingly.

It's like she's forgotten that Christopher was at my front door this morning. Like we're best friends in this high school and everything I do, she gets to do with me. Maybe it's better that she acts this way. That we keep the conversation light.

"Well," I say, pausing because I know my next words could crash every little fake reality Lindsay has built around us. "I'm supposed to meet Christopher at the ice-skating rink later."

As I predicted, Lindsay's cheeks pale at the mention of Christopher. "Oh," she says, twirling her spoon in her coffee. "Are you going to tell me what happened there?" she asks, peering at me through her lashes as she takes another sip of the hot drink.

My tongue sticks to the roof of my mouth, words fumbling around. "Nothing happened. I'm back in town, we saw each other, and, well, you know how much I like him."

Lindsay huffs a laugh at that, and I think she enjoys seeing me squirm. "Penny, you don't have to be nervous around me. I know you like the boy," Lindsay teases. "I just thought that part of your life was over."

My reaction is to say *because you ended it,* but I don't. "Yeah, well, I'm back in town. I'm here and he's here, and it just sort of happened," I say

Lindsay can understand that much, and I know she has questions about how long we've been together since I've been home for months. I know she wants to ask about the future, about what happens when I go back to Frostard.

"I guess it's not a bad thing to have a little fling," Lindsay says. "Take the chance while you have it, you know?"

My face burns red when I realize what she's thinking. That I'm going to go back to Frostard in the fall, that I'm going to leave Christopher behind just like I did last year. She thinks that we're just hooking up while I'm in Rayou. I bite my tongue to keep myself from correcting her. *Let her believe it. She's leaving in a few days.*

I lift my shoulder and look anywhere but at her. "Anyway, I'm meeting him at the skating rink. I guess you could come with us, if you want." I secretly hope she declines. She's never been a huge fan of Christopher.

"Sure!" Lindsay agrees.

My stomach drops all the way to the floor. I didn't think that she would accept, but maybe she really just wants to spend time with me. I remember then that Christopher and I are going to the skating rink for his portfolio. We're taking photos for his contest and I'm going to have to explain that to Lindsay. Admit to her what really brought us back together. I don't know why that makes me nervous. Because Lindsay will think it's lame? But I realize, I don't care what she thinks.

"You can come with us, but I should explain, Christopher and I are actually working on a project for his photography class," I say.

"Really? He's studying photography?" Lindsay asks and I'm trying to decide if her peaked interest is sarcasm.

She knows Christopher loves being behind the camera, but maybe she doesn't realize that was the path he chose for himself. I nod, saying, "He's taking classes at Rayou Community College, and they're having this portfolio contest where he has to present photos that provoke emotion. I've been helping him with the project."

Lindsay looks at me, white light glinting off her eyes, and I wish she would tell me what she's thinking. "Interesting," Lindsay says. "Can I be in it?"

I know Christopher would want Lindsay nowhere near his portfolio project, but I shrug. "Sure." Christopher can just edit those photos out. She won't even be here when the contest ends.

"It's been a long time since I've been skating," Lindsay says, letting the conversation drift another direction.

I agree, remembering the last time I was ice-skating was with Lindsay in high school. "Do you want to go by the library until Christopher is ready?"

Lindsay nods, sliding her empty coffee cup across the counter. "Sure, I could use a good romance to read while I'm home."

I bite back my instinct to tell her I meant to help shelve books and let her... just be her. We pay for our drinks and head towards the library. Lindsay drives down the streets, once again letting the buildings of Rayou pass with little interest, and I try to remind myself that this is not high school. I still have a grip on my life. Lindsay does not control it.

My mom has just turned the open sign around when Lindsay and I approach the front door of the library that sits on the corner of the main intersection of Rayou. The Christmas tree I observed on my first night in town stands tall in the center of the roundabout, but the lights and ornaments have been taken down, leaving a very natural evergreen covered in white snow, still as breathtaking as it had been that night.

We stomp the slush off our boots and walk inside the library, turning to the left and into the enormous space filled with shelves that reach the ceiling.

"It always smells weird in here," Lindsay mutters as she wiggles her fingers out of her gloves.

"You mean it smells like books?" My mom's voice is sharp, and Lindsay looks up to meet her blue gaze, either not thinking my mom had heard her remark, or she wasn't expecting her to be standing there.

A laugh threatens to burst from my pressed lips, and I give my mom a look that says to rein it in. I realize I should have texted her and told her Lindsay was here. I left the house without even updating her on how much everything has changed.

"Good to see you, Mrs. Wilson," Lindsay says, quickly pulling back her surprise.

My mom's watchful gaze warns me she's about two seconds from letting Lindsay know just how she feels. Ever since I admitted to my mom the things Lindsay made me do, the way she influenced and controlled my life, I know my mom has changed her opinion of the best friend who spent as many nights at our house as she did her own. It's not fair that my mom pushes all of that blame on Lindsay. I know a big part of the problem was me, but she's my mom, and I know she would never put any of that blame on my shoulders.

"The books that need shelved are over there," my mom says, nodding to three carts at the other end of the front desk and ignoring

Lindsay's comment.

Lindsay's eyes narrow, and she meets my knowing gaze. "I didn't realize you wanted to come here to work."

"You don't have to help if you don't want to," I say, over emphasizing the word *help*, to contradict her immediate reaction to it being work.

"Oh, I can help," Lindsay counters, curling the ends of her words up.

She follows me across the library, and as I pass my mom, we share a glance that says we're betting on how long Lindsay will last. I take the first of the three carts, and Lindsay follows me as I wheel it toward the Young Adult section of the library.

We work together to shelve the books on the cart. I easily do double—if not triple—the amount of books that Lindsay shelves, but I attest that to the fact that I have these books nearly memorized, knowing exactly where the different letters in the alphabetically organized rows start and stop. It's definitely not because every book Lindsay picks up, she has to examine the cover and read the description on the back. She makes it an entire thirty minutes before I look up and find her curled into the big armchair by the frosted windows, the last book she took off the cart open in her hands. I shake my head, a smile spreading across my face, and return to the front of the library with the now empty cart.

"She's already done?" mom asks, dropping her voice so only I hear her.

I shrug and exchange the bare cart for another full one. "She made it thirty minutes. That's probably a record for her," I tease, knowing Lindsay is no stranger to this library. She's spent her fair share of weekends and afternoons here with me. A lot more when we were younger. Once she got her driver's license and her options of places to spend her time widened, she stopped coming around as much, and by association, so did I, because we had to do everything together. A pain throbs in my chest at the thought of those days being gone, time here with my mom that I can't get back.

"Are you still going to the ice-skating rink?" my mom asks, pulling me from my twisting thoughts.

I nod, slipping my phone from my pocket, her question reminding me to text Christopher and let him know Lindsay will be joining us. I send him a short message, telling him to let me know when he's heading that way and Lindsay and I will leave the library. I know he's not going to be excited that Lindsay's coming, but in order to have as little conflict with her as possible, I'm willing to let her come with us, knowing in a few days she'll be gone, anyway. I continue to shelve the books, and after my second cart, I swear I hear Lindsay snoring when I pass by the chair she's lounging in. Another hour passes before Christopher finally texts me back, letting me know he's on his way to the skating rink, completely ignoring the part of my text that mentioned Lindsay. She wakes when I tap her foot with my boot, swearing up and down she hadn't fallen asleep, but was just resting her eyes. Still, she actually checks out the book she'd been reading and my mom warns her to return it before she heads back to Frostard at the end of the week.

"Sure thing, Mrs. Wilson," Lindsay says, taking the book back from my mom. "I'm sure I'll be over at the house a lot this week. I'll just leave it with Penny when I'm done." Lindsay turns, striding for the exit, acting as if her inviting herself over to my house is completely normal, talking about it like it's her own home.

I blow out a soft sigh and give my mom another glance that begs her not to blow things up with Lindsay. Please just let me keep my taped together life in place a little while longer.

Chapter 34

The sound of ice shaving against the metal blades of skates hisses through the air as Lindsay and I approach the rink. Her car beeps behind us, signaling she's locked it. Bright colored sweaters pepper the ice-skating rink, about ten other people already carving figure eights and large loops across the ice.

"So, is Christopher going to meet us here?" Lindsay says, popping the *O* of his name like it's some cute nickname she's flinging toward me, but I can hear the condescending tone in her voice.

I'm about to tell her that he should already be here, when I find his dark brown hair. He stands an entire head and shoulders above everyone else near the *Welcome Stand*. Lindsay must see my recognition light up my eyes because she turns to the right, finding Christopher on her own. We walk around the rink, following the narrow sidewalk lined with plexiglass on one side and a metal railing on the other.

"Christopher!" Lindsay calls, announcing our arrival a few paces away from him

Christopher turns around, hazel eyes targeting Lindsay first, and then shifting to find me next to her. The muscles along his jawline soften when I meet his gaze, offering him a smile as we take those final steps across the sidewalk.

"I didn't know you'd be joining us," Christopher says, shifting his weight to face Lindsay and slip an arm around my waist.

I tilt my head back to look at Christopher, knowing very well that I told him Lindsay would be coming with me.

"Hmm," Lindsay hums. "If I didn't know any better, I'd say it sounds like you don't want me to be here."

I snap my gaze back to Lindsay, warning her not to push Christopher with my widening eyes. The two have always butted heads, always bickering and pushing the other. I know Lindsay does it because having Christopher means I'm not completely reliant on her. Christopher does it because he hates the way Lindsay treats me.

"I don't," Christopher bites out honestly, a gust of frigid wind raising bumps under the sleeves of my sweater.

Lindsay's brown eyes nearly pop out of her head, not expecting him to be so blunt and honest. Her cheeks tint pink and her mouth opens, a comeback forming on her tongue.

"He's joking, Lindsay," I say, my smile too tight across my face. I lean into Christopher's side, lightly stepping on his foot, and his own fake smile blooms.

Lindsay gives us a breathy laugh that says she's not so sure she believes me, but is willing to run with it. "Penny tells me you're working on some fancy photography project," Lindsay says, shifting the conversation. "Better get my good side." With that, Lindsay turns and strides up to the counter at the *Welcome Stand* to rent a pair of skates.

"What the hell is she doing here?" Christopher asks beneath his breath, stepping out from my side to stand in front of me. His hazel eyes have darkened, the caramel swirls freezing with the edge in his voice.

"She's only here for a few days, Christopher," I breathe, glancing around him to make sure Lindsay doesn't overhear us. "I don't want to fight with her. Let's just pretend everything is okay, and then she'll be gone."

"You just expect me to act like she isn't the reason you were so upset a few weeks ago? That she isn't the reason we broke up in August?" Christopher asks, eyes sweeping side-to-side.

"Please, Christopher. I don't want to confront her right now," I say, my tone on the verge of begging.

Christopher presses his lips together, and I can tell how much he dislikes this by the way his shoulders fall and his eyebrows droop. "I don't want her being back to change *this*," Christopher says, reaching for my hand with hesitant fingers. "Change you," he adds softly, hazel eyes welling with so much desperation it cracks my chest. "Don't let her start deciding things for you again."

"I won't," I whisper, hoping he sees strength in my eyes, feels it in the squeeze I pulse through his hand. "I'm never going to let things go back to the way they were."

He watches me a moment longer before he nods once, letting my hand fall.

"Come on, Love Birds," Lindsay calls, teasing us as she walks away from the stand, white skates in hand.

"This is going to be the longest week of my life," he mumbles, and I elbow him in the side, weak and unsure smiles finding our faces.

We walk up to the stall and Christopher pays for each of our skates, letting the employee behind the counter know that we're working on a photography project. Lindsay doesn't wait for us, and is already out on the rink warming up while I work on lacing up my skates. I stand, balancing on the blades, and awkwardly step around the padded ground next to the entrance of the rink. There's a thud on the plexiglass wall behind me, and when I look over my shoulder, I see that Lindsay has rammed into the wall, grabbing on with her gloved fingers. "Tick tock, tick tock," she teases, her voice singing through the air before pushing back off the wall and making another lap around the rink.

Christopher peers up at me through his long, brown lashes, a fire igniting the caramel swirls. "Penny," he huffs, telling me he's not going to make it the next five days with Lindsay pushing his buttons.

"Come on," I groan, extending my hand to him. Once Christopher has his skates laced up, he places his hand in mine, and I pull him to his feet, squeezing a reassuring burst through our grasp. My smile quirks up at the corner and I say playfully, "Make sure to get my good side," completely mocking Lindsay and I earn a real laugh from Christopher.

He leans forward and presses a kiss against my grin, his lips warm through the winter chill that clings to me. Butterflies come alive in my stomach at our first kiss in public since we've gotten back together. Our first kiss with other people seeing and knowing that he is mine. This kiss feels different from the ones we shared up in the cabin, secluded in the mountains. It feels real and I know Lindsay doesn't miss it.

Christopher steps back, letting a breath of the frigid breeze press in between us. He reaches for my chin, letting his finger rest beneath it, and tilts my head from the left to the right, surveying my different sides, obviously playing off of my joke. "I don't think you have a bad side," he says through his grin. "You make my job too easy."

I giggle at that like a child and awkwardly step further back from him in my skates, nearing the entryway of the skating rink. Christopher follows me, and we glide onto the frozen surface. The breeze picks up strands of my blonde hair that frame my face, twisting them back and sending the curls twirling behind me.

I slide across the surface of the rink, pushing outward with my skates in easy, large strides. Kids in Rayou learn how to skate before they learn how to ride a bike. It's been a year since I've been on the ice, but muscle memory comes back to me instantly.

Christopher stays to my right and Lindsay skates up along my left. We move together to an isolated part of the rink where a cluster of pine trees closes in on the plexiglass railing. Behind the trees, jagged mountains reach towards the rosy pink clouds in the sky, creating a beautiful backdrop for our photos.

"Any instructions, Photographer?" Lindsay asks, obviously teasing Christopher.

She and I look at Christopher together, tilting our heads playfully. Christopher skates back a few strides and lifts the camera up to his eyes. "Just make it look natural," he says, a grin peaking from behind the camera. A bright flash signals for us to move and Lindsay and I skate together in mini figure-eights. Then we try bigger arcs, and moves where we hold hands. We take a break to catch our breath and lean against the railing, and Christopher captures us relaxing and conversing with the winter sun sinking behind the mountains. After a moment, we start skating again. The ice sprays up from my skates when I hit a sharp turn. I can tell by the way Christopher pulls the camera from his face to check the display screen that he caught the moment. Christopher even attempts to skate while Lindsay and I move and takes pictures, claiming he's able to take some pictures with movement.

"Okay, let me see!" Lindsay finally declares after Christopher skids to a stop on the frozen rink, his camera held to his face. He looks up from the display screen to see Lindsay sliding toward him like a bullet. He can't even object before she grabs onto his arm and spins into his side, sliding the camera from his grasp. Lindsay gasps and squeals. "These look amazing!"

"You sound like you had little faith in me, Lindsay," Christopher says, but his tone is no longer sharp, either having warmed up to Lindsay's presence, or he's just too tired right now to care anymore.

"Penny, come look! These are so cute!" Lindsay calls, not looking up from the camera, but waving me toward her.

I skate closer to Lindsay and Christopher, stopping in front of them. "I'm actually not looking at any of the photos until the portfolio is done," I say.

Lindsay's brown eyes catch mine through her lashes, her nose scrunching up. "Why not?" I open my mouth to respond, but before I can, Lindsay answers her own question for me. "Does this have to do with your obsession of hating endings? Like how you don't read the last page of books?" Judgment drips from every word and my cheeks burn a bright pink.

"Something like that," I mumble, crossing arms around my waist.

"That's so weird, Penny," Lindsay says through a laugh that chills my skin more than the winter air, and she shakes her head.

I meet Christopher's hazel stare, catching a muscle in his neck twitch. With the soft shake of my head, I dismiss his unspoken request of wanting permission to knock Lindsay on her butt right here on the skating rink.

"You should use this photo," Lindsay says, holding the camera out so Christopher can see her selection on the display screen.

His features soften, hazel eyes taking in the picture Lindsay chose. He meets Lindsay's watchful gaze, and I can't tell what emotions wash over his face, but it makes the urge to grab the camera and see for myself almost unbearable. I'd expect Lindsay to choose one of herself, some photo that makes her look like a supermodel and the star of his portfolio. Had she done that, Christopher definitely would have responded with some snide remark, but his reaction confuses me.

"Send me some of those," Lindsay adds, letting Christopher take the camera back.

He nods, clicking it off, and lets it hang around his neck. It's now that I realize the portfolio is done. That was the last picture we planned to take for the project. The finality in that threatens to crumble the ice beneath my feet.

"So, now what do we want to do?" Lindsay asks, looking between Christopher and me, the setting sun making the highlight on her cheeks glitter.

I can't believe just this morning I wasn't even thinking about Lindsay. Now she's engrained herself back into my life so fast it's almost like she never left. I don't know if Christopher sees that shock unsettle me, but he answers Lindsay when I don't, saying hot chocolate is on him.

We skate off the rink, Lindsay's arm linked in mine, and I'm sucked back into the moment, feeling like I'm letting that part of my life I just spent the last two months building continue to slip away.

Chapter 35

Somehow, between hot chocolate and dinner, Lindsay invites herself over to spend the night. I walk through the front door and lift a hand, gesturing that Lindsay can enter the house. She steps inside, using the toe of each boot to work the other off, her skinny jeans damp around the ankles. "I can take your coat," I say, my voice hoarse.

The car ride here was quiet, my mind completely exhausted with how Lindsay has swept in and turned everything upside down. The air in the car was stiff, and I know that Lindsay could tell something was bothering me.

"Penny, I've been to your house before. I can hang up my own coat," Lindsay says with a huff, and hurt-filled eyes meet mine as she shrugs off the rose-colored coat, revealing a white blouse with pearl beading around the neckline. Lindsay walks away from me and toward the mudroom off the kitchen on her own, strutting through my house like she owns the place. "Hi Mrs. Wilson," Lindsay sings, her bright tone returning on command, and I assume she just came across my mom in the kitchen.

I hurry down the hall after her, stopping in the archway of the kitchen to meet my mom's wide stare. I texted her that Lindsay was coming over, but clearly she hasn't checked her phone yet. I just shake my head once, before Lindsay comes out of mudroom, arms crossed. "It's okay if I stay the night, right Mrs. Wilson?"

I look between her and my mom, and I can see she wants to tell Lindsay *no*, but she knows this is my battle to fight. "Sure," my mom says. "I'm heading to bed early, anyway. We have a morning event at the library tomorrow." She walks around the kitchen counter and heads for the stairs, a cup of hot tea in her hands.

"You okay, Penny?" Lindsay asks, noticing I'm still staring at the place my mom stood, because my tired mind is still trying to catch up with how much everything has changed today.

I nod stiffly, not meeting her chocolate brown stare and my feet turn on their own. Lindsay follows me back through the house and up to my bedroom. I click on the small desk lamp and sit on the edge of my bed. Lindsay takes the chair at my desk, crossing one leg over the other at her knee. We sit in silence for a second because I'm simply too tired to start another fake conversation with her. It's been a long day, and a nauseous wave settles in my stomach when I realize this is what the rest of the week will be like.

It's now that I ask myself what will happen when the spring semester ends and summer starts? Sure, Lindsay already told me she wanted to stay in California for the summer, but without her classes keeping her there, she'll be able to come back to Rayou whenever she feels like it.

I was stupid to think I could just hold out until this week was over, because with Lindsay, it'll never be over. I pinch my fingers together, trying to rein in the frustration that's beginning to bubble inside of me again. The same heated anger that flared when I saw her on the other side of the front door this morning blooms.

When I look up at Lindsay, teeth grinding together so hard my jaw is locked, I see her eyes are in narrowed slants, her expression sending a cold wave across my hot skin. It's as if she had a mask on all day today too, and it's finally dropped.

"Well?" she snaps, and I realize the conversations we had today, her intervening at the ice skating rink, inviting herself over tonight, all of it was done to chip away at the wall she knew I was building between us. She hasn't forgotten the cold shoulder I gave her when I saw her on my front porch this morning, and she's been waiting until this very moment to try and get the truth out of me.

"I hated it at Frostard," I blurt, letting Lindsay's snapped remark fuel my explanation. I no longer can keep this in, because now that I realize it won't end this week, there's no reason to pretend anymore, and I've come too far to go back to being her shadow. "I hated being away from Rayou. I missed my family, and I had no idea why I was even at that school."

"To get your degree in Business Management—"

"But I don't want a degree in Business Management," I bite out and cut her off.

Lindsay looks at me for a moment, mouth hanging ajar, and slowly brings her lips back together, pressing them into a thin line. After a second she leans back in the chair and says, "I didn't know that."

Her voice has changed, dipping down with concern. It makes a warm wave wash over the walls I instinctively threw up when I saw her outside this morning. Of course she didn't, because I never told her otherwise. Everything that she's ever decided for me, she thinks I wanted. She has no idea all of those moments have been bothering me, because I never spoke my mind.

"I know you didn't," I say, my words gentler. I clear my throat and pull my legs up underneath me in a crossed position. "I needed a break from Frostard to come home and figure out what I really want."

Lindsay's eyes have drifted from me, taking in the walls of my room before settling on my window by the headboard, moonlight assisting the small desk lamp and making the room glow. "And you ignored all my texts and calls because?"

I bite the inside of my cheek so hard a metallic taste fills my mouth. Lindsay didn't believe the quick lie I told her this morning about being back in this small town and getting sucked into the bubble that surrounds it. I hate that what I did the last two months hurt her. I know she's had her hands on the steering wheel of my life for years, leading me down different paths I never wanted to travel, but I don't know how I can be mad at her when I let her do it. I never stood up to her or voiced my opinion. I don't hate Lindsay, I never have.

"I wanted to make sure that when I figured it out, it was my decision," I whisper.

Her brown eyes snap to mine. "And you think that I would have swayed you?"

My sarcastic, breathy laugh seeps from my locked lips. "Yes, Lindsay," I say honestly. "You've dictated absolutely everything in my life."

"That's not true—"

"Cheerleading tryouts in sixth grade," I interrupt her, and continue listing off everything Lindsay has every decided for me, "who I asked to homecoming freshman year, skipping algebra class to go shopping, what dresses we wore to prom, what I ate, when we worked out, going to

Frostard, choosing Business Management as my major, staying on campus over Christmas break, breaking up with Christopher—" I stop when a sheen glitters on Lindsay's eyes. Each thing I fling at her makes my voice raise until Christopher's name is clawing along the inside of my throat, making my own tears bloom. I swallow back the anger that's growing, because it's being misdirected at her. I blink back my tears and sigh. "And that's not entirely your fault, Lindsay. I never said I wanted anything different."

My best friend since sixth grade sits with her legs crossed, arms hugging her waist, and stares at me for a long minute. I can see her throat working on the words she's debating about saying, trying to rein in her emotions before she responds.

"I've been an awful friend," she says, the words cracking through the sobs she couldn't push down and tears flood from her eyes.

My heart shatters at the sight of her crying. We've been through so much together, I know that I would do anything for her, and to see her break at the words I threw her way fills my chest with an ache that throws my world off-balance. "Lindsay, don't cry," I say, my own tears slipping from my eyes. I reach out to her, linking my fingers around her wrist and I draw her from the chair and to the bed beside me. "I should have said something sooner," I admit.

Lindsay tosses her head, sobs still making her body shake. 'No, Penny. There were things I did—"

Her words are interrupted by another wave of tears, her breathing sharp as she tries to steady herself, and it drives the crack in my heart deeper. "Penny, I never should have—" Again she cries before she can finish her words.

I squeeze her hand tighter, wanting her to stop hurting, because I know what she's trying to say. The way she made me feel about my body, that was always wrong. It's something we haven't talked about since we graduated, letting that part of our lives disappear into the forgotten void now that cheer is over. As if we could pretend it never happened because we knew it was wrong. The way we drilled our bodies, made ourselves sick to keep the weight off, we never should have done that. She knows that I never would have if it weren't for her, and she knows it was wrong of her to make me do those things.

"You deserved a better friend," she says through the tremble in her voice.

"Lindsay, please stop crying." I squeeze another burst through her hand before loosening my grip and making her look at me. "I didn't want different friend. I just want…" I trail off, realizing *I don't know* what I want. I hadn't thought this far ahead. Two minutes ago, I was determined to keep all of this a secret and let Lindsay believe nothing was wrong. I didn't prepare myself for what I wanted to do once the truth was out. I look at her, cheeks soaked with tears, loose strands of brown hair stuck to her damp face. Her mascara is smudged all around her already swelling eyes. "You're an ugly crier," I say weakly, letting the joke splinter in my throat, and a laugh tries to bloom at the sight of her.

Lindsay bursts out a breathy laugh, not expecting me to say that. "You don't look so hot yourself," she teases sadly.

We sit here, laughing at the sudden change in the conversation, that natural banter that has always been rooted in our friendship making the air breathable again. When our laughs quiet, I finally realize what I want. I reach for Lindsay's hand once again, linking my fingers with hers. "This is what I want, Lindsay," I say, picking up where I had left off. "I want you in my life. I just want to be in *control* of that life. I want my decisions to be mine."

Lindsay nods, an exaggerated snap of her head, and nudges my shoulder with hers. "Write me up a contract and I'll sign it this instant, Penny. I swear to you, I never meant to control your life the way you perceived it."

"I know," I say, sighing through the reseeding tears in my eyes. "I just didn't know how to tell you otherwise."

"Well, I think you figured it out," Lindsay says, tilting her voice up, talking about my outburst, all those instances bubbling over.

"I could have done it in a better way," I admit.

"But I'm glad you did it, nonetheless," Lindsay says, her voice softening. "I never would have wanted to lose you, especially over something I didn't even realize was hurting you."

"Thank you, Lindsay," I say, squeezing her hand in mine.

The corner of her mouth pulls up in a small smile, and she wiggles her fingers out of my hold on her hand. Lindsay flops back onto the mattress, crossing her arms behind her head, and says, "So, you and Christopher?" The way she draws out her words, like it's the juiciest gossip she's ever heard, makes us both erupt with genuine laughter again.

I scoot across the bed and rest my back against the wall, and Lindsay and I stay up all night talking about the things in my life that I want. The real things that matter to me and where I see myself in the future. I'm honest with her about transferring to Rayou Community College, and everything that will come from that. She listens and supports me with everything I tell her, and I wish I would have done this years ago.

I know this doesn't mean we're best friends again and we can't pretend nothing in the past ever happened, but at least we've repaired our relationship and can form some sort of friendship. At least she's still in my life, and we can work on building something new together. It's going to take time, especially as we continue to go down our own paths, but at least we're trying.

Even though Lindsay and I have been friends since sixth grade, something feels different about her laying in my bed, gossiping about boys and creating our dream weddings in our heads. Now it feels like I have a say in what we're talking about, and when she loves my input, I know it's really because she loves what I've said, not just something I offered because I knew it was what she wanted to hear. For the first time in my life, Lindsay and I are talking about *me* and *my decisions*.

Chapter 36

T he week I had previously been dreading goes by faster than I thought it would. Lindsay and I see each other two more times for coffee at the Snowcapped Diner and an afternoon in the library with my mom. Christopher is nervous about this until I tell him everything Lindsay and I talked about. When second chances are at the root of our relationship, it's hard for him to argue that Lindsay shouldn't get one, too.

Lindsay decides to go back to Frostard on Thursday, claiming it was the cheapest flight and she already promised some of her classmates she'd spend that last half of spring break at the beach house they rented about two hours south of the university. I find myself missing Lindsay's exuberant personality as her car pulls away from the curb on Thursday evening, already looking forward to when she'll be home this summer. So much has changed between her and me, but after everything that was said, we're still going to make this friendship work. She's my person when Christopher can't be, and I think, after all of this, it has the potential to actually bring us closer together.

"It's already quieter around here," Christopher comments, pulling my gaze away from the red taillights of Lindsay's sedan. He sits on the porch swing, dark jeans crossed at the ankles, his denim jacket slung over a white t-shirt.

The boards of the porch creak beneath my steps, their white paint finally showing through the slushy snow. I know that will be short-lived as another snow storm is supposed to come through tonight. I sit on the swing, leaning into Christopher's side, and he drapes an arm around my shoulder, picking up a blonde curl to twirl between his fingers. "Did you want to do something tonight?" I ask, watching Lindsay drive away from the stop sign at the end of my street and turn out of view.

Christopher's fingers that had been twirling my hair freeze. "Actually," he says softly, the cold breeze caring his words across my cheek. "I wanted to do one more photo for the portfolio."

"Really?" I ask, turning to face him. I thought the ice-skating photo would be our last. "Isn't the portfolio due soon?"

"Tomorrow," he says, eyes meeting mine.

"Tomorrow?" I repeat.

He nods, his fingers moving through my hair once again. "That way the judges have a month to review all the submissions."

"Wow," I say, finding myself at a loss for words. "I'm kind of sad that it's over," I admit, though I know I shouldn't be. For a while, the portfolio was a reason for me to see Christopher. I grew anxious thinking about its end because I thought that meant I wouldn't get to see him anymore, but that's no longer true.

Christopher must know that's how I feel because he presses a light kiss to my cheeks, making my heart jump into my throat. After all this time, he can still make my body react like it's the first time. "I'll share my first place prize with you," he says, nudging my temple with his nose and I smile at the implication that he's going to win.

"Do you know what the winner receives?" I inquire, playing along with the assumption that he will take first place.

"I hope it's a camera," he says, and I can hear the daydream in his voice at winning the latest piece of photography technology.

"How would we share that?" I tease, turning to look into his bright hazel eyes, crinkling my nose playfully.

An easy smile spreads his lips, white teeth grinning at me. "You're right, let's hope for a gift-card to the Snowcapped Diner. You're bleeding my pockets dry with that horrible concoction you like to drink."

"Hey!" I shove his shoulder playfully and he laughs into the crook of my neck, squeezing me in a short hug. "So," I begin to prompt him, sitting back and letting the late-March air fill the space between us. "What do you have in mind for the last photo?"

His gaze moves from my eyes to the setting sun, dipping behind the mountains that encase Rayou. "Do you trust me?" he asks, sweeping his hazel eyes back to me.

"It depends what we're talking about," I tease him and his jaw drops open, pretending to be offended. His humorous expression makes me laugh and I nod, saying, "Of course, I trust you."

"Then follow me," Christopher says, standing up and extending his hand to me.

I accept without hesitating and after telling my mom that I'd be back later tonight, we head for his truck at the end of my driveway. The cloth seats are familiar and warm beneath my black leggings. True spring weather is still far off for Rayou, so my mustard coat is buttoned up to my chin, and I angle the air vents in the truck to blast all of their hot air on my face.

Christopher drives slow, taking a scenic route around Rayou to a small park on the eastern side of town. When I call him out for his terrible sense of direction, he explains he was taking his time so the sun would sink even deeper in the sky. The area is deserted, everyone already turning in before the big storm hits in a few hours, and we find a parking spot near the sidewalk that winds through the snow-covered pine trees.

It's a fairly small park, only made up of a single walking path and a playground for kids. Street lamps line the sidewalk, snaking up a short hill and back into the cluster of trees, their branches stretching overhead, creating archways of snow. I have to push the door of the truck to get it to swing open against the strong wind that's picked up. Flurries of large snowflakes have started to fall, a warning that heavier snow is close behind. I drop to the ground and follow Christopher up the narrow sidewalk. His camera hangs around his neck, a folded tripod in his left hand.

Christopher keeps his head tilted back, studying the soft rays from the sunset that are a deep navy and plum. If there's one thing I've learned by sitting in Mr. Riley's photography lectures, it's that lighting is one of the most important aspects of a picture.

After a few minutes, Christopher decides on an alcove of trees that wrap in a half circle around an iron lamp post. It's set back from the sidewalk a few paces. "Go stand over there," he says, pointing to the soft white circle that casts down from the light overhead.

I do as he says, letting the snow crunch beneath my boots as I step off the path. Christopher goes the other way, setting up a tripod for his camera. Usually, he takes his photos handheld, but I guess he wants to eliminate the possibility of any movement in this photo. I watch him closely as he locks the camera on the stand, clicking buttons and adjusting the lens to capture his desired image. I wait for more direction, still unsure what he has in mind for this final photo of his portfolio.

Christopher pauses, examining the preview image he's seeing on the display screen, and then he steps out from behind the camera, making his way across the snow to me, the spiraling flakes peppering his brown hair.

"What are you doing?" I ask as he steps closer, leaving the camera behind.

"Capturing the most important moment in this portfolio," he says, stopping in front of me and beneath the golden rays pouring down from the lamp post. He's framed perfectly in the light, with the tiny snowflakes fluttering around him. Just looking at him makes my lungs weak.

I think back to the first night he told me about the portfolio, about the story he needed to tell, something that would evoke emotion. "Does that mean you know what your portfolio's story is?" I ask through the light chatter of my teeth, knowing he hasn't revealed it to me yet.

Christopher nods, a grin tugging at his lips, and my heart skips at the hint of his smile.

"What is it?" I ask, an anxious wave settling on my skin against the hot desire in my chest.

Christopher raises his hand toward my face, spreading his warm fingers across my cheek. His hazel eyes sweep across every feature, taking me in like I'm a piece of art he's admiring. Finally, Christopher speaks, his words soft. "It's us," he says. "It's our story."

Christopher dips his chin and his lips meet mine. Bits of snow get caught in the kiss, and my heart leaps in my chest at his words. In the distance, I faintly recognize the sound of the camera capturing this moment, but it's muffled by every other sense in my body coming alive.

His fingers curl into the hair at the nape of my neck, his hold on me so sure and loving. I kiss him deeper, wrapping my fingers into his denim jacket that weighs his shoulders down, pulling our chests together.

Coffee and pine flood my nose, his scent strong and consuming. Christopher's mouth moves against mine, warm lips spreading mine apart in a hungry kiss that begs me for more.

I don't know how the girl who was spiraling out of control at Frostard just two months ago is standing here now. I am so unbelievably happy, something I don't think that girl at Frostard ever thought she'd be again.

I tilt our lips apart, so I can speak the words that are dying to get out, gasping a bit for my breath. "I love you, Christopher." I look up through my lashes, snow falling around us in spiraling flurries that frame his beautiful face. "You have no idea how much you've changed my life, but you saved me."

His hazel eyes are wide, black pupils dilated with the matching heat that burns in my veins. He shakes his head slightly, titling my chin up so the light from the lamp post casts perfectly along my cheeks. "You saved yourself, Penny. I'm just lucky enough you chose to include me in your story."

Tears threaten to bloom, and only because of the harsh wind do my eyes stay dry. "Our story," I correct him, repeating what he said this portfolio means to him. "This is our story."

I press my lips back to Christopher's, looping my arms around his neck and I let him wrap his around my waist, pulling me so close to him the winter weather around us fades away. Standing beneath the lamp post, ignited in its yellow glow, snow flurrying around us like flower petals at a wedding, I kiss the man that owns my heart. Who I'm lucky enough to call mine once again. Who I will love until the day I die.

Chapter 37

My steps are slow the next morning as I descend the staircase in my house, letting their carpeted surface mute my approach. Now that the portfolio is completed, that part of mine and Christopher's relationship is over. It's a quick reminder that the next part will be my enrollment at Rayou Community College. After tossing and turning all night, I've finally decided today's the day I tell my mom my plan. Which is why I walk to the kitchen as slowly as possible, wringing my fingers with the nerves that have my heart racing. One of the wooden floorboards in the narrow hall creaks, giving away my arrival, and my mom turns over her shoulder to see me.

A tired morning smile pulls at her lips. "Good morning," she says.

My stomach twists at her bright tone, knowing what I'm about to say will surely darken it. "Morning," I say through a sigh.

My movements across the kitchen are like walking against thick syrup. I take too long to select a bowl, letting the cereal fall inside one piece at a time. My eyes keep flipping to my mom, but she isn't paying attention to me, her gaze down on her bowl of oatmeal. Honestly, I'm not even hungry, but I go through the motions anyway, if only to buy me a few more seconds of the calm before the storm.

Finally, after pouring some milk over my cereal, I place it on the bar and slide up onto the stool next to her. "Mom," I say, not even bothering to reach for the spoon that rests against the edge of the bowl.

"Hmm?" she hums to prompt me, working to clump the last of her oatmeal together on her spoon.

"I don't want to go back to Frostard in August," I admit.

Mom freezes, but only for a second before she continues to scrap the edges of her bowl. "You have to go back, Penny," she says without meeting my watchful gaze. "That was the deal. You can take this semester off, but you said you were going back to finish your schooling in the fall."

My mouth is dry, my tongue heavy as I work out the words. Her immediate denial is a bad start, and it makes me want to second guess myself, to forget I ever had the idea to transfer and just do what she wants. But I don't do what other people want anymore. My life is mine, and I'll make my own decisions.

"I will continue my schooling, I just don't want to continue it at Frostard," I say, choosing my words carefully.

Her spoon clatters to the side of her bowl, leaving the last bite of her oatmeal forgotten. My mom swivels to face me on the barstool, resting an elbow on the counter to prop her head on. "What's wrong with Frostard? It's the best school on the West Coast. You're lucky to have even been accepted there."

Pain grips my heart, anxiety at going against what she wants threatening to choke me. With each word she says, my pulse picks up until my heart is rattling in my chest. "It's too far away," I say, a defensive tone finding my voice. "I don't like the school or the professors. I'm afraid if I go back, things won't get better, Mom."

"So where do you want to go?" she asks, not even hesitating in this conversation. I wonder if part of her anticipated it.

I lick my lips that have gone so dry they threaten to crack. I want my voice to be strong, to sound sure about my answer, but it isn't. It's a weak whisper that lets all the fear flooding my veins show. "Rayou Community College."

The kitchen falls so quiet my head hurts, and when I meet my mother's blue eyes—the same blue as my own—I think I might be sick. She stares at me, eyes wide and a tight jaw. "You can't throw your life away for a boy, Penny," she snaps, her voice sharp and so much louder than my own.

"This isn't about Christopher," I say, seeing that's immediately where she thought this was going.

"It's not?" she asks sarcastically, disbelief flooding a sheen to her eyes.

"No, I want to go to a smaller school. I want to be here in Rayou," I say, listing off all the other reasons of why I want to transfer. "I don't even know what degree I want to get or what job I want after college."

"Then why did we take you there?" my mother asks, and now anger has started to root itself inside of her. "Why did we just spend thousands of dollars for you to go to school there? We took out loans, and moved you across the country, and—"

"Because Lindsay made me," I interrupt her and it makes my mother snap her mouth closed. My breathing is ragged, trying to compete with my skyrocketing pulse. "Because Lindsay made me," I say again. "She applied to Frostard for me. I never wanted to go there."

At the mention of Lindsay, my mom's face softens, her anger

disappearing in an instant. She knows what Lindsay's influence did to me when it comes to my body, what I ate, and how I treated myself on the cheer squad. I never told her the other places Lindsay's control reached.

"Penelope, this is a big decision," she says, using my full name to help emphasize her point. Her tone has softened considerably, and I think she's finally understanding where this decision is coming from. My mom knows this trip home has been a transition for me in more ways than one. It's been a healing process, and I think she understands that I want to start making decisions for myself, now. Transferring to Rayou Community College is one of the first decisions I've made for me, and I can tell my mom is struggling with telling me I can't do the first thing I've wanted to do for myself.

"I want to do this, Mom," I say, and my heart finally begins to rest in my chest, now that the words are out and there's no going back. Telling her was the hardest part, and now that it's behind me, crossing this finish line is up to me. "It's only for a year, and then I'll have my associate degree."

"And then what?" she asks, leaning back in her chair, trying to keep judgment from her tone.

"Then I'll find a school to get my bachelor's degree at," I say. What comes next is truly unknown, but that's okay. That will be another decision I'll make for myself.

My mom stares at me for a long, quiet moment. I wish I knew what she was thinking, as her crystal gaze sweeps across my face, maybe imagining the little girl who's all grown up now, maybe imagining the future she sees for me if I make this choice. My mother takes in a deep breath and sighs, saying, "If it's what you want to do, Penny, I will always support you."

My heart skips at her words, seeing the conversation shift and the tension in the air goes with it. "Really?" I ask, and my mom nods.

"Penelope, it's your life. You have to make the decisions yourself, but as your mom I'll always support you," she says, and I think there may be more that she was going to add, but her words are cut off when I throw my arms around her neck, squeezing her in the tightest hug I can.

"Thank you," I say into her blonde hair. "I'll do, like, double shifts shelving at the library, and organize the next three months of the children's book club."

A soft laugh vibrates from my mom to me, and she runs her hand down the back of my head. "You don't have to do that, Penny," she says, letting me fall away from our hug and back into my barstool. My mom reaches for her bowl of oatmeal, sliding it off the counter and into her hands as she stands. "But you can call your dad to tell him you'll be leaving Frostard."

After the conversation with my mom, everything seems to fall into place, spiraling together like a perfectly wound ball of string. My dad wasn't as receptive as my mom was, and that much I expected. But he's halfway across the globe in London, and there's nothing he can really do to change my mind now.

We spend an hour on the phone talking about the logistics of the decision, and finally he says he understands my choice. He even offers to try and get me a position at his company over the summer to call an early internship, something that would look good on an application to another school down the road, or even, a way to get my foot in the door with my associate degree. My dad not only said he understands my choice, but he wants to help me along the way in whatever way he can.

The transferring process is a bit muddy. Normally, people are taking their community college credits and transferring them to a University, not the other way around. I've been using the contact Maggie and Janay gave me at Rayou Community College, and he's been helpful.

Nearly a month after that breakfast with my mom, and everything is just about to come together like I imagined it would. For thirty days I've kept this secret from Christopher. In theory, it sounded easy, but we've spent practically every day together since spring break, and that has made it ten times harder to keep this to myself. We've have movie nights and dates at the Snowcapped Diner weekly. He's always at the library, helping me shelve books and find ones for us to read together to pass the time, though he always grows frustrated when I won't read the last page with him.

Everything with Christopher is so easy, letting us fall back into that routine we had before I went to Frostard, and of course the chemistry is still there, each kiss feeling like the first time all over again. But today, I think I'm finally going to be able to tell him about my plans for the future, about how I'm not going anywhere. I won't be leaving him again.

I pace anxiously in front of the coffee table in the living room, waiting for my mom to walk back up the driveway with the mail. I know there shouldn't be any issues with me transferring to Rayou Community College, but my new advisor said they'd send me an official enrollment packet in the mail to confirm everything has been set up for me to start classes in August, and today is when they said it would arrive.

The front door swings open, cold air blowing in around my mom, who stomps her boots off on the mat, a stack of envelopes pinched in her hand.

"Well?" I blurt before she even has the door closed.

My mom picks a large black envelope off the top, a shimmery gold ink printed on its border. "It's here!" she says, extending her arm to me.

I snatch it from her so fast I wouldn't be surprised if she suffered a paper cut from my frantic need to know what's inside. My mom laughs at me, closing the door and heading for the kitchen. "Penny, trust me, you got in."

Her words quiet in my racing mind, and my fingers run along the seam, ripping the thick envelope open. I slide out the heavy parchment that's folded three times, and, of course, exhale with relief when I read that I've been admitted for classes this fall. "It's official!" I call to her through the house.

"Told you," my mom sings back.

A smile blooms on my face. Something about seeing it in writing, holding this letter in my hand, makes everything feel real. Now I can tell Christopher, and we can start thinking about our relationship as long term, not having to avoid the subject of our futures any longer.

My phone buzzes in the back pocket of my skinny jeans and I wiggle it free.

Christopher: Hey.

Penny: Hey, you!

Christopher: They announced a winner for the portfolio contest.

My heart pauses in my chest. Those anxious nerves that had been directed at my acceptance to Rayou Community College now repark. I run down the narrow hall and into the kitchen, finding the calendar hanging above the small desk we have in the corner. I confirm that it's the 22nd of April. Four weeks since we took that last photo at the park.

Penny: Well? Did you win?

The three dots appear and disappear twice before Christopher's message finally comes through.

Christopher: Can we meet somewhere?

The air leaks from my lungs, balancing myself in a void of the unknown. I can't decide if it's a good thing or not that he wants to tell me in person, but when I glance down at the black envelope in my hand, I'm reminded that I have my own news to share with him. Something that we can either celebrate with his victory, or we can use to cover the disappointment of the loss.

Penny: Sure, do you want to come over?

After a quick confirmation from Christopher, I turn and see my mom flipping through the other items we had in the mailbox. "Christopher's on his way over."

My mom pauses her shuffle on the letters and looks at me. "Penny, once you tell him, you can't change your mind," she warns, but I blow past her concern.

"I won't change my mind," I say, moving across the tiled floor and into the mudroom. I reach for my coat, buttoning the silver studs up to my chin and lace my brown leather boots. As an afterthought, I tuck the letter from the community college inside my coat, knowing I want to time the reveal correctly.

I trek back through the house and decide to wait on the front porch for Christopher's arrival. As I open the front door, the afternoon sun sprays a warm, orange light across my face, and I can't keep the wide smile from materializing. It pulls at my lips, so tight dimples form at the corners. I'm finally going to tell Christopher I'll be in Rayou. I'll be with him, for every day moving forward.

Chapter 38

The wooden porch swing creaks beneath my weight as I sway back and forth. Snow-covered pine trees knit themselves together around the neighboring houses and Olive Street seems to be caught in a frozen snow globe.

Christopher is taking longer than it should to drive to my house.

When my fidgeting fingers are about to give in to the temptation to call him, I hear the rumble of his truck approaching from the right. At the sight of the familiar truck—the rusted spot above the passenger side front tire and fogged windows—the ball of nerves in my belly finally fades. Christopher parks his truck at the end of the driveway and, after turning off the ignition, drops from the cabin.

I launch off the swing with excitement, bouncing on the balls of me feet while I wait for him on the porch.

"Hey!" I say, my breath fogging the space in front of me.

Christopher's smile is loose when he reaches me, brown hair falling across his forehead. "Hey," he says, and immediately the softness of his voice puts me on edge. He doesn't meet my gaze, those hazel eyes dark tonight. "Can we sit out here?"

I study him for a moment, trying to assess the situation. Even though it's the end of April and the cold breeze still bites my cheeks, I had felt like a warm ball of sun was burning in my chest, the excitement about my surprise to Christopher keeping my body thawed.

We must have lost the portfolio contest.

Well, even more the reason why I'm glad I have good news. Maybe it will make him forget about the competition. I shift my weight and the thick black envelope hidden beneath my coat pokes me in the side.

"Sure," I say with a sharp nod and we both move to sit side-by-side on the porch swing. I pull my feet underneath me in a crossed position while Christopher uses the toe of his shoe to rock the old swing back and forth while he perches on the edge. "So?" I prompt him, forcing my tone to stay bright.

Christopher's mouth parts, and he lifts his head to look at the line of trees across the street. After a moment, he sighs, letting his back slump against the swing, and he shakes his head. "Penny, I don't know how to say this."

For the first time since he climbed my porch, Christopher turns and looks at me. My eyes dart across his face, seeing worrisome lines creasing his forehead, a sheen growing at the corners of his eyes. My stomach sinks further, seeing how much this is upsetting him. It takes everything in me not to blurt out my good news, wanting him to give me his news first.

"Say what?" I ask softly, knowing he's struggling to tell me that, after all the effort we put into the portfolio, it wasn't enough.

"Well," Christopher starts, tilting his head back to look at overhang that glows orange in the setting sun. His lip begins to tremble as he sucks in a deep breath, and when he dips his chin to meet my watchful eyes, he finally tells me what happened. "I won."

I blink at him. "You won?" I repeat, and when I say the words aloud, they finally process. "You won!" I exclaim. "Christopher, that's amazing!" I throw my arms around his neck, welcoming the familiar warmth of him wrapping around my body. The porch swing groans and sways against my movements and I laugh into the crook of his neck. "You had me so worried!" I say, thinking his saddened eyes and drooping shoulders were an act so he could surprise me with the victory.

I sit back from him, and my heart clenches when I see the tears that were building in his eyes now streak his cheeks. Not happy tears, but ones heavy with sadness, shaking his body. "What's wrong, Christopher?" Honest, bone deep fear has gripped me at seeing him cry. "I thought we wanted to win."

"I thought I did too," he says, his voice trembling so badly that he has to pause to take a breath, aggressively wiping away the tears, leaving his cheeks pink.

"What happened?" I ask. Something obviously changed in the last twelve hours since I saw him for our movie night. I've never seen Christopher so broken. Not since that night in August—

"The first place prize is—" He takes in another shuddering breath, and I visually see the pain his next words cause him, his face crumbling.

I'm losing my patience with him, my panic making my throat close up. "Christopher," I say, his name sharp on my tongue. I reach up, holding his face between my hands, and the heat from his flushed cheeks burns against my cold fingers. "Talk to me," I say, my wide eyes locking with his.

He sits there and stares at me, letting his heart slow and his voice settle before speaking again. "The first place prize is a full ride scholarship to Rhode Island School of Design."

My hands fall from his face, arms heavy with shock. *A full ride.* "Wait…" I say, voice broken as realization sweeps through me. "Oh my God." My heart picks up, rattling in my chest.

"I know," Christopher whispers, running a hand through his brown hair.

A full ride to Rhode Island School of Design.

Rhode Island.

He's moving across the country to his dream school.

I'm so overwhelmed with emotions I have absolutely no idea how to react to this. I want to cry and let the pain creeping up my throat rip an angry wave through my body. I want to shrug my shoulders and say it doesn't matter, that once I tell him about me transferring to Rayou Community College, he'll turn down his full ride. I want to be happy for him because it's his dream school. He'd told me about it that first day I went with him to his photography class, and he said he'd never get to go because it was too expensive.

After all of this rushes through my mind, everything finally settles in with the cold truth of what is happening. Christopher just received a full ride scholarship to his dream school on the other side of the country. The tightly wound ball of string is unwinding before my eyes, our relationship dissolving between my fingers.

"You're leaving me," I whisper, tears rushing to my eyes.

Christopher looks at me with honey colored swirls in his gaze, and I see how hurt he is by what is happening. I know he didn't choose to go to school in Rhode Island, it's just an opportunity that's presented itself, but I can't keep the blame from shifting to him. After all this time, *he's* leaving *me.*

"You're leaving," I say again, my voice stronger, an obvious crack of betrayal shattering the cold air between us.

"Penny, I didn't mean for this to happen." The words fumble from his mouth, but when he reaches for my hand, I snap it back.

I know my anger is misdirected but… but dammit, *no*, this can't be happening! If I could, I would scream at the universe for ruining my life after I just put it back together, but my anger tinted eyes only see the boy in front of me, dropping my glass heart the same way it fractured last time.

"You're leaving!" I yell at Christopher, tears breaking free from my eyes, and I lose my grasp on my racing heart, my breaths panicked. My mind rushes to find a way to fix this, to pull in the fraying string and go back to just a few minutes ago when everything was right.

Christopher's broken face hardens before my eyes, his own anger blooming at my directed blame. "You're leaving too!" he says, raising his voice to match mine. "You're going back to Frostard in August. What the hell did you think was going to happen to us, Penny? This was never going to be forever. We were just pretending on borrowed time."

For a moment, I forget he doesn't know about my plan to stay in Rayou. I'm about to scream at him that I just gave up everything to come back home, but the words freeze on my tongue, my mouth hanging ajar. I want to tell him, to let him know that I wasn't going to leave this time, that I kept my promise to him that I wouldn't break his heart again, but I can't.

I can't tell him I'm staying in Rayou, because then he'd feel obligated to give up his scholarship to stay with me, and I won't be the reason Christopher loses this dream. We stare at each other through the tense quiet moment, both of our chests rising and falling with racing hearts. His tears have drawn back, but mine still flow down my face, freezing to my cheeks.

"I wanted it to be forever," I say instead of the truth that I know I can never speak. My voice falls to a whisper and my chest splits open, the cold, Colorado mountain wind pouring in and spreading ice through my veins.

Christopher's sharp jaw softens, and I can see him struggle with the anger that matches my own. Struggling to be mad at the person sitting across from them when we love each other so much. And because of that, I have to let him go. My legs shake beneath me as I stand, trembling hands shoving their way into the pockets of my coat.

"Penny, don't walk away," Christopher says, rising and blocking my path on the porch. He towers above me, looking down at me through the brown waves that frame his face. "Please, don't go like this." A single tangerine beam casts a shadow across his sharp jawline, making his hazel eyes glitter. "We haven't even talked about trying long distance."

Long distance. The idea burns like acid in my throat. Is it fair of me to say that isn't good enough? Because that's not us. Christopher is supposed be my warmth in the cold, the smell of coffee and pine, the sound of rich laughter. He can't be the crackle through the phone, a frozen picture on social media, a memory that becomes fuzzy.

And there's no possible way I can be in a long distance relationship with him and not be honest about the fact that I am transferring to Rayou Community College. The only way I can keep that secret and make sure Christopher gets to go to his dream school is to walk away and let him go.

"I can't, Christopher." The words cut my throat, a heaving sob making my lungs throb.

He raises his right hand, cupping my damp cheek and I feel his heartbreak in his frantic movements. "Please, Penny."

I shake my head against his grasp, more hot tears burning tracks down my face and in between his fingers. His brown eyes are wide with defeat, and in a final attempt to make me change my mind, Christopher dips his head and presses his mouth to mine. The kiss is hard and wet with my tears. I squeeze my eyes shut and lean into him, begging myself to memorize the feel of him, the love that is crashing into me.

Christopher speaks against my mouth, his breath raising bumps down my arm. "Penny Wilson, I love you so much."

"I love you, too," I say through a steadying breath. When I open my eyes, they burn from my tears meeting the frigid wind. I have to raise a hand and rest it on his chest, physically pushing myself away from him to put space between us. "But I know what it's like to be gone from Rayou and you, and I can't do it again."

I try to look Christopher in the eyes when I say it, but my focus gets caught on the single tear that creeps down his cheek. I follow it to his jaw and shudder when it drops onto my hand that still rests against his chest. "I can't do it, Christopher," I whisper and snap my mouth closed. I have to bite my tongue so hard a metallic taste fills my mouth to keep from telling him that *I'm* not the one leaving. *He* is. But when I look up at Christopher, at the man I'd give everything for, I know, for him, I'll walk away.

I step around Christopher as another wave of hot tears pours from my eyes, biting trails into my cheeks. I keep telling myself that this is the right thing to do, even though it feels so incredibly wrong. Against my aching heart, I leave Christopher standing on my front porch in the exact spot I stood that night in January when I saw him drive by in his red truck. And if I could, I'd go back and tell myself to look away. To never see his shadowed figure behind the steering wheel, to never let myself wonder about him, because then, maybe, we could have avoided this inevitable heartbreak.

Chapter 39

With the side of my face pressed into my furry pillow, I study the cork board at my desk, tracing the faded squares where those pictures of Christopher and I used to hang. This time yesterday, I may have been daydreaming about hanging new ones in their places, but now I know they'll always remain empty.

My cheeks are raw from crying all night, the tears finally running dry only a couple of hours ago.

Christopher is leaving.

I can't shake that thought out of my head. It just keeps rattling there, making my chest ache each time I have to reprocess this horrible, twisted fate.

"Penny, are you not getting up today?" My mom's voice is muffled on the other side of my door.

I know I should respond, tell her that I'll be down in a second, but I can't get words to form. She must worry from my lack of response because I hear the knob on the door jiggle, and the hinges creak as she eases it open. "Penny, what's wrong?" Her voice is soft, so much care hanging on her words that it thaws the empty, vast void of sadness that built up around me last night. She crosses the room and sits on the edge of the bed, her hand instinctively going to my forehead like I might have a fever.

I wish this was just a cold. Something that I could heal from and forget ever happened after a week.

"Christopher's going to Rhode Island School of Design," I say, my voice nasally from my stuffy nose after all my crying. "He's leaving, Mom."

Her hand pauses on the top of my head. "What?" she asks, the same shock finding its way into her as it did me.

I rock my head against her touch and the pillow. "He won the portfolio contest, and the prize was a full ride to that school."

My mom only lets the surprise linger for a second before her hand is moving in soothing strokes down my back. "I'm so sorry, Penny."

New tears form, traveling in skinny trails down my cheeks. After last night, they don't even phase me, and I just let them roll free.

"It's going to be okay, Penny," my mom whispers. She reaches for my hand tucked under my pillow and pulls it free, tugging me up so I'm sitting and facing her. "It's going to be okay," she says again. Her fingers are cold as she wipes the tears I've neglected from my cheeks. I can see her eyes moving, searching for a way she can fix this, to do something to make me feel better because she's my mom, and she feels like it's her job to heal me.

"Did you tell him you were transferring?" she asks, and I follow her gaze to my desk, where that black envelope rests against the cork board. I tossed it there last night when I got inside before sinking into my mattress and crying until sleep found me.

I shake my head, hair that's damp with tears slipping around my shoulders. "I couldn't. I don't want him to give up the chance to go to his dream school," I say through my hollow throat.

My mom brings her blue eyes back to me, understanding why this is so difficult for me. Because I know I could get him to stay if I wanted to, if I wanted to be selfish and take this opportunity from him. It feels like my hands are breaking my own heart just as much as Christopher's are.

"Well," my mom says through a sigh, "you could always go back to Frostard in the fall. Christopher will never know that you were going to transfer. It could be like it never happened."

I know she means for her words to make me feel better, but they just open a pit beneath my stomach and a nauseous wave follows them. I don't want to forget everything that's happened, and even after my relationship with Christopher has fallen apart, I don't want to go back to Frostard.

My gaze lingers a moment longer on the black envelope with gold foil boarders. Yesterday, I had seen it as the letter sealing my future with Christopher, but now, I see it as my own future. Meant for me and what I want.

I shake my head and look at my mom. "I still want to go to Rayou Community College in the fall."

"Even though Christopher won't be here?" she asks. I had told her that I didn't choose to transfer because of Christopher, but I don't think she ever really believed that.

I'm not sure I did either. "That's still what's best for me," I say, taking a deep breath that makes my whole body shudder. I exhale, letting my shoulders slump forward and a bit of that weight that had been suffocating me all night lifts. I still have my life to figure out, these decisions I'm making are sculpting my future. My chest still aches when

I force my mind to see that future without Christopher, but I think that's just something I'm going to have to live with for a while.

My mom reaches up and cups my cheek. I lean into her touch, and make my lips pull up in a small, sad smile to match her own. "It's going to be okay, Penny," she says once again, and each time she does, I slowly start to believe her.

Snow sprays away from the tires beneath the SUV as my mom turns onto Main Street. I lean against the passenger side door, watching the colorful shops pass by, the icicles hanging from their gutters dripping and melting in the spring sun that's trying to take over Rayou.

It's been a week since Christopher told me he was going to Rhode Island. He must know I need space right now because he hasn't texted or called. I'm not really sure if that's helped with the ache in my chest, but today is the first day I've left the house, so that's progress.

I probably I would have stayed locked in my room until August if my mom hadn't found me that morning, coaxing me out of the pit my heart was sinking into. She's the one who got me out of the house today, saying she could use my help at the library since Sarah is on vacation this week.

When we drive by the Snowcapped Diner, I close my eyes and face away from the window, not wanting to look at it and think about the memories that will always linger there. After a few more turns to maneuver around the block, we can park at the back of the Library, and my mom and I slide out of the SUV.

We enter through the employee entrance and I help her flip on the lights, hearing them buzz to life overhead. She turns up the heater, filling the space with that cloud of warmth that always makes me want to live inside the library forever. I walk down the back hallway to the main entrance and twist the open sign around. The enormous pine tree that grows in the center of the Rayou town square is blurry through the old glass door, but I can still tell all of the snow that had hung to its branches that first night I arrived in Rayou is gone. A sign of how much time has passed, how many things have changed since that night. The frozen world outside is melting, and it reminds me of the waterfall we hiked to at Estes Park. I wonder if its waters have thawed and are flowing once more. Just like how my life had been balancing in a frozen, perfect moment, until it all came crashing down, rushing forward, and leaving that perfect moment behind.

I turn around and walk down the narrow hall, loving the way the old floors groan and shift beneath my leather boots. I stride through the archway to my left, entering the heart of the library. The lights glow a warm yellow overhead, making the dark wooden shelves look timeless. Every time I walk beneath this entryway, I lose my breath at the beauty of the library, instantly becoming consumed with all the colorful spines of the books that are pressed tightly together.

But today, it's different. Today I look out at the sea of shelves, the smell of worn pages thick in the warm air, and I feel an overwhelming anxiety swell up in my chest. All these books, all of these last pages, and endings, surround me. The end of mine and Christopher's relationship is so fresh, so raw, that it makes me want to live through all the endings I've neglected my whole life. I've spent eighteen years avoiding final moments of movies and songs, never wanting to close doors and seal off parts of my life.

I'm afraid of letting things go, but with Christopher, I never had a choice. It was ended for me, and it makes me want to scream at all the time I wasted hating endings for this very reason.

I walk up to the closest shelf, pulling off a fantasy book that I read years ago. The pages fan out in my grasp and I flip to the very last page, and I read it.

I read those final words, letting myself finally know how it ended all these years later, because it did end, and I never realized how insane it was for me to ignore that, to pretend these characters kept living after the ink had dried. I grab the one next to it, another fantasy book I had loved as a kid, and again, I read the last page.

And another, and another. I spend the entire day walking down the shelves, pulling old books free and finally learning what I had tried to deny for years. Everything ends.

Maybe that's all Christopher and I were. An ending I refused to believe was over months ago. I came back to Rayou and let myself ignore that our final page had already been written. Instead, I traveled down that same story, hoping for different words on that last page, but they were the same.

As I read the endings of the books around me, I begin to accept the ending fated for Christopher and me. I start to understand that it's over, and maybe, one day, I'll be able to close the book. Because no matter how many books I snap shut and slide back onto the shelf, that part is still the hardest to do, to accept the end written there and let it go.

Some of the endings are happy, the couple getting married, or reuniting after being torn apart. Even more are sad, though. Final pages filled with goodbyes and death and yes, ends.

After hours pass and I've read so many pages my eyes are throbbing in my head, I fall into the plush armchair by the wall of frosted windows, letting my mind go numb as I watch the dust dance in the beams of sunlight. I sit here for a moment before my mom finds me, walking up with a black book in her hand. I'm about to tell her I can't read another last page, something I know she was watching me do while she worked behind the front desk, when I notice that this book isn't like the ones on the shelves. It's taller and not as thick. Its pages are black, not the cream paper I'm used it. She extends it to me, and I take the heavy book in my hands, my heart swelling when I realize what it is. It's a portfolio.

"Christopher dropped it off at the house earlier this week," my mom says gently. "I wasn't sure if you wanted to see it."

I can't bring my gaze up to meet hers, still completely consumed by the black leather binding of the portfolio in my hands, so, I just nod. She leaves me alone with the binder and it takes me a few minutes to work up the courage to open it. When I do, tears rush to my eyes at the first picture. An empty bench, surrounded by pine trees, their branches hanging heavy with snow. I remember the night Christopher took this like it was yesterday.

Actually, I think the point of this photo is for the bench to be empty.

His words still drive a crack in my heart, and I feel myself hit rock bottom all over again. The point of this portfolio was to evoke emotion, and he's done that with a single picture. The photo is dark and somehow cold, and it completely captures how I felt three months ago when I had left Frostard.

I turn the page slowly, letting the thick, black cardstock linger between my fingers. The next page has three photos placed across its surface from the night at the lookout spot. The first has my back to the camera, the girl in the photo far away and shadowed by the dark night. In the distance, just beyond the wooden fence I lean against, is Rayou, the Christmas lights still glittering.

I'm looking over my shoulder in the second photo, a curious gaze that makes me want to ask the girl in the photo what she was thinking, a mysterious aurora wrapping around her. A plane soars overhead in the last photo, a white dot in the dark sky, red lights caught flashing in the frame, and my neck is craned back, looking at it soaring overhead.

On the next page, I'm caught by surprise with the single photo he's chosen, one I didn't even know he'd taken. I'm sitting in the same plush armchair I rest in now, a book propped open on my knee, just seconds before I know I closed it to keep from reading the last page. I think back to that day, remembering how I looked up from the book and saw Christopher standing by the desk with my mom, but I hadn't realized he'd already taken his photo for the portfolio. I trace the edge of the picture, loving how he captured me in the moment, not staging or acting out the picture. It's real.

I run my finger across the top of the portfolio, my featherlight touch slipping behind the black cardstock and turning to the next page. I suck in a breath when the bright white images pop off the page. Two of them, from the day at the hot springs. A smile pulls my lips in an open grin, wide eyes sweeping across the pictures.

The first is absolutely stunning. He's captured the moment he ran up behind me and pulled me into his arms, leaping into the hot spring. Hot steam curls up to reach our feet as we jumped, fully clothed, into the pool. That was such a good day.

My gaze slips down to the second photo, a wall of water arcing through the air. The splashing war that commenced after we'd jumped into the hot spring. We're both laughing, wet hair hanging around our shoulders. My eyes are squeezed shut, arms crossed in front of my face to prepare for the wall of water to hit. These photos have so much movement even though everything here is motionless, captured, remembered, and saved here forever.

The next page sends tingles down my arms. My chest lightens and the air in my lungs seeps out. The sunset is a bright orange, sinking behind the mountains that surround the ice-skating rink. Christopher's caught me in mid-spin, the ice from the rink spraying up around my skates. He must have been moving when he took it, because everything around me is blurry, drawing the eye to me, to the focal point of this photo, and, now that I realize it, the focal point of the entire portfolio.

Christopher had told me he wanted to portfolio to be our story, but the way he's placed these photos, the way the camera captures me and nothing else, makes me wonder if maybe my story was the one he was telling all along.

When I flip the page again, my heart spreads open, warmth and ache filling me all at once. It's from the night at the park, and it's just a single photo, printed so large it fills the entire page. A small black boarder from the cardstock beneath it clings to the dark edges of the image from that night. Christopher and I stand beneath the lamp post, yellow light casting a perfect circle on the snowy ground around us. Snowflakes drift through the air, tiny white dots that pepper the image. Our kiss is caught here, frozen like the world we're standing in.

The story Christopher is telling with his portfolio begins to become clear to me, because I lived it. It is my story. The first photo of that empty bench was dark and lonely. The library photo showing who I was; someone caught up in their delusion of avoiding endings, still learning how to make choices for herself.

The photo at the hot springs is the turning point, reflected in the bright snow and the light that filled the images. The day I stopped letting my past define me. The day I finally understood that I wanted things to change, and that I had the power to change them. The ice skating photo, completely focused on me, paints me as independent and confident. Finally finding the girl who was inside me all along. And this page, with the captured kiss, it's magical, but also final.

When my finger runs along the top of the portfolio, my heart pauses in my chest. The next page is the last page. My damp eyes look up, scanning all the shelves filled with books I just read the final pages of, and I decide that I can do one more.

I look back down at the portfolio and turn the page. It's heavier then the others, and when I have it spread wide, I realize why. It's littered with pictures, so many of them, cut and pieced together in a collage that it fills the black cardstock from corner to corner.

It's all the images Christopher hadn't included on the first pages. There's a picture of me walking up to the lookout railing, tons from that day in the library when I peered at him through the shelves and we ran around the aisles of books like children, smiles spread on our faces. Tears begin to sting the edges of my eyes, but I keep scanning every single image, wanting to see all the moments captured here. I find some more photos from the hot springs with the splashing war captured in beautiful frozen arcs. He even included the picture we took in front of the fireplace at the resort, the fluffy robes we had been wearing looking as silly as I remember them.

The ones of the cabin we stayed in are a bright white, the freshly fallen snow making the images glow amongst the rest of them. I find pictures of the snowball forts, and of me and Maggie and Janay on the porch. There's some from that day we found the frozen lake in the woods around the cabin, but my favorites are the ones we took on our drive. Pictures we'd captured on his phone of us eating burritos the size of our faces and pointing out signs that went with our alphabet game.

Tears break free, sliding down my cheeks, but a smile tugs at my lips. I love everything he's put here, these moments, the memories from the last three months. It hurts my heart and makes it beat all the same.

My fingers slide across the glossy pictures, pausing at the center of the page where a blue piece of paper has been taped at the corners, a dedication written there.

To Penelope Wilson, who taught me how to live in these moments instead of only capturing them.

A cry breaks through my tightening throat, hot salty tears finding the corners of my broken smile. He really did put this entire portfolio together for me. For the person I've become over the last three months. I stare at the collage of photos for what feels like hours, finding new details in each image. Deep in my heart, I know that Christopher is still going to Rhode Island in August. Our story really is over, and this portfolio is proof that the tale we'd been living the last three months is over, too.

And here I am, doing exactly what I told myself I would never do. I'm reading the last page. Not only that, but I'm *living* it. I thought that would break me, so I avoided endings of any kind and I let myself be blinded by all those things that lead up to the final page. Like when I got that feeling, that spark, the swoop of my heart. It happened in the moment I knew I was about to fall for Christopher, and I took a breath. I breathed in all the possibilities and I prepared myself for all the ways it could go right or wrong. And I jumped. Christopher jumped.

But I couldn't have been more wrong when I assessed what I was getting myself into. I knew we could end this story in heartbreak—I honestly would have bet money on that—and when the time came, when I saw the cracks fracture in the mirror of my heart, I reminded myself of what I used to always say. *Don't read the last page.*

Because when you do, it's over. Done. There's no more hoping he'll come back, or that you'll try again. But I did it anyway, and what I read on that last page, what I'm seeing now, aren't the words I thought I'd find. Words of sadness and grief and reflecting on what we had. No, instead they are words of hope, of wisdom, of the image of the woman I am. Simply put, it's a call to collect the broken pieces and keep moving.

So, don't read the last page.

Pick up a pen and write your new beginning.

Epilogue

T he clattering of porcelain coffee cups rings in my ears as the afternoon rush at the Snowcapped Diner buzzes around me. I let the sounds of one of my favorite places in Rayou engulf me, leaning back to swivel in my barstool as I overlook the kitchen. Willie offers to get me a refill, but I slide the empty cup to her and tell her I'm done. I pull my hand back, tapping my fingers on the pocket pamphlet that sits in front of me on the bar, a plane ticket tucked inside that my mom surprised me with the other day. I know I need to leave soon, so I'm ready when the shuttle to the airport picks me up, but I can't get myself to move. The leather seat seems to attach itself to my skin, the first day I've been able to wear shorts since I came home in January.

I take in the Snowcapped Diner one more time, telling myself I'll be back soon enough. Just as I'm about to stand, the scent of coffee intensifies, followed by a hint of pine that makes my heart pause. An arm brushes mine as someone slides into the barstool beside me, and when I twist in my chair to look at them, I meet his hazel gaze.

"Christopher," I breathe his name. It's the first time I've seen him in two weeks, the last time being that night in April when everything fell apart.

"Hey, Penny," he says, the corner of his mouth twitching up in a nervous grin. His gaze sweeps over me, taking in my straightened blonde hair and cherry red blouse. I know he notices my make-up, the eyeliner crisp and the mascara thick. "How are you doing?" His tone is borderline cautious, knowing he's asking a loaded question, but I think he's surprised to see how put together I look, all things considered.

My knee brushes his as the barstool twists beneath me. I reach up to tuck my hair behind my ear, my own nerves hitching in my throat. "I'm doing okay," I say, flashing my gaze to meet his through my lashes. He's wearing a tight, white shirt, his dark jeans a stark contrast, and his denim jacket is missing, probably put away for the season.

Christopher folds his bottom lip back between his teeth, and nods, looking like he's struggling for the words he wants to say, so I fill the gap in our conversation. "How about you? What have you been up to?"

He exhales, shoulders falling a bit. "Busy getting ready for my classes this fall," he says. It's a cold reminder of the fissure that split our relationship, but in the two weeks that have passed, his leaving no longer hurts me the way it did the first night I learned of it. "My dad is helping me find an apartment out there," he adds.

"Your own apartment? That's exciting," I say, letting my smile come easily.

"Yeah, well, I'm not technically a freshman since I'm transferring in as a sophomore, so I don't have to live in the dorms," he says, resting his arm on the back of the barstool.

"Trust me, you're not missing anything," I say, shuddering at the thought of the tiny room Lindsay and I shared for a single semester.

Christopher's laugh is short, but it still makes goosebumps raise on my arms. "Yeah, I didn't think so."

Our conversation pauses, my chest tightening in the tense air that forms. We both look away, finding something on the walls of the diner to study as the silence lingers for another minute.

"Are you here for you daily coffee or..." I say, searching for any words to fill the lingering silence.

Christopher meets my gaze, and shakes his head. "Maggie and Janay just told me you were planning to transfer to Rayou Community College. I wanted to talk to you, and I figured you be here," he says and my heart stops beating in my chest. "Since we broke up, they..." Christopher trails off, the mention of our separation causing his words to falter. "They thought I already knew." He looks at me, and a sense of hurt radiates in his eyes.

"I was going to tell you that night," I explain, and my voice cracks as my mouth turns dry. "But after I found out about your scholarship, I didn't want you to change your mind." Christopher opens his mouth, but no words follow. I think his first reaction is to tell me that, if I had told him that night, I wouldn't have changed his mind, but he stops himself from saying it, realizing he'd be lying if he did.

"I'm excited for you, Christopher," I say, nudging his knee again with mine and I welcome the sparks that shoot up my leg from the brief contact. "Rhode Island School of Design is your dream."

The caramel swirls in his eyes are bright this afternoon. He glances away from me, blinking through the harsh sun that shines across his face. His chest rises and falls, the muscles tight under his shirt, and it looks as if he's still struggling with the idea of leaving, that talking about Rhode Island has upset him. An ache has taken root in my chest too, and our next words are spoken in unison, subconsciously racing the other to say it. "I miss you."

Christopher's brings his gaze back to me when we speak, and we look at the other for a second before a warm laugh escapes us. "Penny, I've been thinking," Christopher says, interrupting the soft laughter. "I understand you didn't think we could do long distance before because you had to keep your decision to transfer a secret, but now I know. Now, could it be an option?"

That ache in my chest only grows at his words, the idea making me sick. "That's not how our story is supposed to be," I say softly, sadness hanging on each word. I've given the idea some thought, but every time I do, it just hurts my heart. To be with him, but not *with* him, would drive me crazy. After all the time we spent apart, all those wasted months, I don't want to lose another second with him. In my head, in my heart, our story has always been moments we share together.

"That story is over, Penny," Christopher says. "That was our high school story. Maybe that's our problem. We keep trying to read the same book, expecting the ending to change, for the story to continue, but what if we accept that it's over? Accept that was our last page?" He reaches for my hand, his fingers warm as they wrap around mine, and my breath eases out of my lungs. It's the same realization I had made myself that day in the library. He squeezes my grasp reassuringly, my heart skipping with the gesture. "And then we open a new book and start a new story. You in Rayou and me in Rhode Island. Could that be our next story?"

"No, it can't," I say, my throat tight around the words.

Christopher's grip on my hand loosens, mirroring the drop of his heart. I let his hand fall and his eyes darken at my blunt rejection to his proposition.

"Because I'm not going to be in Rayou this fall," I add, explaining why his idea of our new story wouldn't work.

"You're not? Did Lindsay talk you back into Frostard?" His voice turns up defensively, worry creasing the corners of his eyes.

"No," I say, stopping him before he can continue theorizing what I mean. "I make my own decisions now."

He smiles at that, a brief grin that makes the butterflies in my chest reawaken. "So, where are you going to be?"

"That depends," I say, wringing my hands together, a bit nervous about what I'm about to do. "Do you need a roommate?"

Christopher blinks a few times, mind trying to unravel my words. "What do you mean, Penny?"

I dampen my lips, a heat rising to my cheeks as I prepare myself to lay all my cards out for him. This is all I can offer him, the last chance I have to be with Christopher. "My classes at Rayou Community College are all online. I can take them anywhere."

He looks at me like I might be speaking a foreign language. Hazel eyes wide, mouth slightly ajar. "Were you not going to tell me?" he asks, hurt filtering through his words.

"I was," I quickly explain, "but I'm leaving today. I was going to tell you when I got back, to see if you still…"

"Still want to be with you?" Christopher asks, filling in where I let my words fail.

I nod once, my heart picking up in my chest, making me so nervous the room starts to spin. I don't know if I can accept Christopher telling me he doesn't want to be with me. Not this soon. I didn't plan on letting him know any of this until I came back from my trip, but now he's in front of me and it all came out, putting the ball in his court.

"Penny," he whispers, reaching for my face and running his warm fingers across my cheek. He tilts my head back so I'm looking right at him, right into the depths of his marbled eyes. "I think it's obvious my heart is, and always has been, yours."

Christopher leans forward, taking away the space that was between us, and kisses me. His lips are warm against mine, and the kiss is passionate, strong, translating the words he just said into a spark that travels through my entire body. I take in the feeling of him against me and the scent of pine and coffee. In the distance, I hear the whistles and applause from the other people in the diner who are witnessing the entire exchange, but they fade away as I kiss him back, bringing my hands up to his face, running my fingers into his brown waves.

Christopher tilts his head, pressing his forehead to mine, and lets me suck in a short breath, my heart erupting in my chest.

"Penny, I love you today, I'll love you tomorrow, and I'll love you every day of my life." He whispers the words against my lips and I have to fight the urge to press another kiss to his. "Come with me to Rhode Island and every adventure after that." His eyes shimmer as he watches me react to his words.

In all the time we've spent together and spent apart, my heart has never strayed from Christopher, and to hear that his heart still wants me, it makes tears dampen my eyes. His acceptance is everything I'd hoped it would be, everything realigning and coming together as it's supposed to be.

"To our new story," I say, my lips meeting his, kissing him through my smile.

"To our new story," Christopher says through our kiss.

Because we're sitting in the middle of the Snowcapped Diner, I pull back, the sounds of the crowd breaking through the tunnel-vision on my mind. Christopher laughs softly, noticing them too.

The watch on my wrist begins to ring, startling me and nearly making me jump out of my barstool. I look down, seeing my alarm is going off. If I don't leave now, I'm going to miss my shuttle. "I— uh," I start to say, my breathing still hard as my heart tries to settle in my chest. "I actually have to go or else I'll miss my ride to the airport." I pick up the pocketed pamphlet from the counter and stand, slinging my purse over my shoulder.

"When will you be back?" Christopher asks.

"In July," I say, almost regretting the words.

The last thing I want to do right now is walk away from him, but this trip is important to me. My mom put this together to cheer me up, and it's giving me the opportunity to take myself to the one place I've always wanted to go as a way of celebrating the person I've found after these last three months. The old Penny wouldn't have dared to take a trip for herself. She would have been content on just dreaming about it and hoping it would come true one day.

"Maybe we can plan a visit to Rhode Island in July then," Christopher offers. "Find our new apartment," he adds with a smile that glitters in the sun.

"Sounds like a date," I say, curling my fingers around the strap of my purse. "I'll see you soon." I take a step back, finding it harder to turn away from him than I want it to be.

"Penny," Christopher calls a second later, and I glance over my shoulder, seeing him still leaned back on his barstool. "Where are you going?"

The corner of my lip tugs up, and I'm unable to hide the smile that floods my face. I look at Christopher, at the boy who has been my biggest supporter for years, who helped me find myself after I had gotten so lost.

"London."

The End

Can't get enough of
Christopher and Penny?

OUR FIRST PAGE is a short story detailing moments from
the beginning of Penny and Christopher's relationship.

Read it now by subscribing to author Catherine Downen's
newsletter!

ALSO BY CATHERINE DOWNEN

THE MARKINGS (Book 1)

CROWNING KEYS (Book 2)

SHATTERED VISIONS (Book 3)

COMING SOON:

ENDING IN CADENCE (YA Portal Fantasy)

SPELLBOUND LIES (YA Fantasy Retelling)

LEAVE A REVIEW TODAY!

YOU CAN MAKE A DIFFERENCE

Thank you so much for reading DON'T READ THE LAST PAGE! It would mean the world to me if you could take a minute to leave a review for my book. In a world with millions of amazing stories, reviews are how books reach new readers, how authors connect with their target audience, and how distributors know which books to recommend their users. By spending just a minute leaving a review, you are impacting lives of hundreds of people that love to read and were involved in the publication of this book!

READ THE FIRST CHAPTER FROM
CATHERINE DOWNEN'S
BEST-SELLING NOVEL,
THE MARKINGS.

Chapter 1

My frail fingers curl around the jagged rock. I press it into the stone wall and drag it up and down until a small groove forms. I drop the rock and step back, glancing over all the lines I've made. It is day 2,436 of being in this prison with my mother and younger brother.

"Adaline, you've got to stop tallying. You've filled the entire cell with your lines," my mother, Rosa Sagel, groans. She sits with her back against the opposite wall, and her eyelids threaten to fall closed as she blinks slowly.

"I need to keep track so I'm ready when we escape," I say in a hushed voice. It may have been nearly seven years of being locked in here, but I've almost finished my escape plan.

"Addie," my younger brother sings in his childish voice.

"Don't call me that, Titus," I say, taking a seat next to him on the old ripped up mattress.

"Will you tell me the story about the rocks again?" Titus asks slowly. He has a hard time finding the words he wants to say. I know he means the story about the asteroids that reset civilization on this planet nearly 100 years ago. When we were arrested Titus was just a baby, and I was only nine years old. I've been trying to teach him about our history and how to read and do math, but he's still far behind where a seven-year-old should be. I really only blame myself.

"Don't you have that story memorized by now?" I joke, poking him in the stomach. He laughs, and just as I'm about to start the story my mother jumps up, alarmed.

She starts spinning around the room and asks me, "Adaline, what day did you say it was?"

"2,436," I say, scanning her worried face.

"Are you sure?" she asks sternly.

"I'm pretty sure," I say gently.

"It's fine. I'll just count them," my mother brushes me off.

"I can help," I say, and together we move around the cell, counting all of my tally marks until we get to the one I made this morning.

"2,436," my mother whispers, tracing the last line with her thin finger. "It's time. It's finally time."

"Time for what?" I ask, my voice trembling.

"You are nearly 16 years old, Adaline. It's time to be strong," my mother says, sitting me down on the mattress with my brother.

"Actually, I'm 15 years and 363 days," I correct. Ever since we were put in prison, I've become a numbers person. I'm always counting up to dates and back from them. It helps to keep time moving in here. Usually, my mother scolds me for correcting her or for bringing up my numbers, but right now her eyes fill with tears, and she gently cups my face with her hands.

"You did such a good job, Adaline," my mother says, looking deep into my emerald eyes.

"I don't know what's going on," I choke out and give my head a soft shake. She seems to focus a bit and rubs her damp eyes.

"It's time I tell you a secret," my mother says.

Titus leans in and his eyes widen, "A secret?" My mother lets out a dry laugh before pulling an old, black diary from her grey prison shirt. "What's that?" Titus asks.

"I am a Future Holder," my mother says gently.

"You have a gift?" I ask, shocked. We never talked about gifts before. I learned about them in school once. A select group of people were infected during the fall of the world before ours, giving them magical powers. As a kid, I'd always wondered what it would be like if my family was gifted, but I had never thought it would be a reality.

"Yes, and so do you." My mother hands me the diary, and I notice a small lock on its cover.

"What gift do I have?" I ask quietly.

"You are a Force Lifter, Adaline. You control whatever you see," my mother says. "There is so much I never told you about how the gifts work. If someone is born with a gift, they will have a sense that is enhanced in a certain way. You have an enhanced sense of sight that lets you control what you see."

All of the information my mother is telling me loses me, and I feel a confused glaze settle on my face. My mother pauses and must notice she's lost me. "I have an enhanced sense of sight as well, but my powers are different. I can see into the future."

"So I can save us?" I ask, as the idea of having magical powers fully processes.

"No!" my mother almost shrieks back to me. "You have to wait to use it until the time is perfectly right."

"I don't understand," I draw out my words, confused.

"You just have to promise me, or else we will all be killed. Do you promise, Adaline?" she asks urgently, her hands squeezing my arms.

I hesitate and look into her icy blue eyes. "I promise," I choke out in a small, almost inaudible, voice. "So you've seen this all happen?" I ask, starting to piece together my mother's information about our powers.

"Yes, as a Future Holder, I've had visions of how our lives play out," my mother explains.

I glance at the ticks in the wall and ask her, "So what does day 2,436 mean?"

"Today you escape," my mother whispers. The ringing sound of the metal prison door slamming open makes me jump. I had completely forgotten it was Parting Day. "I love you both so much," my mother says, tears escaping her eyes.

"Why are you crying?" my voice breaks. I hear cell doors being thrown open as the guards start dragging select prisoners to their executions. An officer appears in front of our cell, and I scream in protest. It can't be one of us, not now.

"It's your time Ms. Sagel," the guard announces before unlocking our cell. My mother stands to go, and Titus begins to scream and sob. They can't take her. I can't lose her.

"Mother what do I do now?" I ask between cries. I hope she tells me she was wrong and that I need to use my powers now. I need her to tell me how to use them, and how to save us.

She looks at me very calmly and says, "Hold your brother's hand, Adaline." I turn to Titus and see him squeezing the air between his shrieks. I grab his hand tight and he continues to squeeze three times, then a pause, and then three more. I had taught him to do this when he got upset and couldn't find the words he wanted to say. It was his way of communicating with us.

I look back to my mother who walks out of our cell and the door closes behind her. "Count Adaline," she instructs. I catch one last glance of her blue eyes and her long brown hair before the guards take her with the other prisoners, and then she's gone. My mind races trying to figure out what I'm supposed to do now. She isn't gone. She can't be gone. "Count Adaline," her voice reminds me again. I do this every Parting Day. It's the same every week. From the moment the guards leave with that week's group of prisoners it's exactly 1,876 seconds until the guards will drag the dead back through the prison so we know the killings were successful, and then bodies are disposed of.

So I start to count softly and evenly. *1. 2. 3.* I now know what my mother had meant when she said I had to wait until the time was right to use my gift. After Parting Day most of the security and help at the castle get the evening off. This will be my best opportunity to escape.

11. 12. 13. Titus continues screaming and squeezing my hand. Three squeezes, then a pause, and then three more. He does this every Parting Day, but today it is so much worse. Parting Day is a way for the King to make room in the prison. Once a week seven or so prisoners are removed and executed in the large coliseum, and everyone in the entire city of Garth, the city I used to live in and the capital of our island, has to watch.

98. 99. 100. Everyone is supposed to attend the killings and is forced to watch us die as a sign to show what happens when the laws are broken. Then, the bodies get brought through the prison to the disposal room to remind us what we have to look forward to.

245. 246. 247. As I count I imagine my mother walking farther and farther away from us. *451. 452. 453.* I have to be strong. I am a Force

Lifter. I am a gifted. I can escape and save my brother. *777. 778. 779.* Titus has finally quit screaming. He sits quietly beside me while we wait for the dead to be brought to the disposal room.

1,206. 1,207. 1,208. I wonder if she's gone already. Was she one of the first to go or did they make her wait and watch everyone else die first? I hope it was quick. *1,505. 1,506. 1,507.* They'll start wrapping up now.

1,874. 1,875. 1,876. I stop and the prison seems to balance on a silent beam. Just a beat later and the doors slamming open rings through the concrete tomb. 93 seconds to the disposal room. 1 body. Then 2. 3. I count as they carry the dead, wrapped in dirty white fabric by the cells. 4. 5. 6. There's a pause, a lag in the line, and then finally my mother's body is carried by us. Her eyes are closed and her skin is pale. She could just be sleeping. "Mother," my voice chokes out. I know what Parting Day is, I've seen this happen hundreds of times, so why did I let my mother go with them? I had thought it was a plan she had. If she had seen this in the future why would she let herself die?

"Count Adaline," her distant voice echoes to me. *83. 84. 85.* I continue, tears rolling down my cheeks until 93 and the guards have cleared the prison and enter the disposal room. We sit in the cell completely shocked. Titus has begun to cry again, but I don't feel upset. I feel anger pound through every inch of my body. Anger at the guards that took away my mother, but mostly anger toward myself for letting her die. She told me I had a gift. Why did I do nothing? I glance down to the black diary she had handed me. When I try to open it, the small lock resists. She gave me a diary I can't read, told me not to use my gift, gave me no other instructions except to count, but there was one more thing. She had said to wait. Now she would say to move.

Before I can act I try and calm myself down, just enough to be able to think straight. I breathe in very slowly until I can't take in any more air and then release it. I do this a few more times until I feel the muscles in my body relax. "Breathe Titus," I mumble and he takes in shaky breaths through his cries.

I don't even have the first clue as to how to do this, but I rise, not wanting to waste any more time. I place the small black diary into the pocket on the inside of my grey prison button-up shirt and take in another deep breath. I waited as mother had instructed and now I need to move. "Run now and mourn later," I instruct to Titus and myself.

I lift my hand and hold it out in front of me. She said I just need to picture it. I see the caged door so I can control it. I can open it, but I feel the nerves building up inside. What if my mother was wrong? What if her visions were wrong? What if she didn't have visions at all, and was just trying to keep me hopeful for when she was gone? I know what this prison does to people, it drives them crazy. For a second I doubt my mother and her visions, and I wonder if she had just completely lost her mind in her last minutes. I look from my shaking hand to the barred door. I clear my thoughts of doubt and just try to believe. I close my eyes and imagine the door sliding open.

"Please work," I whisper. I slowly let my eyes open and I feel my heart drop when I see the door is still closed. "No," my broken voice lets out. I have to get out. I stare into the barred door and squeeze my fists as tight as possible. "Move. Move. Move," I repeat in my head over and over again. I focus harder and harder until my hands shake and my eyes water with tears of frustration, and then I see the bars start to tremble.

"Yes," I breathe, overcome by hope. I continue to think and beg the door to move in my head, and I see it continue shaking and shaking. As the frustration and tension build inside of me I hear myself scream, "Open!" and watch as the barred door flies to the right.

I almost fall over at the release of all the tension built inside me. I did it. I exhale and can't help but feel relief. I do have the gift. My sense of sight is enhanced so that I can control whatever I see. I am a Force Lifter.

The second this thought crosses my mind I'm hit by another wave of panic. I won't only be wanted as an escaping prisoner, but also as one of the gifted. King Renon forces everyone with a gift to work directly under him. I can't get caught. My heart starts to quicken at the thought of the guards catching me and turning me into King Renon crosses my mind. Images of how my mother may have died flash in my head.

I won't let her death be for nothing. I turn to Titus who sits frozen on the mattress.

"Run now, and mourn later," I instruct him again and help him to his feet. "Time to go Titus."

"Addie, how'd you do that?" Titus asks, but I don't answer because I don't know.

I grab his hand and drag him from the cell. I begin to turn right to go toward the only entrance and exit I know of, but Titus begins to pull my hand left and toward the disposal room.

"No, that's the wrong way Titus," I say, but he shakes his head hard.

"Mother is in there. We need to save her too." His words crawl across my skin.

"Oh Titus," I say softly and kneel in front of him. Even though nerves and anxiety run through me I try to deliver my words as calmly as I can. "Mother is dead, Titus." His face sets in a stone line. "Today was Parting Day and they took her." I can see his eyes shifting. His brain knows what happened, but he's trying to deny it.

"No Adaline," he says, getting my name right. That's how I know he's serious.

"Come with me, Titus. She wants us to go now." Titus gives one more glance over his shoulder, down the hall toward the disposal room. After a second he takes my hand and we move toward the exit. I just have to picture it. I can do this. It's just like I've dreamed about every night for as long as I can remember.

Out of the corner of my eye, I look in the cells of other families. At first, they all look shocked, especially when they don't see a guard with us. Then, they start pleading for help. When I don't offer any they start screaming, "Guards! Guards!" Usually, the prison is filled with guards, but on Parting day there are only ever two.

The two guards turn around the corner, swords pulled and ready to attack. In my head, I try to command the guards' swords to move away from their hands, but it's not that easy. The swords start shaking in their hands and I watch as the guards try to use both hands to steady them. I look around the room at other things to control, but everything in the dungeon starts shaking. Stones in the walls and ceiling fall, crushing the guards in my path. Innocent people in their cells start screaming and huddling for safety from the destruction I'm causing. I stop trying to control things and the prison becomes still again. I tell myself to start running and Titus and I take off down the dungeon hallway to the metal staircase I was brought down seven years ago.

We climb up the stairwell and to my right is a door that will lead into the castle itself. We turn and proceed through it. The hall is dimly lit with lanterns that hang on either end.

"I remember this," I whisper softly. As my eyes adjust to the dim light I feel my heart drop. I look forward and everything looks the same as it did the night we arrived, except for the fact mother is no longer with us. The night we were brought here is replaying in my head over and over again, but I know I have to keep moving, for mother's sake.

I walk forward down the short hallway. The walls are a simple white with gold and red swirls and floral designs. Beneath my bare feet is a beautiful velvet purple carpet lined with gold. It's a rare luxury in Garth, my family could never afford it. Once I reach the end of the hallway I lift my hand and picture the locks on the other side of the door turn and the doors open. I can't tell if the locks on the other side of the door flip open or if I simply just shake the door until it breaks free.

"That's so cool," Titus breathes and I see his eyes light up. He knows what this means. We get to start over and be free. We step out into the main foyer of the castle. Everything looks the same here as in the last hallway except for the hints of purple and blue running through the walls. I squeeze my eyes shut, trying to recall the way out, but it's been far too long. My gut tells me to turn right so I stop trying to force my memory, and just follow what feels right.

Quietly, we move down the hall, our feet silently floating over the lush carpet. Trying to get out on Parting Day was the right decision. The castle seems to be empty after today's events. Everyone from Garth who came to view the killings have returned home, and the majority of security has been off duty. Titus and I continue to move through the castle undetected. We walk past a hall to our right when something catches my eye. About halfway down the hall hangs a large painting of a palm tree. I stop suddenly and focus on it. I remember it from the night we were brought here. The memory from that night surfaces and I see myself and my mother walking by the painting with Titus in her arms. I remember the guards practically shoving us down the hall, and I had peered at the painting through tear-filled eyes.

"We're close Titus," I say softly. We turn and move down the hall with the painting. The way out starts to come back to me and I know the front of the castle is just around this hall.

A slam of a door back the way we came causes my heart to pause. "We need to move faster," I whisper and Titus and I pick up our pace to a jog. Another slam off in the distances sends me into a sprint. I glance over my shoulder and see Titus falling behind.

Then, a guard emerges into the hall behind Titus. "Run!" I scream as the soldier draws his sword. I stop in the middle of my stride and switch to running back to him, but the guard's blade drives through Titus's chest before I get there. Through clenched eyes I picture the blade flying back into the guard and effortlessly it does. I drop to my knees, into the damp, purple carpet next to my little brother under the palm tree painting. The guard I threw the sword into makes unidentifiable noises as he falls to the floor and silence returns to the castle.

"Titus," I say gently, tears filling my eyes. He takes my hand in his, wet with red blood, and tries to speak. "It's okay Titus," I try and quiet him.

"We need to go find Mother," Titus gets out.

I drop my head. "You'll be with her soon Titus," I say and meet my younger brother's dying eyes. "You and mother will be free soon." Titus's lips curl into a tiny smile before he takes in his last small breath, and his hand becomes limp in mine.

I fight the urge to make a sound. I clench my teeth and fill my head with internal screams. *1. 2. 3.* I count and squeeze my brother's hand.

1... 2...3

ABOUT THE AUTHOR

Catherine Downen is a Young Adult author in both fantasy and contemporary romance. She graduated from Bradley University with a degree in Mechanical Engineering. Currently, Catherine is working as an engineer in St. Louis while writing her books.

Connect with me:

Author Newsletter

Book Playlists on Spotify

Tik Tok

OTHER SOCIAL MEDIA: